"Carries readers away into a vivid new fantasy world . . . entertaining and suspenseful . . . full of lively characters . . . The intriguing new system of magic and politics provides plenty of potential for sequels."
—*Publishers Weekly*

"Filled with vivid details of everyday life, a strong and admirable heroine, and a plot with as many twists and turns as the mighty river that threads through the story, Shinn's latest novel should appeal to her avid readership and to lovers of the genre. Highly recommended." —*Library Journal* (starred review)

"Will be enjoyed by readers who like stories with hints of western European aristocracy and elemental magic, with a happy ending." —*Booklist*

"A lush new world that is peopled with fascinating characters . . . Shinn once again demonstrates her considerable facility for creating a richly developed world peopled with intriguing characters blessed with remarkable powers."
—*Night Owl Romance*

"Character-driven fiction with fantastical and romantic elements. Shinn has created a world that is completely believable and magical at the same time." —*Fantasy Literature*

"A great opening political fantasy that is filled with a strong cast; wonderful, refreshing laws of magic; and court intrigue . . . Shinn affirms what her fans already knew from the Twelve Houses saga: that the author is one of the best fantasists." —*Alternative Worlds*

READER AND RAELYNX

DARK MOON DEFENDER

continued . . .

THE THIRTEENTH HOUSE

"Outstanding . . . a lyrical grace and deep appreciation of camaraderie reminiscent of Diane Duane at her best . . . [a] superior fantasy series."   —*Publishers Weekly*

"Lyrical and entertaining fantasy . . . peopled by well-drawn characters that readers can really bond with . . . abounds with subtle romance and high-spirited adventure. Ideal for readers who like a little romance with their fantasy." —*Kirkus Reviews*

"Set in a world of noble houses, shape-shifting mystics, and dexterous swordsmen, the sequel to *Mystic and Rider* further develops Shinn's new series characters and introduces new plot elements. Shinn provides a wealth of action and a balanced cast of genuinely heroic and admirable characters."
                                                        —*Library Journal*

"Shinn is a strong literary writer [and is] especially good at writing realistic characters. Readers who enjoy romance and strong characterization will enjoy this book and the Twelve Houses series."   —*SFRevu*

MYSTIC AND RIDER

"Engaging . . . an enjoyable yarn with characters who leave you wanting more."   —*Locus*

"Shinn is an engaging storyteller who moves believable characters through a fascinating landscape and interesting adventures, [and] manages to do it with deep insights that make us reach into our own souls and wonder: If we were placed in the world of these characters, what would we do and what would we believe in?"   —*St. Louis Post-Dispatch*

"*Mystic and Rider* . . . is that rarity, the opening book of a series that stands solidly as a read-alone novel. Well-developed and engaging characters, an intriguing plot, plenty of action, and unforeseen twists make *Mystic and Rider* a great book."
                                        —Robin Hobb, *New York Times* bestselling coauthor of
                                                        The Inheritance & Other Stories

TROUBLED WATERS

Sharon Shinn

ACE BOOKS, NEW YORK

THE BERKLEY PUBLISHING GROUP
Published by the Penguin Group
Penguin Group (USA) Inc.
375 Hudson Street, New York, New York 10014, USA

Penguin Group (Canada), 90 Eglinton Avenue East, Suite 700, Toronto, Ontario M4P 2Y3, Canada
(a division of Pearson Penguin Canada Inc.)
Penguin Books Ltd., 80 Strand, London WC2R 0RL, England
Penguin Group Ireland, 25 St. Stephen's Green, Dublin 2, Ireland (a division of Penguin Books Ltd.)
Penguin Group (Australia), 250 Camberwell Road, Camberwell, Victoria 3124, Australia
(a division of Pearson Australia Group Pty. Ltd.)
Penguin Books India Pvt. Ltd., 11 Community Centre, Panchsheel Park, New Delhi—110 017, India
Penguin Group (NZ), 67 Apollo Drive, Rosedale, Auckland 0632, New Zealand
(a division of Pearson New Zealand Ltd.)
Penguin Books (South Africa) (Pty.) Ltd., 24 Sturdee Avenue, Rosebank, Johannesburg 2196,
South Africa

Penguin Books Ltd., Registered Offices: 80 Strand, London WC2R 0RL, England

This is a work of fiction. Names, characters, places, and incidents either are the product of the author's imagination or are used fictitiously, and any resemblance to actual persons, living or dead, business establishments, events, or locales is entirely coincidental. The publisher does not have any control over and does not assume any responsibility for author or third-party websites or their content.

TROUBLED WATERS

An Ace Book / published by arrangement with the author

PRINTING HISTORY
Ace hardcover edition / October 2010
Ace mass-market edition / October 2011

Copyright © 2010 by Sharon Shinn.
Cover illustration by Jonathan Barkat.
Cover photo © Shutterstock.
Cover design by Judith Lagerman.

ISBN: 978-0-441-02089-8

ACE
Ace Books are published by The Berkley Publishing Group,
a division of Penguin Group (USA) Inc.,
375 Hudson Street, New York, New York 10014.
ACE and the "A" design are trademarks of Penguin Group (USA) Inc.

PRINTED IN THE UNITED STATES OF AMERICA

10   9   8   7   6   5   4   3   2   1

For Robin,
with her elay *soul*
and her sweela *crown*

Random Blessings

ELAY (AIR/SOUL)	HUNTI (WOOD/BONE)	SWEELA (FIRE/MIND)
joy	courage	innovation
hope	strength	love
kindness	steadfastness	imagination
beauty	loyalty	clarity
vision	certainty	intelligence
grace	resolve	charm
honor	determination	talent
spirituality	power	creativity

CORU (WATER/BLOOD)	TORZ (EARTH/FLESH)	EXTRAORDINARY BLESSINGS
change	serenity	synthesis
travel	honesty	triumph
flexibility	health	time
swiftness	fertility	
resilience	contentment	
luck	patience	
persistence	endurance	
surprise	wealth	

Quintiles & Changedays

The calendar of Welce is divided into five quintiles. A quintile consists of eight "weeks," each nine days long. Most shops and other businesses are closed on the firstday of each nineday.

The first quintile of the year, Quinnelay, stretches from early to deep winter. It is followed by Quinncoru, which encompasses late winter to midspring; Quinnahunti, late spring to midsummer; Quinnatorz, late summer to fall; and Quinnasweela, fall to early winter.

The quintiles are separated by changedays, generally celebrated as holidays. Quinnelay changeday is the first day of every new year. Since there are five changedays, and five seventy-two-day quintiles, the Welce year is 365 days long.

Money

5 quint-coppers make one copper (5 cents → 25 cents)
8 coppers make one quint-silver ($2)

5 quint-silvers make one silver ($10)
8 silvers make one quint-gold ($80)

5 quint-golds make one gold ($400)

ONE

Navarr Ardelay's body was laid to rest in a blazing pyre, as befit a *sweela* man who owed his allegiance to flame. Zoe stood numbly within the circle of mourners, unable to speak, as she watched her father burn away to ashes. Even as he had wasted away for this past quintile, growing thinner, more frail, uncharacteristically querulous with pain, she hadn't really believed he would die. How could there be a world in which Navarr Ardelay did not exist?

She was so cold that not even the leaping flames could chase away her chill; the weak winter sunlight offered no warmth at all. Doman hovered close, his hand always half-outstretched. Zoe wondered if he thought to catch her when she fainted or to yank her back if she attempted to throw herself into the fire. Doman was the unofficial leader of this little village; he made himself responsible for the well-being of every soul in the small cluster of houses, and he had been tireless in his efforts to ease Navarr's passage out of this life. He had even sent to Chialto for surprisingly effective medicines that would soothe pain and keep the mind clear. Navarr had been awake and lucid as recently as two days ago, continuing to dictate to Zoe how he wanted her to distribute his few items of any worth.

"Doman must have anything he wants from the house, of course," her father had said late that night. "He will probably choose my desk or fountain."

That had caused Zoe to look up in surprise. "But—I want to keep both of those."

Navarr had lain back against the pillows, his face thin and drawn, his body weak, but his mind, as always, working working working. "It will be too much trouble to transport them."

She was even more surprised. "I'm not going anywhere."

His eyes were closed. "Of course you are. It is time you remembered that you are part of your mother's family as well."

She had not bothered to answer that because, as soon as he spoke the words, he was asleep again.

And because she was too astonished.

He spoke of her mother rarely, and her mother's family not at all. He blamed the powerful Lalindar clan for his fall from grace ten years ago, for the long years of exile and poverty. Zoe didn't even know if her grandmother was still alive, and which of her aunts or uncles or cousins would have inherited Christara Lalindar's title and property if the old woman was dead. Not that she cared. She would not be seeking any of them out, even if the unthinkable happened. Even if her father died. She doubted if any of them remembered her more clearly than she remembered them—or thought of her more often.

This village was her home now, this house the place where she belonged. She already knew, as her father lay there so quietly, that the tiny house would seem enormous once his spirit had flown it. She did not know how she could possibly fill its entire vast emptiness with her own limp and tired soul.

Zoe would have thought her father's body would sustain any flame for a quintile at least—his swift, questing, inexhaustible mind should have been fuel for a nineday all by itself—but in fact the fire began to die down sooner than she would have thought possible. Most of the villagers had lingered for about fifteen minutes and then drifted away, although three women who had been in love with Navarr at various times still stood weeping around the pyre. Zoe herself was prepared to stand here watching until her legs buckled under her, and then she planned to kneel before the fading embers until the world itself ended.

But Doman would have none of that. He put his hand on her shoulder, avuncular, insistent. "Come inside now," he said, nudging her away from the circle of stones, back toward the stand of houses. "The fire is almost out. It is time to go in."

"Not yet," she said, planting her feet.

He turned his free hand palm up. "It has started to rain," he said. So far the drops were thin and misty, hardly an inconvenience, but the pale sunlight had been blocked out by a slowly building mass of heavy gray clouds, and the air felt like it was gathering itself for a tantrum. "Your father would not want you to be drenched in the tears of the world for his sake."

Since this was true, she allowed him to turn her away from the pyre and lead her to her small, sad, utterly abandoned house.

Together they stepped into the *kierten*, the tiny room set just inside the door. In great houses, Zoe knew, a *kierten* might be enormous—a huge, echoing chamber big enough to accommodate fifty people. A *kierten* was always completely empty; it was a homeowner's way of saying he was so wealthy he could afford to waste space. Poor villagers could not make such a boast, of course, but none of them were so destitute that they did not have a *kierten* at their front door.

Doman stepped into the main room right behind Zoe, and she glanced swiftly around to see the place through his eyes. She hadn't had much time to clean up the detritus of death, so the room was predictably messy. Bed linens were balled up on the floor, clothes and dishes were scattered across various surfaces, and books and papers were stacked in haphazard piles wherever she had tried to get them out of the way. A faint odor of rotting food drifted in from the only other room in the house—the small narrow kitchen that doubled as Zoe's bedroom. She hadn't had time to take her trash to the composting field for at least four days, perhaps longer.

"Would you like me to send Miela over to help you?" Doman asked. "You know she is a reasonably organized woman."

It was a small joke, but Zoe found herself incapable of smiling. Doman's wife was magnificently capable. She had raised ten children and served as a great maternal presence to everyone in the village, even Zoe's father, who had been the last man in the world in need of mothering.

"Thank you, no," Zoe said, speaking with an effort. "If I have something to occupy my hands, perhaps my heart won't hurt quite so much."

"You must come and spend the night with us, of course," he said.

Zoe shook her head. "No. Thank you, but no."

"Then Miela will come here to sleep."

She shook her head again, but it was reflex. She knew if Doman decided she should not be alone tonight, one way or the other, she would not be alone. Doman was all *hunti*, all wood, stubborn and immovable. It did not matter how much you leaned against Doman, how many burdens you piled on him; he would not change and he would not break.

The rain had started to fall with a bleak and heavy steadiness; it was the kind of rain that could go on for days. Even less light spilled in through the small, high windows of frosted glass, so Zoe stepped over a pile of soiled clothing to light a lamp. Instantly the clutter of the room was even more visible.

She made an indeterminate gesture to indicate the whole room. "My father wanted you to pick something to remember him by," she said. "Anything in the entire house."

It was a common enough tradition, a way for the living to remember the dead. Doman must have realized that he had been given the supreme honor of being the first to choose among Navarr's possessions, for he nodded once, suitably solemn. He was a tall man, thin and sinewy, with brown-bark skin and thick gray hair, and the colorful overrobe he had worn to the funeral made him look like some kind of oracle.

"I am happy to bring a piece of Navarr Ardelay into my own home," Doman said. "But I wouldn't want to take anything that you held especially dear."

"The things I want to keep I have already moved into my room," she said. "Take what you like."

Doman glanced at the carved desk—a huge, ungainly piece of furniture, bought five years ago from a peddler selling a strange assortment of quality merchandise from the back of his wagon. Next he studied the bronze fountain, a miniature replica of the one that played in the great hall of the royal palace. But then he stepped toward the back wall and pointed at the three pieces hanging over the rumpled bed.

"I would take the random blessings, if you could stand the loss," he said.

For the first time in four days, Zoe almost smiled. "Doman," she said. "Your trait is wood. And you covet the blessings of a man of fire?"

He indicated the first item hanging on the wall. It was a square of hammered copper, perhaps five by five inches, with the symbol for courage embossed in it from behind. He had no trouble summoning a smile. "That is a blessing that should fall on a *hunti* man," he said.

"True enough," she said.

"And endurance is a blessing for a *torz* woman, and Miela is certainly that," Doman added.

The symbol for endurance was the most beautiful of the three blessings, embroidered in shades of blue on a crisp white background and contained in a frame of carved wood. "Yes, I know Miela has always liked that piece," Zoe said.

Doman gestured at the third blessing, a stylized symbol vividly painted onto a long narrow bolt of stretched canvas. "And who could not use triumph in his life?" he asked. "I shall be the envy of everyone in the village."

Triumph was the rarest of the extraordinary blessings—everyone knew that—and Navarr had always considered it exquisitely ironic that it had been one of the gifts bestowed upon him at birth. Or perhaps the irony had only become clear to him during those last ten years of his life. Certainly, when he was younger, when he lived in Chialto and had the ear of King Vernon, he had been considered one of the most successful men of his generation. Maybe different blessings exerted their power at different points in a person's life, Zoe thought. Triumph had governed Navarr's existence for twenty or thirty years, but it had given way to endurance at the end. Zoe supposed that there had been times during his political career when her father had displayed great courage; thus, in their way, as they always did, the three blessings had proved themselves to be true.

"I will be happy to think his blessings are now blessing you," Zoe said formally.

Doman turned to give her a sober inspection. "Although perhaps I should leave them behind to nurture you instead," he replied.

Zoe shook her head. "I will draw strength from my own blessings," she said, extending her left hand and giving a slight shake to the silver bracelet that held three charms.

"Beauty, love, and power," Doman said, for of course he had seen the blessings dangling from her wrist every day of the past ten years. "At least one has been true your whole life. Love and power will surely come."

"Surely," Zoe echoed, though she had never believed it. In fact, she knew the first blessing wasn't true, either. She was tall, thin, and serious, with straight black hair, fierce black eyes, and faintly olive skin that quickly tanned dark in the early days of summer. If she had had to pick an *elay* trait that described her, she thought she would have claimed honor instead. But no one had any say in their own random blessings.

"When shall I send Miela to come help you?" Doman asked.

Zoe glanced around the room, at the piles of clothes and papers and general disarray. For a moment she could not imagine how the whole mess could be reorganized into something tidy and respectable and *bearable*. She could not imagine how to restructure the house into a place she could live in without her father.

"I don't know," she said, suddenly too weary to stand. "Later. An hour or two from now. I have to lie down. I have to sleep. Maybe it will all make sense when I wake up."

Doman crossed to her side and kissed her very gently on her forehead. "Perhaps not today when you wake up," he said. "And perhaps not tomorrow. But soon enough you will heal. It is the way of the world."

As soon as Doman was gone, Zoe curled up on her mat in the kitchen, but despite her exhaustion she remained awake for a long time. Idly, she played with the charms on her bracelet, fingering them one by one. She had always thought there could hardly have been three blessings that suited her less, but she cherished them anyway. Mostly because she loved the tale of how her father had sought them out, inebriated with happiness.

He had been so excited at her birth—so the story went—that he could barely wait for her to be five hours old before he rushed out into the crowded streets of Chialto, looking for likely strangers to bestow blessings on his newborn daughter. She had come squalling into the world shortly after midnight, so it was scarcely dawn when the clock struck that fifth hour, and the only people patrolling the street at that time were late drunks, early servants, and women who sold their favors. He had excitedly begged a token from someone in each category.

The cheerful, dizzy man, who had just stepped out of a tavern, fished in his pocket and pulled out a cheap blessing coin stamped with beauty. "It's the only kind I carry," he confided with a smile. "Every girl deserves to be beautiful."

The servant, a rushed and unsmiling woman of exceeding plainness, had dutifully stopped and dug through her bag and come up with a bent and dingy coin that held the glyph for love. "We can go to a temple if that's not one you like," she'd said, but Navarr had been delighted to think that his tiny little girl would receive so great a gift.

It was the prostitute, weary and young, who had fulfilled her role in the traditional way, accompanying Navarr to the nearest temple, where he paid the tithe for both of them to enter. They didn't waste time sitting in one of the five pews, inhaling the incense-heavy air and meditating themselves back into a state of balance. They just stepped up to the big, heavy barrel in the middle of the chamber and plunged their hands deep into its rich bounty of coins.

The prostitute had pulled up a token first. "One for your daughter," she said, and dropped it into Navarr's hand.

"Power," he had said, when he had identified the symbol by the murky light. He'd laughed. "It seems like such a heavy blessing for such a tiny creature!"

"Maybe it will suit her better when she is my age, or yours," she'd replied. She dipped into the barrel again, not as deeply this time, and pulled up a second token. "And one for me," she said. Her voice was wistful when she added, "Wealth. That would be nice."

Navarr pressed a few quint-golds into her hand. Random blessings were supposed to be freely given, and most people refused payment for the service, but this girl quickly pocketed her bounty. "Did you pull a coin for yourself?" she wanted to know.

He nodded and showed her. "Change," he said.

It was a *coru* trait. "Is your daughter born to a woman of blood, then?" she asked.

He was laughing again. "Yes, but this blessing is for me, I fear," he said. "An infant in the house changes everything, don't you think? I have been told that my life will never be the same."

"I hope you come to love her," the prostitute had said.

"I already do."

Zoe had heard this story so often she could recite it along with her father by the time she was five years old. Her mother had never seemed quite as amused by the part where Navarr and a woman of the streets searched the city together for a temple, but that was the point of random blessings: You were not supposed to show caution or discrimination about the people you approached. You were supposed to rely on the people who had been sent to you by the unchoreographed currents of the universe. You were supposed to understand that wisdom could be imparted by anyone, no matter how unexpected, that everyone had a gift to bestow.

Zoe squirmed on her mat and turned over to try for a more comfortable position. Everyone had a gift to bestow; everyone had a lifespan to complete; the world would change whether you wished it to or not. These were among the immutable truths that she could not alter by weeping. She closed her eyes and finally managed to summon a haunted and unsatisfactory sleep.

It was still raining a couple of hours later when Zoe woke up. As a woman born to a *coru* mother, the trait of blood and water, Zoe had always liked rain. She loved its many moods—from gentle and romantic to wild and unrestrained—and she loved the fresh, newly washed scent it always left behind. As a practical matter, rain was a welcome visitor here in the village, refilling cisterns and replenishing underground aquifers. Zoe was not the only one who loved the rain.

She pushed herself to her feet and then stood there a moment, trying to decide what to do. Caring for her father had taken up almost every waking moment for the past quintile, especially during the final days of his illness. What would she do now that she did not need to make his food, coax him to eat, and clean away the messes his body produced? Whom would she speak to, now that that great restless mind had shut down? What purpose could she have to go on living?

Foolish thoughts. Her father would be distressed to think she considered her own existence so dependent on his. Zoe shook her head and forced herself to look around.

The kitchen was a mess. A long room with the cooking hearth tucked into the far right corner, it was so narrow that two people could barely pass each other to work. Next to the hearth were clustered all the implements used for cooking—the baking stones, the baskets and sealed crocks of ingredients, the pans and dishes. Near the far left corner of the room, Zoe had hung a gauzy purple curtain to create her own small private space. It held little more than a sleeping mat, a trunk of clothes, and a few useless but beloved treasures.

Now the mat was a tangle of bedsheets and discarded tunics Zoe had been too busy to wash. The kitchen held piles of dirty dishes and scraps of forgotten food. The floor had not been swept clean for days.

There was no purpose to Zoe's life, not now, but at least she could put it back into some kind of order.

So for the next two hours she began the slow, methodical repair of the small house. She made a pile of all the items that needed washing; she put fresh linens on her own bed, which would be used again, and her father's, which would not. She brought in a bucket of rainwater and scrubbed the kitchen, cleaned the dishes, wiped the floors, and even freshened up the *kierten*. She made the place habitable again, but it was hardly a home.

It was still raining at nightfall when Miela stepped in, careful not to track in mud. "I've cooked dinner and made up a bed for you in my daughter's old room," Miela said. The consummate tactician, Miela never bothered asking you to accede to her plans; she just told you what to do next. "Bring your night-clothes and come with me now."

So Zoe stuffed a few items in a bag and obediently followed Miela out into the wet night. Only when she felt the drops on her face did she realize she had been crying all afternoon. The tears were hot on her cheeks, but the rain was cool; it did not wash away any of her grief, only gave it a different temperature against her skin.

Miela worked with Zoe for the next two days to clean out the house. Zoe felt sometimes like a spinning doll set in motion by someone else's hand. If Miela had not been there to animate her, Zoe thought she might not have moved at all. Grief shrouded her thoughts and muffled her mind. She felt utterly blank. She could not even summon the energy to consider how long this state would last.

Miela, by contrast, was a bundle of competent bustle. A large woman, with broad hands and a wild aureole of curly gray hair, Miela projected calm and purpose, and both were equally soothing. At the same time, Miela kept up a steady stream of conversation that helped Zoe tether her consciousness to the physical world. Miela never asked Zoe for an opinion; she simply stated her decisions.

"You will not need all these clothes of your father's, so we will just set aside a few pieces for you to keep, and the rest we will give away . . . Once you are living here by yourself, you will want to rearrange the furniture. I will have Doman and one of my sons move the desk, and you'll see how everything is opened up. You will move out of that corner in the kitchen. That will become a place for storage . . . Perhaps we will buy you fabric and you can begin to sew. You have some skill with a needle, I think, or you would if you practiced enough."

Implicit in Miela's words was the notion of a future, which would require Zoe to think, to act, to support herself. Zoe couldn't imagine it, but she didn't have the strength to protest.

"My cousin's neighbor's son, he's about your age," Miela went on, neatly folding a pile of Navarr's trousers. "He has a house that's way too big for a man alone! Doman and I will invite him for dinner one night and you can see if you like him."

Miela had tried more than once to pair Zoe with some young man to whom she had a remote connection, but Zoe had never been much interested. Despite the love charm hanging from her bracelet, Zoe had never believed marriage and a settled existence were in her future. After a lifetime of conversation with her brilliant, erratic father, she could not imagine being satisfied with a simple man's dull observations on crops and the weather, no matter how kindhearted he was or how ambitious. So perhaps she should consider becoming a professional seamstress, after all. She should start thinking about what activities would inform the rest of her life.

"And there's a man in the next village—his wife died a year ago," Miela went on. "Older than you, but you might like that. You've never really been a young girl, even when you first arrived here. You were wise as an old woman even when you were thirteen. So maybe a mature man would suit you better."

Zoe didn't answer and Miela opened her mouth to make another observation. Then she paused and turned toward the door as if listening to someone step into the *kierten*. At first, all Zoe heard was the endless thrumming of the rain, but then she caught the foreign noises above that familiar sound—heavy wheels, creaking wood, raised voices.

"A trader's caravan, traveling in this kind of weather?" Miela asked. "I'd have expected them to stay safe and dry in whatever town they'd found last. Let's go see what they have to offer."

She started toward the door, then stopped to look around appraisingly. "If they're looking for a place to bed down, this would not be a bad room to offer them," she said. "You could ask for a little extra coin if you made a meal for them as well. The back of a wagon gets mighty soggy in wet weather."

Zoe found the strength to protest. "I don't want a lot of strangers sleeping in my house."

"It might do you good," Miela said. "Give you something else to think about."

Zoe followed her through the *kierten* and out the front door, still protesting, but silently by now. If Miela thought Zoe should act as innkeeper for a group of itinerant merchants, innkeeper she would surely become.

But once they stepped outside into the chilly drizzle, it was clear this was no peddler's wagon come to seek shelter for the night.

All the inhabitants of the village had spilled out of their huts to stand in a ragged circle, staring at the vehicle that had arrived. It was the length of two ordinary wagons, made of a painted, polished wood that would not be out of place inside the king's courtyard, and its six wheels were enormous. Windows set into the polished walls were covered with painted blue shutters, shut against the rain just now. At the front of the vehicle, where an ordinary wagon would have a bench for the driver and a hitch for a team of horses, there was only a small, enclosed chamber. Two men sat inside it, looking out through panels of glass.

There were no horses. It was impossible to imagine what had powered the conveyance down the roads.

Or perhaps not. A faint, unfamiliar odor emanated from the front of the vehicle, and a thin line of white smoke drifted between the small enclosed section and the huge back portion. Zoe's father had loved to read reports of inventions being tested in Chialto, and he had been fascinated by the self-propelled vehicles that were fueled by compressed gasses. Surely this contraption was one of those.

"Why don't they come out and tell us why they're here?" Miela murmured to Zoe as they all stared at the two men sitting in their enclosed bubble. The men stared back but made no move to disembark.

Zoe was watching the central panel of the larger cabin, where a door opened up and folded downward, so that its top edge rested on the ground. A shallow set of steps marched down the lowered door, and down this makeshift stairway a man slowly descended.

He was a little more than medium height, with black hair cropped very tight to control a renegade curl. His face was long, thin, and pale; his eyes were a sharp and restless gray. Everything he wore was black—leather shoes, silk trousers, silk tunic, and an unadorned wool overrobe that swept all the way to his ankles.

He looked like a walking manifestation of wealth and power.

He set his expensively shod foot into the mud of the road without seeming to notice, and his expressive eyes flicked from face to face. Zoe, still a pace behind Miela, instinctively drew back to conceal herself behind the other woman's ample form. Everyone else stood utterly motionless, utterly silent.

After considering the villagers for a moment, the man headed directly toward Doman. Zoe was impressed. That quickly he had assessed his entire audience and determined who might speak for the group.

He said, "My name is Darien Serlast, and I am looking for someone I believe lives in your village."

At the name *Serlast*, Zoe caught her breath. There were five great families in the country of Welce—powerful clans that for generations had amassed wealth, consolidated property, and advised royalty. Depending on the generation, depending on the king, different clusters of the Five Families had risen to greater prominence or fallen to disgrace. The Serlasts—all of them *hunti*, all of them unyielding as wood and bone—had been among the favorites of the current king since before Zoe and her father fled Chialto.

The only person a Serlast could possibly be looking for was Navarr Ardelay.

"Too late," Zoe whispered, so quietly not even Miela could hear. "He is already dead." He could no longer be forgiven and reinstated, or condemned and executed. He was safe from the king's wrath, out of reach of the king's remorse.

Doman nodded gravely. He did not seem at all discomposed by the elegant visitor; he wore his usual somber dignity without unease. "Who are you looking for?"

Zoe braced herself to hear her father's name, and so she did not immediately recognize the name Darien Serlast actually spoke.

"Zoe Ardelay."

Slowly, as if she moved through a medium as sticky as mud, Miela turned to stare at Zoe. She even took a step sideways, so Zoe was no longer hidden by her body. Just as slowly, all the other villagers shifted in her direction, their eyes wide and blank, their faces slack. Only Doman did not bother to turn in her direction, but instead kept his gaze on the stranger's face.

"What do you want with her?" Doman asked.

Darien Serlast's restless gray eyes had noted where the crowd was staring, and now he, too, was focused on Zoe, standing alone and frozen in the muddy road. There was nothing at all to be read on his narrow face. "I must take her back to Chialto with me," he said, "so she can marry the king."

TWO

The conveyance traveled over the muddy, rocky road as if it were a length of silk passing over a piece of polished glass. Zoe supposed its elegant design included an incomparable suspension system invisible to the casual viewer.

If so, it was the vehicle's only invisible luxury. Once Darien Serlast had handed her up the carpeted steps, she had found herself inside a small chamber whose opulence rivaled anything Zoe could remember from the houses she had visited in Chialto. The floor was covered with a profusion of gaily colored rugs, and the whole space was stuffed with plush furniture layered with pillows and cushions and embroidered blankets. Real crystal was displayed in glass cabinets; wall sconces burned with flickering fire, fed by oil or some other fuel. Despite the outside chill, the interior of the coach was warm, rich with incense, and sybaritically comfortable.

Zoe had scarcely said a word since Darien Serlast had installed her inside the coach. She had scarcely said a word since he had pronounced her name and all the villagers had gasped, and Doman had said, "Zoe does not leave this place unless she agrees to go with you." She had not been able to articulate to him how much she appreciated his gesture even as she recognized that it was useless. Darien Serlast was the king's ambassador and a man of wood; not even Doman would be able to stand against him.

Besides, Miela was appraising her with wide, thoughtful eyes and nodding her head. Miela was afraid of no one—not a king, certainly not a Serlast—but she had already decided Zoe needed drastic change to break through her lethargy and grief. "Zoe wants to go," Miela had said. "She needs to go."

"She has no choice in the matter," Darien Serlast had replied. He was so supremely confident that he didn't even seem arrogant; he could have been discussing something as absolute as the arrangement of the stars in the night skies. "The king has sent for her and she must come."

"If she agrees to go," Doman repeated stubbornly.

Zoe didn't waste time speculating what sort of retribution this powerful man could bring to anyone who tried to thwart him. "I agree to go," she said in a faint voice, but everybody heard her.

"Good," Darien Serlast said briskly. "Get into the coach."

Even Miela protested at that. "She must gather her things! She must set her house to rights! She will not be able to leave for a day at least!"

Darien did not even bother to look annoyed. "She may gather what she needs," he said. "We leave within the hour."

A fter all, the few things Zoe needed could be gathered up in five minutes; what took time was saying goodbye. Miela and a few of the other women accompanied her back to the house, where Zoe packed what she wanted. Some changes of clothing. Two small journals in her father's hand. A few loose copper and quint-silver pieces that might come in handy on her journey. The warm, colorful, densely patterned shawl that had been her mother's, hung with cheap metal and glass charms that chimed merrily together and covered the clinking sound of the gold coins sewn into the border.

"You and Doman can do what you want with the rest of the furniture," Zoe said to Miela as they stepped out of the *kierten* and closed the door behind them. "You will know who needs the clothing and the cooking pots."

"I can't believe you're to marry the king!" one of the other village women exclaimed.

"But I thought the king already had a wife," piped up a young girl.

"He has four," Zoe said.

The girl stared. "But then how can *you* marry him?"

Miela hushed her. "He's the king. He's different," she said. "He may have as many wives as he likes."

"And why would he want to marry *Zoe*?"

There was a conspicuous silence; the question had obviously vexed everyone. What did these people know of the politics, the shifting alliances of power in Chialto? Zoe glanced down at the girl, a thin, scrappy blonde with huge brown eyes. "Because my father used to be a very important man," she said gently. "It is quite possible King Vernon has been looking for him the entire time that we lived here."

Her mouth forming a soundless *O*, the girl stared back at Zoe. But even Miela seemed startled at that news. Oh, she had always known that Navarr Ardelay was a great man who had fallen on hard times. But clearly she had not given much thought to just how great he was or how far he had fallen.

"Will you be safe, then, in your new life at the palace?" Miela asked, seeming for the first time to wonder if it was a good idea to thrust Zoe into a new and glamorous existence. It might be better, after all, to mourn in obscurity.

"I suppose I will," Zoe said, her voice indifferent. To be honest, she didn't care. She could live here and grieve, or make her home at the palace and grieve; it simply didn't matter. Wherever she was, her life would be bounded by insurmountable pain. "I don't think you need to worry."

Wrapped in her mother's festive shawl, Zoe made her rounds through the gathered villagers, accepting their hugs, their whispered words of farewell. Doman pressed on her a blessing coin, no doubt one of his own that he had hoarded through the years. It was stamped with the symbol for courage, which seemed particularly appropriate as she was about to embark on a journey with a *hunti* man.

"If the king is unkind to you, return to us," he said loudly enough for everyone, even the Serlast man, to overhear. "We will give you shelter from any cause, from any weather."

"Thank you," she said, leaning forward to receive his kiss

on her cheek. "I have been most happy during these years my father and I lived in your village."

"We must go," Darien Serlast said, his impatient voice overriding their quiet goodbye. "I would like to travel some distance before nightfall." He gave an unfriendly glance at the louring skies. "Which would be easier if it was not raining." He said it as if he considered the bad weather a personal affront.

Zoe turned away from Doman to give Darien an incurious look. "It has been raining here for two days," she said.

"Well, the rest of my journey was dry," he said. "Once we get five miles east of here, we will no doubt be clear of the storms."

"Then let's go," she said and, without another backward glance, climbed up the stairs.

She took her seat in the deep, soft chair that Darien Serlast suggested and felt the vehicle ease into motion before proceeding in an utterly smooth fashion. She tried to stir up some emotion at the thought that she was returning to Chialto to become the fifth wife of the king. But she simply didn't care.

A t first, Darien Serlast attempted to make conversation. "I doubt you have seen such an amazing conveyance before in your small village," he said. He had seated himself across from her in what Zoe realized was supposed to be a sort of parlor, with sofas and chairs and small tables. A few feet over was an area that mimicked a kitchen, with its cabinets of dishes, its central table, its stone casks that no doubt held reserves of food. The coach—or whatever it might be called—was so long and roomy that there were actually doors at either end of this central space. She wondered if they led to simple closets or additional rooms, maybe even bedrooms. One for her, one for her host.

"No," she said.

"You must wonder what powers it," he added. When she said nothing, he frowned slightly, but went on. "It runs on a combination of compressed gasses and a carefully controlled ignition system. The gas itself is owned and mined by the Dochenza family. There are only about a hundred vehicles so far that are equipped with this propulsion system, but more are being manufactured all the time. The Dochenzas will become exceedingly rich in a few years' time."

The Dochenzas, although one of the Five Families, had always been considered a little odd. Well, most of them were *elay*, of course, people of soul and air. The women frequently were great philanthropists and social reformers, always working to improve the lot of the poor, while the unmarried daughters often went off to serve in the temples. The men tended to be philosophers or tinkerers or writers—hopeless at running a household, so her father had always said with a laugh—but now and then one would come up with an idea so breathtaking that it redefined commerce or transportation. Zoe supposed it only made sense that a man of air would be the one to figure out how to turn a naturally occurring gas into a source of profit and innovation.

"Kayle Dochenza calls these vehicles *elaymotives*, but the word has not found much favor," Darien Serlast went on. If she'd had the energy, Zoe would have been annoyed at the lecturing tone of his voice. "Everyone else calls them *smokers*, because they seem to run on a fuel as insubstantial as smoke. Most are so small they only seat three or four people. But because the cabin that you and I are riding in is so large, it must be pulled by a bigger engine powered by a specialized motor, and it requires the attention of trained mechanics. The three men riding in the controller car up front are experts at mixing the ingredients in just the right proportions to keep the motor functioning."

"I only saw two men," Zoe said.

"There is a small bunk within the controller car, and one sleeps while the other two drive," Darien replied. "Thus, we do not have to break our journey, as we would if we were relying on horses."

Zoe thought that the men in the front car might wish to halt from time to time, if only to step out of that confined space, but she didn't bother to make the observation out loud. "How long will it take us to get to Chialto?" she asked.

He looked pleased that she was interested enough to ask. "If all goes well, six days."

It had taken Zoe and her father half of a quintile to make it from the city to the village. But they had traveled on foot and in carts; they had taken detours and debated where they might settle down. From time to time they had lain in hiding when it seemed patrolling soldiers were looking for fugitives, possibly them.

When she made no answer, he went on as if she had asked another question. "When we arrive in Chialto, I will take you directly to the palace so you can meet the king."

She gave him one slow, level look. "I have met King Vernon. Many times."

His gray eyes were suddenly sharp. "Yes, but you were very young," he said. "Back when your father was in favor." When she did not reply to that, he went on. "It is the Serlasts, now, who hold the position Navarr Ardelay once had. His property belongs to us now."

Zoe only nodded. Her father had known that, somehow; he had received news from mysterious sources over the years, and shared some of the more important bits with his daughter.

"My mother and sisters live in the house where you grew up," Darien added. "It is a beautiful place, with exceptional gardens."

She wondered if he was trying to be kind, offering praise of a well-loved place, or trying to be cruel, making her envision new tenants in those gardens, in those halls. Perhaps he was just trying to force her to show any emotion at all. But she had never felt much attachment to the city house. It was the place where her mother had died, where Zoe had mostly been alone because her father was always at the palace with the king. She had preferred her grandmother's house in the northwest territories, and she had loved the small house in the small village. She would be much angrier to have a Serlast take over *that* little property.

Because he so obviously expected an answer, she made an effort to speak. "Do you live with your mother and sisters?"

"No, I keep a house on the western edge of town," he said. "But I also have quarters at the palace."

That was not so impressive; many members of the Five Families had rooms at court. Navarr and his brother each had a suite there, and Zoe herself had spent more than one night under the palace roof. But it did mean this Darien Serlast was as powerful as he appeared. It did mean he had the ear of the king.

"Why does the king want to marry me?" she asked abruptly. "He has four wives."

Once again, Darien bestowed upon her all the intensity of his undivided attention. "Four wives and three children, one of them an infant," he said. "He feels the numbers are out of balance. It would be better to have five wives and three children to achieve the number eight in the proper ratio."

"As soon as another baby is born, he will be out of balance again," Zoe pointed out, her tone a little tart.

Darien rewarded her with a small smile, but in it she read intense amusement. "King Vernon will worry about that when the next child is announced," he said. "Perhaps *three* of his wives will become pregnant at once. Perhaps two of his wives will become pregnant, and he will add three more brides, and then the palace will be full of fives and eights."

"There are other ways to achieve balance," Zoe said.

Darien was still smiling. "Surely you've heard of old King Norbert, who had twenty-four wives and seventy-one children," he said. "Not all of his efforts could produce that seventy-second child—a most propitious number, eight times three times three. There was a great deal of unrest in the kingdom, and famine, and skirmishes at the borders—all due to the fact that his household was out of balance. He finally appropriated an infant born to his brother and named it his own child. And all was well throughout the kingdom."

Zoe rested her head against the pillowed back of the chair and felt a faint stir of interest. This might almost be a conversation she could have had with her father. "And do you believe that?" she asked. "That unless the numbers add up, the kingdom is in peril?"

Darien Serlast made a broad gesture with his hands. "You could say that we are a nation that lives with a specific and entrenched superstition," he replied. "Is it true? Perhaps not. But if I *believe* that superstition, and I can accumulate my fives, my threes, my eights, then I feel invincible. I act from confidence and certainty instead of fear and disquiet. My own belief turns the superstition to truth. If I believe."

"And do you believe?" she asked again.

He laughed. "Let us say, I do not go out of my way to try to disprove the notion. And I pull my random blessings anytime I need guidance."

She regarded him for a long moment. If he had not been all wood, all *hunti*, she would have thought him *sweela*, for there was a burning intelligence behind the attitude of unshakeable certainty. She found herself offering an unsolicited observation, groping a little to get the exact phrasing correct. "My father always said it was ridiculous to believe that any random assortment of digits had control over the movements of the stars, the spinning of the planet, or the strivings of individuals, but that there existed so many documented instances of their—their felicity that it would be foolish not to heed their power."

Darien Serlast listened closely and nodded when she was done. "Exactly. A rational man would claim his life could not possibly be influenced by fives and threes. And yet he might find a life full of twos and tens and sixes to be ragged and unfulfilling." He held his hand out as if presenting her to someone. "Therefore, our king has determined that he needs a fifth bride."

"Chialto is full of marriageable women," Zoe said. "Why choose *me*?"

Darien Serlast was instantly serious again. "He wants an alliance with the Ardelay family. He believes it is time the old rift was healed."

"He could marry one of my cousins instead."

"He could," Darien acknowledged. "It was a course of action he was willing to consider if we had been unable to locate you."

Her father had been so certain that no one would ever be able to track him down. Zoe had not been positive that anyone had been looking for them, but now she wondered. "How did you find me?"

He gave her a smile that she was already beginning to recognize—gracious enough, but unyielding, giving nothing away. A *hunti* smile. "I had resources. I had informants. Eventually I learned where Navarr Ardelay had taken up residence when he fled the city ten years ago."

"Navarr Ardelay is dead," Zoe said bluntly.

"I know," Darien said.

"Did you know that before or after you arrived in my village?"

"Several people mentioned that fact to me while you were gathering your things," he said. She noticed that the carefully worded answer did not actually answer her question, but she was too exhausted to press for a more definitive response. She thought Darien Serlast was probably fairly adept at not giving away information. At any rate, he gentled his voice and added, "I am sorry he is dead."

I am sorry, too, Zoe thought, but she did not bother to speak the words. Her little flare of interest in the conversation had drained away, her little spark of energy. She closed her eyes, not caring if it was rude, and allowed herself to fall asleep under Darien Serlast's speculative, dissatisfied gaze.

THREE

The rain followed them for the entire length of the journey.

Not that the rain was a particular inconvenience. Indeed, Darien Serlast's carriage was so well-constructed that Zoe had to fold back the blue shutters and peer out the windows to ascertain that the rain was still falling. Once they made it off the rutted mud road that served the village, and onto the westernmost of the paved roads that crisscrossed Welce, the rain wasn't much of a hindrance to the *elaymotive* drivers, either.

Still, they kept encountering obstacles that slowed their progress. On the third day of their trip, they passed through a good-sized town that was overflowing with people dressed in festive attire and celebrating in the streets, despite the wet weather. It took Zoe a few minutes to realize that it must be Quinncoru changeday, the first official promise that spring was on its way. She smiled wistfully at the beribboned little girls tossing flowers to passersby, the teenage boys competing in footraces and feats of strength. She had plenty of leisure to observe them, since it took the drivers almost an hour to negotiate the crowded streets. But Darien Serlast didn't suggest they pause to enjoy the holiday, so neither did Zoe.

Periodically they did make stops, especially if they were

passing through some sizable town, so the drivers could refill their fuel tanks at some Dochenza-owned facility. They also took on water, since the *elaymotive* came with its own system for drinking and washing up. It was an unexpected and welcome luxury, which Zoe appreciated at least as much as the tiny bedroom she had all to herself.

The stops to replenish water and fuel were planned and efficient, but as the journey progressed, the drivers pulled off the road increasingly often for reasons that didn't seem as clear. On the fifth day, they halted for the second time before the noon hour had even arrived.

Zoe and Darien were sitting together in the main cabin and he had just asked her if she was hungry. By this time, he must have realized that her answer was always going to be *no*, but he continued to ask the question, continued to make up plates of food for her, continued to watch her until she ate at least half of everything he served her. She could tell that her passivity was beginning to alarm him, but she didn't care. Let him turn her into the king's fifth wife; she didn't care. Let him starve her, or throw her out on the road and run her over with the wheels of this monstrous, movable house. It simply didn't matter.

She did look up, though, when the smooth, rocking motion came to a halt. Darien was frowning.

"I see we have stopped again," he said, coming to his feet and pushing open the door to stare with reproach at the drivers' car. There was just enough space around his body for Zoe to see that they were in another of those midsized towns—large enough to sell all the supplies they needed, small enough that a vehicle like theirs would draw a great deal of gawking attention.

Glancing back at Zoe, Darien said, "Stay here," and took the stairs in two leaps. Zoe didn't stir, not so much as lifting her fingers from her lap, and in five minutes Darien was climbing back inside. His hair and the shoulders of his fine tunic glittered with moisture.

"There's some trouble with the valve on the fuel line," he explained. "One of the drivers says there is a Dochenza shop here where it can be fixed, though it might take a little time."

"Or perhaps they merely want a chance to step out of that

tight space for a couple of hours," Zoe said. "It seems like it would be very confining."

Darien lifted his head, sifting for some meaning she had not intended. "Would you like to step outside as well?" he asked. "This town is too small to have a Plaza, but I saw a row of shops, and one or two places to eat. You might enjoy a stroll around." *You might regain some of your energy,* she was sure he was thinking.

Zoe didn't move. "It's raining," she said.

He smiled at that, and the laughing look made his stern, narrow face much more likable. "A *coru* woman should not be bothered by a little rain. Anyway, it's mostly stopped. Right now it's more like mist."

It seemed like an immense effort to pull up out of the chair, but Zoe managed it. "Let me get my shoes," she said.

She put on her sturdiest pair of walkers, wrapped herself in the jingling shawl, and allowed Darien to help her down the steps. The damp air was chilly and clingy but not as cold as Zoe had expected. Well, of course, it was Quinncoru now; soon enough, the warm weather would arrive again.

They had stepped out into the muddy yard of some kind of industrial housing—the place where the gas was stored or obtained, Zoe guessed. Darien left instructions with the drivers, and then hurried to her side. "I told them we will be back in two hours and I expect us to leave immediately," he said.

"Then I hope the recalcitrant machinery behaves," she said.

He gestured to his right and they started forward, stepping carefully until they reached the relative security of a paved walkway. "That's the first time you've made a joke," he observed. "That's the first time you've shown . . . anything—at all."

His pronouncement was so startling to her that she lapsed back into silence.

She had the sense that Darien Serlast was the kind of man who always strode through life; but here he allowed her to set the pace, and she was capable of no more than an amble. There was little to recommend the small town until they made their way past the industrial buildings and a few grim blocks of workingmen's houses. Next came the larger houses, the places where the wealthier people lived, and then in the very center of town, one short street of commerce. There were perhaps fifteen or sixteen individual storefronts—a cobbler, a jeweler, a moneychanger, a bookseller, a dressmaker, an apothecary, a toolmaker.

A row of lampposts marched down the center of the street, flickering into light against the grayness of the day. They looked utterly new, and Zoe guessed that these were the first gas-powered lighting fixtures to be installed in this town, courtesy of that useful Dochenza fuel. Her father had told her that gaslights could be found all over Chialto by now, though smaller towns were only slowly adopting the new invention.

"Let's eat something," Darien said, making his way toward the storefront of a retail kitchen. "It will make a nice change from the sad meals I have put together every day."

Zoe followed him into the warm, aromatic building, where customers were already lining up at a glass counter near the back and filling the dozen or so tables set up front. Her mouth was tugging itself into a semblance of a smile. Darien was not much of a cook; he had clearly been at a loss when she had showed no disposition to make meals, either for herself or for him. She wondered what he had eaten during the long journey to find her. Had he subsisted on bread and dried meat, assuming that he would be well-fed on the return journey with the king's intended bride preparing elaborate meals? Her father would have relished such *hunti* arrogance. Imagining him laughing was almost enough to make Zoe laugh.

Almost.

Behind the glass counter was an excellent assortment of baked goods, fresh vegetables, and cooked meats, and Zoe was surprised to feel the stir of hunger. She ordered everything that looked appetizing, which caused Darien to give her a sideways glance full of amusement. He ordered almost as much, and then asked for a basket to carry any uneaten portions back to the wagon. They would have decent meals for the next few days, at least.

They found a table near the window and watched the townsfolk hurry past, heads bowed against the rain that had started up again. Zoe saw a circle of children splashing enthusiastically through a particularly big puddle, and several adults who paused and turned their faces up to let the water sluice down their cheeks.

"It's good to see children playing in the rain," Darien said, gesturing toward the streets. "The Marisi River is lower than it has ever been, though snowmelt still comes down from the mountains. A few of the smaller towns have been hit very hard, since the farms that feed them have essentially shut down. This is the first time they've seen rain here in a quintile." His mouth twisted into a sardonic smile and he added, "I could wish its timing was better, since it has slowed our journey to an intolerable pace, but I am glad to see it."

Zoe swallowed a mouthful of a deliciously flavored meat-and-rice dish. "You must welcome bounty whenever it comes, *hunti* man. It is often inconvenient. But if you insist on accepting it only when it suits your schedule, you will find yourself very poor."

He laughed and then crossed his arms and leaned back in his chair, watching her. "I knew Navarr Ardelay a little, and that sounds like something he would say."

She nodded. "All the time."

"So are you like him?" Darien pursued. "You have been so quiet that I have not been able to form a sense of your personality. Your mother was a woman of blood, your father a man of fire. Which personality do you favor, or have you developed an entirely different one on your own?"

"I am *coru*," she offered.

"And when did you decide that?" he asked.

In Welce, it was believed that all children came into the world receptive to one of the elements. Most often a child would take after a parent, or perhaps a grandparent, who exhibited a certain set of traits. But, really, there were no sureties. All children were encouraged to discover their own internal sympathies. A girl born to two *sweela* parents might find herself drawn to air; a boy with primarily *hunti* relations might be entirely *torz*. It was assumed that, at some point in his ancestry, there would be a *torz* forebear, and the affinity had merely skipped generations. It was just a matter of discovering what kind of longing was in the blood, what kind of certainty was stamped into the bone.

"Very young," she said. "I cannot remember a time I did not consider myself *coru*."

"So you are a woman of blood and water," he said. "But

what else is there to know about you? Is there curiosity in you? Kindness? Greed? I cannot tell."

Zoe took another bite before answering. "I'm not sure I can answer that."

He leaned forward. "Why not? Was your father such a strong personality that you had no room left to form your own?"

She raised her eyebrows, her expression sardonic. "Would that please you if it were so?" she asked. "Wouldn't that be the right personality for the fifth wife of a king?"

He settled back against the chair again, his gray eyes even more intent. He was clearly finding her more of a puzzle than he had expected, Zoe thought. It would have been amusing if she had been trying to confuse him, but she hadn't even made that much effort.

"It might make life simpler for *you*," he said slowly. "The king's second and third wives have strong personalities—very—and there is much subtle feuding between them. A new wife who was scheming and ambitious might find herself with two seasoned enemies."

Zoe knew the prospect should be alarming. She knew she should feel dread and uncertainty about her new position; she should ask this court insider for advice on how to navigate the treacherous palace waters. But she merely shrugged. "I am not at all ambitious," she said. "I don't think they will find me much of a threat."

"Alys sees everyone as a threat," he replied. "And Seterre is not much better."

"I don't think anyone has ever hated me before," she said. "It will be an instructive experience."

He watched her for a long time in silence. "I believe I am seeing glimmerings of it," he said at last.

"Glimmerings of what?"

"Your true personality. There is humor in you, is there not? A deep appreciation of the ridiculousness of the human condition. And a certain tolerance for the vagaries of human nature."

It was hard to know if his assessment was accurate or not. She had never spent much time on self-analysis—not even back when she had time and energy to think about herself. "My *sweela* father used to say that he had passed on to me the gift of clarity. From my *coru* mother, I inherited a certain amount of resilience. I think this means that, no matter what my situation, I can look about me, I can appreciate what it offers, and I can adapt."

He listened closely. "Then this—this docility that you show is your true self, not some mask that has descended over you as a manifestation of your grief."

She blinked at him. *Your grief.* Such a casual way to describe such devastation. "I suppose that in general I am not a contrary sort of person," she said, her voice muffled.

His eyes were narrowed; he was making no attempt to disguise the fact that he really wanted to peer inside her soul. "And yet you are the daughter of a *sweela* man," he murmured. "You cannot be as tame as you appear. There must be passion in you that can be roused by *something*. There must be something you would fight for, or against."

"I am a woman of water," she replied. "I am more likely to slip away in stealth than to blaze up in wrath."

He looked dissatisfied. "All men and women have a little wood and bone in them. Somewhere, from some ancestor. Something that will not back down. Something that will not give way."

She turned her right hand palm up and studied the faint lines. "There must be bone in me somewhere, or I could not hold my shape," she said. "But these days all I can feel is blood."

They passed the rest of the meal in silence, which suited Zoe just fine. The rain had slimmed down to a faint gray drizzle by the time they left, and the gaslights had been put out.

"There's a temple around the corner," Darien said. "Would you like to stop in for a blessing?"

It was a practice city dwellers honored more often than country folk. Zoe knew that after they had moved to the village, her father had missed having constant access to the blessing barrels. He was delighted whenever they visited a town large enough to hold a temple, so he could pull out a blessing for the day. She had always thought it was the ritual that appealed to Navarr, or perhaps the folly; how could a man really expect to receive guidance from a message presented to him entirely by happenstance? But he had taken advantage of every opportunity that came his way.

"Yes," she said, and they turned their steps toward the temple.

It was a small and pleasant round stone building filled with incense and lamplight, heated and dry on this chilly and wet day. The five benches lining the perimeter were painted in traditional colors—white for *elay*, blue for *coru*, black for *hunti*, green for *torz*, red for *sweela*. The space was so small, and the benches were so close together, that their edges almost touched, turning the interior into a pentagon. Darien tossed a tithe into the box at the door, and then he and Zoe went straight for the blessing barrel that was set squarely in the center of the floor.

"You first," he said.

Zoe plunged her hand deep into the pile of coins, enjoying the cool, sliding sensation of the metallic disks against her wrist and forearm. She wanted to close her fingers over a whole pile of blessings, shower herself with gifts of strength and endurance, but she resisted. Instead she pinched a single coin between her thumb and forefinger, and brought it slowly up.

They looked at it together. Its utter unsuitability would have made Zoe laugh, if she were capable of laughing. "The blessing of surprise," Darien said. He inspected her. "It might have been the very last one I would have bestowed upon you at this moment."

"Perhaps that is why I need it," she said. She slipped it into her pocket. Some people tossed blessings back into the barrel, particularly if they didn't like what they'd been given, but Darien had paid the tithe, and a handsome one at that. It would more than cover the cost of minting new blessings to make up for any they walked out with today. "Now you."

He grinned, a surprisingly boyish expression. "I will, but I can tell you already what coin I will draw," he said. "It will be resolve or power—perhaps loyalty—but it will be a *hunti* trait. It always is."

That actually roused her interest. "Always? Even at your birth?"

His grin widened and he nodded. "My father went to the

nearest temple and found three strangers to draw blessings for me," he said. "All three pulled out the symbol for determination."

She tilted her head to study him. "If I had been your parents," she said, "that might have made me a little uneasy."

Now he laughed. "You think such blessings would portend a stubborn and difficult child?"

"Yes."

"You would be right," he said. "But they were both *hunti* themselves, so they didn't have much right to complain."

She gestured toward the barrel. "Show me. Very quickly, so you don't have time to finger the embossing and pull out the one you want."

He gave her a derisive look that was easy to read—*as if I would stoop to anything so petty*—and dipped a hand into the barrel. Smiling, he offered her the token. Determination. "I told you."

She felt her face relaxing into a faint smile. "Again. Deeper this time."

He obliged, and retrieved a second coin from what very well might have been the bottom layer. Determination.

"That's remarkable," she said. "A third time?"

This time the coin he secured was stamped with the sigil for resolve. "You have to be cheating in some fashion," she said. "But I can't see how or why."

"Come here," he said, although she was standing right beside him. He guided her over until she stood with her spine nearly touching his chest. He extended his right arm so it rested on top of hers, his open palm grazing the back of her hand. Carefully, he laced his fingers through hers and folded them down.

"*You* plunge your hand into the coins and *you* pull one out for me," he said. "See what you choose."

Its very oddness was irresistible. She actually smiled at him over her shoulder. "Very well, then, I will." She narrowed her fingers and plunged them into the metallic bounty, blessings spouting up and curling away from their entwined hands. His skin was so much warmer than her own; it was almost a shock to realize that some people maneuvered through the world without the constant chill that had dogged her for the past nineday. It was tempting to back up a pace, to collect more of his heat along the other planes of her body. She was sure he had plenty to spare.

Instead, she let her fingers close over a coin—and then let it go, and chose another one. She drew their arms up before she changed her mind again, the token clutched inside her fist so she could not drop it. He released her the minute their hands emerged from the barrel, and she half turned, so they could both see plainly when she showed off the treasure she had retrieved.

Power.

He was laughing outright. "I told you," he said.

Her own thought was so ridiculous she did not bother to voice it. *What if this was a blessing meant to fall on me instead?*

They were three more days upon the road, since the malfunctioning gas valve did not prove entirely amenable to repair. Darien grew increasingly impatient, but Zoe was entirely unaffected. She slept later every day in the impossibly soft bed in the impossibly tiny bedroom, turned drowsy and content by the ceaseless rocking of the smoker coach. Sometimes she tried to lie awake and imagine life at the palace as the fifth wife of a man old enough to be her father, but she couldn't make the picture form. It was so much easier to drift back into dreaming.

On the last two days of the journey, they passed through bigger and bigger cities. The smaller towns they'd seen earlier had rarely featured a building taller than two stories, and most of the houses had been constructed of wood and plaster. In the cities, there was usually a cluster of buildings five or six stories high, and stone was in evidence just as much as wood.

By this time, they were also encountering real traffic— single riders on horseback, caravans of horse-drawn wagons, even a few other *elaymotives*, though none as elaborate as their own. Their pace therefore slowed considerably, when it did not stop altogether because of the imperfect valve.

On the seventh day of their journey, at an enforced halt, the drivers announced they would need a few hours to replace some key part. Darien took the news with relative sanguinity. He had just told Zoe they were only a day from Chialto. She assumed he could hire some other conveyance to get him that far, if he had to, which made him feel more cheerful.

They had arrived in this town in the early afternoon, and naturally it was raining. Nonetheless, Darien proposed they go shopping.

"I'd rather stay here and sleep," Zoe said.

He appraised her. "What do you plan to wear when you meet the king?"

She gestured at her clothing. Loose gray trousers, a faded red tunic, and the ever-present beaded shawl. "This or something very like it," she said. "By now, you have seen all the clothing I own. Pick the outfit you like."

"I like none of them," he said. "You should buy something else to wear."

"I wouldn't know what to choose."

"I will advise you."

She protested, but without much hope. He was not the kind of man to suggest a plan of action and then not follow through. Out into the rain they went and strolled through the respectably sized shop district. At least three small storefronts catered to women, displaying their wares in tall windows. Darien studied them critically before picking one based on criteria that Zoe couldn't determine—perhaps current fashion, perhaps level of quality. She wondered if he had a wife back in the city, someone for whom he purchased fine ensembles in a fit of romantic affection.

She must be starting to heal a little. The very thought of Darien Serlast in the throes of desperate passion was funny enough to make her truly smile. He very likely had a wife, but she would be some carefully chosen political bride with connections to the right families and a deep well of ambition herself. Probably *sweela*, brilliant and scheming. Zoe imagined her very tall, a little homely but impeccably attired. Living in her house would be like living in a museum. If there were children—though how could two such coldhearted individuals manage the mating process?—they were kept out of sight, perhaps at a country estate, and given over to the care of well-paid servants.

"Zoe." The sound of her name jerked her from this detailed picture and painted a flush of guilt on her cheeks. Darien was standing in the doorway and regarding her quizzically. "*Do* you have a color you prefer?"

"Green," she said breathlessly and followed him inside.

It was not the most unpleasant way to spend an hour or two, she decided later—being fussed over by professional seamstresses who had a clear monetary incentive to please their wealthy patron. They assembled five complete outfits for her of soft, colorful trousers and various tops—a long tunic for casual wear, a tighter-fitting bodice for formal occasions, a filmy overrobe printed with a bright design. They even sold her a pair of shoes made of such fine beaded leather that she could never wear them outside for fear of ruining them. She was sure she saw the clerks exchange horrified glances at the state her feet were in—callused and rough, the nails needing a trim—but they made no comment, at least not while she was within hearing.

She didn't care, of course. Let them whisper about her. Let them wonder what her relationship was to this powerful city man—she who was so obviously an unsophisticated west-province girl without the least hint of social grace. It amused her to think what their faces would show if she said, "I'm to marry the king once I arrive in Chialto." But she didn't bother. She didn't care.

"This should see you through the first two days at least," Darien said as they left the shop, their arms piled up with bundles. "You'll need more, of course, but Seterre and Alys can guide you in those purchases."

"Seterre and Alys," Zoe repeated. "Those are the two wives who will hate me most?"

He glanced down at her, an arrested expression on his face. "Yes. Well. They will not want you to embarrass Vernon in front of company. They might scheme against you behind his back, but you can trust their taste in clothing." And then he laughed out loud.

"I cannot wait to meet them," she said politely.

• • •

Nevertheless, Zoe was wearing some of her oldest clothes, and her thickest pair of shoes, when she joined Darien in the common room late the next morning. He frowned as he looked her over.

"Why didn't you put on one of your new outfits?" he asked. "That green one was particularly pretty."

Zoe curled up in one of the plush chairs and waited for him to bring her a plate of food. He had done so every morning. She kept expecting him to make some kind of pointed remark, like, "I am not in this coach to wait on you. Why don't you feed yourself?" But it hadn't seemed to occur to him, even though he did not seem like the kind of man who habitually served others. He either thought she was so helpless she couldn't care for herself, or so precious she shouldn't have to.

Or so stupid she would waste away if no one looked after her.

Or so indifferent to life that she would just as soon starve as not.

Indeed, in about two minutes he carried over a plate of bread and eggs and sliced oranges. They had been out of fruit last night; the coach must have made a stop this morning while she was still asleep. "Also, the red tunic was very nice with those blue trousers," he added, taking a seat across from her.

"The material is too thin," she said. "I'd be cold. I'll change before we get to the palace."

"We should be there by late afternoon," he said.

"And I'll have to wear my old shoes," she added.

Because of course it was raining. The new soft leather shoes would melt before she took five steps from the carriage to the door.

"Wear the new ones," he said. "I'll carry you through the puddles myself."

But she hadn't bothered to put on any of her new finery by the time they pulled into the city limits. And at that point, Zoe was too dazzled and delighted to think about going back to her bedroom and changing.

Instead, she knelt in a sturdy chair and peered out one of the windows set into the coach walls, folding the shutters back so she could see. The rain was warm and misty, shrouding the whole city in a soft, romantic fog, and she just stared.

She *remembered* that deep, murky canal that curved three-quarters of the way around the city, crossed in five places by wide bridges. She *remembered* the low, rosy-blond granite of the foothills that stood guard at the northern border of Chialto. She remembered how that landscape changed colors as the sun changed its angle, icy taupe in bright morning, warm cinnamon at sunset. She remembered the irregular horizon line of the buildings, crowded and sooty in the outer ring of the city, taller and more gracious in the center, where the wealth and commerce of Chialto were concentrated. And there was the palace, an impressive, crenellated structure of golden stone, posing on a wide plateau halfway between the mountain peak and the flat ground of the city—visible from all points, beautiful from every view.

And she remembered the river.

It plunged down the mountaintop in a spectacular fall of foaming white, calmed itself to blue in a wide pool that glittered just beyond the palace courtyard. A much more sedate drop brought it to the deep channel that lined Chialto's eastern border, and then it made a leisurely loop to connect to the canal before it gathered its strength and hurried southward toward the sea.

"The waterfall is so beautiful," she murmured, resting her chin on her crossed arms where they lay on the narrow sill. The air working its way inside was damp and chilly; she had wrapped herself in her warm shawl, but she could still feel the cold along her shoulders. "But it looks smaller, somehow. I remembered the river as broader and more—ferocious."

"I told you," Darien said. "There has been such drought for two years that the river has shrunk in its banks."

She felt a twinge of alarm. A complicated system of aqueducts brought fresh water to every neighborhood; the Marisi River supplied all of Chialto's needs. "Is it so low that anyone is worried?" she asked.

"Not yet," Darien said. "And since it seems like it's been raining for the past nineday, I expect the levels will rise."

They had crossed the canal at one of the southwestern

bridges, so they would have to traverse virtually the entire city before making it to the winding, steeply ascending road that would take them to the palace. The first couple of miles were the diciest, as they moved through the crowded neighborhoods just past the canal. Here in the southern district, the streets were too narrow, the buildings too close together. The whole place had a discarded, noisome feel, like an abandoned house where neighbors had tossed their unwanted junk to rot, and dangerous, half-broken weapons moldered in the corners. When she was a child, Navarr had made it very plain that Zoe was never to visit the southern neighborhoods, which were full of desperate women, unscrupulous men, and lost children. Even now she felt a thrill of danger as their large, ungainly vehicle made its slow passage down these undesirable streets.

She imagined that even Darien Serlast breathed a little more easily once they turned onto the broad drive of the Cinque, which served as the border between the slums and the more civilized portions of Chialto, at least in this part of town. In fact, the five-sided boulevard looped around the entire city and carried the bulk of Chialto's daily traffic. Unfortunately, that meant it was always clogged with carts and coaches and pedestrians, and today was no exception. The *elaymotive* managed little more than a crawling forward motion, giving Zoe plenty of time to stare.

On the inner edge of the Cinque, she could spot the beginnings of the nicer neighborhoods, the houses owned by merchants and tradesmen and bankers. They were mostly tall, mostly stone, and invariably well-kept. At the northern boundary of the city, she knew, would be clustered the private houses, the sumptuous mansions where the Five Families lived. Darien's carriage would have to drive right through that neighborhood on its way to the palace.

But first it would have to get clear of this district. Traffic had come to a complete standstill, and through the open window, Zoe could hear the irate shouts of one of their own drivers. "Out of the way! We're on the king's business!"

Darien came to stand behind Zoe and stare out over her shoulder. "What's the problem?"

"I think a cart has just stopped in the middle of the road. We're too big to drive around it like the smaller wagons can."

She glanced back at him. "I don't think we'll be moving any-time soon."

"We certainly will," he said, and strode toward the door. Quickly lowering it to the ground, he took the stairs in two hops and fought through the crowd to deliver a stern order to the men who had abandoned their wagon.

Zoe moved away from the window and stood very still for a moment, considering that open door. Then she lifted the bright scarf to protect her hair from the rain and stepped outside, carefully negotiating the unfolded steps. Darien was still arguing with the drivers. She turned away from him and mingled with the crowd, instantly becoming a part of the busy, bustling tide of humanity. Within a few paces, she knew, her figure was completely lost to view. She did not once look back.

FOUR

S
unset on the banks of the Marisi River presented Zoe with
a perfect image of peace.

Once the rain stopped, life in Chialto, even for a vaga-
bond, could be very pleasant indeed. Here in the opening days
of Quinncoru, the sun spent all day heating the huge, flat
stones that lined the southwestern edge of the river, so they
were warm enough to lie on comfortably at night.

The city's poor gathered on the riverbank to sleep.

It was something Zoe had remembered from her long-ago
life in the city. An entire community lived in this corner of the
city, camped upon the stone apron that ran for almost a half
mile along the edge of the river. The wide, flat space had been
hollowed out alongside the river nearly a hundred years ago, a
place for the floodwaters to spill when there was too much rain.
No one was allowed to build any permanent structure here. It
was just a big vacant stretch of stone—Chialto's own *kierten*,
some arch political observer had said once. Proof of the city's
wealth.

So it was empty; its slight depression below the rest of the
city foundation protected it from wind and weather; and it had
unending access to water. Inevitably, it collected its own
ragged tenants, all of them poor and with no other homes to

go to—hundreds on an average day, more during seasons with kinder weather. A complex system of rules governed behavior among the squatters who made their homes along the flats. Everyone knew you scooped drinking water from the upper reaches of the river, did your bathing in the middle section, and threw refuse in the very last few feet before the Marisi went rushing south.

There was surprisingly little crime along the river, mostly because the squatters had nothing to steal, and a loose sense of community. The residents looked out for each other, sharing food when they had it, sympathy when they didn't. There were women who acted as nurses and midwives when medical emergencies arose. There were men who patrolled the flats daily, making sure no one grew too rough, though you had to pay them a few coppers every nineday to make sure you were one of the ones they watched out for.

All of them had a love for the river. It was said not a soul camped out on the Marisi who was not *coru* to the core.

Zoe and her father had spent a couple of ninedays with the river squatters shortly after he'd lost the house, lost his position, lost everything. At the time, she had thought it was rather an adventure, sleeping outside by the river in the hot, dreamy nights of Quinnatorz. Navarr had been preoccupied, absentminded, but not particularly unhappy during that period of time, at least as she remembered it. Later she had realized that he must have known his fall from grace was coming; his worst days had been the ones leading up to the ouster. Once he had actually been stripped of his money and his power, he had not seemed to mind so much. He had said once, "There is a kind of glory in freedom, which to me is wholly unexpected." She hadn't really known, at the time, what he meant.

But Zoe had never forgotten those nights at the river.

And now that she was back in Chialto with a desperate need for haven, she remembered that city on the bank of the Marisi.

Stepping out of the *elaymotive* had been an act of sheer impulse; she had no plan. Should she go to her aunt's house and ask for succor? Seek out her father's brother and hope for rescue? Continue on to the palace and fling herself at Darien Serlast's feet, begging for mercy? Stop at a temple and pray for guidance?

The last time she had stepped inside a temple, all the guidance she had received was the word *surprise*. She supposed, after all, the blessing must be read as true. This time, she had even surprised herself.

After a few hours of drifting through the streets, pausing in doorways, and reacquainting herself with the city, Zoe was cold, tired, and extremely thirsty. That was when she thought of the river—and the little city that gathered on the flats.

So, as sunset drew near on that first day, she made her way cautiously to the southern edge of town and the great, flat bowl of stone that seemed to offer the hope of safety. And she stepped up to the lip of the depression and gazed down at the colorful patchwork of mats, tents, drying clothes, running children, and sparkling fires, and felt her face curve into a smile. The river, broad and lazy in its perfectly carved channel, was so red with sunset that it appeared to have been painted with a prodigal hand. She set her feet on the hard-packed path that led from the edge of the city and headed down without a moment's hesitation.

That first night she paid a few coins to the river patrol and then bedded down on the flats with nothing but her scarf to keep her warm. She was chilly and hungry, but at least the rain had stopped. When she woke the next morning, stiff, sore, and a little disoriented, she found that someone had left two oranges and a wrapped loaf of bread by her head. She was hungry enough to devour the food immediately, all the while looking around to see if anyone came forward to claim the kindness. No one did.

Once she had eaten, she took a few minutes at the river's edge to wash her face and try to comb some order into her tangled black hair. Then she sat for a while regarding her reflection in the rippling water.

She couldn't count on anonymous offerings of food every day, and she would grow ragged and grimy very quickly if she did not have another change of clothes soon. No matter how long or short her stay here in the river community, she would need a few essentials to make her life agreeable, and eventually she would have to come up with a more permanent plan.

But not today. Today she merely had to figure out how to survive until tomorrow.

There was no hope of privacy along the river flats, so Zoe climbed back into the city proper and wandered, looking for a doorway or a culvert where she might be unobserved for five minutes. Finally she found a damp, shadowed alley where a row of merchants dumped their trash, and she flattened herself against a wall that had no windows. It was the work of a few moments to slit one of the seams in her wool scarf and catch a coin as it slid into her hand.

It was a gold piece, the largest possible denomination. A careful woman could live for a quintile or longer on such a coin, if she needed nothing but food. Zoe had fifty of these coins sewn into the border, each one in its own secure pocket so that they did not all come clattering out at once.

Of course, dressed as she was, she could not spend such a coin in any respectable outlet. She would be instantly branded a thief and hauled before the city guards—and, almost as quickly, turned over to Darien Serlast. No doubt he had lodged her description with every authority in the city. She needed to find a moneychanger, someone with flexible standards and a complete lack of curiosity.

Wrapping the shawl more tightly around her shoulders, Zoe exited the alley and headed straight toward the Plaza of Men.

The heart of Chialto was the shop district, which featured dozens of specialized boutiques that had, in many cases, stood in the exact same spots for hundreds of years, run by an unbroken succession of merchant families. But the Plazas, one on each end of the shop district, formed the two halves of the city's soul.

It was relatively easy to navigate the city, since a variety of public transport vehicles made a continuous circuit around the Cinque. Zoe found her way onto a crowded horse-drawn omnibus, but traffic was thick with small carriages for hire and a few smoker coaches that looked big enough to haul fifty people at a time. The Plaza of Men was at the northern edge of the shop district, so the ride was long, though endlessly interesting. Zoe watched the neighborhoods unroll on either side of her, the poor, disreputable homes on the outer edge of the boulevard, the fancier, prettier ones on the inside. Not wanting to ask anyone for directions, she guessed at which stop was closest to the Plaza, and ended up having to walk a good two miles before arriving at her destination.

Despite its name, the Plaza of Men was full of traders happy to do business with women. It was just that more of their enterprises happened to appeal to the other sex. A handful of permanent, semi-open structures delineated the outer perimeter of the Plaza. One was the betting booth, which had been there ever since Zoe could remember. There, clients could enter wagers on any possibility that intrigued them: from how many children King Vernon might sire to how many women they might induce to kiss them before the day was over. It was said that the family who owned the booth kept leather-bound books with the records of all the bets made there for more than two hundred years.

Another enterprise that had been at the Plaza for centuries was the promise booth, where a man might swear before witnesses he would achieve a certain task by a certain time, or stand with a potential employer to agree to a set of tasks and a code of conduct. Nearby were three or four horse-seller stalls, two very large swapping tables, and metalworking outfits that would repair knives and jewelry.

Clustered in the middle of the Plaza were the more transient purveyors of services that might have some masculine appeal. Most of these merchants were sitting or standing beside wheelbarrows or small carts with huge wheels. Some were entrepreneurs looking for financial backers. Some were politicians trying to drum up interest in their causes. Some were scribes or accountants, selling their services. Some were moneylenders. Some were moneychangers.

Zoe was not in any particular hurry, so she lingered for a few minutes before each of the moneychangers, eavesdropping on their conversations with other customers. Her goal was to find one who would be fair, if not scrupulously honest—one who would give her good value for her coin without wondering too hard where she had acquired it.

Eventually she chose an older fellow with rumpled gray hair, a rumpled reddish face, and rumpled clothes. "I'd like to change this into coins of smaller denominations, please," she said, handing over the gold piece.

He shot her one quick look, inspected the coin closely for authenticity, then named a sum on the low end of her acceptable range. "And that's firm," he added. "But I'll throw in a leather purse if you want it. Long strap. You can wear it under your clothes so it won't get snatched."

It hadn't even occurred to her to wonder how she would carry around a large pile of small coins, so her opinion of the moneychanger went up a notch. "Thank you," she said. "Let's do business."

He stacked up the copper and silver coins for her—quite a lot of them—and let her count them before sweeping them into the sturdy bag. "If you find yourself with more golds like that," he said, "I'll be happy to change them, too."

She slipped the strap over her head and settled the bag on her hip, where it was mostly covered by the shawl. "I'll look for more, then."

Now that she had money in reasonable denominations, she could make a few necessary purchases. First, of course, was food; except the bread and fruit, she'd eaten nothing for nearly a day and a half. Some of the vendors at the Plaza of Men sold meat on a stick and fried bread and huge, misshapen apples that tasted sweeter than honey. Zoe kept a few coins in her pockets so she didn't have to draw attention to the purse. Everything was cheap and tasted wonderful.

Next she had to have at least one change of clothes, a sleeping mat, and a carrying bag. She knew she wouldn't find what she needed in the shop district, since most of these merchants catered to the wealthy. But since she had to travel past the shops to get to the Plaza of Women, she let herself idle as she strolled by the open storefronts and eyed the merchandise inside.

The shops were like a beggar's children, crowded shoulder to shoulder along the sidewalks and shouting for the attention of the rich passersby. Most were about the same size, maybe thirty feet by thirty feet on the bottom story, and built of a sandy brick or mortared stone. Most of them featured a second story—sometimes a third—where the owners lived. Almost every shop had a colorful awning that stretched from the front window to the edge of the street, so that even on rainy days, patrons could travel a whole block and not feel a drop.

Boys and girls, young men and young women, stood in the doorways or perched on the sills of the open windows and called out to the steady stream of traffic. *Fine wool! Fine silk! Best prices in the city!* Or, *Shoes made of the softest leather! Fancy boots for men and women!* Or, *Watches! Bracelets! Rings for your loved ones! Shop here, best quality!*

Zoe eyed the fine bracelets, sighed over the apricot silk, but her feet rarely stopped for long. These wares were too dear for her circumstances. On to the Plaza of Women.

In shape and size, it was nearly identical to the Plaza of Men, but there was an entirely different feel to it. Where the Plaza of Men possessed a buzzing kind of energy, a sense that at any point someone might start shouting or jostling or brawling, the Plaza of Women was at once more purposeful and more playful. First, there was more commerce—this was the place everyone came when they needed an item and couldn't afford shop prices—so there were dozens of little kiosks crammed together, selling cheap fabric, secondhand clothing, and worn but serviceable shoes.

Second, there was more camaraderie. Mothers and daughters strolled through the marketplace together, picking out flowers for a dinner party or a family wedding; friends and neighbors gossiped as they shopped, and vendors and patrons shared stories and recipes and news. There were very few men at the Plaza of Women. Zoe remembered that her father claimed he never felt so out of place as he did there. *I'm too big, too loud, too awkward, too mute. How is it that women always know what to say to each other?* But it had been the place that Zoe and her mother most liked to visit together, back when her mother was alive.

And *that* had been more than twelve years ago . . .

Zoe shook her head and began a slow, pleasurable stroll around the Plaza. It was Quinncoru, and before long it would be Quinnahunti; she could probably make do with a couple of pairs of lightweight trousers, two or three tops, and an over-robe in some neutral color. She spent a long time picking through an assortment tumbled together on three short tables, holding the items up to her neck or her waist to see how they would fall, debating how practical each piece was. Would the dye run out the first time she washed the black trousers in the cold waters of the Marisi River? Could she wear the loose blue trousers with both the pink tunic and the cropped red top? Should she choose the sensible overrobe of gray or the prettier one in patterned blue?

In the end, she was only a little frivolous, buying just one item that wasn't eminently practical. The shirred, close-fitting top of purple silk was not the sort of thing she would wear as she made camp on the river flats, yet it was so pretty and so cheerful that she could not pass it by. She supposed that, after the nineday she had just had, she deserved to buy something simply because it made her happy.

Or perhaps she was still operating under the blessing of surprise.

A sleeping mat, a blanket, and a carrying sack were much quicker purchases to make, and then she paused at food booths to pick up staples that would last a couple of days. She didn't have cooking utensils, so she had to buy ready-made meals—bread, nut butter, strips of dried meat, and a bag of apples.

And, again on impulse, a bag of sugared candies, flavored with almond and citrus. Zoe popped one in her mouth before the vendor had even tendered her change. She couldn't remember the last thing that had tasted so good.

That final purchase completed, she made one last circuit in case something else caught her eye. A sight claimed her attention; she came to such an abrupt halt that two women bumped into her. She apologized, then stepped out of the way of pedestrian traffic, still staring.

She had forgotten about the blind seers.

There were three of them, all women of indeterminate age—sisters as they claimed, maybe, or possibly an aunt and her nieces—younger women replacing the older ones as the generations turned over and no one could tell the difference. They were all large-boned and soft-skinned, with dark and rather ragged hair curling around their moon faces. They sat on a little dais at the center of the Plaza, their backs to each other so that they formed a sort of triangle. Yet there was enough space around each of them that they could have low-voiced, private conversations with clients, and none of the others would overhear.

It was said that the three of them knew everything about everyone who lived in Chialto. You could ask any question and receive the true answer. *Is this man honest? Is this woman faithful? Who bought the house that used to belong to my uncle?* It was not that they had any occult powers to divine such matters; it was that all information regarding the workings of the city inevitably passed through their hands. You could ask a question and pay for the answer with gold—or with information the seers did not already possess. They traded in knowledge, and they were the richest women in Chialto.

Zoe stood for a long time, watching the seer who was most visible to her. The woman's smooth face could have belonged to a thirty-year-old or a sixty-year-old; her blank eyes were rolled back just a little as she listened to whatever story a well-dressed matron whispered in her ear. The seer nodded slightly every time the woman paused for breath. At the end of their session, Zoe saw the seer hand back the coin that the customer had deposited in her hand. Apparently whatever information the customer had had to share was worth the knowledge she had come to seek out.

After the matron descended from the dais, no new customer immediately came forward, ready to hear or relate news. Zoe took a step forward, hesitated, stepped back. There was certainly a great deal she would like to know, and she had enough money to buy almost any information. But she was not quite ready yet to sort through what she needed to learn and what no longer mattered. And she was still too tired, too sad, too lost to try to figure out how to piece her life back together. The three seers would be here the next day, or the next year, or whenever Zoe was ready to ask her questions. She would come back then.

The afternoon was fairly far advanced as Zoe wended her way back toward the river flats. A rising wind turned the dry air chilly, and she was glad she had invested in the blanket as well as the mat. If it continued to rain, she would have to investigate the possibility of a small tent as well. Something to think about for another day.

Just like yesterday, she was cheered by the sight of the colorful community laid out before her on the stone apron at the river's edge. Aiming for the same general area where she had slept last night, she handed a few more coppers to the guards, then picked her way carefully past tents and campfires. When she had found the spot—as best as she could figure—she unrolled her mat and set out her bag of candies and waited.

It was nearly sunset before anyone came calling, and then it was a reedy old man, pale-skinned, white-haired, smiling. Instead of wearing trousers and a tunic, he wore an overrobe so long it fell to his ankles; it had been sewn from a garish fabric that had softened over many washes in hard water, but it still looked like the sort of thing few people would choose to own. His smile was wide enough to display several gaps between his teeth.

"Welcome!" he said in a raspy voice. "You've come back for a second night."

"I have," she said. "I find the river pleasant, and I have no other home to go to just now."

"The river is happy to have you back," he said. "My name is Calvin."

"I'm Zoe," she said, not having any reason to hide it. "Are you the one who left me food this morning?"

"My wife," he said.

She offered him the bag of candies. "May I repay you with something equally delicious, though hardly as nutritious?"

He laughed and happily took two pieces. "No repaying necessary, but I do love sweets," he said. "Would you like to join us tonight for dinner? We eat simply, but there's enough to share."

She offered her bag of apples, lighter by the three she had reserved for herself. "Only if you will let me bring something."

"Gladly," he said and waved her to her feet.

She had so few possessions that she just bundled them all into her carrying bag before she stood up. The jingling shawl she tied tightly around her shoulders, since it was the thing she could least afford to lose. "The nights can be so chilly," she explained, and he nodded.

"My wife wraps herself in piles of covers so deep I can't even tell if she's there under all the layers," he said. "Some days I wonder if she's crept away to amuse herself with a handsome young man, while I make conversation with a stack of blankets!"

His silly words were so charmingly uttered that Zoe actually laughed aloud.

She couldn't remember the last time she had done that.

Calvin's wife was not, in fact, swathed in blankets, though she was snugly wrapped in a heavyweight wool robe that covered a worn and faded set of clothing. She was as thin as Calvin, with a seamed brown face and black hair so short it was scarcely more than a fuzz of color along her scalp. She moved efficiently through a campsite that had the faintest air of permanence about it, as if it had been set up in this exact same spot for years, though it was obvious it could be dismantled in minutes. The low tent, barely big enough to hold two people, was stretched over a couple of sleeping mats. Two enormous soft-sided bags were half-open at the front of the tent—one holding Calvin's possessions, Zoe guessed, and one holding his wife's. A small round brazier was surrounded by a tattered collection of seating mats. None of those items was so valuable that it could not be abandoned if it became necessary to leave camp very quickly, or if it was stolen. Calvin and his wife had accumulated a few luxuries, but it was clear they were not weighed down by them. Zoe guessed there was nothing here they could not walk away from with very little regret.

"Zoe, my wife, Annova," Calvin introduced them. "Annova, our guest has brought apples to complete our meal."

Annova looked over and smiled, but did not step away from the brazier, whose small grill was crammed with two pots and a few potatoes, baking over the heat. "Excellent. I have cinnamon, so we can flavor them."

Her accent wasn't from any of the regions Zoe was familiar with—Chialto, the northern provinces, or the far western villages. She guessed Annova was from one of the southern cities near the ocean where the Marisi ended its journey. "Thank you for inviting me to share your meal," she said.

Calvin stepped closer to his wife and tapped her lips. She opened her mouth and he dropped the second piece of candy onto her tongue. "Zoe brought us another gift," he said. "Isn't that delicious?"

Annova closed her eyes in a mock swoon. "Very! You must have been at the Plaza of Women today. I know the booth where you bought this."

Zoe felt herself smiling again, just a little. "I was. I bought a lot of things there, but the candy might be my favorite."

Calvin waved his hands toward the mats on the ground. "Sit, sit, sit! Everything is almost ready. Did you bring your own cup with you?"

"I don't have one."

Annova gave Calvin a reproving look. "We have extras," she said. "But it is common, along the flats, for people to carry their own."

Because there was so little room for anything except the barest necessities. Because it would be rare for people to have enough for anyone but themselves. "I'll get one tomorrow," Zoe said.

Soon enough they were all seated and sipping water. Annova served a simple dish of seasoned rice sparsely flavored with small chunks of meat. Potatoes and spiced apples completed the menu.

"What impulse brings you to the city, Zoe?" Calvin asked when they had all had a few bites and complimented the cook. "And when did you arrive?"

"Yesterday afternoon," she said. *And I did not come here on any whim of my own.* Impossible to say that, of course. "It seemed like time to look for a new life. My father died a little more than a nineday ago, and the grief seemed too great back in the house I shared with him."

Annova nodded sympathetically. "It is best to turn your back on tears," she said, "once you have shed enough of them."

"Still, to arrive in the city without a plan—and with no friends to advise you—that can be a tricky road," Calvin said. "You are lucky you found your way to the river. There are parts of the city that are much more dangerous for a young woman alone."

"Not luck so much as memory," Zoe said. "My father and I lived in Chialto years ago. Part of that time we spent down here on the flats."

That intrigued Calvin. "How long ago? Perhaps I remember you from that time."

She hesitated, but, really, would it matter if this man remembered her—or her father? Would it matter if he knew she was Zoe Ardelay? Did he have acquaintances up at the palace to whom he could sell the information? Would he even recognize the Ardelay name, if she was foolish enough to pronounce it?

"Ten years ago," she said.

He shook his head. "No, that was before we took up residence on the flats."

She didn't ask what reversal of fortune brought them here; she didn't want to be asked for her own story in return.

"I was only thirteen then," she said. "I thought it was a marvelous place."

Calvin laughed. "I still believe that, and I'm no child."

"But now that I'm here," she said, "I'm not sure what to do next." She gestured at the dented metal plate lent by her hosts. "How do I earn enough money to eat? I don't require much, but I must live on something."

Calvin nodded. "Some of the people on the flats go begging—you'll see them at the Plazas, or the shop district, or along the Cinque. But many of them work. Some travel with the caravans for a season or two before returning here until their money runs out again. Some take day jobs at the warehouses. Some work at the factories south of the city. The Dochenzas have been hiring a lot of people to build those new smoker coaches you might have seen driving around."

Zoe took the last bite of her rice. "You mean some of those vehicles that don't need horses?" she said. "I saw some on the Cinque. I'd be afraid to ride in such a thing."

"I'm not," Calvin said, so earnestly that both Zoe and Annova laughed. "I'm not! I ride one every chance I get. Stick my head out the window and grin like a fool."

"I think they seem dangerous," Annova said. "There was an explosion not long ago at the well where they get their gas. One of these days there will be an explosion in one of those factories, too, just wait and see."

"I don't think factory work is for me," Zoe said.

"Sometimes there are jobs in the shops," Annova said. "You

have a cultured voice and a soft way about you. You could probably hire on as a salesgirl."

"I would have thought those positions were taken by family."

"When there's family to be had," Annova said. "When the sons and daughters don't run off, wanting a more exciting life."

"I might be able to do that," Zoe said cautiously. "Work in a shop." She liked the idea, actually. It sounded friendly and productive. Something that would occupy her mind and her hands so the days didn't seem so empty.

"Let me know when you're ready to look for work," Annova said. "There are one or two people I could introduce you to."

Zoe felt her smile returning. "I'll bring you another bag of candies if you find a job for me!"

"Then I hope you want to work soon!"

They finished the meal and parceled out some of the sweets, Calvin taking two at a time and chewing them with exaggerated ecstasy. Annova gathered the dirty dishes and laid them aside, scoffing when Zoe offered to take them to the river to wash.

"I'll do it tomorrow. Something to make me get up in the morning," Annova said.

Zoe gestured at the Marisi, just now sparkling with glints of garnet and amethyst as the fading sun scattered it with jewels. "It seems much lower than it did ten years ago," she said. She remembered that Darien Serlast had complained about drought here in the eastern half of the country, though they'd always had plenty of rain in Zoe's village. "Smaller."

Calvin nodded. "It is. You see that dip there, along the river's edge?" There was a shelf that dropped a couple of feet below the flats where most of the squatters were camped. Zoe nodded. "That's how high the river used to be on an ordinary day. Of course, when it flooded, this whole area would be underwater."

"I can remember a night or two when we all had to pack up and scramble out with barely an hour's notice," Annova put in. "Sometimes the water kept rising, anyway—one summer it covered the streets a half mile inland."

"You never saw such a mess when the water went down," Calvin said. "Of course, *we* didn't lose anything. We didn't have anything to lose."

"Did everybody down here get out safely?" Zoe asked.

"Oh, we had plenty of warning," Calvin said. "It had been raining the whole quintile, so everyone was watching the river, to see what it would do."

Annova turned to him. "And none of us were here the second time it flooded, remember? They'd already cleared us out."

"That's right, I'd forgotten."

"Cleared you out? Who did? Why?" Zoe asked.

Calvin waved his hand in the general direction of the palace. The deepening twilight was thick enough to obscure the building from view, but not yet dark enough for the candlelight in the windows to shine brightly against the black. "The king—or rather, his guards," he said. "Whenever some important visitor comes to the city, we're always rounded up and shoved out of the flats. We're too *unsightly*, camping out here like a troop of vagabonds."

"You can see the flats from the palace windows," Annova said. "And whenever ambassadors come from other countries, we're hidden away. But it's not so bad. There's usually a place set up for us on the western edge of town, just outside the canal, with water and shelter made available."

"It's almost like a festival," Calvin added.

"And we're always allowed back here as soon as the rich visitors are gone."

"I like the sound of that," Zoe said with a smile. "Maybe we'll have some dignitaries come to the city while I'm living here."

They finished off the bag of candy while night rolled slowly down out of the mountains. Small lights sprang up all around them—campfires, mostly, with the occasional lamplight turning a whole tent into a softly glowing mound of color. The air was rich with scent—smoke, onions, meat, wine—all overlaid with the heavy damp odor of the Marisi itself. Zoe watched the river turn from red to silver to murmuring black, and surrendered herself to a feeling of remarkable contentment.

FIVE

Zoe spent the next three ninedays merely existing.

She slept late, ate any food left over from the day before, washed her dirty clothes and pegged them out to dry beside her sleeping mat. She usually paused to speak to Calvin and Annova, sometimes meeting other river folk at their tent, and then she would set out to wander through the city again. Often she strolled through the shop district, studying the storefronts with more interest, wondering where she would like to work if she could have her pick. Sometimes she returned to the Plaza of Men just because she liked the energy of the place; mostly she spent her time at the Plaza of Women, where she listened to gossip and sorted through clothing and bought food for the rest of the day.

Every afternoon she paused for a few moments to watch the three blind sisters share information with their clients, and every day she turned away without posing any questions of her own.

Twice she stopped at temples, paid the tithes, and pulled blessings from the center barrels. Each time, *coru* traits came up in her hand: first change and then resilience. She figured she had already encountered plenty of the first, but she was happy to see the second. Her new life was still so amorphous, so unsettled, that she would need to muster all her resilience to successfully adapt and thrive.

About midway through Quinncoru she realized she was running low on funds. She had been careless with her money, not just purchasing necessary items like food and clothing, but buying another pair of shoes in the Plaza and indulging herself in sweets whenever she wanted them. So she cut another gold piece from the shawl and returned to the Plaza of Men to swap it for more manageable denominations. Although she was positive that he recognized her, the rumpled old moneychanger gave no sign that he had done business with her before, which she supposed was the way most of his clients preferred to operate. She slipped the change into her leather purse and turned away.

She had not made it three steps from his booth when a great commotion started building up from the northern edge of the Plaza and spread through the crowd like ripples speeding through water from the impact of a boulder. Like everyone else, she pulled back toward the perimeter, curious but cautious. She half lifted her bright shawl to shadow her face, then changed her mind and tied it around her waist, where no one wandering by would be likely to see it. Instead, she wrapped her head with a cheap blue scarf she had just bought because she liked how closely it matched her tunic.

The crowd pressed back even farther toward the outer edge of the Plaza, obviously clearing the way for some procession. It did not take much intuition to guess that a royal party had descended from the mountain to make an expedition through the city. Zoe wondered if she would see the king, whom she remembered only hazily from her few encounters with him more than ten years ago.

At first it was hard to tell who rode at the heart of the convoy that moved slowly into view. It was ringed by marching guards all wearing shoulder patches featuring the king's rosette—the five intertwined colors of the five elementals. At the center of the procession was a vehicle about the size of a horse cart, though much plusher and completely devoid of horses. Another one of those smoker coaches, thought Zoe, standing on tiptoe to see over the shoulders of the men in front of her. And sitting inside it, on what appeared to be velvet cushions, were one man and three gorgeously dressed women.

Zoe caught her breath. These had to be three of the king's wives. Which three? Where was the fourth wife and why had she been excluded? What would they say if they knew that lurking in this crowd was the woman who had been chosen to be the king's fifth bride?

The smoker coach came to a halt and the man vaulted out so he could help the women disembark. Zoe could hear the whispers of the other fascinated watchers in the crowd.

Is that Alys?

Yes, and Seterre and Romelle.

Where's Elidon?

They say she won't go anywhere if Alys is included.

She's beautiful, don't you think?

Alys? Yes, but don't you think she looks cruel?

She's all sweela. *All ambition and fire.*

Zoe could only guess which one was Alys, but the choice seemed fairly obvious. One of the women was small-boned and elegant, with dark red hair that curved perfectly around her heart-shaped face. She wore loose scarlet trousers that fit tightly at the waist and ankles, so that she seemed to swirl when she walked, and a white overrobe so short it showed off the thinness of her waist. Even from a distance, it was possible to see the darkness of her eyes, the redness of her lips, and the perfection of her complexion.

Zoe didn't get much more than an impression of the other two wives, both of them fair-haired and smiling. Alys, even with her small frame, seemed to block both of them from view. Alys said something to them over her shoulder and then laid her hand possessively on the arm of the man who had helped them from the car. The whole procession began to move in a leisurely fashion toward the booth of promises.

Zoe stopped paying attention to Alys once she realized that the queens' escort was Darien Serlast.

His face offered no expression at all as he strode beside Alys through the Plaza, though his head was tilted slightly in her direction as if he was listening to her conversation. Indeed, Zoe could see Alys's red lips moving in what appeared to be a constant stream of observations. Her beauty, her graceful motions, and what Zoe supposed was witty conversation all appeared to be wasted on Darien Serlast. He did not look bored, precisely, but neither did he look as if the king's wife had engaged all his attention. His stern face did not relax into a smile; his restless eyes flicked ceaselessly over the crowd. Zoe drew back even farther as the group grew even with her and then passed by.

She knew she should slip away before there was the remotest chance Darien Serlast would see her, but an ungovernable curiosity kept her in place another five minutes. They were indeed headed to the booth of promises—all three queens, Darien Serlast, and their cadre of guards. Zoe amused herself by wondering what possible vow Darien was planning to wring from the king's wives—or they from him—what promise was so critical that all of them felt it had to be sworn and recorded in front of witnesses.

Then she wondered what kind of pledge she would require of Darien Serlast, should she ever see him again. *Promise you will never again threaten to make me marry the king.*

She stood there a moment, so amazed by her own revelation that for a moment she forgot she was spying on members of the royal court. It turned out she did *not* want to become one of the king's wives. It turned out she *did* have some notion of what would make her happy and what would make her miserable—and she cared enough to pay attention to the difference.

Two days later, when Zoe browsed through the Plaza of Women, she stood for a long time before the low dais that held the blind sisters. At that moment, all three of them were in consultation with visitors, but soon, one client rose to his feet and descended, so deep in thought that he almost bumped into Zoe. She hesitated only an instant before climbing the shallow steps and settling herself onto the serviceable brown mat laid in front of the seer. It was the kind of day that Zoe had always thought of as blond and blue-eyed—the sun was so yellow it gave the whole world a golden cast, while the clear sky could not have been a deeper shade of cyan. Here in the fifth nineday of Quinncoru, the air was deliciously warm; the sunlight on Zoe's back felt like a hand resting between her shoulder blades.

"Sister," she said, "I have a question."

The woman tilted her head slightly, listening to the cadence of her voice. "Have you consulted with any of us before?"

"My father did, some years ago, but I never have."

"Then I will tell you how we proceed. You give me a coin and state your question. If the coin is not large enough to pay for the answer, I will keep my hand extended. You may also pay for the answer with information of your own."

"I don't think I know anything of value."

The seer smiled a little. Her face was doughy and pale, though she spent so much time outside she should be tanned dark as leather. It was almost as if the fact that she could not actually see the sun meant its light did not fall on her; it was as if she curled in a dark burrow, restful and relaxed. The notion was enhanced by the serenity of her expression. For someone who must know some truly horrifying secrets, Zoe thought, this was a woman who seemed deeply at peace.

"You might be surprised to learn what information is valuable and what is not," the seer replied. "Everyone knows something that is worth paying for."

"Some other day I might realize what that is," Zoe said, handing over a silver coin.

"What do you want to know?"

"I have been gone from Chialto a long time. But when I was here last, Navarr Ardelay was an advisor to the king and the rest of his family was highly respected. I know he was disgraced some time ago, but has that trouble extended to all his relatives? If I had business to transact with the Five Families, should I avoid the Ardelays?"

"The Ardelays have been absent from court, but they have not lost all their connections. Nelson Ardelay is still prime—the head of the family—and he still maintains friendships with the Serlasts," the seer said. "You would suffer no taint by trading with the Ardelays, but you would win no favor with the king, either."

"And what about Navarr Ardelay? What happened to him?"

The seer extended her hand again and Zoe laid a quint-silver in the palm. She wasn't willing to pay more than that for an answer she already knew, but she was curious to learn how her father's exile had been viewed in the city.

The seer weighed the coin and seemed to decide, reluctantly, that it was good enough. "He quarreled with the king ten years ago and left in disgrace. He disappeared with his daughter and was not heard from again. I have heard it said he recently died in exile."

"What did they argue about?"

"Navarr Ardelay had counseled the king against making a treaty with the Soeche-Tas nation across the mountains. Other advisors considered them valuable potential allies, and there was even some thought that King Vernon would take one of the viceroy's daughters as his fourth wife. But Navarr Ardelay did not trust the viceroy and resisted the notion of another wedding. The arguments grew so heated that Navarr Ardelay was barred from court. Even so, no alliance was ever finalized—and no wedding, either."

Zoe was almost disappointed. It did not seem like the sort of disagreement that should have cost her father so much, but perhaps she simply didn't understand politics. "But the king has four wives now," Zoe said.

"Yes, he married Romelle three years ago. A *torz* girl."

"Tell me about his wives and his children," Zoe said, preparing to hand over another quint-silver.

But the sister waved off the money. Zoe supposed this was such common knowledge that the seer couldn't justify being paid for the information.

"Elidon is the king's first and most beloved wife," the seer said. "She is all *elay*, gracious and kind, and the king loves her greatly. But she was never able to bear him an heir. Seterre is the second wife—a *hunti* girl—and she has one daughter, who is now fourteen. But there was no second child, so the king married Alys with the hope of producing more heirs. She, too, has one daughter, who is eleven years old. Romelle was delivered of a baby girl in Quinnelay, but she is fussy and not very strong, and Romelle has not conceived another child."

Zoe's attention had been caught by one salient fact that Darien Serlast had never bothered to mention. *Elay, torz, hunti* . . . and she would bet she knew the answer to this question. "Is Alys *sweela*? I glimpsed her in the market and thought she looked to be all fire and mind."

"She is, and her daughter as well."

And I am not only Ardelay, I am coru, Zoe thought. No wonder the king had been so eager to bring her to the marriage bed. His house would be in balance indeed. "If Romelle is *torz*, perhaps she will prove more fertile," Zoe said.

"Yes, and she is quite young," the seer replied. "Elidon is past the age of bearing children, and Seterre nearing it. But both Alys and Romelle could yet produce many more heirs for the king."

There was a moment of silence while Zoe reviewed what she had learned and how much more she needed to ask. But not today; there were some answers she wasn't yet prepared to learn. "I do have one more question," she said slowly. "Yesterday, three of the king's wives strolled through the Plaza of Men to the promise booth. They were accompanied by a man I did not know. What kind of vow were they making—to each other or to their escort?"

The seer promptly put her hand out again, and when she accepted two coppers for the answer, Zoe figured she was not the first person who had asked this question. Indeed, half the people who had witnessed the procession through the Plaza of Men had probably hurried to the Plaza of Women the very next day—and the vendor who recorded vows had probably sped through the crowds to the seers' stage the instant his transaction was completed. In a city that thrived on gossip, *that* particular bit of news was so useful the seer might have paid *him* to relate it.

"They were exacting a promise from the king that he would not bring a fifth wife into the household without their approval and consent."

That was so funny Zoe felt her ribs expand with laughter. The laughter felt so odd inside her constricted chest, as if it was a cough that had been surprised into something else. Had the queens gotten wind of Darien Serlast's expedition? Or did a disappointed king make such a fuss over Zoe's escape that eventually everyone in the palace knew what Darien's commission had been?

"A promise from the king!" Zoe exclaimed ingenuously.

"Was that the man who traveled with them? I wish I had taken a better look."

"They were accompanied by Darien Serlast, who frequently acts as the king's agent. He signed the note in proxy for the king."

And who is Darien Serlast? How much influence does he have with the king? Is he a good man? A wise man? A dangerous man? A reformer, a schemer, a cipher? Instead of asking the questions, Zoe rose to her feet, brushing the dust from the back of her trousers.

"Thank you," she said. "You have been most informative."

"Come back someday when you have more questions."

"Oh, I will. I have so many questions that I will have to think hard about which ones I want answered first."

During the next nineday, Zoe returned three times to the trio of sisters on the seers' pavilion. She was trying to get a better idea of the politics of the city and the Five Families who were such a crucial part of the city government—something she had only dimly grasped when she lived there before.

The Dochenzas, all *elay*, were currently the richest of the Families, mostly because their gas-powered smoker coaches were in such high demand. But Kayle Dochenza, prime of the clan, was an odd and reclusive man who spent little time at court. His nephew often served as his emissary instead, though he was just as odd as his uncle, if somewhat more social.

The Frothens—mostly *torz*, though a few had produced *coru* offspring who were unreliable and interesting—were also enjoying a time of ascendance, due in large part to the fact that Romelle had just given birth to the king's third daughter. On the other hand, the Lalindars, who had been so powerful while Christara was alive, had slipped somewhat in power and influence.

"Her death left them disorganized, and it seems that neither her son nor her daughter will take on the responsibilities of the prime," the seer said.

Of course, Christara had produced *two* daughters. Alieta, the oldest, had been willful, unpredictable, headstrong, and capricious; and she had married Navarr Ardelay even though her mother expressly forbade it. After Alieta had died—after her body had been sent down the Marisi River, as befit a *coru* woman—Zoe had never seen any of her Lalindar relatives again. Navarr had told her they didn't care enough about her to come and visit her in exile, so it was hard for her to feel any sympathy for them now.

"Well, I don't suppose it matters to anyone except the Lalindars that they do not have their affairs in order," Zoe said.

"It is never good when any of the Five Families are out of balance," the seer said. "The rest of the world falls out of balance as well. Some people even believe the country has seen such drought over the past two years because the Lalindars still have not recovered from Christara's death."

Zoe widened her eyes. "Surely no *coru* family, even the Lalindars, has that kind of power."

The seer shrugged. "It is only what some people say."

There didn't seem to be much else to discover about the Lalindars. Zoe pretended to cogitate a moment. "Who is left to talk about? Oh—the Serlasts. When I lived here last, Damon Serlast was the prime of the family. Is that still the case? Or has the title passed to that Serlast man who advises the king? For some reason I cannot keep his name in mind."

She didn't know why she said that. Of course she remembered very well what the king's advisor was called. She couldn't understand why it pleased her so much to hear his name on someone else's lips.

"Darien Serlast—Damon's son," the seer said. "No, Damon is dead, but the title has gone to Damon's sister Mirti. She is not the richest of the Five Families, but she has a great deal of influence at court. She and the king's first wife are close allies. She has also befriended Nelson Ardelay in an attempt to repair the king's breach with that family."

"Why would she do that?"

The seer shrugged. "She is a practical woman, and she always advocates balance, or so she says. If she has other motives, who knows? But *hunti* and *sweela* make for a tricky alliance, for fire can burn wood and bone can batter brain. There is always a chance at great turmoil when those traits are brought together in a room."

"That is a chance that exists whenever a *sweela* man or woman is invited through the door," Zoe said, unable to suppress a smile. "No matter if it is *torz* or *coru* or *elay* on the other side."

The seer smiled back. "I thought I sensed some *sweela* energy in you," she said, "though it is burning very low."

"Brighter every day," Zoe replied.

"But not all fire, all mind," the sister said thoughtfully. "You are a woman of blood and water, as well, unless all my senses have been blunted."

"My mother was *coru*," Zoe acknowledged. "But *coru* supplied none of my random blessings."

"It is better that way," the seer said. "Each energy has its own strength and its own weakness. It is best to be in balance."

Zoe remembered Darien Serlast and how every blessing he pulled from the temple barrel had been some *hunti* variation. She supposed there wasn't much balance in *his* life. But she was not up to asking about him today. "Indeed, I strive for just such a thing in all my dealings," Zoe said and rose to her feet.

"Come back when you have more questions."

"Sister, I will."

SIX

Zoe was making a brief detour through the shop district before she went home, admiring the merchandise she could not afford to buy, when she was approached by an agitated man. He looked to be a year or two older than she was, dark-haired and wild-eyed, and he appeared to have spent at least the last day in the same stained overrobe. But the cut of the cloth was expensive and the set of his face bespoke intelligence, and Zoe felt no fear when he reached out as if to take her arm, although he did not actually touch her.

"My wife has had—two of them, babies, *two*—and I must get blessings for both," he said, stumbling over the words. "I—can you?—and for each of them? Or must I find six people? I don't know, I don't know."

She wanted to laugh but she also wanted to soothe him. "Blessings are easily come by," she said in a reassuring voice. "Are the babies healthy? Or is some of your concern for their well-being?"

For a moment, his anxiety disappeared behind a beaming smile. "Oh! Quite healthy! Beautiful! Both girls, you know, and I love them so much already, although I had thought—and the one has already smiled at me, though the nurse says I am mistaken. I did not want to leave but they are five hours old and I must find strangers—how does one do this? It is so very odd."

Zoe would have had to ask him to be sure, but she had to think this was an *elay* man, all air and spirit, entirely ill-suited for mundane, everyday tasks. She had never done this, either, but she understood how the ritual was supposed to work. She gently took his arm and guided him down the street, under the colorful shop awnings, back toward the Plaza of Women.

"I know where a temple is," she said. "There are sure to be people there meditating. We will draw all the blessings for your little girls."

Indeed, when they stepped into the small shrine, there were five or six others sitting on the benches, their eyes closed and their breathing slow as they attempted to restore themselves to a state of harmony.

"Oh, but I can't disturb any of them," the new father whispered in a voice loud enough to carry.

"It will be all right," Zoe said quietly, and led him to the blessing barrel. "Which daughter was born first?"

"Anna," the man replied. "She's the one who smiled at me."

Zoe skimmed her hand across the surface of the coins, sleek and cool and sliding away from her fingers. It seemed to Zoe that she should choose a coin from the very top layer of the barrel to bless an infant so newly brought into the world. Before she could think about it too long, she closed her fingers over a disk and pulled it out. It was pristine and freshly minted, as if it had never been culled from the barrel and tossed back in, as most of the blessing coins were, over and over.

"Grace," she said with a smile and handed it to the young father. "That is a lovely gift for Anna to have at the beginning of her life."

"Yes! Perfect. Grace," he repeated, holding the coin as if it were struck from gold.

"Perhaps you should put Anna's blessings in your left pocket, and your other daughter's in your right pocket, so you do not get them mixed up," Zoe suggested.

"Excellent! Of course! How thoughtful—well, then—and for Elle?"

For the second twin, Zoe drew a blessing of serenity. The girl's father seemed much impressed by this.

"Yes! Of course! For Anna has been . . . very vocal—crying, you know, even though she is fed—but Elle seems much more *peaceful*. From what I can tell after five short hours," he added hastily.

"I am sure both of them will have their moods," Zoe said, smiling. "Now, would you like me to help you choose two more people to bestow the other blessings?"

"I would be so grateful," he said. "I don't know—I mean, how can you tell who would be pleased and who would be annoyed at such a request?"

To Zoe, one choice was fairly obvious. A short, matronly woman had opened her eyes and come hopefully to her feet as soon as she realized that random blessings were being handed out. She had probably participated in such a ritual dozens of times, Zoe thought, and seemed like the type of woman who would enjoy it even more if she could actually cradle the newborn in her arms.

"The woman in the black tunic—yes—the one smiling at you," Zoe whispered to the young father. "Gesture to her and I'm sure she'll come over."

Indeed, the motherly woman moved with alacrity to join them in the center of the temple. "I do love to bestow a blessing, but I've never had the chance to do it for twins," she said, cheerfully rummaging through the whole barrel. "Oh! See that? I pulled up two coins with one hand. And they're both joy," she said, smiling even harder. "Two girls blessed with joy! It could not be better."

"I don't suppose you'll get those two mixed up, no matter which pocket you put them in," Zoe said.

She studied the other people sitting quietly in the temple, while the young father earnestly thanked the matron and she exited through the nearest door, still beaming. Two of the visitors still had their eyes closed and seemed oblivious to any other activity, but the other three were watching them, openly or covertly, ready to do their duty if they were called upon. One was a man about her father's age, dignified and thoughtful; another was a harried-looking woman who probably had a houseful of her own children waiting for her. Either would be a safe and reasonable choice, but the one who caught Zoe's attention was the skinny redheaded boy who looked to be about thirteen, wide-eyed, fascinated, and burning with curiosity.

"Pick him," she whispered to the father. "He will choose some interesting blessings for your girls."

Surprised but clearly incapable of making any choices on his own, the twins' father beckoned the youth over. He practically bounded through the temple, almost knocking the barrel over.

"I get to pick blessings? Really?" he demanded. He was obviously trying to keep his voice down, in deference to the place and the occasion, but he was so excited he didn't quite succeed. "I've never done it before! What must I do? What if I pick the wrong ones?"

"There are no wrong blessings," Zoe said tranquilly, when the father looked at her with a quirk of nervousness. "Every random blessing is the right one for that child at that moment."

She nodded at the father, who said, "Please pick first for Anna."

The redhead drove his thin arm deep into the barrel and pulled out a slightly battered coin. "Wealth," he said, handing it over. The relief in his voice was palpable. He must realize everyone welcomed this particular coin.

"Wealth! Wonderful! My aunt has money, and she has not decided on an heir—of course, Anna is just a baby—and, anyway, I mean, Elle should certainly have as much as Anna, not that I expect them to be identical—"

"And for your other daughter?" Zoe prodded gently.

"Yes! Of course! Will you pick for Elle?"

A little more confidently this time, the boy plucked a second coin from the barrel. His face was drawn into a slight frown as he showed the glyph to Zoe. "I don't recognize that one," he said, slightly uneasy.

"Time," she whispered, as the father took the coin reverently into his hand. It was one of the three extraordinary blessings that belonged to no category and were rarely bestowed. "A marvelous gift for such a young girl."

"Then I did it right?" the boy asked, bouncing eagerly.

Zoe couldn't resist reaching out to tousle his already untidy red hair. "You did exceptionally well."

The father was fumbling in his pockets, searching for more

prosaic coins. "Do I—I'm sorry, I can't recall—should you be paid for your services?" He swiveled around to look with some dismay at the door where the matronly woman had already disappeared. "Except—oh, dear—but I didn't think of it in time—or is it an insult?"

"You may offer small thanks, but you are not compelled to do so," Zoe told him. Her father had explained this to her once, fortunately, or she would not have known how to answer. "And those who have bestowed their blessings may accept your thanks, but they do not dishonor you if they refuse. Though some choose then to toss those coins in the tithing box," she added.

She was not surprised when the hungry-looking boy happily accepted the quint-silver pressed into his hand and then went skipping out the door. But she shook her head when the new father tried to give her the same wages.

"I have been paid," she said, smiling. "I have been touched with all their blessings, and your happiness, too."

"Is it—I have heard it was customary—should I pull a blessing for myself as well?" he asked.

Zoe laughed. "I would think you need a blessing now more than you ever did," she said. And she laughed even harder, trying to muffle the sound against her palm, when the coin he chose was stamped with the symbol for patience.

"No doubt that is something you will have very great need of with baby twins in the house," she said merrily.

His grin was lopsided but genuine. "Perhaps you should pull a blessing for yourself," he suggested.

"Perhaps I will," she replied, and picked up the first coin her fingers encountered. "Clarity," she said, and smiled a little. It had been the blessing her father coveted most, though she remembered it coming into his hands only once or twice during their ten years of exile. "I do believe my mind is starting to clear."

The young father looked faintly intrigued by that, and Zoe had the sense he might have followed up with questions on any other day when the tasks awaiting him at home were not so urgent. "I can't—you have been—thank you," he said in his disordered way.

She smiled. "And you have been as well," she said. "May

all blessings fall on you and yours for the remainder of your days."

Zoe had fallen into the habit of joining Calvin and Annova for dinner three or four times every nineday, usually when she had bought herself a treat and was embarrassed to think she might eat the whole thing on her own. On her way home that night, she purchased a shockingly expensive bag of chocolate drops imported from a country she couldn't even pronounce. Annova almost gasped when Zoe handed it over.

"I know how much these cost, and if you can afford them, you shouldn't be sleeping down here at the river," she said. That didn't stop her from scooping up a candy and sliding it instantly in her mouth. Her eyes closed and she made a small sound of satisfaction.

Zoe laughed. "I had to celebrate," she said. "I was approached in the streets and asked to bestow random blessings on a set of twin girls. After such an event, you cannot live an ordinary life. You must be extravagant."

This explanation seemed perfectly reasonable to Annova. "What did you draw for them?"

"Grace and serenity."

"Excellent virtues."

Zoe smiled. "Ones that I sometimes wish had been bestowed upon me."

They had long ago compared their own blessings. Annova's were all *torz* and *coru*, which Zoe would have been able to guess; she was a nurturing sort of woman.

"Your own blessings will serve you well," Annova said.

"Beauty and power?" Zoe said a little derisively. "They do not seem to have hovered over me so far."

Annova reached up to fool with the untidy locks of hair falling into Zoe's face. "You are not a conventional beauty, it is true. But neither am I, and I very much like the way I look," she replied. "I'm sure your father was a fine man, but it usually takes a woman to help a girl learn how to enhance her looks."

"And my mother died when I was eleven," Zoe said.

"Let me cut your hair and show you how to wear cosmetics," Annova said. "Different ones from the kinds I use. Your skin is much fairer."

Zoe widened her eyes. "That's kind but—" She gestured at the whole expanse of the river flats, filling up with their nightly quota of transients. "Who is there to impress with my new beauty?"

"You will not spend all your life camping here," Annova said with conviction.

"Even if I don't, why is it that suddenly *today* you think I need to improve myself?"

Annova's voice was gentle. "Because suddenly *today* you are laughing, and I see what a pretty girl you could be."

Zoe was so surprised that she simply sank to the ground, reviewing the state of her heart. Yes—she had felt deep amusement once or twice as she consulted with the seer, and she had felt actual delight as she participated in the blessing ritual. She would not have gone so far as to say she was feeling joyous, but she felt looser somehow, limber, as if the joints of her soul had warmed up after seasons spent locked immobile. She was beginning to remember what it felt like to be herself.

Clarity.

The coin she had pulled from the barrel was, like every blessing, proving itself to be true.

A middle-aged woman named Sima helped Annova cut and style Zoe's hair, though Zoe had not been so certain about the cutting part. "Nonsense, you're as ragged as an alley cat," Sima had said so matter-of-factly that Zoe couldn't bother to be offended. And apparently there was no cutting without washing, and if you were going to wash your hair, you might as well scrub your whole body. So the day of Zoe's transformation began with the three of them flinging themselves into the chilly Marisi during the morning hours reserved for the women to bathe.

It was the first time Zoe had wholly immersed herself since arriving at the river flats. A few of the more enterprising residents set up bathing tents along the banks every day, and a couple of times every nineday she had paid her five coppers for a tub of clean water and a modicum of privacy. But Sima and Annova had no inhibitions about completely disrobing and stepping into the water, staying close enough to the bank that they were never more than waist deep. Dozens of other women were already bobbing in the current, some of them holding babies and toddlers, others swimming out with long, sure strokes into the deeper, faster waters.

Annova's body was long and sleek; Sima's was full and pendulous, the pale stomach showing stretch marks and scars from numerous childbirths. It didn't bother them that anyone could stare at them, note their imperfections—and their attractions—judge their weight, their health.

"Come on, *coru* girl!" Annova shouted when Zoe lingered too long on the bank. "You cannot be afraid of the river."

Zoe took a deep breath, then dropped all her clothes on the ground and stepped into the Marisi.

She had expected it to be icy from its plunge down the mountains, but apparently its long, somnolent pause in the pool beside the palace allowed it time to heat up under a strengthening sun. Not that it was actually *warm*. Zoe felt her skin prickle with goose bumps as she held her breath and ducked her head under the unquiet surface.

For a long moment, it was as if she had suspended the need to breathe.

The water swirled around her, almost as if gathering her in an embrace. She felt as though silken hands brushed along her bare arms, stroked down the length of her thigh. Muffled voices murmured at her ears, speaking words just outside of her ability to comprehend. She felt buoyant, liberated, energized, and at peace. She felt, for a brief, glorious stretch of time, as if she belonged.

Then her lungs burned with protest and her mind clamored with alarm. She shot to the surface, taking in great gasps of air, and beating her arms against the water to warm up her skin.

Sima and Annova were splashing over with big, messy footsteps. "How can you stay under so long?" Annova demanded. "I thought maybe you'd been swept away."

Zoe was still panting, but she felt incredible. As if she had run swiftly down a mountain, as if she had spun herself into dizziness, as if she had drunk glass after glass of wine, suffering no effect except euphoria. She laughed. "*Coru* girl," she said, because really, there was no other explanation. "Water is my natural element."

"Well, water is the element that will get you clean," Sima said practically. The heavyset woman was holding a bar of some rough soap that smelled surprisingly fragrant. "You can use this to wash your skin *and* your hair," she said.

They all commenced to lather up and rinse off with great efficiency, since the longer they were in the water, the colder it seemed. Two little girls chased each other in and out of the river while their mother called to them sleepily from the bank; other women jumped in, scrambled out, and swam by while the three of them worked. It was a lively, happy scene, and Zoe found herself smiling the whole time.

Once they were out and dried off and back at Annova's campsite, Sima combed out Zoe's hair and began to make careful cuts. "I would *like* to trim it short around your face, but Annova says you aren't ready for drastic changes," Sima said. "But see how you like it when there is just a little styling."

The "little" styling also involved heating slim rods over the brazier and wrapping locks of Zoe's hair around them, a process that Zoe viewed with alarm. "That's why I keep my own so short," Annova said, running a hand over her crisp black hair.

While Sima worked, Annova began fussing over Zoe's face with a motley assortment of cosmetics—cracked and nearly empty pots of rouge, dry end-sticks of kohl, crumbled cakes of eye powder. Zoe was surprised to learn she *wanted* to see what she could become under someone else's hands. She had always been simply Navarr Ardelay's daughter. Who else might emerge when that persona was pushed aside?

Annova had insisted Zoe change into a deep red tunic, more tightly fitted than most of the ones she owned. "You don't wear enough *sweela* colors," she scolded. "They're the right ones for your complexion."

"I like blues and greens. Shades of *coru*."

"Those are good, too, but they must be the right shades."

Finally she was dressed to the satisfaction of the older women, her face made up, every strand of hair arranged just so. "There," Annova said with satisfaction. "*This* is how you are meant to look when you live up to your blessing of beauty."

Sima had brought a mirror, something Zoe had consulted only rarely during the past ten years. It was about the size of her palm and not really useful for getting a good look at her overall image, but what she saw in bits and pieces looked nothing like the person she remembered.

Her black hair lay perfectly against her face, curling at her chin. Her dark eyes looked huge, the lids shadowed with subtle sweeps of charcoal. Her thin mouth was fuller, redder, and curved in a smile. The gold and scarlet colors of her ensemble reflected deeper color into her sallow skin.

She was not a beauty, but she looked striking. Clear-eyed. Confident. Slightly mysterious.

"A *coru* girl with a *sweela* heart," Annova said with satisfaction. "And what do you get with that?"

Sima was the one who replied. "Steam."

SEVEN

Three days later, Zoe had a job.

A few more shopping trips to the Plaza of Women, a few investments in the bold colors that Annova approved of, and Zoe found herself exchanging her third gold coin for more reasonable denominations. A quick count of the lumps still left lining her shawl made her think she would race through her inheritance in little more than a year if she continued at this pace. So the next time Calvin and Annova invited her to dinner, she expressed her intention to seek employment.

"Come with me to the shop district tomorrow," Annova said. "I'll introduce you to some friends."

The next day, Zoe and Annova spent a pleasant couple of hours strolling by the storefronts while Annova pointed out the boutiques where she knew the owners. They discussed the advantages of working for a vintner, a bookseller, and a woman who made fashionable women's clothing, but in the end Annova decided Zoe should offer her services to a cobbler and his wife. "*Torz*, both of them, but she only bore the one son, and he's proved to be restless," Annova said. "You can be useful to them, I believe. *Coru* sustains *torz*. Water drenches earth."

The instant they entered the little shop, they were inhaling the distinctive scents of leather and dye. The day was cool but sunny, and the yellow awning stretched above the door threw a warm golden tint into the front room. The space was small and incredibly crowded. All four walls were lined with shelves that stretched to the ceiling, and every shelf held dozens of small wrapped bundles that Zoe assumed were pairs of completed shoes. A short wooden counter was set close to the back wall, a stool behind it and another bank of shelves behind that. A golden curtain hung over a doorway very close to the counter; Zoe supposed the workroom was behind that, for she could hear the cheerful metallic sound of a hammer tapping a chisel or a nail.

"Ilene?" Annova called. "Melvin?"

The curtain brushed back and a short, thin woman stepped through. Zoe guessed she was in her late fifties, ropy and sinewy, with stringy gray hair pushed back behind her ears.

"Annova," Ilene said, offering a limited smile. Zoe did not get the impression that this was a particularly effusive woman, despite her *torz* traits. "Have you come for a new pair of shoes?"

Annova extended her right foot, clad in a cushioned half-boot. Zoe had never bothered paying much attention to Annova's footwear before. "No, these are holding up remarkably well," she said. "I may never need another pair." She laughed. "Perhaps you do your job too well, my friend."

"Other folks require more than a single pair of shoes to get them through their lives," Ilene retorted. "With those customers, high quality guarantees additional sales."

Annova looked around the shop. "Has Barlow joined the family business yet?"

Ilene's gaunt face clouded over. "No. In fact, he has expanded his trade route, and he is sometimes gone for quintiles at a time."

"Barlow is her son," Annova explained to Zoe, as if she hadn't shared this fact before they stepped inside the shop. Zoe nodded and Annova continued. "Still, he must be successful in his trading ventures if he's going more places."

Ilene brightened a little. "Yes—and he has brought us back some remarkable goods. White leather so soft it feels like silk. Fleece to line winter boots. Dyes that I have seen in no other storefront in Chialto. Even the king's wives have come to us to buy belts and shoes and bags."

"I'm glad to hear Barlow is so successful, but sorry to learn that you are without his assistance," Annova said. "Are you looking for someone to help you out in the shop? I've brought my friend Zoe to recommend in case you are."

Ilene gave Zoe a sharp, thorough inspection. Her dusty brown eyes were narrowed; her expression was skeptical.

"We've hired workers from time to time, but we've always been disappointed," Ilene said. "One of them stole from us. One was so lazy we had to push him out the door—he was too lazy even to walk out on his own!"

"You wouldn't have any of those problems with Zoe," Annova assured her. "She's honest and hardworking."

Ilene still looked skeptical but not entirely set against the notion. "What have you done before?" she asked Zoe.

"Only domestic work, I'm afraid," Zoe said. "I helped my father with his correspondence and his accounts, and I nursed him when he was sick. I managed the household budget, kept the property clean, and cooked for both of us."

It was a meager enough set of skills, but Ilene did not look displeased. "So you know how to count and handle money, and you can read and write?" she asked. When Zoe nodded, Ilene said, "Show me."

Writing materials were quickly produced, and Zoe carefully lettered her first name, the names of everyone in her village, and the names of all the king's wives.

"Very pretty handwriting," Ilene said, her voice warming up to cautious approval. "Now let me see you do sums." She rattled off numbers for Zoe to add and subtract, and then pulled out a coin box and had her make change.

"I don't know anything about shoes, though," Zoe confessed when the shopkeeper actually started to look pleased.

Ilene waved away this deficiency. "We're not looking for an apprentice. Melvin and I do all the cutting and sewing. But we need someone watching the front of the shop to wait on customers and prevent anyone from stealing. If one of us has to sit here all day, we can scarcely get our work done."

"I'd be happy to sit here," Zoe said, "if you'd have me."

"Then it's settled?" Annova asked.

Ilene was still unconvinced. "I'll ask Melvin."

She disappeared through the curtain, reappearing moments later with her husband in tow. He was a big man with a short brush of thick gray hair still holding traces of brown. He was a little stooped and, despite his size, radiated an air of supreme gentleness. He was wearing a workman's apron stuffed with tools, and his sleeves and clothing were streaked with dyes.

When Ilene introduced him, he looked Zoe over with watery green eyes that were more accustomed to focusing on objects than on faces. She held herself very still, thinking too much animation might confuse him.

"Take her to a temple," he said to his wife, turning back toward the workroom. "See if any of the blessings make sense."

Ilene looked relieved. "I'll do that," she said, adding to Zoe, "You're willing?"

"Of course," she said.

"I'm coming with you," Annova said.

They ended up at the same temple Zoe had visited when she pulled blessings for the twin girls. That seemed propitious, but she didn't want to be overly optimistic. She wasn't quite sure how this would work. It was difficult to pull a negative coin from the barrel since, of course, the very word *blessing* was meant to be reassuringly positive. What particular character trait might Ilene view with doubt and suspicion?

There were, Zoe knew, a few coins tumbling around in the depths of the barrels that were so old and so worn their glyphs were impossible to read. People called these ghost coins; they were usually considered unlucky, hinting at a future too dire to predict or a personality too debased to describe. When drawn for an infant, they were sometimes believed to forecast a very short life. The acolytes went to some trouble to sift these ghost coins out of the temple barrels, but unless they dumped the entire contents on the floor and refilled the barrel piece by piece, there was no way to screen them out entirely. A ghost coin might be unlucky in this instance, she thought; she wouldn't pull out any disk unless she could detect some pattern raised into the metal.

"You choose a blessing, and then I will," Ilene directed.

Zoe plunged her hand into the cool metallic bounty, found a piece clearly stamped with some design, and pulled it out. She handed it to Ilene without looking.

"Honesty," said the shopkeeper. For the first time she showed Zoe a genuine smile. "That is a very good trait to possess."

"And now you," Annova said.

Ilene buried her hand wrist-deep in the barrel before pulling out a single coin. "Wealth," she said, and now she offered an even wider smile. It didn't make her look particularly pretty, or even more rested, but it was an inviting expression. Zoe smiled back.

Ilene said, "My husband and I would like to hire you to work at our shop."

Zoe slipped into this new phase of her life like a raindrop slipping into the sea. It was so effortless. It required so little of her except that she simply be.

She liked having a reason to rise in the morning and to spend a few extra minutes improving her appearance. She liked the ride on the crowded bus down the wide boulevard, followed by the walk through the shop district just as all the doors were opening, before any customers had arrived. She liked having her days filled with just enough responsibilities that they could occupy all her attention, leaving her no time to think about the bigger questions that always crouched at the back of her mind.

She felt like a groggy sleeper who had just awoken from a long and troubled dream and was not yet ready to face the living nightmares waiting in the other room. If she could have, she would have fallen back to sleep, but it was too late. The best she could do was to refuse to leave the bedroom for as long as possible.

Ilene made it very clear what Zoe was expected to do. When no customers were inside the cobbler's shop, she was to stand at the open door, smiling and waving at little girls, offering compliments to the well-dressed women. *What a lovely tunic that is—we have a pair of shoes that would match it perfectly.*

When customers did step inside, Zoe either retrieved their shoes from the shelves, took their money, and noted the transaction in a huge ledger, or she learned that they wanted to buy a new pair. If ready-made shoes were good enough, she would pull a few samples off the shelves for the customers to try on. If they wanted to be fitted for a new pair, she called for Ilene. The cobbler's wife would instantly step through the curtain, carrying her measuring sticks, offering her thin smile, and asking dozens of questions. Was this to be a boot, a sandal, a formal shoe, a casual shoe? Did the customer want the finest imported leather or the sturdy domestic kind? Did the client prefer a sober black or a whimsical red? A low heel or a higher one? Fancy stitching or plain? When was the shoe needed? Zoe was surprised to learn how much fashionable, custom-made shoes could cost; she was frequently handling gold and quint-gold pieces as clients handed over their deposits.

When the shop closed at night, she added up the numbers in the ledger and the coins in the money box to make sure they tallied. Then she brought the money to the back room and waited while Ilene counted it again. Zoe would stand very still and just let her eyes wander around the workroom with its long benches, neatly aligned rows of tools, spools of thread and cord, and shallow shelves of stretched leather. Along the main workbench, wooden lasts lined up in a row like so many upside-down feet.

Against the back wall, under a narrow horizontal window, was another table and a row of small cauldrons. On dyeing days, these would be boiling for hours as Ilene mixed pigments until she was satisfied with the colors. She would carefully set out the sections of leather and brush on layer after layer of color with long, smooth, flawless strokes. The sharp scents would fill the workroom and drift into the front room and out into the street. When she was coming back from lunch, Zoe could smell the cobbler shop for blocks before she could see it.

Some of the boutiques in the shop district never closed, but

Melvin and Ilene shut their doors on firstday. Zoe was always glad to finish that eighth day of labor, knowing that what came next would be a day of rest. Ilene would hand over her wages—three silver pieces—and Zoe would go directly to the Plaza of Women. She usually spent two coins buying food for the next nineday and special treats she could share with Calvin and Annova. The third one she would sew into the hem of her shawl.

Because who knew when she might need to run away again?

Zoe had worked at the cobbler's for two and a half ninedays before there was even a ripple of trouble. It had been a particularly busy afternoon, with customers filling the shop four and five at a time, all of them wealthy, most of them imperious and not used to waiting. Ilene had had to leave off the dyeing and help Zoe at the sales counter, where most customers were retrieving shoes they had ordered some time ago.

"Everyone wants shoes for the holiday," Ilene said to Zoe during a rare quiet moment. "It's always like this right before Quinnahunti. And sometimes right before Quinnasweela. Our two busiest times."

"I hadn't realized Quinnahunti was so close," Zoe admitted. It was the loveliest time of year, late spring melting into early summer, and at the village they'd always celebrated the changeday holiday with food and games.

"Oh, yes! Just four days away now! There will be fairs in both the Plazas, and celebrations at the palace," Ilene said. "Everyone wants to wear their new clothes, so we'll have crowds of people for the next few days."

Which didn't bother Zoe in the slightest, until she tried to balance her accounts that night. In the press of people, the scramble to make sales, it appeared that she had failed to record a transaction—or, worse, failed to give someone the right change. The money box held one more quint-gold coin than it should.

Frowning, Zoe methodically redid the arithmetic and recounted the coins. No, there was still one extra quint-gold in the box. She supposed Ilene could have made the mistake just as easily as she could have, since Ilene had been waiting on customers half the day, but she certainly wasn't going to point that out. She gathered the ledger and the coin box and slipped past the curtain into the back room.

"How did we do?" Melvin asked. He was using an awl to punch holes in a strip of leather. He was often still working when Zoe left, though she didn't have a sense that he stayed on the job because he was worried about finishing projects by a promised deadline. No, she thought he simply loved the tools and accessories of his profession so much that he did not want to put them aside. "The place seemed full from the minute we opened."

"It was our best day since I've been here, but there's a problem," Zoe said.

Ilene, who was standing by the shelves, counting sheaves of leather, quickly turned. "What's wrong?" she asked.

"We have more money than we should," Zoe said. "A quint-gold. Either I didn't give someone change when I should have, or I forgot to write down a sale."

For a fleeting moment, Ilene's face showed satisfaction before she smoothed the expression away. "Oh! Not your fault. I thought we would run out of small coins, so I added a handful of silvers and coppers to the box. I meant to take out a quint-gold, and I forgot."

"Good," Zoe said. "Then everything adds up."

Ilene took the box from her hand. "We'll see you tomorrow, then. I hope it doesn't rain."

Zoe laughed. The sky had been threatening all day, with low clouds bunched in angry gray clusters, and the wind had picked up considerably since they had closed the windows for the night. "I hope so, too, but I think it will," she said. "I'll see you in the morning."

Not until she was hurrying home, head bent against the wind, did it occur to her that Ilene had set a trap for her. Certainly Ilene could have added the coins for just the reason she gave—but just as easily she could have seeded the box to see what Zoe would do. A quint-gold matched to no receipt! Surely that would be a powerful temptation to most girls with little money and few prospects. Ilene still didn't trust Zoe; there might be other tests like this in the future.

Zoe shook her head, smiling faintly. If only Ilene knew how unlikely it was that her new shop worker would steal money or shoes or *anything*. Ilene might find a few things in Zoe's life to surprise or displease her, but larceny wouldn't be one of them.

EIGHT

The Quinnahunti changeday dawned sunny and calm after three days of miserable weather. Even Zoe, who liked rain, had found it unpleasant to camp on the river flats in the unending wet. About half of the squatters disappeared in stormy weather, seeking shelter in alleys and under bridges or with friends and family members who would take them in briefly. Through Annova, Zoe had met a severe and silent older woman named Barra who owned a tent big enough to hold three people. On rainy days, Zoe and another young woman brought their mats to Barra's to sleep, paying three coppers for the privilege. It was better than sleeping in a downpour, but barely. The quarters were cramped, the company unfriendly, and the nights long.

If Zoe planned to spend much more time on the riverfront, she would need to invest in her own tent. But such a commodity was expensive, a couple of quint-golds at least. Not at all worth it if she would be living somewhere else before the year was out.

But would she be? And where?

Zoe closed her mind to the questions and simply handed over her coins.

And Quinnahunti changeday was so gorgeous that she didn't have to think about vexing problems like tents. She took advantage of the mild weather to immerse herself in the river, getting wholly clean, then put on her favorite purple top to celebrate the day.

Ilene had been right—the city turned into one big festival on changeday. The Cinque was just as crowded as the Plazas, brimming with vendors selling food and hats and *hunti* trinkets like wooden whistles and fantastical animals carved out of bone. There was no hope of catching a ride on one of the omnibuses, which were so full that people seemed to spill out of the open sides anytime the wheels hit a bump, and certainly no horse-drawn vehicle could force its way through the pedestrian crowds. Performers of wildly varying levels of sophistication stood on corners and offered music, magic tricks, and acrobatics, while thieves wound through the watching crowds and lifted jewels and purses.

Zoe allowed herself a handful of quint-silvers to spend on the day and wandered happily through the streets, watching more often than spending. She did make one wholly frivolous purchase, a small, twisting fish carved of white bone and painted an iridescent purple. She liked its color as well as the happy flirt of its body. Besides, it was lucky to buy a *hunti* object on Quinnahunti changeday, and a fish was *coru*, which made it luckier still for Zoe. And anyway, it made her smile. She threaded a cord through the closed loop made when its tail touched its glimmering side scales, and she wore it for the rest of the day.

She returned by nightfall, loaded down with candies, and found the whole expanse of the flats turned into one grand feast. Every campfire simmered with some special meal, and the air was so laden with smoky spices that it was a treat just to inhale. Following Annova's advice, Zoe carried her own plate from site to site, asking to taste whatever was cooking. In payment she offered a handful of candies or a quint-copper, whichever her hosts preferred. She ran out of candy first, but by then she was so full she only made it to three more campfires before deciding she could not eat another bite.

It was nearly dark, anyway. She made her way back to Annova and Calvin's tent, where maybe a dozen of their friends already were sprawling on blankets and passing around bottles of wine.

"Any of those lemon sweets left?" Calvin asked hopefully, but she laughed and shook her head.

"Next time I'll buy twice as many," she said.

She lolled back on her own mat, dropped off hours ago for just this purpose, and watched the sky overhead darken to true black. Around her, at varying distances, she could hear bursts of laughter and snatches of music, and now and then a rhythmic clapping that she supposed indicated dancing, though she was too lazy to sit up and strain to see through the dark.

She had been lying there for nearly an hour, growing increasingly sleepy, when she heard Calvin say, "There it goes," right before the collected crowd produced a murmur of delighted approval. So she sat up and turned her attention toward the palace, ensconced high above them in its mountain nook. Normally, by this time of night, the whole building was set with flickering lights at enough windows and turrets that its shape was visible as a series of white dots against the grainy darkness of the mountain. But tonight virtually all of those lights had been doused and there was nothing to see but the hulking, undifferentiated bulk of the mountain itself.

Then a sudden wash of blue light played over the palace, illuminating it and shadowing it in almost equal measures before just as abruptly fading. A moment's pause, and then its shape was exposed in a burst of scarlet light that turned orange as a blast of yellow overlaid the red. The first color disappeared, leaving behind a twinkling golden glow that did not seem to vanish so much as evaporate like steam from a heated stone.

"What is that? It's so beautiful," Zoe murmured as patches of sapphire and amethyst and emerald bloomed along individual towers and doorways in rapid succession before just as quickly fading.

"Some Dochenza invention," Calvin answered. "They make light out of gasses and pigments, but it doesn't last very long, as you can see. Amazing to watch, though."

"They've been doing this for the past three or four years on

Quinnahunti changeday," Annova said. "It's amazing, isn't it? I could sit here all night and watch."

And, in fact, they did. At some point, the broad strokes of color gave way to more complex and intricate patterns, punctuated at times by great swooping shadows that looked like animals—a diving hawk, a running fox, a lumbering bear. It was all quite extraordinary. The show went on till nearly midnight, and even then nobody was ready for it to be over.

Changeday fed straight into firstday, and most of the city had a two-day holiday. Zoe slept till almost noon and found herself disinclined to do much even after she'd rolled to her feet and slipped off to the river to wash up. She was not the only one. There was very little activity along the flats from sunup to sundown. Zoe spent her time making small repairs in her clothing, napping, and staring idly at the river. It was a very good day.

The first two ninedays of Quinnahunti were unremarkable except for the slow heat that began to build in the little shop— enough so that Zoe started to look ahead to oppressive Quinnatorz with a certain amount of apprehension. "It won't be so bad on the street level," Melvin told her one afternoon when he saw her fanning her face with her hand. "Upstairs, that's where it's sometimes so hot you can't sleep, even with every window open and a breeze blowing through."

"*That's* the time to be living down by the river," Ilene added. "We'll be envying you by the middle of Quinnatorz."

Zoe smiled. "Buy yourselves a couple of mats and come sleep down there by me," she invited. "I'll cook you dinner."

She could only make such an offer, even in jest, because her relations with her employers had warmed up considerably since the holiday. Specifically, her relations with Ilene—Melvin didn't seem to have strong feelings for Zoe one way or the other. But Ilene had started to like her, and she had demonstrated this fondness by bestowing small, practical gifts on Zoe. One day it might be a sleeveless tunic in a bright color. *I saw this on the Plaza—they were practically giving it away! Of course it doesn't fit me, but it will look very good on you.* Another day, it was food. *I made this last night and there was so much left over. Why don't you take it for your dinner tonight?* There had been no more tests of Zoe's honesty, though now and then Zoe had the sense that Ilene was trying to determine how well Zoe met her qualifications on other key measures.

For instance, one afternoon they had the responsibility of watching after Ilene's niece, Darray. The girl was nine, skinny and shy, and Ilene insisted she stay out in the front room with Zoe all day "because there's just too much trouble to get into on this side of the curtain." Zoe figured there were at least as many risks in the front half of the shop—such as the open front door, which might seem inviting to a little girl when her keeper was busy with a customer—but she didn't voice the thought. Instead, she kept Darray close at all times, pinned behind the counter with her, amusing the little girl with whatever tasks and games she could think up.

"If only I had someone who could count all the quint-coppers for me!" Zoe lamented early in the afternoon. "There are so many, and I need to keep track."

"I can do that!" Darray piped up.

"Oh, would you? That would be such a help." Quint-coppers were worth so little that even if Darray lost a dozen of them, it wouldn't cost Zoe much to make up the difference, and the chore kept the little girl occupied for nearly an hour.

After that, Zoe had her count the blue shoes on the shelves and draw portraits of some of the customers who came in and demonstrate how long she could hop on one foot and tell her the names of all her friends. Frankly, it was an exhausting day, and Zoe was glad when, near sunset, Ilene's sister came to fetch her daughter.

After seeing Darray and her mother off the premises, Ilene came to rest her elbows on the counter. "Isn't she precious?" she asked Zoe, who was straightening up the day's receipts.

It was obvious how to answer *that* question. "Adorable," Zoe said. "And very well-behaved. Her mother has taught her excellent manners."

"You were very good with her. Do you like children?"

"Usually. I taught math to some of the boys and girls in the village where I used to live. I didn't like *all* of them, of course," she added.

"Well, no. Children have different personalities, just like adults do," Ilene said. "Do you have any nieces and nephews?"

Zoe shook her head. No siblings, no nieces and nephews. Her cousins might have a few children by now, but it was unlikely that Zoe would be getting to know them anytime soon.

"Do you want children of your own?" Ilene asked.

"I never really thought about it," Zoe said blankly, which was the truth. But in situations like this, a conventional answer was always safest. "But if I found the right man to be husband and father—of course I would want them."

Ilene nodded, looking pleased. "Of course."

Three days later, Ilene invited Zoe to dinner.

It was unusual, Zoe knew, for a worker to be allowed into the home of a merchant trader, and she was a little surprised at being admitted so deeply into her employers' lives. Nonetheless, she was honored and strove to show it. She wore her purple top to work on the day she would stay late for the meal. On Annova's advice, she also brought a bag of the expensive chocolates to share with her hosts. "Because even if they don't like chocolate, which would be something unfathomable to me, they will recognize the cost of the item and realize that you are showing gratitude by bringing it to the meal," Annova had said.

In fact, it turned out that both Ilene and Melvin loved chocolate, and Zoe laughingly had to hide the bag from them or they would have consumed every last drop before the workday had even ended.

"It will take me just a little time to get the meal ready, so, here, you take a few quint-silvers—take them, take them!— and wander around a bit and buy yourself something nice," Ilene said. "Come back in an hour, and then we'll eat."

That was certainly an agreeable way to pass an hour, though Zoe thought hard about how to spend her bonus. If she was supposed to lavish the coins on herself, Ilene might be unhappy if Zoe bought a gift for the house instead, and she could hardly purchase something else to supplement the meal, because that would look like she didn't expect much from the food. In the end, she bought an armload of flowers from a booth at the Plaza of Women. A purple blossom to set in her own hair, a small golden bloom for Ilene, and the rest to sit in a vase over dinner and go home with Zoe that night.

She could not help but feel it was another test, and she hoped she passed it, though she was not certain why Ilene had devised it.

Ilene met her in the *kierten* that opened off the back stairs, a narrow little space barely big enough to hold both of them. She exclaimed over the flowers while Zoe enthusiastically inhaled the delicious smells wafting in through the door that connected directly to the kitchen.

"Ilene! Whatever you're cooking smells wonderful!"

Ilene tucked the gold flower behind her ear and preened a little—or, no, she just looked so good because she had taken a little trouble with her hair and her clothing, and there was a smile of pure happiness on her face. "It's Barlow's favorite meal," she said. "He'll be here in a moment. Come inside, straight through the kitchen."

For a moment, Zoe couldn't remember who Barlow was. Instead of asking, she stepped through the door and looked around the kitchen. It was narrow and low-ceilinged, but spotlessly clean and laid out with Ilene's usual affinity for shelves and containers. "This looks like an excellent place to cook," she said.

"Let me show you the whole place," Ilene said.

All in all, the living quarters above the shop weren't much bigger than the cottage Zoe had shared with her father—and, true to Melvin's prediction, a little too warm. The main room opening off of the kitchen was clearly where the family did most of its living. The furniture was neatly arranged, but there was too much for the small space—a dining table and chairs, a cluster of more comfortable chairs set by the windows, mats and pillows on the floor. More of those useful shelves lined every wall, stocked with an unending variety of household objects. A few closed doors probably guarded closets and at least one bedroom, Zoe thought, but she guessed that all of them were cramped.

Still, the colors were muted and pleasing, the ambiance was tranquil, and the place had a prosperous, contented feel that instantly made it seem welcoming.

Ilene put the flowers in a vase and set it in the middle of the table, while Melvin pulled his big body up from one of the chairs at the window. "I hope he gets here soon," he remarked. "I'm hungry."

As if the words had conjured their guest, there was a rattle on the back steps as someone stepped into the *kierten*. Ilene's smile grew even brighter.

"Barlow," she said happily, before calling, "we're all in here!"

Moments later Barlow stepped into the room, and that was when Zoe remembered who he was. He had the same lumbering bulk as Melvin, though he was not quite as tall, and the same brushy brown hair, though none of his had turned to gray. His eyes were more like Ilene's, dark and curious, taking in the room, the company, the situation, in one quick scan. He had, Zoe would guess, his father's shape and his mother's soul.

"Dinner smells great," he said.

"Zoe, this is our son, Barlow," Ilene said, taking him by the arm and leading him over. "Barlow, Zoe has been helping us out in the shop and working very hard."

Barlow nodded to Zoe, assessing her with a little more attention. She couldn't tell from his expression if he'd expected her to be here or not. "Learning how to make shoes, are you?" he asked.

She decided she simply would not allow herself to be ill at ease. She would not think about why Ilene had invited her here, why Ilene had asked if she wanted children, why she had encouraged Zoe to wear her prettiest top and the trousers with the smoothest, most flattering fit. She smiled faintly. "Not so far," she said. "I have my hands full just keeping track of the sales and the money."

"That's a big part of any merchant's job," he agreed. "Doesn't matter what you're selling. If you price it wrong, or don't watch your inventory, you won't stay in business very long."

"Barlow's a trader," Ilene explained. "He buys and sells goods all over Welce! He's been from the southern ports to the northern mountains and everywhere in between."

"Where have you found the most interesting merchandise?" Zoe asked.

Before he could answer, Melvin interrupted, humorously plaintive. "Could we talk about it while we eat?" he said. "I'm too hungry to wait."

"Of course! Barlow, you help me get out the food. Zoe, will you pour water? There's a pitcher on the table."

After five minutes of bustle, they were all seated, Zoe and Barlow facing each other over the plates and glasses and steaming platters. Barlow—whom Zoe supposed was used to being the focal point of any conversation with his parents—immediately resumed the discussion where it had been interrupted.

"Well, every place has interesting merchandise, if you know where to look," he said. "At the southern coastal towns, you can find all the spices and gems and imported silks you'd expect, but anyone else can find them, too. You need to look for merchants who carry the unexpected treasures." He took a large bite, chewed quickly, and swallowed. "But that's only half of it. You have to know the markets that will buy the unexpected treasures as well."

"Like what?" Zoe asked. "What did you buy and sell that was so unusual?"

"In a northern port I once found a man selling hunting birds from Soeche-Tas. Smaller than a hawk and faster. He took me out to a field and showed me how they would dive on their prey—absolutely soundless. The most chilling thing I ever saw, and the most beautiful." He paused to take another mouthful of food. "But I was able to buy the birds for an excellent price because none of the other land traders could figure out where to sell them."

"Tell her where you found your buyers," Ilene said.

"The Dochenzas," Barlow said with satisfaction. "Kayle Dochenza is a hunter himself, and I thought surely an *elay* man would feel an affinity for a creature of the air. It was a gamble, of course it was, but it paid off. He paid me double my cost for every one of those birds."

"That was smart," Zoe said, sincerely impressed.

"Oh, Barlow has hundreds of stories like that," Ilene said.

"Have you ever been to the southern ports?" Barlow asked. When the rest of them all answered in the negative, he said, "It's nothing like Chialto here, I'll tell you that," and launched into a long description of its wharves and markets.

He seemed taken with the freighters that carried merchandise from far-off countries, for he spent an inordinate amount of time noting the size and hull capacity of all the vessels with which he did any business. "Have you ever thought about sailing to one of those other ports and buying merchandise directly from the dealers?" Zoe asked.

He laughed and shook his head. "*Torz* man through and through," he said. "I don't like to get too far from land."

"Where will you be going when you leave the city?" Melvin asked him.

"And how long will you be gone?" Ilene added.

Barlow swallowed another bite. "I have a few short trips I need to make in the next couple of ninedays. First I want to go southwest to pick up some wool that a sheep rancher promised me. I can swap it to a trader who will be in the city toward the end of Quinnahunti, bringing painted glass he hauled in from Berringey. I'm taking the glass up to the northwest provinces. Lalindar territory."

"How do you keep it all straight?" Ilene demanded with a laugh.

Zoe smiled at her. "You have two hundred customers you can call by name," she said. "How do you keep *them* all straight?"

"That's different. I know them."

But Barlow was nodding. "That's how I feel about the goods I trade for. I might have twenty pelts in one trunk and six different bolts of fabric in the other. But I bought each one, a piece at a time—I could tell you where the flaws are, I could tell you what the weight is. It's as if they have faces or souls. They're individuals to me."

That's actually a poetic way to put it, Zoe admitted to herself. Certainly it would never have occurred to her to think in such terms. She thought Barlow might seem like a very interesting man if she knew him for any length of time.

"Who are you going to see in the northwest?" Melvin asked. "Thought all the Lalindars were here in the city. All the ones with any money, anyway."

"Some of them," Barlow agreed. "The big estate is still

empty, but there are a half dozen other Lalindars with smaller houses near the river property." He laughed and glanced around. "Well, I say they're *smaller*, but they could fit this whole space in their *kiertens* alone."

Zoe felt a small frown pucker her forehead. The big Lalindar house was empty? Christara's lovely, elegant mansion overlooking the Marisi River? Zoe remembered that the polished wood floor in the *kierten* had been buffed to such a high glow that it looked as wet as the sparkling river. She and her cousins had skated across it in stockinged feet, skidding into the walls and tumbling over each other like clumsy puppies. The seer had told her the Lalindar family was still in disarray since Christara's death, but it was hard to believe that neither her aunt Sarone nor her uncle Broy had claimed the house, even if they had not yet settled who should be prime.

"And when do you leave for that trip?" Ilene asked again.

"Before Quinnahunti is out, I hope. I'll leave the day after tomorrow to pick up my wool."

"I wish you would stay with us whenever you were in the city," Ilene said.

He grinned, and once again Zoe felt a certain liking for him. His voice was teasing as he answered, "I like having my own place. A man can't behave the way he likes when he's under his mother's watchful eye."

Melvin snorted and then laughed out loud. Ilene batted him playfully on the arm and looked over at Zoe. "Can you believe it? He's nearly thirty and he still hasn't picked a wife or provided me with grandchildren."

"I'm not a settled kind of man," he said. "I'd need a wife who likes to wander as much as I do, and so far I haven't found her."

"Probably won't find her among the *torz* women," Zoe said with a smile.

"Or the *hunti*," Ilene added. "I don't know where he got his wandering blood, unless it was from Melvin's *coru* grandmother."

Zoe had never felt like her own *coru* heritage had been stamped more visibly on her face. This, clearly, was why she had been invited to dinner—so Ilene's restless son could look her over and see if he found her attractive. Zoe was surprised to think that Ilene approved of her enough to present her to Barlow as an option, but maybe Ilene liked the alternatives even less. Who knew how Barlow spent his time on the road or in his bachelor's lodgings in the city? Who knew what kind of unworthy women caught his attention? At least Ilene knew Zoe was honest and clean—and steadier than the average woman of blood and water.

Zoe was clasping her hands together tightly in her lap in the hope that the mild pain would prevent her from bursting into semihysterical laughter. All things considered, Barlow might be a husband preferable to the king; no doubt Ilene would believe Zoe sacrificed nothing by making such a swap. At any rate, Barlow would not expect Zoe to share him with four other wives. *That* was definitely a point in his favor. She was sure she would find other advantages if she tried. *Don't laugh. Don't laugh.*

"A *coru* woman might do," Zoe said, her voice only slightly strained. "But *elay* and *sweela* are lively girls as well. Don't despair of finding someone who suits you."

"Zoe has traveled a little," Ilene said, gesturing in her direction.

"Really? Where have you been?" Barlow asked.

"I lived for some time in the southwest provinces," Zoe said, "but I have done very little traveling except to make the journey here. My life has not been nearly as interesting as yours."

That easily was she able to persuade Barlow to begin telling more of his own stories; he was a man who seemed to prefer talking to listening. That, again, might be one of his attractions. He would not require much of a wife except that she appear rapt by his conversation. Zoe didn't suppose that would be difficult at all.

Before long they had finished the meal and Ilene wasn't letting anyone help her clear the plates. "Is it time for some of those chocolates Zoe brought?" Melvin asked hopefully. The women laughed.

"*That's* what you should be trading for," Ilene called to her son from the kitchen. "Chocolate. That'll make you a rich man."

Barlow laughed with the rest of them but said, "I'm going to be a rich man no matter what I buy and sell. You just wait. You'll see."

The rest of the evening ran along much the same lines, Barlow basking in the attention of his parents, Zoe keeping a smile on her face and her true thoughts in shadow. But she was anxious to bring those thoughts out of hiding and examine them one by one. Therefore, when Ilene made the offhand comment that perhaps Barlow should walk her home, Zoe courteously refused and quickly took her leave before Ilene could insist.

Fairly quickly she realized that it might have been a good idea to accept an escort. Although it had been fully dark for at least an hour, the streets were still almost as crowded as during the day. But these nighttime pedestrians tended to be younger, a little rougher, than the daytime visitors—less likely to be workers hurrying to and from jobs and more likely to be teenagers looking for trouble or pickpockets looking for an easy target. Zoe pulled her festive wool scarf a little more tightly around her shoulders; *that* was the one thing she could ill afford to lose. But she supposed she didn't look rich enough to rob or seductive enough to assault. A few people bumped into her in passing, mumbled excuses, and moved on. Otherwise, no one troubled her.

She wound her hands in the ends of the shawl and contemplated Barlow and the notion that he might consider her for a wife. Over the years, she had given very little thought to marriage. It had just seemed so remote and unlikely. While living in the village, she had had her share of adolescent infatuations with some of the more popular boys. She had been wildly excited when one of Doman's nephews had spent a summer with his uncle; during secret trysts he had introduced her to some of the more pleasurable aspects of kissing. She had also nursed a secret affection for one of the peddlers who stopped at their village every quintile, a handsome yellow-haired man with a flashing smile and, no doubt, a litter of illegitimate children stretched across the western territories.

But she had never thought she *loved* any of those highly

ineligible men. She had never thought about marrying them. It had seemed clear she would never marry at all. She was an Ardelay. Her father would not have countenanced her union with anyone not related to one of the Five Families, and it had been highly unlikely that any of them would track her down while she lived in exile.

But now her father was dead and she was living in Chialto. There were still no Five Family scions lining up along the riverbanks to woo her, but there were plenty of other men in the city whom a woman could marry without feeling she had betrayed her name: politicians, professionals, merchants, tradesmen.

Melvin and Ilene's son.

The wind blew a little more coldly and a drunken girl careened into Zoe under the light of a gas-powered lamp. "Sorry," the girl squealed, then hiccupped and laughed. Zoe gathered her shawl even more tightly around her shoulders and hurried on.

So what did she think of Barlow? He was a little self-important, but he had displayed a cheerful attitude and a certain intelligence; he generally seemed like a companionable sort. He clearly had some business acumen, and probably made a reasonable income. His restlessness was no drawback to Zoe, who liked the idea of travel, either around the country or across the ocean, if Barlow ever got over his irrational fear of water. At the same time, she was adaptable, as any *coru* girl should be. She would not mind staying behind in some small city dwelling, if that made more sense once the children came along. Ilene would help her out—probably even more than Zoe would like—while Melvin would play with the babies and teach them how to hold an awl and hammer before they were two years old . . .

At the thought, Zoe almost burst out laughing. She pressed her hands to her mouth and had to force back the giggles that could quickly become all-out hysteria. What was she thinking? What was she planning? On the strength of one passably successful dinner, how could she be envisioning her life as this man's bride, down to the house they would own and the children they would raise? What was the matter with her? Was her existence so empty of meaning that any opportunity, however remote, suddenly lent it contour and substance, no matter how imaginary?

She had no desire to be a tradesman's wife. She wasn't even sure what desires she *did* possess; her future still looked blank to her when she tried to peer into its shadowy corridors. But a life beside Barlow was not one she was tempted to pursue.

Which then left her with a very important question . . .

NINE

Barlow did not make another appearance at the cobbler's shop during the next few days, but his presence certainly informed the place. For one thing, Ilene was happy just knowing he was near. She smiled much more often, and Zoe thought she looked less gaunt, as though love had plumped up her lean cheeks and thin lips. For another, Ilene couldn't conduct a conversation without mentioning his name. Zoe listened patiently, agreed anytime it seemed necessary to corroborate a statement about Barlow's general excellence, but otherwise kept her own counsel.

She was relieved when endday arrived, because it meant she would have a day's respite from stories about Barlow, but then it turned out she would have other things to think about over firstday.

"We're packing up and moving off the river," Annova informed her when Zoe arrived at the campsite that evening.

"What? Why?"

"The king's guards are closing down the flats, moving us all away," Annova answered. "Must be special visitors coming to town. That's always when they make us go somewhere else."

Despite the fact that her wardrobe had steadily expanded since she'd arrived in the city, Zoe didn't have much to pack, but the inconvenience still left her feeling disgruntled. "Where do we go?"

Annova waved a hand. "If you've got another place to stay, go there. Otherwise, they let us settle on the fairgrounds at the west edge of town. It's not so bad. They haul in water and provide big trash pits. They didn't used to do that," she added, "but one summer, a couple of people died from dehydration, and the squatters almost started a riot. There was such a mess left behind that it took a couple of ninedays to clean it up. So now they make sure we're taken care of while we're displaced."

"Wait for me to get my things together, and I'll travel over there with you."

Zoe wasn't looking forward to a long trek through the crowded streets carrying all her possessions in a couple of sacks, but it turned out the city officials had provided transport as well. For the next two hours, three ramshackle horse-drawn shuttles made a torturously slow loop between the Marisi and the fairgrounds, depositing river folk on wide, bare acres just outside the western canal. Annova was right: A semicircle of large, official-looking vehicles defined the northern edge of the fairgrounds. Two were enclosed privies—one for men, one for women—to keep the river folk from fouling the camp-grounds. Two more of the vehicles were marked with the *coru* sign for water and already had dozens of people queued up to fill casks and jugs from an array of spigots.

Some of the river folk were grumbling about the king's high-handedness, others about the location of the fairgrounds, but most seemed content to settle there for a few nights at least, as long as their basic needs were taken care of.

But not Zoe. As night fell and she stretched out on her mat, listening to the murmur of camp sounds all around her, she found herself edgy and dissatisfied. It was hard to sleep on the open land, away from the sunken contours of the riverbed, away from the drowsy chuckle of the river. The stars were too close and the sounds of the city too far away. She felt more unmoored than at any point since she had stepped out of Darien Serlast's vehicle and onto the crowded streets. She stayed awake a long time, her body tense as she strained to hear the idle running of the water through the canal; but its passage was too smooth and artificial. She had held herself so rigid, she had been filled with such yearning, that she almost thought, as dawn swept stormily in, that her very longing had brought the rain.

The king's representatives had thought of everything. The rain had been falling for less than an hour by the time they had strung yards of canvas over the fairgrounds, providing a modicum of shelter for the hundreds of people camped there. Still, it was a damp and wretched morning, and more of the displaced squatters were beginning to look as miserable as Zoe felt.

"So who's here visiting?" Zoe asked Annova during their shared breakfast. "If this person is going to disrupt our lives so much, we should know who he is."

Annova waved a dismissive hand. "I don't care."

But Zoe was curious. So she dressed in her most comfortable clothes, draping her scarf over her head to keep off the continuous drizzle, and crossed the nearest bridge back into the city. She caught one of the smoker cars that ran in a continuous loop around the Cinque and rather admired the view of streets she rarely saw as it traveled along the western leg of the boulevard. Multistory buildings were interspersed with squares of green parks and occasional fountains, and everything was scrupulously well-maintained. *This must be where the wealthy live,* she thought. Not the Five Families, who clustered closer to the palace, but the scholars and lawyers and occasional business owners who had planned right or gambled well.

This was where she and Barlow might buy a home if he turned enough wool into Lalindar glass. She choked back a laugh and continued to watch the scenery flow by.

By the time they got near the Plaza of Women, the crowds were so thick in the streets that the shuttle couldn't get through. "Everybody out!" the driver bawled, and Zoe hopped to the ground along with all the other riders.

While most of the shop district closed down on firstday, nothing stopped commerce at the Plazas, but Zoe had never seen either of them as crowded as this. "Why are so many people here?" she asked an older man who had been riding the shuttle alongside her.

He looked surprised. "To see the parade, of course," he replied, and hurried off.

Well, now, that was worth a little effort. Zoe pushed through the gathering throng that had congregated along the north-south stretch of the Cinque. She made it close enough to the front to see that both sides of the street were lined with guards wearing the king's gaudy rosette. They stood shoulder to shoulder, holding the crowd back.

She'd only been standing there about fifteen minutes, shifting from foot to foot to try to see better, when a procession pulled into view. A smartly dressed contingent of royal soldiers was followed by four open wagons, each holding its own queen. Zoe assumed they rolled by in order of rank, and she stared at each one in turn.

Elidon sat with her hands folded in her lap, wearing a bright yellow dress that made her appear to be clad in sunshine. Her expression was warm as she smiled benevolently at the masses. She had been queen for close to thirty years, and it was clear by the cheers that she was popular. The crowd's reaction was progressively less enthusiastic as Seterre and Alys passed before them, though the applause picked up a bit for Romelle, or perhaps for the squirming princess she held on her lap.

After the queens came a gas-powered smoker car, with King Vernon sitting inside on a raised stage, four attendants below him. Zoe studied the king, thinking he looked very much as she remembered. His body was slight; his hair was dark and a little thin, ruffled in the damp morning wind. His features were finely made and handsome enough, though at the moment he was frowning a little. He must be past fifty by now, Zoe thought, though the years sat on him lightly. He did not look stooped under too many cares or debauched from excessive indulgence in the perquisites of power. He merely looked like a fussy middle-aged man annoyed that rain had marred what should have been a more enjoyable day.

The king's car passed to a dutiful level of applause, but the parade watchers expressed more genuine enthusiasm for the vehicle coming right behind his. It was another smoker car, this one carrying two girls standing toward the back and waving at the crowd. The older princesses, Zoe realized. One looked to be about ten and the other thirteen or fourteen; they both wore serious expressions. It was as if they were performing a grave and solemn duty, or one that they endured even though they greatly disliked it.

The girls' wagon was almost past her before Zoe realized there was a third person in it, sitting with his back to the driver, his expression closed and sober. Seeing him gave her a sudden and violent start; she stepped back into the crowd so he wouldn't see her. It was Darien Serlast. Zoe supposed it was a mark of high favor for him to accompany the girls, but he didn't look happy about it. Perhaps he had thought it was a bad idea for them to be so publicly exposed. Perhaps he had argued against their inclusion in the parade at all. Perhaps he had insisted on being the one to sit with the girls, ready to protect them with his own life if danger threatened from the masses.

And perhaps she was romanticizing. He might be wearing that scowl because he had been excluded from the king's car, and for no more noble reason than that.

At any rate, he did not see Zoe, or change his expression if he did. She felt an odd squeeze in her stomach when a cluster of the crowd put him out of her sight. She told herself the feeling was relief, though it seemed closer to disappointment.

The last wagon was more gaily decorated than all the rest, a brightly painted wooden platform with flags flying from the front bench and ribbons woven through the spokes of the wheels and into the manes of the horses. The man sitting on a thickly padded bench looked older than Vernon, but more robust and cheerful. He had white hair, a ruddy complexion, and a wide smile, and he was dressed in gorgeously embroidered red and gold robes. *He* clearly wasn't bothered by the damp weather or the slow pace; he smiled and waved and now and then tossed coins into the crowd, which caused everyone to scramble after them. Despite his genial expression and apparent generosity, Zoe conceived a dislike of him. He was too satisfied and well-fed. He looked like a man who indulged his appetites, whatever those appetites might be—and had enough money and power to disregard anyone's attempts to keep his more unseemly behavior in check.

She shook her head. Where were these thoughts coming from? How could she think she knew what was in Darien's mind, or in this visitor's heart? Did she really believe she could judge a man's character by his smile and his clothes—judge a man's motives by his frown and his posture? *Maybe if you were an* elay *woman,* she scoffed to herself, *a creature of air and soul. But you are a* coru *woman of no special insights and only ridiculous notions.*

After the brightly painted wagon passed by, there were more soldiers, this time in the foreigner's livery, and then, a few tumblers to amuse the crowd. But Zoe had lost interest. She pushed her way through the throng of people and headed back to the Plaza of Women.

So many people were watching the parade that the Plaza was practically deserted, though a few hardy shoppers were picking up bargains. Only one of the blind sisters was entertaining a client, so Zoe climbed the five steps and immediately got an audience.

She handed over a couple of coppers. "What visitor is the king entertaining and how long will he be in the city?"

The seer nodded; this was common knowledge, not very costly. "He is the viceroy of Soeche-Tas, over the mountains. He and the king have entered into an alliance to share troops in the event of an invasion from Berringey, over the sea."

"Is such an invasion likely?"

"Who knows? But the king and the viceroy have signed trading alliances in the past and might make more agreements in the future. This is just a way to cement their friendship."

That called for another small coin. "What other agreements might they make?"

"There is some talk that the king might marry one of the viceroy's daughters."

Zoe frowned. An argument about the viceroy's daughter had cost her father his place at court. "I thought that was a plan the king abandoned ten years ago. Surely the woman is already some other man's wife."

"Ah, but the viceroy has an abundance of daughters. Eight or nine—the reports vary."

Zoe had remembered another obstacle. "And I thought the king recently promised his wives that he would not take another bride."

A sly smile lit the woman's plain, doughy face. "He promised he would not take a bride unless they *approve* of his choice," she said.

"And do they?" Zoe asked.

The seer was still smiling. "I have to assume they do not, since the deal has not been finalized."

Zoe couldn't help a snort of laughter. "I foresee another hasty trip to the Plaza of Men in the morning. The queens will make the king promise that he will not take a Soechin bride. They will have some reason to dislike *all* of the viceroy's daughters, I am sure."

"I expect you might be right!" the seer said with a laugh.

"Perhaps this time the wives will insist the king make his own vows at the booth of promises instead of allowing Darien Serlast to speak on his behalf," Zoe said.

"It is possible."

Zoe toyed with a quint-silver coin, running it back and forth between her thumb and forefinger. "But who *is* Darien Serlast?" she asked at last, giving the coin to the seer. "What kind of power does he wield in the court?"

But the seer shook her head, letting a small smile come to the corners of her mouth. She reached out, found Zoe's hand, and dropped the quint-silver back onto Zoe's palm. When Zoe started to ask another question, the seer merely put a finger to her lips as if to enjoin silence. Then she drew a scarf up over her head and refused to speak another word.

TEN

It was still raining the next day when Zoe made her way to work. Her shoes were drenched and the hems of her trousers were soaked through when she stepped inside the cobbler's shop. She left wet footprints all the way to the counter.

"There won't be much business today," Ilene grumbled when two hours had passed and only three customers had stepped inside. "No one comes out in weather like this."

"Just as well," Zoe said from her perch on a stool behind the counter. She was yawning so hard she thought she might topple off. "It was too wet to sleep last night, so I'm having a hard time staying awake."

Ilene gave her one quick, uncertain look. "Yes—I thought about you around midnight when the rains came down so heavily. What do you do on such nights? Where do you stay?"

"Usually I find shelter in a borrowed tent," Zoe said. "Of course, right now all the river folk are huddling under this enormous tarpaulin the king's men have put up for us. But when it rains that hard, the water just comes sluicing down the ground."

"I hate to think of you so damp and wretched," Ilene said.

It was the first time the cobbler's wife had shown any concern about Zoe's accommodations. Zoe was moved but a little amused. "I don't mind so much," she said. "I like being out-doors. I like being close to the river. I even like the rain—*coru* girl that I am. I might feel differently when the cold weather comes, but I might have found a more permanent place by then."

Ilene's face showed sudden decisiveness. "You should stay here," she said. "On stormy nights. You can sleep in the work-room. It's dry and warm, and there's a sink where you can wash up."

"Why, Ilene! That's so kind!" Zoe exclaimed. "But are you sure?"

"Yes, of course I'm sure. I know you won't steal anything, and why shouldn't you stay down here? It's not luxurious, I know, but it has to be better than camping on the ground in the rain."

"It will seem palatial to me," Zoe said with a smile.

"You could stay here every night, if you wanted to," Ilene said, with such studied nonchalance that Zoe realized she was making an extraordinary offer. "Not just during the bad weather."

"Let's first see how well we like the arrangement on rainy days," Zoe said gently. "I'm so used to my freedom now that I'm not sure how well I will sleep under a roof. And you may find it makes you uneasy to know I am roaming around below you. You might find that I intrude on your private life."

"It is not as though our private life was ever that noisy or exciting," Ilene said with such uncharacteristic tartness that Zoe dissolved into laughter. Ilene watched her, finally letting a small smile curve her mouth. "Well, it wasn't," she added.

Zoe managed to contain herself, though she still felt suf-fused with merriment. "In any case, I thank you deeply for your generosity, and I will definitely take you up on your offer tonight!"

"And who knows?" Ilene said, as if her next observation logically flowed from their previous exchange. "Barlow might be back before the rain ends."

Zoe spent the next three nights sleeping on her mat in the back room, wedged between Melvin's workbench and one long wall of tools. She drowsed in the imperfect dark, inhaling the aromas of hide and tannin and dye, listening to the skittering of rain across unfamiliar surfaces. This situation was *infinitely* preferable to huddling under the huge tarp with hundreds of damp, discontented squatters. And yet, the instant the rain stopped and the viceroy rode out of the city, she was happy to return to the river flats under the open sky.

"If the offer still stands, I would love to be able to sleep here whenever there is inclement weather," she told Ilene when she gave the older woman her sincerest thanks.

In return, Ilene handed her a key to the front door that was locked only after the shop was closed for the day. "Come even if it starts raining at midnight," she said.

Zoe was astonished and humbled. "Ilene! A key! I'm so honored."

Ilene was embarrassed enough to try a joke. "I'll just have the lock changed if I decide I can't trust you."

"Oh, I can imagine how dreadful *that* would be to discover in the middle of the night in the middle of a storm!"

Ilene smiled. "I don't think it will happen."

Impulsively, Zoe gave her a hug. "I don't think it will, either."

From that day on, no matter where she went, she wore the key on a cord around her neck, just as she wore her coin-encrusted shawl around her shoulders. Poor as she was, these were the two objects that conferred on her specific and complementary kinds of wealth: independence and safety. She knew very few on the river who could claim resources to equal her own.

In the middle of the following nineday, Zoe was in the back room, hunting through a bin of discarded shoes for a dye match, when there was a commotion at the front of the shop. First there was the sound of many booted feet, then came the singing of a trumpet. Astonished, she spun around to gape at Melvin and Ilene. He was already laying down his hammer and she was smoothing back her stringy hair.

"What's going on?" Zoe demanded.

"The king," Ilene said. "From time to time he has been a

patron of our shop." And, holding her head in what she clearly imagined was a regal pose, she swept past the gold curtain into the front sales area to greet her exalted customer.

"You can come, too," Melvin said. "Not every day a river girl gets to meet the king."

But Zoe had no intention of exposing herself to curious royal eyes. She could hardly believe she had been lucky enough to be out of sight when he first arrived. "Oh—I couldn't—I would be too nervous—and say something stupid—" she stammered.

Melvin grinned. "Ilene does all the talking anyway," he said. He pointed at a small rectangle of glass set into the wall between the workroom and the sales area. "Looks like a mirror from the front, but it's a window from this side," he told her. "You can watch. See what it's like to have the king as a customer."

Then he, too, stepped past the curtain just as she realized that Ilene had probably used this disguised window to observe Zoe when she was first employed. Well, Zoe had nothing to hide from *Ilene*. But she would gladly skulk back here and watch King Vernon through the trick piece of glass.

A tall stool was helpfully set under the window to enable easy spying. Zoe could hear Ilene welcoming the king to the shop; she could hear the sound of the customer's chair scraping across the floor as someone adjusted its angle. There were more footsteps, possibly the guards and the herald distributing themselves around the room. A self-important voice—the herald, Zoe guessed—announced, "King Vernon has come to be fitted for a pair of boots."

Ilene answered, calm as you please, "We are honored to have the chance to serve his majesty again. Sire, if you would remove your shoes, my husband will measure your feet."

It had taken this long for Zoe to settle herself on the stool and cautiously peer through the glass. Its odd construction made the view a little murky, as if she were watching the participants through a haze of smoke, but she could see well enough to count bodies and read faces. Yes—five liveried soldiers were pushed up against the shelving units. A slim and supercilious man was strutting across the floor, clutching a trumpet in one hand and sneering at the crowd of curious onlookers who had clustered just outside the front door. The king was sitting in the deep-cushioned customer's chair, one stockinged foot extended toward Melvin, who knelt before him with tapes and rulers in hand. Ilene and two others stood near the customer's chair, intently watching the serious business of determining the size of the king's foot.

Zoe took a moment to stare at Vernon. He looked much as he had on the parade route, though less damp, of course, and in a slightly better humor. Close up, it was easier to see the marks of age on his face—creases around the corners of his mouth and vertical lines between his eyebrows—and they deepened as he offered his hosts a royal smile.

"I very much liked the black shoes I purchased here last year," he said. "Quite comfortable and yet stylish. Now I need boots—brown, I think, and with a fashionable buckle."

"Will these boots be for riding or walking?" Ilene asked, her voice very professional. "If for walking, will you be indoors or outdoors? Do you want them to be understated or ornate? With boots, we recommend a slight heel so the shape is pleasing, but the heel could be made higher if you like."

Instead of being annoyed by the flurry of questions, the king seemed to enjoy giving his attention to each separate consideration. "I will be wearing them outdoors, but they shouldn't look too casual, even so," he said. "I should be able to wear them inside if I like. And I would prefer a taller heel if it could be discreetly made."

He had more to say, but Zoe lost interest. One of the men standing beside Ilene had shifted his weight, which put him in her line of sight. Darien Serlast.

She caught her breath and jerked her head back. She should not have been surprised to see him; she was beginning to get the impression that none of the royal family ever set foot outside of the palace confines without Darien Serlast in tow. But this was the closest she had been to him since she slipped away from his opulent vehicle more than a quintile ago. She could not help staring at him now, reacquainting herself with the details of his appearance: His narrow face. His stern expression. His gray eyes—quick, impatient, taking in everything. They flicked toward the mirror and held a moment, as if he could see through the frosted baffle, and then moved on.

"What do you think, Darien?" the king was asking. "A higher heel than that? It would give me an advantage the next time we entertain the viceroy. He is taller than I am, which I do not like."

"You may ask your wives how easy it is to walk in a tall heel," Darien said. "I don't know that it would give you much advantage to wobble and fall down."

"True," said the king. He bestowed another royal smile on Ilene. "A *hunti* man is a good advisor because he is always practical," he said.

"I myself would choose comfort over looks, but we can make boots for you that combine both," Ilene answered as she proffered a tray. "Take a look at our buckles here—each one is available in gold and silver and figured brass. Do you see one you like?"

The king appealed to his advisor. "Is gold too elaborate for footwear? I must admit, I like that buckle."

"It would be suitable for a court shoe, but not a riding boot," Darien said seriously. "I would opt for the brass."

"Yes, that was my second choice."

Zoe had a hard time containing her amazement. This was Darien Serlast's weighty role? Advising the king about fashion? She had imagined him guiding Vernon through thorny issues of diplomatic policy, helping him think through new laws and their corresponding punishments. But picking out boot buckles and recommending against a certain type of sole? She never would have pictured Darien Serlast acting in such a capacity.

"Will this be a winter boot?" Ilene was asking now. Melvin had finished measuring the king's right foot and now was working on the left one, methodically laying his tape around the ankle, across the toes, from front to back, and writing notations in a little notebook. "We can line the inside with fleece for additional warmth—but it then becomes unsuitable for summer wear."

"The fleece sounds very good," the king said uncertainly, glancing at Darien. "My feet are often cold."

Darien nodded. "You are unlikely to be wearing boots during the summer, in any case."

"So, then, the fleece," the king said happily.

"How long will it take before the boots are ready?" Darien asked.

"If the king needs them in two days, we can have them ready in two days," Ilene said. "Otherwise, we like a nineday to work with the leather."

"I would not like you to rush," the king said. "One nineday will be perfectly acceptable. I will send someone to pick them up."

The transaction appeared to be concluded. The second man who had hovered behind the chair now scurried around to the front, dropped to his knees, and began to ease the king's feet back into his shoes. This must be the royal valet, Zoe guessed. He treated the king's footwear and the king's person with a care that bordered on reverence.

Eventually the royal party had organized itself to exit the shop, and Melvin and Ilene bowed as the king and his escort filed out. "Thank you so much for your patronage," Ilene said, bowing again. "These will be the finest boots ever made."

When the shop was finally empty, Zoe collapsed on the stool, too nerveless to try to stand. Melvin slipped back through the curtain, his notebook clutched in his hand, and grinned.

"Kind of knocks your feet out from under you, doesn't it?" he said. "He's been here three or four times, and each time I just lose the ability to speak. Good thing Ilene's so good at talking."

"It never occurred to me that he might just walk down the streets like an ordinary man, buying clothes and shoes."

"It's one of the things I like about him," Melvin said. "He comes out of that palace and lets people see him."

Zoe came experimentally to her feet and found that her legs would hold her. "Well, next time I hope I have a little more warning."

She stepped through the curtain to the sound of Melvin's laughter. Ilene was sitting at the sales counter, carefully filling in big block letters on a heavy sheet of pressed paper. Zoe looked over her shoulder and had to hold back a laugh. Ilene had written: THIS IS WHERE THE KING BUYS HIS SHOES.

As the warm Quinnahunti days edged toward the extreme heat of Quinnatorz, Zoe found herself so relaxed, so at ease with the direction her life had taken, that she was almost always smiling.

"You look so pretty these days," Annova commented one evening over a shared dinner. "What's different? Your hair? Your clothing?"

Calvin gestured at his own cheekbones. "Her face has filled out," he said in his raspy voice. "She's eating the right food."

Zoe shrugged and smiled. "Maybe," she said.

But she knew what it was: the slow lifting of grief, the gradual budding of contentment, and the lack of any day-to-day worries. No sick father to nurse, no fear about money. Someday—and fairly soon—she knew she would have to take a hard look at what she wanted from her future and then formulate a plan for attaining it, but right now she didn't even have that responsibility to weigh her down. She simply was, and she was happy.

"People have started to notice," Annova said, nodding wisely.

"Who has noticed what?" she asked.

"Young men. Have started noticing *you*."

"I thought I saw Derek stop by to try one of those orange candies the other night," Calvin said.

"Yes, and Mitchell brought you a loaf of bread two days ago," Annova added. "Said he'd gotten too much and couldn't finish it before it got stale, but he bought it to give to you. I'm sure he did."

"Really?" Zoe murmured and fought back a grin. "I like them both a great deal."

"Mitchell's the better prospect," Annova told her. "Has a job four seasons out of five *and* is careful how he spends his money. Derek's better-looking, but he'll always be a squatter. No ambition. He'll never be able to buy you a house."

"Hey," Calvin said, turning on his wife in mock indignation. "All of a sudden you think a man's worthless unless he can own a little property?"

"Living on the river is good enough for me," Zoe said.

Annova was shaking her head. "If you're old, the river's a place to stay because you love it. But if you're young, the river's a place to stay when you're out of options. You can't waste your life here, drifting from day to day, building nothing, leaving behind nothing of value."

Zoe shrugged. "*Coru* girl."

Annova came close enough to put her hand gently on the front of Zoe's tunic. She said softly, "*Sweela* heart."

Of course Zoe had realized that Mitchell and Derek were flirting with her. She'd liked it. She had been aware of the changes in her face, in her body; it was nice to hear that other people had noticed, and approved. In the past two ninedays, now and then she had attracted attention when she was simply walking down the street. Old men smiled at her; male vendors gave her an extra portion when she bought candy or fruit. Men her own age gave her long, appraising stares and then sometimes turned to whisper something to their companions. Some made excuses to speak to her, if only to ask for directions; one or two asked for her name.

She smiled back at all of them and allowed herself to bask, just a little, in the brief but potent sunshine of youth and beauty. It was not a chance she'd had very often up till now.

A few days before the Quinnatorz changeday, she walked home from work instead of trying to catch one of the crowded shuttles along the Cinque. The heat was starting to build in the city; every structure of stone or brick or cinder block retained every degree it had absorbed from the sun all day and slowly released it into the air as night drew on. Within another eighteen or twenty-seven days, the heat would be truly oppressive, but last night's rain had washed down the whole city and left the temperature relatively bearable. Zoe even thought she caught a hint of a breeze tiptoeing across her face as she left the shop district and made her way toward the crowded residential neighborhoods that lay between her and the river.

She got caught in a knot of human traffic when she tried to cross an east-west stretch of the Cinque as it followed the southern edge of the city. When she pushed her way to the front of the road, she found her progress blocked by a contingent of the king's guards. Apparently there had been an accident in the road, and pedestrians and drivers had all gathered to give their vociferous advice on how to mend the broken vehicle.

Hot and impatient, Zoe stepped off the edge of the boulevard and tried to pick her way around the onlookers. She was fanning her face with one hand and pushing her hair back with the other when a small boy darted by her and neatly twitched her shawl from around her waist.

"Hey!" she cried and dashed after him as he dove through the crowd. Panic and very real fear gave her unwonted speed; she was almost able to keep up with him as he flitted past bystanders and ran toward the warren of dank streets that made up the southern ghetto. "Stop that boy!" she cried, but no one lifted a hand to intercede. The thief kept running, and Zoe kept chasing after him.

With a shocking suddenness, they were in a foreign and frightening corner of Chialto. From tumbledown storefronts spilled young toughs and sullen girls and quarreling children and mounds of odorous debris. Zoe tried to detour around murky puddles in her path—pools of urine or blood or spilled spirits—without losing sight of her assailant. Once, an old woman in a filthy dress grabbed at her as she passed, and once, a middle-aged man with a ravaged face swiped at her arm, but she dodged and twisted away and kept running. The heavy heat made it hard to breathe, or maybe here in the southern neighborhood the air was simply no good. Zoe felt herself panting; she was not sure how much longer she could keep up.

Then the little thief made a critical error. He turned to look over his shoulder, trying to see if he had eluded her, and he stumbled into one of those potholes filled with foul liquid. He howled as he went down, landing on his knees in the filthy water, and Zoe jogged up and snatched the shawl from his flailing hands. It was sopping wet, but she didn't care. She tied the soaked ends around her waist and exclaimed, "You awful boy, this is *mine*! I *need* it!"

"Here, now, are you stealing from a child?" called a voice behind her, and she whirled around to see three teenage boys closing in, intent to cause harm clear on their gaunt faces. Terror shot fresh strength into her exhausted limbs. Zoe didn't pause to explain or argue, just took off again as fast as she could manage through the hot and hazardous streets.

She had no idea where she was, no clue where safety might lie. Behind her she heard shouts and pursuing footsteps. Almost blindly, she kept pounding forward, zigzagging around staring onlookers, piles of trash, broken carts upended in the road. Over the yells from behind her and the sobbing sound of her own labored breath, she thought she heard the whispered invitation of running water. Unthinking, she turned in that direction.

Suddenly she almost somersaulted over a broken railing embedded into an apron of poured concrete. She slid down an embankment that was half weeds, half cracked stone, hearing the teenagers behind her loose shouts of triumph. Before her was the wide trough of the city canal, filled with calm, silty water moving slowly past a series of frets and filters.

"She's trapped!" one of the boys shouted. She could hear him skidding down the embankment. "I've got her!"

Wrapping her arms around her body and closing her eyes, Zoe stepped off the concrete lip of the bank and plunged into the water.

For a moment, it was as if all thought, all motion, all sound, sheer existence, was suspended. She could not hear or see or think or move or breathe. The water lapped around her in a dozen individual currents, some cool, some warm, some gritty as sandpaper against her skin. A hand seemed to tap against her cheek, each finger as huge as a sausage, as insubstantial as rain. Another palm pressed against her heart. A cool stream of water brushed across her lips, offering a passing kiss.

Above her were voices, muffled by water and distance.

Where is she?

She jumped in!

I can't see her! Did she drown?

How can she stay under so long?

Maybe she hit her head.

I think she drowned!

She heard them, she understood them, but she couldn't bring herself to care. The water held her in a careful but joyful embrace, as if she were a beloved child unsteady on her feet as she rose from a bed of sickness. It was impossible to worry while being so closely guarded. It was impossible to be afraid.

I need to get to safety, she thought, but she couldn't bring herself to swim. *I probably need to breathe.* But she did not push her head above the water, and her lungs did not burn from lack of air, and her blood did not protest.

Home, she thought, picturing the stone flats, the broad and gently rumbling expanse of the river as it flowed away from the city. It was as if the canal itself could pluck images out of her mind. She felt the water coalesce around her with a little more substance and intent. Still underwater, still making absolutely no effort of her own, Zoe began moving through the canal at a steady pace, against the southerly direction of the current.

She tried to guess the route the water would take her. The river ran along the eastern border of the city, between the mountain and the flats; the canal made a great C-shaped ring to connect with the river at northern and southern points. But there was a vast network of underground pipes, feeding water to various parts of the city and carrying away waste. She would not particularly like to swim through sewage, and she was fairly certain that at many points in the subterranean system there were grates and locks through which she could not pass.

But it did not seem to matter. Volition had been taken away from her, or she had discarded it without a protest. She turned her cheek against the water as if it were a pillow covered in satin, and she lay unresisting on a changing, restless bed. She could not tell how fast she was moving, or in what direction. Sometimes she could sense sunlight against her closed eyelids; other times she was in deep shadow, either passing under a bridge or moving through an underground tunnel. Then the light would return, weak but welcome.

For the longest time, she heard no more voices, at least none that were distinct. Now and then she could catch echoes of laughter or distant conversations; sometimes, unnervingly close at hand, she heard the steady hum of machinery or the bubbling of air being forced through a purifying mechanism. Once, she heard a shout of alarm, and she wondered if some observer had seen her submerged body pass by. It was fairly clear that the street toughs, at least, had been left behind some time ago.

She could not say how long she had been traveling when she sensed the water shift below her and begin roiling with a wilder current. At the same time, the temperature cooled down; she could almost feel the bottom dramatically deepen as the artificial surface of the canal gave way to the natural bed of the river. Overhead, the light against her eyes grew stronger. She was possessed by a sudden, ungovernable impulse to thrash in the water, kicking her way toward the choppy surface. When her face broke clear, she sucked in deep gusts of air and whipped her head around, trying to orient herself.

She was just upstream from the river flats, passing between high, unfriendly banks on both sides but heading down toward calmer and more familiar waters. Once she had her bearings, she let the Marisi carry her forward but began a slow, methodical stroke that would bring her into the shallower waters of the western bank. In another ten minutes, she was able to drop her feet to the riverbed and walk the last dozen feet toward shore, splashing heavily. Her soaked clothes weighed her down, particularly her heavy, waterlogged shawl; her skin prickled with chill, even on this warm day. It was almost more effort than she could manage to pull herself out of the water's possessive grasp and then drop to the baked stone of the flats, where she lay spread-eagled on her back.

She had been in danger of her life, but the river had saved her.

She did not know how to make sense out of such an impossible thing.

ELEVEN

Zoe told no one about her misadventure, though both Ilene and Annova commented, during the next two days, on her unusual quietness. "It's like the old Zoe has come back for a few days," Annova said.

"The old Zoe?" she asked.

"The girl who first came to the river, silent and afraid. I thought she had run away forever."

There was no way to explain, so Zoe said, "I'm just tired."

"Well, I hope you catch up on your sleep very soon, because I think Mitchell will be joining us for dinner the day after tomorrow, and I want you to feel your best."

Ilene did not ask personal questions, but Zoe sensed her concern. She tried to reassure the older woman by smiling a great deal, though it took an effort, and showing tireless goodwill. Even so, she knew it was worry that made Ilene let her go early one day, claiming that business was so slow that Zoe might as well treat herself to a lazy afternoon sleeping by the river.

Instead, Zoe went straight to the Plaza of Women and waited patiently behind four other petitioners until one of the blind sisters was free to talk. Then she climbed the dais and sat on the low mat.

"I stood on the banks of the canal the other day and I saw a woman jump into the water," Zoe said. "Ten minutes went by and she did not raise her head to breathe. Another ten minutes went by and another. When she finally broke the surface of the water, she was laughing and smiling, but she never once took a breath in all that time. How is such a thing possible?"

"It's not," said the seer, "unless the girl is the Lalindar prime."

Zoe shook her head. "She isn't. True, she is a *coru* woman, and even a Lalindar, but she is not the prime."

The seer cocked her head. Even her blank eyes looked interested. "How do you know? Christara Lalindar's heir has not stepped forward in the two years since the old woman died."

"But—then—who *is* Christara's heir? Why hasn't her son or daughter taken over the title?"

The seer held out a hand and Zoe dropped a handful of quint-silvers in her palm. Let the woman think Zoe was curiously ignorant for a Welce girl; she had no idea how the laws of inheritance worked.

"It is not such a simple thing, naming the next prime," the seer said. "Only the primes themselves understand exactly how the process works. It is said the Dochenza prime whispers a name to the wind, or the wind whispers a name to him, and they speak one name after another until they both agree. The Ardelays swear they see a name written in fire. The Serlasts see it carved in the trunk of some old tree." The woman shrugged. "But only the prime can say aloud the name of his or her heir."

"And then—that's it? The next prime is suddenly instated?"

The seer gave a skeptical chuckle. "Oh, they will claim there is more ritual than that. Mirti Serlast says she had to walk through a grove of plum trees on her brother's estate—a grove she had visited many times during the past twenty years—but once she was named heir to the title, the trees embraced her. She felt their branches lean down to touch her shoulder—she felt the leaves sweep across her face as if memorizing its contours. The Lalindars say that the new primes are not recognized until they are wholly immersed in the Marisi River." She shrugged again. "Each family has some such ancestral touchstone."

Zoe could hardly breathe. She remembered the afternoon

that she had gone bathing in the river with Annova and Sima. She remembered how long she had stayed underwater, not needing to breathe, feeling the river run curious fingers over her face, her arms, as if reacquainting itself with someone who had been long missed and was greatly beloved.

It was the first time she had immersed herself in the Marisi since she and her father had been exiled.

But did that mean . . . Could it mean . . .

"Does no one know who Christara wanted to be prime after her?" Zoe managed to choke out.

The seer nodded, holding out her hand again. Impatiently, Zoe gave her a quint-gold, surely enough to cover any question she might ask for the rest of the session. "Christara's daughter, Sarone, says her niece, Zoe, was her mother's choice. But everyone wonders if that is true, since Sarone never said a word about Zoe until Darien Serlast went off to find the girl. Zoe Ardelay was long in exile with her father and no one knew where she was," the woman explained kindly.

"And why did Darien Serlast want this—this Zoe Ardelay?"

The quint-gold had loosened the blind woman's tongue. "He thought she would make a suitable fifth wife for the king. He was still out of the city when Sarone stepped forward to claim Zoe was prime. All the gossips anticipated a clash of wills between Sarone Lalindar and Darien Serlast—"

"Why?" Zoe interrupted.

"Because the king cannot marry a prime, of course. All of a woman's property is forfeit to the king when she marries, so no family ever would allow the heir to go to the royal household."

"And did Darien Serlast find the missing girl?"

"He says he did, but he cannot produce her. He claims the Lalindar heir is alive and living in Chialto, but no one has seen her and no one knows if he is telling the truth. So the king has no fifth wife and the Lalindar house sits empty, and no one knows if the Marisi has, in fact, anointed the next Lalindar prime or if Sarone Lalindar was lying."

Zoe slowly gathered her feet below her and stood up, pleased that she was actually able to stand. "I have a message you can give to Sarone Lalindar and Darien Serlast and anyone else who may care to hear it," she said.

The seer tilted her head to one side, her face brightening in anticipation. "Yes?"

"Zoe Ardelay is not dead. Darien Serlast found her and brought her to the city, but she slipped away from him. She is still here, and she is trying to decide exactly when to make her presence known."

It was the first time Zoe had seen one of the sisters dumbfounded. Her blind eyes fluttered; her wide mouth parted slightly as if otherwise she could not draw in enough air. "You're certain," she said, but not as if she had the remotest doubt. Zoe supposed she must have an extraordinary ability to determine when someone was telling her the truth.

"Entirely," Zoe replied.

Without speaking another word, the seer reached out for Zoe's hand. She returned all the coins Zoe had given her, folding Zoe's fingers over the smooth, round edges. This was information worth far more than gold.

It was a short enough walk to the temple, and Zoe felt the need for a quiet space to sit and think. But even when she paid her tithe at the door and collapsed onto the blue *coru* bench, she could not calm her jangled nerves or slow her racing mind. She was numb with disbelief, stupid with shock, but she was surprised to find that her dominant emotion was rage. Against Christara Lalindar, for being too stubborn to maintain relations with Navarr Ardelay after her daughter died. Against her Lalindar relatives, who had made no effort to locate Zoe and inform her of her inheritance, hoping instead to find some way to win it for themselves.

Against her father, who, she was beginning to suspect, had known all along that Zoe was Christara's heir. *It is time that you remembered that you are part of your mother's family as well,* he had said to her, only a few days before he died. Not simply part of it, oh no. The head of the family. The Lalindar prime. He had known, and he had said nothing, because he was careless or because he was vain or because he felt so much spite for Christara he wanted to make her suffer.

Zoe could not calm herself enough to sit there and meditate back into a state of balance. Already, the dozen or so other people who had taken up contemplative poses around the temple were sending her glances of irritation as she kept squirming on her pew and clenching her hands and shaking her head as if to shake away her anger and befuddlement. Abruptly she got to her feet and headed for the door, then changed her mind and strode back to the blessing barrel in the middle of the room. Plunging her hand deep into the pile, she churned the coins with such vigor that she earned a few more dark looks. She let her hand close over three coins and pulled her arm free. Not until she was outside the temple doors did she pause to see what blessings she had wrested from the fates.

Travel. Change. Surprise.

All three *coru* virtues.

All three perfectly suited to her mood.

When Zoe returned to the cobbler shop the next morning, her main purpose was to tell Ilene that she would be quitting soon for reasons she could not discuss. But Ilene had more pressing matters on her mind.

"Barlow will be back tonight," she said, fluttering around the shop, happiness brushing color into her face again. "Of course, he leaves again in two days, but it will be so nice to have him nearby tonight."

"Yesterday I pulled the blessing for travel," Zoe said. "You may tell him that I will extend that blessing to him as well."

"Oh—why don't you tell him yourself?" Ilene said. "Join us for dinner tonight. It was so pleasant the last time you ate with us."

Zoe opened her mouth to refuse, then a sudden inspiration made her change her mind. "I will," she said. "Thank you."

Accordingly, in the hour between closing the shop and returning for dinner, she strolled through the Plaza of Women, looking for specific items. The first was a dramatic red tunic that fit snugly over her bosom and fell to her knees; gold embroidery around the hem and the neckline drew attention to her figure. The second was a gold clasp for her hair, and the third was a set of cosmetics that the vendor's daughter agreed to apply for her, since Zoe still had few skills in that area.

Naturally she had to buy chocolate drops as well, since the

last time they had all dined together, Barlow had liked them almost as much as his parents had.

She wanted Barlow to like her.

"Don't you look pretty!" Ilene exclaimed when she admitted Zoe to the *kierten*.

"I probably spent too much, but I just couldn't resist this tunic."

"And a good thing you didn't! It's perfect for you."

Soon enough, they were all seated around the table, handing around dishes and listening to Barlow talk. This time, Zoe thought, she was paying even more attention to Barlow's words than his mother was, as she waited for him to drop information that she could use. She wasn't too interested in his account of his recent trades, but when he started describing his upcoming journey, oh, she couldn't hear enough about that.

"The northwest provinces seem so far away," she said. "How long does it take to travel there?"

Barlow laughed. "Much less time than it used to! My partner and I just invested in one of those new *elaymotives*. You can hitch two carts to it—one to carry your merchandise and one to carry your own gear. When the weather's good, you can cover the ground in almost half the time it used to take."

"And when the weather's bad?" Melvin asked.

"Well, then you slow down, just like everyone. You still have to be careful getting through the mud. You still have to clear away trees and branches in the road. You can't ford a river any faster than the ferry runs. But on the open road—" Barlow held his hand out flat in front of him and then moved it through the air to indicate smooth and rapid progress. "Nothing slows you down. We'll be at the headwaters of the Marisi in a nineday."

"I didn't know you had a partner," Zoe said.

Barlow nodded. "We sell different products to different buyers, but we split travel expenses and earn a higher profit percentage. He won't be ready to leave until the day after tomorrow, which is why I'm stuck here until then."

"We'll be glad of your company," Ilene said.

"So it's just the two of you traveling all that way?" Zoe asked.

Barlow's face clouded over. "We used to bring Jaker's

nephew along until he took a job with a sheep farmer. It's a help having a third person on the trip, because you have to leave someone behind with the merchandise. If it's just the two of us, we have to take turns doing our business. You lose time. And the trade business is all about time."

Zoe made her face laughing and her voice light. "I'd *love* to see the northern provinces! Too bad you can't take *me* with you!"

Barlow's eyes narrowed; he gave her one long, analytical look. Zoe had the thought that her careful choice of clothing and makeup had been wasted, and Ilene's subtle matchmaking as well. He wasn't looking at her as a prospective mate. He was trying to determine how hard she worked, how honest she was, how successful she might be at fending off thieves who tried to rob his wagons.

"And why *couldn't* I take you with me?" he said slowly.

She pretended to be unnerved, at a loss, a woman who had not meant her little joke to be taken seriously. "Well, because I—I have a job and I—you'll be gone so long and—"

"Two ninedays," he said. "Three if the weather is impossible. That's not so long."

Zoe glanced nervously at Ilene, whose face was drawn into a frown of concentration; she was thinking hard. "But your mother and your father need me! I could never leave them so abruptly."

"You'll be back," he said. "They'll hardly notice you're gone."

Ilene had made up her mind. "It's a wonderful idea," she said. "It will be good for you to see some of the world, Zoe. A pretty girl like you wasting her life away on the river flats! Go with Barlow. Visit the northern lands. Then when you get back—well—we'll see, won't we? Maybe a lot of things will have changed by then."

Maybe my son will have fallen in love with you, Zoe knew she was thinking. The possibility seemed more remote all the time, but Zoe wasn't about to say so. "If you're sure," she said uncertainly. "I would hate to feel like I've abandoned you."

Ilene smiled and put her hand on Zoe's arm. "You're hardly abandoning me when I'm pushing you out the door."

Zoe turned back to Barlow, trying not to seem too brisk

about it, as if she had successfully completed a first, inconsequential task and was now getting to important matters. But that was how she felt. "Then—what would my responsibilities be while I traveled with you?" She paused, trying to imagine the journey itself. "Do you camp out along the way? Stay at inns? Stay with clients?"

"We camp out or sleep in the second wagon," he said. "Quarters are tight, but you could sleep in the merchandise wagon, where Jaker's nephew used to put his mat. We all take turns cooking. If you know how to drive a vehicle, you could take your turn at that, too. But mostly we just need you to stay behind and watch the merchandise when we're off trading."

One part of this speech had caught her attention in a wholly unexpected way. "Drive an *elaymotive*?" she repeated. "A smoker car?"

Barlow grinned. "It takes some getting used to," he admitted. "But I like it."

"I'd *love* to learn," Zoe said, wholly sincere for the first time tonight. "I can't wait! I'm ready to leave tomorrow!"

There were goodbyes to say, loose ends to tie up, but all in all Zoe estimated that she could have packed her belongings and been ready to depart the city within twelve minutes of receiving Barlow's invitation to join him on the road. The whole conversation had gone more smoothly than she'd anticipated; she'd thought she might have to convince Barlow to take her and overcome Ilene's disapproval. But everyone, for radically different reasons, had been pleased by the plan.

Annova and Calvin also were wholly in favor of Zoe's trip. "Good for you. You need some fresh excitement," Annova said. "And traveling with an eligible young man! Nothing could be better. Don't just concentrate on being beautiful. Show him how indispensable you can be. A workingman looks for a partner, not just a lovely face."

"I will be traveling with *two* eligible men, though I don't know anything about this Jaker," Zoe said. "So my chances are doubled."

"I don't know this Jaker, either," Annova said. "But stick with Barlow. His parents are good folks. He can be trusted."

Impulsively, Zoe gave Annova a fierce hug. "If I don't come back before the end of Quinnatorz," she said, "assume I have found somewhere better to stay."

Annova returned the embrace with fervor, but pulled back to give Zoe a long look of appraisal. "You'll be back, I think," she said, "but you'll be changed."

"*Coru* girl," Zoe said. "Always looking for change."

"*Sweela* girl," Annova said. "Too smart to let it destroy you."

TWELVE

Journeying across the kingdom with Barlow and Jaker was nothing like traveling with Darien Serlast. The only thing their vehicles had in common was that they were powered by compressed gas and they ran on wheels. All similarities stopped there.

For one thing, there was no team of Dochenza drivers on hand to make sure the motor assembly functioned smoothly, and at least once a day the wagons came to an abrupt halt as the supply lines fouled or the ignition system failed or some other problem surfaced. Jaker, the more mechanically minded of the partners, would climb into the small, odorous compartment and curse loudly and make a lot of mysterious banging sounds, and soon they would be on their way again.

Despite Barlow's boasts, they did not cover ground very quickly. Zoe didn't know much about such things, but the engine in the Serlast carriage seemed to have been more powerful than this one; at any rate, their own small caravan did not bowl along at the same brisk pace she'd enjoyed on her eastward journey. And the level of comfort between Darien's car and Barlow's wagons could not even be compared. The trade wagons jounced along, even on the smoothest roads, as if they wanted to eject all merchandise and passengers with the maximum amount of violence. When progress was slow enough—on highly pitted roads or in heavily trafficked areas—Zoe opted to climb out and walk. It was a far more pleasant way to travel; and she had worked for a cobbler, so she owned excellent shoes.

Despite the unending low-level wretchedness, Zoe enjoyed the trip immensely. Jaker proved to be a lean, long-limbed, and friendly fellow somewhere between forty and fifty years old. His blue eyes brightened a weathered face and bald scalp tanned dark by constant exposure. Everything interested him, from the way a fellow traveler hauled a water keg to news about the viceroy of Soeche-Tas. He seemed happy to talk to Zoe on any subject she introduced without once asking prying questions. He was one of the most comfortable people she'd ever met.

He was the one who taught her the basic mechanics of driving the *elaymotive*, explaining how to speed up, how to slow down, and how to cut power to the engine if she couldn't figure out any other way to make the wagons stop. She was fascinated but tentative; she didn't trust her newfound skills enough to be the driver if there was any other traffic on the road. But on clear days, when they were between towns, Zoe loved to take the wheel and feel the bunched power rumbling behind her in the engine box, loved to know that it was her will, her decisions, that would keep them going forward or tumble them into a ditch.

"You've got some aptitude for this," Barlow said on their third night out as they made camp. Something else Zoe had not known was that campsites existed up and down the main roads of the kingdom, places where all sorts of travelers, not just peddlers and traders, could pull over for the night. These usually offered only the barest amenities—a well-cleared circle of land, a water pump, perhaps permanent privies, and a trash dump. However, a few of the more well-stocked ones sold oats for horses, meat and bread for humans, and canisters of gas for the new engines. "If you ever decide the city life isn't for you, you could hire on with some merchant and travel for the rest of your life."

She smiled at him. On the road, Barlow seemed like a different man altogether—happier, more relaxed, more expansive.

Torz heritage or not, this was a man with a *coru* heart. He would never be able to sit still, adding up accounts and fawning over customers at his parents' shop.

"Maybe I'll hire on with you and Jaker," she suggested.

"If you decide that's what you want, we'd both be glad to have you."

She was more relaxed with him as well because it had been clear from the very first day that he had absolutely no interest in her as a potential wife. He had no interest in any woman, and neither did Jaker. People who preferred to take lovers of their own sex were a largely ignored subset of Chialto society; she had seen a few such couples down on the river flats but none of them had been her particular friends. Zoe had to hide a laugh at the thought of how disappointed Annova would be that her *two* unmarried men both turned out to be wholly ineligible.

That first night, she had watched as Barlow set up a small tent, scarcely big enough for one, and Jaker had carried in a single sleeping bag. Her eyes were still wide with a question when Jaker crawled back out. He gave her a barely perceptible nod, his blue eyes considering her; she had replied with a slight shrug and a small smile. Everything had been easy between the three of them from that minute forward.

"Well, if I decide I want to go adventuring across the kingdom with the two of you, I'll handle my own merchandise," she said. "Jewelry, maybe, or—no! I'll sell shoes! I'll have Ilene and Melvin make up dozens of pairs in fashionable sizes, and I'll sell them in all the small towns where girls dream of luxuries that their local cobblers can never provide."

"Not sure you can make much profit on shoes," Jaker commented.

"Oh, I'll make a profit. You have no idea how much country girls long to be as fashionable as city girls. They'll pay twice what the shoes would go for in the city."

But she was just talking. Spinning dreams she had no intention of pursuing. She was a *coru* girl, true, who thrived on change and travel. But, strange and surreal as it seemed, she was the Lalindar prime. She would not be traveling the countryside selling footwear out of a wagon. She had no idea what the rest of her life might hold, but she was sure it would be far more complex than that.

W eather was good for the entire length of their trip, though it was the opening nineday of Quinnatorz and the air simmered with the promise of heat. For the first three days, they passed through land that was broad and level, prairie and woodland taking over any stretch of soil that hadn't been cleared and cultivated by human hands. Water was abundant, though this apparently came as a welcome surprise to many of the travelers they met on the way.

"Drought been along here for the past two years," an old man observed to Zoe as they waited to fill containers at the water pump of a campsite. "The first year, they rationed how much water you could take at any campground. Last year, none of the camps had water at all. It makes me crazy to see water spilled on the ground—look at that, those boys don't even stop pumping while they put down one bucket and pick up another one!"

She smiled at him. "I don't think we're going to run out. Not today."

"You wouldn't say that if you'd ever lived through a drought," he grumbled.

"I suppose not," she said. "But I never have."

Coru girl. Lalindar prime. Of course she'd never seen a time without water, but until now she had never realized why.

As they pushed farther north, the land began to change, growing hillier and rockier, sustaining hardier crops and more stubborn trees. Not long after that, mountains began taking a dusky shape on the northern horizon, curving up from the southeast to create a serrated spine from the city to the northwestern coast. The river, Zoe knew, ran alongside the mountains all the way to the southern sea.

"The air smells different here," she said on that seventh morning. She was carefully piloting the wagons along the empty road that rose at a shallow but insistent angle all along the visible horizon. "It smells like snow. I'd forgotten that."

"Forgotten?" Jaker said. "You've been to the northwest provinces before?"

"Not for years. We used to visit my grandmother there when she was alive."

"It's the prettiest land in the whole kingdom, I've always thought."

"I loved it when I was a little girl."

"Is any of your family still alive up here in the northern parts?" Jaker asked.

Zoe thought about it a moment. "Maybe."

He gave her a shrewd look from his blue eyes. "Is that why you're along on this trip? To find out?"

She smiled at him. "Maybe," she said again.

He nodded and asked no more questions.

The day was blissfully sunny when they finally reached their destination, a small, picturesque town nestled against the mountain foothills like a kitten curled up against a rumpled pile of blankets. Smaller and more playful here at its headwaters, the Marisi chortled in its banks between the steep slope of the mountainside and the flat acres of the town. The place was barely a crossroads for travelers planning to journey on to the coast and for tradesmen swapping goods with local merchants who served the great manor houses nearby. The town boasted little more than one inn, a modest campground, and a couple dozen houses and storefronts.

"You might as well take a room for the night," Barlow told Zoe. "We've got to haul the wagons to the three estates where I've promised deliveries—can't transport the glass any other way. We'll probably end up pitching a tent on one of the properties, depending on where we are by nightfall. We'll be back sometime tomorrow to pick you up and start on home."

Smiling, she shook her head. "I won't be going back to Chialto with you."

Barlow was surprised, but Jaker wasn't. He said, "I thought you didn't know yet if any of your folks were still here."

"They're here," she said. "I just don't know what they think of me."

A little bewildered, Barlow looked between Zoe and Jaker. "If you're not sure of a welcome," he said slowly, "we could wait a day or two. You can still come back with us if things don't go the way you hope."

Impulsively, she kissed him on the cheek—and then, because it felt right, she kissed Jaker, too. "It'll take me more than a day or two to sort it out," she said. "I'll find another way back to the city if I have to."

"What do I tell my mother and father?" Barlow asked.

She laughed. "Well, first you have to tell your mother that you are *not* interested in marrying me." He groaned and she went on. "And then you can tell them that I thank them very much for the trust they put in me and the opportunities they gave me. And that when I have a chance, I will pay them back eightfold."

That raised Jaker's eyebrows, but Barlow was still focused on more immediate explanations. "They'll want to know why you didn't come back."

"Tell them the truth," she said softly. "I have family here. And I'm going to see how much we like each other."

"*Coru* family?" Jaker said.

"Yes," she said. "Lalindar."

She spent the night at the inn, taking a small, cramped room that seemed infinitely luxurious after the sleeping mat laid between crates and boxes in Barlow's wagon. As much as anything, she wanted to wash away the grime of travel, to beautify herself for Christara's house, much as she had beautified herself for Barlow that last evening in Chialto. She paid extra money to have hot bathwater brought to her room, and she took extra time to wash her hair and rub oil into her hands and feet. As Sima had showed her, she tied her damp hair in scraps of rags so it would froth with curls in the morning. She lay down on the narrow bed and slept fitfully, and the seductive murmur of running water ran all night through her dreams.

In the morning she dressed in her most formal black trousers and her favorite purple top. It was too warm to need an overrobe, but she carried her festive jangling shawl with her anyway. She did not want to approach her inheritance destitute and pitiful. She would bring with her whatever wealth she already owned, and a lifetime's worth of pride.

The innkeeper arranged for her to hire a driver and a small cart to take her to Christara's house, perched halfway up the mountain on the other side of the Marisi. She sat motionless in the back of the cart and watched the house as the driver negotiated the short, narrow streets of the town—as they took the bobbing ferry across the gurgling waters—and as he began the winding ascent up the pine-scented road. Now and then the house disappeared from view, only to reappear larger and closer. It was a long, three-story structure built of yellow stone that so closely matched the color of the mountain that sometimes only the blue shutters, the blue flags, and the great double-hung blue entrance door distinguished it from its surroundings. The entire bottom story featured what seemed to be an unbroken line of windows, higher than the height of a tall man. From any room with a southern view, Zoe knew, you could look out and see the river.

She could feel the pressure of elevation singing in her ears by the time the road leveled off and took a straight line toward the house. Almost immediately, the sound was accompanied by the cheerful patter of falling water. The entire estate was ringed by a fountain—a narrow band of ornamental stone set into the ground and concealing jets of water that leapt and danced in a choreographed display. Only one twenty-foot section of the fountain was habitually turned off to allow carriages to pass through without getting soaked, but at night even that section was usually spouting water.

As they trotted through the break in the fountain, catching stray droplets on their faces, the driver was moved to speak. "They say old Christara Lalindar could turn that water against someone if she didn't like whoever was arriving at her door," he said. "She could call up streams of water so hard they could wash a man right off of his horse or out of his coach."

"Did you ever see her do it?" Zoe asked.

"No, but I believe it."

"I believe it, too."

He pulled up at the doorstep and helped her out. She gave him a quint-gold, far more than the transportation service was worth. He widened his eyes, and then narrowed them to give her a more thorough appraisal. She merely smiled and turned toward the door. Carefully climbed the five steps. Pulled three times on the rope that sent chimes chasing each other through the house.

When the door opened, she saw eight servants lined up just inside. Seven were bowing; the eighth held his hand out in a gesture of welcome.

"Zoe Ardelay Lalindar," he said. "It is good to have you home."

For the first nineday back in her grandmother's house, Zoe spent most of her time in the *kierten*. It was an enormous, high-ceilinged space with ten-foot windows on three sides and wood floors so brightly polished she could see her blurred reflection.

Now she stood in the center of the bank of windows that overlooked the river and did not think she could ever look away. From here, by turning her head a little to the right, she could see the headwaters of the Marisi, jetting up with a joyous rush. The river still churned with delight, but was already much tamer, by the time it passed directly before the Lalindar house. If she turned her head to the left, she could watch it for another mile as it curled and lapped along the base of the mountain range, as if eager to explore but unwilling to travel too far from familiar paths.

At every time of day, it was a different color—frosty silver in the morning, luscious blue at midday, glancing gold at dusk as the sun laid down horizontal bars of fire. On nights when the moon had much shape or substance, the river sparkled with random lights that seemed to skate along its moving surface.

Zoe felt as if the blood in her own body mimicked the river's surging currents. As never before, she sensed the head-long flow down through artery, back through vein, bubbling up through her heart like the waters themselves. She could picture every inch of land that the Marisi traveled through, knew every juncture where it skipped under a bridge or coiled around an outthrust foothill. She was almost dizzy as she felt herself plummeting down that long fall of stone behind the royal palace to collect and swirl and calm herself in the deep pool nearby. She wanted to wave and call out greetings as she flowed past her friends on the river flats, but she was in too much of a hurry; she had to pick up speed and race down those final miles to the sea. Then came the plunge into icy water, the shock of brine, the disintegration of self.

And suddenly she was back at the headwaters again.

Had anyone tried to describe this sensation to her, she would have believed he was mad.

But it was this remarkable connection with the Marisi that finally began to convince her that she was indeed prime. She was certain Christara must have had the same visceral bond. She wondered if it was something that came awake in the dormant blood only when the new prime stepped for the first time into the ancestral home. She wondered if she would lose that awareness of water, of blood, when she left this house and traveled down the mountain.

She could not decide if it was something she would welcome or fear.

Quiet footsteps behind her signaled that Hoden had entered the room and wanted to speak to her. In truth, she had caught the pattern of his pulse before she heard the slight sound of his shoes. She supposed it should be more eerie, this sudden ability to know where all the servants in the house were located merely by the sound of their heartbeats.

All this time, she had remembered she was *coru*, but she had forgotten that her gift was blood as well as water.

Indeed, in ancient days, when people first identified themselves by their five intrinsic traits, it was believed that men and women were blessed with distinct and complementary strengths. Men were known by the elementals—air, water, wood, earth, fire. Women claimed the corporeal—soul, blood, bone, flesh, mind. A *coru* woman might be a midwife or a healer; she would work in blood. A *coru* man would be a fisherman or a sailor who loved the sea. Zoe had forgotten all that—and, indeed, these days the traits seemed so blended together that no one separated them out by gender anymore.

But she was reminded now of where her separate strengths lay. And—at least while she resided in this house—she was unlikely to forget.

"You have company," Hoden said.

She remembered Hoden from her grandmother's day, or perhaps she remembered his father, for his family had served her family for as long as the river ran through Welce. He was neat, small, unobtrusive, efficient, and utterly indispensable. It was Hoden who had escorted her through every room of the house, explaining what work had been done since she had been there last, more than ten years ago; it was Hoden who had sat down with her in her grandmother's study to show her how her accounts stood, which investments had prospered. She was, it turned out, a very wealthy woman.

"Why didn't you send for me after my grandmother died?" she asked him that first afternoon.

"I didn't know where you were."

"But you knew I was alive. And that I was prime."

He paused a moment, as if at a loss for how to explain. "The house knew," he said at last. "Both of those things."

And though he served a *coru* family, Hoden was a *hunti* man. Wood spoke to him as water called to Zoe. Naturally, he would believe whatever story it had to tell.

"You have been so faithful. I am not sure how I will repay you for your years of exceptional service to the house while I was away."

His face had flickered with surprise. "There was nothing else I could have done."

She believed that, too.

Now she turned slightly to see him standing motionless by the doorway. "Yes, I heard someone approaching," she said. *Heard the heartbeats of the horses and the humans. Four horses, two humans, one no doubt a coachman.* "Who is it?"

"Keeli Lalindar."

Zoe's eyebrows rose. Aunt Sarone's daughter. "My cousin. I thought she was living in the city."

"Yes. She is here visiting her uncle Broy. His estate, of course, is an hour south of the village," he added. It was something she ought to know, but probably didn't; that was what Hoden meant every time he dropped a smooth *of course* into their conversation. She appreciated his tact.

"By all means I will see her." She glanced around. "Here? Or is another room more appropriate?"

He never seemed discomposed to be consulted even on such tricky matters, and during the past nineday he had answered dozens of odd questions. "To receive visitors in the *kierten* is to indicate that you wish them to acknowledge your status and your power," he said. "It might not be a hostile reception, but it is not a warm one. It signals that you might not trust them. That you judge their worth to be less than yours."

"Ah," she said. "Not the message I want to send to Keeli."

"Perhaps the green sitting room that overlooks the garden," he suggested. "I will bring refreshments."

She smiled at him. "That sounds perfect."

A few minutes later she was standing in the green room, a place that seemed to exist for no other purpose than to provide people with somewhere to sit. There were two chairs drawn up before the tall windows—which did indeed provide a view of the garden, which no one looked at because the windows also provided a view of the river—and a narrow table between them. The rest of the room offered more chairs in small groupings, some accompanied by footstools and occasional tables. That was it. No bookshelves, no statuary, no musical instruments. Zoe thought it might be almost as much of a statement as the *kierten*, with its vast expanse of wasted space. Only this room said, *I am so wealthy, I am so pampered, that I need do nothing all day but sit and stare.* It was not a philosophy that generally appealed to Zoe.

She heard Keeli's heartbeat coming closer—and then suddenly it was overlaid by the sounds of rustling clothing and hasty footsteps. "Keeli Lalindar," Hoden announced at the doorway, but the visitor brushed past him to step impatiently into the room.

Then she came to a dead halt and simply stared. "They were right," she said. "It *is* you."

Zoe signaled to Hoden to withdraw, and for a moment the cousins gazed at each other in silence. Keeli didn't look much like the playmate Zoe remembered from childhood. She was taller than Zoe, heavier, with a voluptuousness not at all concealed by the ornate gold jacket and wide-legged gold pants that Zoe guessed were the epitome of fashion. Her heavy hair was also golden and pulled back from her face in a thick, braided knot adorned with jeweled flowers. Her eyes were river blue, her skin sunrise pink. By now Zoe knew enough about footwear to realize that the beaded leather flats she wore had probably cost an entire gold coin.

Thanks to Hoden, Zoe's appearance was not quite that of a river squatter attempting a masquerade. The day after she arrived, he'd brought in the house seamstress to take her measurements and alter a few of the more classic pieces from Christara's wardrobe. So now she wore an embroidered red tunic over matching trousers with a narrower silhouette than the ones Keeli wore. She'd put a few clips in her black hair and brushed rouge onto her cheeks, but she knew her appearance could not compare with Keeli's. Anyone would know, just by looking at them, which was the cousin who had grown up with all luxuries at her command and which one had grown up in exile.

"Hello, Keeli," Zoe said. "Yes. It's me."

Keeli came forward into the room, still staring. "Christara always said you weren't dead, but nobody knew where you were," she said. "Where have you been all this time?"

"With my father," Zoe replied.

Keeli shook her head wonderingly. "Banished. Away from all your family and all your things. And the *house.* Didn't you miss it? Didn't you want to come back?"

Zoe wasn't sure how to answer. *No one invited me back.* "I thought it was important to stay with my father. I thought he needed me."

Keeli's pretty face drew into a frown. "Is he dead now? That's what Uncle Broy said."

Unexpectedly, Zoe's throat closed, choking down the words that would confirm the news. She merely nodded.

"Well, I'm sorry to hear it," Keeli said. "My mother said he was the most interesting man any Lalindar had ever married, even though Christara hated him."

And that—even more unexpectedly—made Zoe laugh. "He certainly was, even at the end."

Now Keeli offered a tentative smile. "When you laugh, you look just like I remember you," she said. "I think I was only ten the last time I saw you. We were running through the fountains, trying to time it so that we would jump out onto the grass before the water shot up again."

At the description, Zoe suddenly had a complete memory of an afternoon she had wholly forgotten. "Yes! And we were absolutely drenched!"

"And we tracked water through the *kierten* and down the hall and up the stairs to our rooms."

"Christara was furious," Zoe added, "but we couldn't stop giggling."

Keeli took a step closer. "I feel like I should give a hug to the girl I used to know," she said. "But I can't tell if the woman you are now would welcome such a thing."

Zoe caught her breath. "I think I would," she said, and closed the distance between them.

Keeli's embrace was quick and light, but Zoe was amazed by the degree of comfort it conveyed. Or—no—something more. She was flooded with a sense of kinship, of connection, for that brief moment that her heart rested against Keeli's. *This is a blood relation,* her body seemed to be saying, overjoyed by the news. Zoe felt a little dizzy when she pulled back, a little giddy. She was relieved to hear Hoden approaching, so she could have something else to think about.

"Come in," she called before he knocked, and he pushed an elegant wooden cart through the door. It was covered with cups and carafes and cakes and candies. One plate held a carefully arranged pyramid of chocolates. She had mentioned once that she loved the sweet confections, and ever since then, they had appeared anytime the servants brought Zoe food.

"Thank you," she said as he set the cart up in front of the two chairs nearest that spectacular view. He bowed and exited, and Zoe took Keeli gently by the arm. "Let's sit and talk awhile. There's so much you can tell me."

In fact, Keeli was an invaluable source of information, and she chattered happily for the next hour. Zoe poured drinks for both of them—cool river water that still carried the taste of the mountain, flavored with rinds of fruit. They both nibbled on various foodstuffs while Keeli filled her in on the state of the Lalindar family. *This* cousin was married to a sadly inferior Dochenza man; *that* one had gone into business and prospered, though his wife was unfaithful to him and there was no telling who had fathered his youngest child. Their uncle Broy lived nearby on a sprawling estate; Keeli's parents owned property in the city.

"It used to be Christara's house, but she gave it to my mother outright before she died," Keeli said a little anxiously. "*This* house is yours, of course, but not the one in Chialto."

Zoe smiled. "I remember the city house and it's far too big for me," she reassured Keeli. "I wouldn't want the responsibility of trying to maintain it. It even has a pool inside, doesn't it?"

Keeli was laughing. "It does. I swim there almost every day."

"I'd like to come to Chialto, though, at least to visit," Zoe said. "Maybe I'll look for a small place to rent."

"I'll help you look at properties," Keeli promised. "I could also—well—if you were planning to do any shopping for new clothes—"

Zoe laughed. "You think that I shouldn't be wearing my grandmother's clothes, even if they've been altered to fit me?"

Keeli giggled. "You wouldn't be denied admittance at the door, but everyone would talk about you as soon as you left."

"I would be most grateful for your fashion advice. And your time. I imagine it could take days to assemble an entire wardrobe." Not for the first time, Zoe spared a thought for the outfits Darien Serlast had purchased for her two quintiles ago as they traveled from the village. She quickly closed her mind to the memory.

"We can get started even before you leave for the city," Keeli said. "I have all the latest patterns, and Christara's seamstress is very good."

"Excellent," Zoe said. "I am already feeling more confident about my eventual return to the city."

"So when do you plan to come to Chialto?"

"I'm not sure yet. It's been so long since I've been in this house that I think I want to stay here awhile longer. Maybe for the rest of the quintile. I want to remember what it's like to be a Lalindar and learn what it's like to be prime."

For a moment, Keeli studied Zoe out of her dark blue eyes. "So where *were* you?" she asked, as she had before. "All this time?"

Living in penury, in isolation, in a village so far from here you would never find it. Camping on the river flats in the city. Sleeping on the floor in a merchant's shop. "My father and I had a house in a village in the far southwestern territories," she said. "We lived very simply. You wouldn't have liked it."

Keeli sighed. "And now he's dead, and Christara, too, after all their fighting."

"I never did know what they argued about," Zoe said. "Just that they hated each other."

Keeli was staring. "You," she said.

For a moment, Zoe was distracted by the sound of her own suddenly thundering pulse. "What do you mean?" she said faintly.

Keeli spread her hands. "They fought about *you*. Christara wanted to keep you here. Raise you to your duties as prime. But your father refused, and your mother sided with him. They would not give you up. They almost refused to let Christara see you again, until she promised she would not try to lure you to stay."

"But—me—she knew—she picked me as her heir that long ago?" Zoe stammered. "No one ever told me that! And why? I was a child. What would even make her think I would be suitable to be prime?"

Keeli leaned forward and plucked at the bracelet dangling, as always, from Zoe's wrist. She sorted through the three charms until she came to the one she wanted. "Because of this," she said. "None of her other descendants were given such a random blessing."

Zoe bent her head to see which charm Keeli had singled out, but she knew what it would be even before she looked.

The one that held the symbol for power.

THIRTEEN

After Keeli left—promising to return in the morning with patterns and sketches—Zoe paced through the house and up the open stairway to the long corridor that ran the entire length of the second story. Like the sitting room, the hallway itself faced out over the river; the twelve doors opening off it led to bedrooms that overlooked the mountain. Only the prime's room, directly above the *kierten* on the far western edge of the house, was so huge that it had windows on three sides—one that showed the river, one that showed the mountain, and one that faced toward the western sea. Everyone else who slept in Christara's house had to rise from their beds and step out of their private rooms in order to get a glimpse of the Marisi.

Decorating the long wall of this corridor were colorful patches of art that Zoe had always thought represented Christara's one slight concession to whimsy. But now she realized that these images, like everything else in Christara's life, were purposeful, calculated, and emotionally stark.

It was a blessing wall.

The first three blessings had been painted next to the doorway to Christara's room. They had been done by a master artist; each separate glyph had been rendered as a trellis that vines and flowers twined around and birds perched upon to sing. Winding through the triptych and tying the separate images together was a narrow blue river. Christara's three blessings were all *coru*: persistence, resilience, luck.

Along the rest of the corridor, scattered between the bedroom doors, were the blessings for Christara's children and grandchildren. Zoe couldn't discern any pattern in how they had been laid out—certainly not by chronological age, or gender, or claim to a particular bedroom. So here were the blessings that had been bestowed on her aunt Sarone, and below them the blessings for one of Broy's daughters.

The style of artwork for each separate set was completely different. One series of blessings contained nothing but the symbols themselves, drawn on the wall in a flowing calligraphic hand with no other ornamentation. Another series was presented in childlike blocks of bright color. The one Zoe liked best showed each blessing as an animal; surprise was conveyed by an owl's wide eyes, imagination sprouted a butterfly's wings, and the symbol for contentment was curled in the fur of a sleeping lamb.

She had always known where her own blessings appeared; Christara had shown them to her when she was very young and made sure she visited them whenever she came to the house. They had been painted between two doors in the very center of the hall, and now they were at eye level. When she was a child, someone had had to pick her up so she could touch them with a cautious finger. There was nothing about them to indicate that Christara had considered them any more meaningful than the blessings of any of her other descendants. In fact, they were rather simple—traditional, unadorned blessing glyphs laid over squares of summer blue. Zoe lifted her hand and very gently traced their lines and curves.

Beauty. Love. Power.

No other piece of artwork on the entire wall showed the glyph for power.

It took her some time to find the set of blessings she wanted suddenly, desperately, to see. At some point, she was sure, she had known where they were, but apparently she had not returned to them as faithfully as she had checked on her own. At last she located them, very low to the floor, small monochrome squares no bigger than her hand. They looked like etchings or woodcuts, with thin, precise lines printed directly on the wall itself in a sepia-colored ink. Creating a background pattern behind the lovingly crafted symbols were tangles of stems and briars and the occasional wistful rose.

Resolve. Intelligence. Love.

Two *sweela* traits for Alieta Lalindar and one *hunti* blessing. No wonder she had fallen in love with a man of fire and clung to him so stubbornly that her *coru* mother disowned her.

No wonder she would not give up her only daughter.

Unexpectedly, Zoe was overcome with grief for the bright, fierce, laughing, quarrelsome, irresistible creature that she remembered as her mother. Flattening her hand against the wall, centered on the trait for love—the blessing that they shared, the blessing that bound them together—she sank to the floor and began weeping. She had cried so hard when her mother died, cried so hard that no one had been able to soothe her. Twelve years later, it was as if that long-healed wound was raw again; all the complex memories crowded once more to the forefront of her mind. An old despair should not feel so new, but a new despair could haul an old one out of hiding. She wept for her mother, for her father, for the lost little girl she had been and the bewildered woman she had become.

When she was too tired to weep anymore, she laid her body down on the floor, there in the hallway, with her back pressed against the blessing of her mother's love. Facing the river and drawing strength from its ceaseless benediction, she closed her eyes and fell asleep.

The next nineday was full of chatter and motion and outings both pleasant and tense. Keeli, it seemed, had decided to make herself responsible for transforming Zoe into a proper prime, and she was taking her duties very seriously. She arrived at the house every morning carrying swatches of fabric and sketches of current fashions and trivial bits of information about the other Five Families.

"Kayle Dochenza has made a fortune with this compressed gas business, but it's made him even more peculiar than he was before," she told Zoe. A little later she observed, "Taro Frothen is big and brown and stupid-looking, but my father says you should never underestimate him. And there's something likable about him, even though to look at him you would think he was the dullest man in the kingdom."

Finally she introduced the name Zoe was most interested in hearing. "Mirti Serlast is plain and unfashionable—I never saw a woman give *less* attention to her hair—but very clever. Don't ask her opinion unless you really want to know what she thinks, because she doesn't bother with the usual political niceties."

"Are the Serlasts in favor with the king these days?" Zoe asked casually.

"Oh yes. He turns to them for everything. He won't make a decision without consulting Mirti—or, more often, Darien."

"Who's that?"

"Darien Serlast? Mirti's nephew. He can't be more than thirty-one or thirty-two, but he acts as if he's fifty. So serious and stern and—*weighed down*, I sometimes think. He's the king's closest advisor and you *never* see Vernon unless Darien is along."

Zoe toyed with one of the sketches Keeli had brought over, showing a fantastically ornate ensemble. "Does he seem like a *good* advisor?" she asked. "Someone you trust to counsel the king?"

Keeli shrugged indifferently. "I suppose so. At any rate, you never hear anyone say anything against him."

Zoe remembered the blind seer at the Plaza of Women, who refused to discuss Darien Serlast at all. "Maybe people don't talk about him because they're afraid of him."

"Maybe they don't talk about him because he's boring," Keeli said. She took the sketch from Zoe's hands. "Yes, I love this, but it's too grand for everyday wear, even at the palace," she said. "You might wear it to a coronation or a wedding." She held it up in Zoe's direction and squinted, as if imagining Zoe in the completed outfit. "Have it made in gold and scarlet. You'll look beautiful."

Apparently they were done talking about Darien Serlast. Zoe swallowed a sigh and toyed with the charms on her bracelet. "I don't think I ever quite manage to be beautiful," she said, "despite my blessing. When I make the effort, I'm attractive enough, but it takes some work."

Keeli made an inelegant sound. "It takes some work for everyone! When I first get up in the morning, I look like mice have been nesting in my hair, and I'm so pale I look ill. And yet generally everyone considers me a very pretty girl," she added without a trace of self-consciousness. "But *I* have to style my hair and put on rouge and pick the most flattering colors. *Everyone* does. Just because you have a charm for beauty doesn't mean you're naturally gorgeous. It means you have potential."

Zoe laughed aloud. "So I suppose I have the *potential* for love and power as well?"

Keeli grinned at her. "That's right. You'd better get to work on those, too."

W hen they weren't choosing a wardrobe for Zoe—and the occasional new piece for Keeli—they were making the rounds of nearby estates so Zoe could meet the Lalindar relations she had not seen in ten years or more. She was nervous on those occasions, having no reason to think these aunts and uncles and cousins would welcome her reappearance. Indeed, none of them was as warm as Keeli. More than one eyed her with disfavor; she was sure she read resentment in their faces when they were forced to acknowledge her as the new Lalindar prime.

"Why didn't one of them move into the house while I was gone?" she asked Hoden one day as she fretfully waited for Keeli to arrive and take her to another awkward social engagement. "Why didn't one of them claim the title and the power? Christara was dead—who would gainsay them?"

He answered in his careful, unalarming way, making impossible things seem wholly reasonable. "No one ever attempts to usurp the power of the prime," he said gravely. "It is said a man who masquerades as the Lalindar prime will drown the minute he attempts to step into the Marisi. A man who pretends to head the Ardelays will be quickly consumed by fire. There is a tale of a Frothen imposter who was killed by a falling boulder. It is not so easy to assume an unmerited rank."

That explained why the house was still hers, she supposed, but it made her just a little leery of sticking so much as a fingertip in the river, in case, after all, she did not deserve the title she had assumed.

She couldn't tell if she was disappointed or relieved to learn that her ability to hear someone else's heartbeat faded almost completely once she stepped outside of the fountain that encircled the estate. Oh, if someone in the room was excited about a piece of news, Zoe could often catch a faint eager thrumming, and when her uncle Broy took her hand, she was instantly aware of the race of blood through his body. Not only that, she could tell, as if she were a scientist relying on impossibly sophisticated analytical tools, that the composition of his blood was in some way the same as hers. He did not look especially happy to meet her and his face was pulled into what might have been a sneer, yet she could tell that they were related. Bound together, whether he liked it or not.

"You don't look nearly as wild as my sister," he said. "Are you?"

"I might have been, had I lived a different sort of life," she said coolly. "But a wild heart would not have served me very well."

"It didn't serve Alieta well, either, but that wasn't enough to make her change her ways," Broy retorted. "I am glad to hear you are a little wiser."

She hesitated when, a few days later, Broy invited her out on a boating expedition. "I think he'd like to push me over the side and see if the Marisi takes me," she confided to Keeli, but her cousin laughed.

"Oh, Broy's all spite and sourness, but he wouldn't actually hurt you," Keeli said. "Anyway, no prime has ever drowned in the history of the Lalindars. I think you're safe."

If I'm really prime, Zoe wanted to say. But she supposed she would have to go out on the water eventually, or the question would always linger at the back of her mind.

Accordingly, she joined Broy—and, as it turned out, his wife, his two daughters, and Keeli—for an afternoon on the river. The Marisi showed no disposition to upend the boat and dash Zoe's head to pieces against the banks. Even Broy seemed a little mellower once they were out on the water.

The sun was directly overhead, fat and yellow and contented; the breeze off the water was playful and curious. Below the hull, Zoe could sense the endless lazy rocking of the current. She found she was not at all afraid for her life.

"Can you take the Marisi all the way down to Chialto?" Zoe asked Broy.

He shook his head. "There are three impassable places—one a dam fifty miles downriver, one a natural rock hazard that would shred any boat that tried to go through. And then there are the falls that drop into the city behind the royal palace. There are portages by the first two, but nothing crosses the mountain pass but water."

"Have you ever taken a boat out on the ocean?"

"Not this one, but yes, I have a schooner built to cross the sea. Someday I'm going to sail to the other edge of the world just to feel the water beneath me the whole time I'm traveling."

"I'd like to make that journey sometime," Zoe said. "I'd like to see the other side of the world."

Keeli shook her head. "You can't go wandering," she said. "You have to go back to Chialto."

Zoe celebrated Quinnasweela changeday with her newfound relatives and then bid them goodbye. Most of them flocked to Chialto once cooler weather made the tall buildings and densely populated streets bearable again.

"When will you be coming to the city?" Keeli asked.

"Soon," Zoe promised.

But the Lalindars left, and the leaves turned so red it appeared that the whole mountain was on fire, and still Zoe waited. One nineday passed, and then another. It was the middle of the third nineday of Quinnasweela, and she had been in Christara's house for more than a quintile, when she heard the sound she had been listening for.

First it was as faint as the breath of a sleeping child, and then it was only as loud as far-off rain. By sunset, it sounded like footfalls down the corridor, and Zoe slept all night with that unhurried rhythm tapping steadily in her ear. She rose early and put on all her finest new clothes, a top and trousers and overrobe all made of a gold-edged blue. Hoden's wife helped her with her hair, but Zoe applied her own makeup with a light hand.

All the while, she felt that heartbeat growing louder, coming nearer, until it was finally ascending the hill to Christara's house. She was in the *kierten* before the carriage horses trotted through the break in the tall fountain. She pressed herself against the bank of windows on the far wall, the ones that showed the mountain face angling up toward the sky, half bare *torz* dirt and half bright *sweela* color.

The door chime rang three times and Hoden answered it, bowing very low. Zoe heard a man's voice say, "I am here to see Zoe Ardelay Lalindar."

"She is awaiting you," Hoden said, making a gesture of welcome.

Darien Serlast stepped across the threshold. He looked straight at Zoe as if he had known, before the door even opened, exactly where she stood.

"Prime," he said, offering her a very slight bow.

Not until Hoden left the room did she answer him, her face showing no hint of a smile. She said, "I've been expecting you."

FOURTEEN

They stared at each other a good long while. Zoe was not sure if they were reminding themselves of features they'd forgotten or checking for changes they could not have anticipated. The day was sunny, and light fell dramatically through the windows, burnishing the wood floors to a blinding luster. Zoe did not offer to bring Darien Serlast to a friendlier room in the house; she did not ask if he would like refreshments. After that first greeting, she didn't say a word. She simply watched him, simply waited. He was *hunti*, he could be as stubborn as oak itself, but she was not going to yield. She was not going to be the first to speak.

Finally he nodded, as if conceding something, and took three steps deeper into the room. "So," he said. "The girl who ran away from me to hide along the river finally finds her way home."

"Still alongside the river," she pointed out. "But how did you know that was where I took refuge?"

"Because I looked for you, of course. Every day, until I found you. I went to the houses of your Ardelay and Lalindar cousins, hoping to surprise you in a parlor or a kitchen. I went to the tenements by the southern canal. I checked the infirmaries. I checked the morgues." He shrugged. "Before the first nineday was out, I thought to seek you on the flats, and there you were. After that, one of my men went by every few days to make sure you were still in place."

Although she was pleased to find that he had been worried enough to watch out for her, she was deeply irritated to learn that he had known her whereabouts all this time. "You should have dropped by some evening," she said, "and shared a meal with me."

His mouth formed a soundless laugh. "If you had stayed on the flats much longer, perhaps I would have. If you had seemed to be in danger, I certainly would have stepped forward and taken you to a more sheltered place."

"Whether or not I wanted to go." When he shrugged instead of answering, she went on. "It would be just the sort of high-handed behavior I have come to expect of you."

His eyes narrowed at that. "I suppose, then, that you have come to consider me some kind of villain."

She turned away from him and began a slow, measured pacing, coming to a halt when she was along the shorter wall, where the windows faced west toward the sea. Darien took a few steps forward, so he stood almost dead center in the room, and pivoted slowly to follow her progress. It was as if they were engaged in the stateliest of dances, where every step, every gesture, was weighted with significance.

Half of the room still lay between them, gleaming with refracted sun.

"I have come to think of you as . . . someone who is prepared to go to extraordinary lengths to bring about an outcome he believes is desirable," she said, choosing her words with care. "I do not think it matters to you if the outcome is so desirable for everyone else who gets caught up in your machinations."

"There is some truth to that," he said. "But my motives are not sinister. Or selfish. I serve the king, which means I serve the kingdom. And everything I do, have done, or will do has had the goal of keeping the king and the country strong."

"It *sounds* admirable," she said. "And yet a ruthless champion is still ruthless. The people he tramples still generally feel bruised and resentful."

He gave a slight laugh. "Well, I did wonder," he said, half to himself.

She was annoyed with herself that she could not resist saying, "Wonder what?"

He gestured at her. "What personality you would show when you emerged from your cocoon of shock and grief."

"It is a personality that changes," she said. "Even I have been a little surprised to discover that. But it is not a personality that seems to harbor a great deal of fear. Leading me, perhaps, to do things and say things that other people might not."

"So you have a little courage, a fine *hunti* trait," he said.

"And anger, which is not one of the random blessings," she said.

His eyebrows rose. "Anger at me? In what possible way did I hurt you?"

She began pacing again, in those slow, stately steps. Again, he pivoted to watch her, not attempting to come closer. She rounded the corner and swept majestically by the great southern windows that overlooked the river. "You did not see fit to tell me something I cannot believe you did not know, which was that I was heir to Christara Lalindar's estate."

"I had no reason to believe *you* did not know it as well," he countered. "Every other prime of the Five Families is perfectly well-informed on that point."

He was right, of course, except she was pretty sure he was lying. "You had every reason," she said. "You knew I had lived isolated from society for ten years. You knew my father had quarreled with my Lalindar relatives—yes, and you knew no Lalindar prime had stepped forward since Christara died! A quick-witted man would have concluded that I had no idea where my proper destiny lay. A kind man would have shared that information instead of trying to lure me to the city with promises of a marriage he knew I could not possibly consummate. Yes, I think it is entirely appropriate that I feel a little anger for you."

He seemed to weigh his answer carefully. She wished she was like one of the blind sisters at the Plaza of Women, able to discern from a man's tone of voice whether or not he was telling the truth. "It is true that when I found you in your father's village, you were stunned and docile, and I knew you would not have the strength to resist any plan of action I proposed," he said. "And it is true that I had come there to find you and bring you back, and I would have done so even *had* you resisted. My mission was to bring you to the king. But I do not think," he said, raising his voice to drown hers out when she attempted to interrupt, "that I thereby injured you in any way. It was clear you were not thinking rationally. It was clear that you could barely care for yourself. I would not have let any harm come to you—I was prepared to care for you as long as it took you to recover some measure of yourself."

"You wanted to *marry* me to the *king* before I had the sense to think it through!" she exclaimed, balling her hands into fists and taking a hasty step toward him.

He gazed at her gravely. "There would have been no marriage," he said. "I never expected that transaction to be completed."

"You acted very certain of it at the time!"

"It was posturing. It was a ruse. In the first place, I knew that as soon as the rest of the Lalindar family learned of your whereabouts, they would be swarming over the palace, snatching the prime out of the royal clutches. In the second place," he added—and then paused, as if once again he needed to consider how to phrase his words. "I was not particularly interested in promoting any fifth marriage for the king. At the time, he was looking to obtain concessions from his wives. If he seemed intent on acquiring another bride, they would be more willing to make those concessions. You were a threat. And threats," he added, "are generally not informed of how they are about to be deployed."

She watched him with narrowed eyes. He might be speaking the truth—or he might be trying to portray himself in a less culpable light. "It is hard to see exactly how *I* would be a threat to the king's wives," she said in a calmer voice.

He smiled suddenly, an expression that unexpectedly warmed his serious face. "It is an ongoing game between Vernon and his wives," he said. "No man, not even the king, is a match for four women. He is constantly making plans to bring another woman into the household—not because he wants a fifth wife, but because it is something they want even less. Thus, they negotiate. It is a delicate and ongoing dance."

She made an impatient motion with her hands, as if brushing away rain. "And no doubt it is entertaining for all of you, but why draw me into your game? If you knew the Lalindars would step forward to claim me the minute I reappeared, why even go to the trouble of bringing me back to the city?"

"Because I promised your father that I would."

She stared at him. Nothing he could have said would have astonished her more. For a moment, she wished they were in any other room—one that offered chairs, for instance—but she stiffened her back and tried to keep amazement off her face.

"I am afraid you will have to explain," she said, making her voice very cold so that it didn't shake.

"It was, actually, my father who made the promise," Darien said. "He and your father had long been allies, and my father did not believe Navarr should have been banished. They remained friends once Navarr left Chialto, and my father promised *yours* that he would fetch you if something happened to Navarr before he regained the king's favor." Darien shrugged. "But my father died before yours did. And so the responsibility of looking after you passed to my hands."

Zoe was trying to remember what Darien had said all that time ago when she had first met him, when she asked if he had known about her father's death. His reply had been evasive; that was all she could recall. "You never told me how you tracked me down in the village where my father and I lived," she said slowly.

"I had a letter from your father, telling me he was dying," he said. "I had hoped to arrive while he was still alive, but he timed his letter very well."

Her anger had returned. "Do you begin to see the reasons I am inclined to distrust you?" she said. "Why didn't you tell me who had brought you there, what my inheritance was, how you planned to use me once we arrived in the city? Instead, all your actions are cloaked in secrecy, all your motivations are questionable. Why not simply tell me the truth?"

"You might fling the same question at your father," he shot back. "He lied to you for ten years or more. *I* merely failed to expose the lies. Direct your anger at Navarr, not me."

"Oh, there is plenty of anger for both of you," she said. "You are just closer to hand."

"Your father was *sweela*. Always thinking, always scheming," Darien said. "If he concealed things from you, he had a reason—though it might not be a reason you would appreciate."

"Indeed, and I can guess it very well," she said. She was so furious that she could not stand still. Again, she embarked on that slow promenade, reaching the corner of the room and turning north, walking along the single solid wall broken only by a door that led to the rest of the house. Again, Darien Serlast turned to watch her as she moved. It was as if she revolved around him, the painted outer border of some dizzy, spinning top; Darien Serlast was the weighted balance at the center, nimble and much less frantic. "He was banished, and he wanted me to be company for him while he was in exile. So he did not tell me a different life was possible. It is no more complex than that."

"It would take a very selfish man to deny his daughter her birthright only because he could not share it with her."

"I assure you, my father was just that selfish."

He studied her as she paced, very slowly, along the wall of windows that showed the autumn mountainside. "And yet, if I am to judge solely by the great grief you showed upon his death, you loved him very much," Darien said. "He must have loved you extravagantly to earn so much affection from you."

"He did. He indulged me and challenged me and encouraged me and taught me, and I adored him. *Adored* him. I wouldn't have left his side no matter what kind of power and position I was offered as Lalindar prime. He knew it—or he *should* have known it. And yet he did not tell me the truth. He did not trust me to choose him over my grandmother. It will be a long time before I will be able to forgive him for that."

"I hope you forgive me sooner."

She came to a flat halt and glared at him. "*You*," she said, "have done nothing but earn my suspicion. And not a word you have spoken today inclines me to begin trusting you."

"I'm sorry to hear that," he said. "What can I do to reverse your opinion of me?"

"Can you promise not to lie to me again? To tell me the truth at all times—whether or not I have explicitly asked for it?"

He hesitated a long time and then answered, "No."

She was surprised into a laugh. "Only a fool would say no to that question, even if he did not intend to keep his word."

"Only a rogue would lie when he was asked if he would be truthful," Darien retorted. "And you already think badly enough of me."

"You have given me no reason to change my mind! You have admitted that you will continue to lie to me!"

"I am in a delicate position," he said. "I serve King Vernon, and sometimes I must conceal information from almost everyone. I have gotten in the habit of telling the truth only when nothing else will achieve the results I need. That is not admirable, perhaps, but it has enabled me to walk the steps of a very dangerous maze without stumbling into any disasters. I do not see my way clear of the maze at this point. So I do not see my behavior changing anytime soon."

She was still staring, but now she was more fascinated than furious. "Such an admission makes me wonder just exactly what is transpiring at the palace."

His smile was a little lopsided. "And well you might. Though I presume it is no worse than the intrigue that plays out at any royal court."

"I do not like the idea that you feel you can lie to me with impunity, just because your life is complicated," Zoe said. "Just because you have told me you might."

His smile grew broader, more genuine. "What about this?" he said. "I will lie when I feel I must. At any time you can *ask* me if I am lying, and if I am, I will confess—though I will not then be compelled to tell you the truth that I am concealing. But you will be able to judge how much you can trust me."

"Although a liar would lie even about such a bargain," she pointed out. "So a quintile from now, I might say, 'Is that the truth?' and you would say, 'Yes,' and I would believe you because *today* you claimed that you would not lie in such a situation."

He laughed out loud. "That is *sweela* reasoning," he said. "A *coru* woman would have simply strolled out the door by now. Would already have moved on."

She caught her breath, for he was right. But her answer was stiff. "A *coru* woman seeks and seeks for passage through an unnavigable space," she said. "She will rise to any level or turn into any channel. And if you attempt to block her way, she will flood the banks and sweep everything ahead of her. Just because I argue with you today does not mean I will not force my way past you someday when you have tried to throw one too many boulders in my path."

"I admit, I think that would be an interesting thing to witness."

"On the contrary. I think you would be sorry that day had come."

He held his hands out as if in surrender. "The fact that you are even quarreling leads me to hope that you are not so angry you will refuse to return to the city with me. You will make me pay for my perceived sins, but to do that, you must be somewhere in my vicinity."

He made her want to laugh, and at the same time he made her want to hit him. It was hard to remember that less than a year ago she had passed nearly a nineday in his company and had never been moved to do either.

"I have always planned to return to Chialto," she said frostily. "Your invitation has no influence on my actions."

"No, I'm sure it doesn't," he said. "But you have not heard the extent of the invitation yet. King Vernon would like you to temporarily take up residence at the palace."

That made her open her eyes and take a step backward, until she felt the smooth surface of the glass against her spine through the heavy fabric of her robe. "Why?"

"It is common for the primes of the Five Families to keep quarters at the palace so that they may easily come and go," Darien said. "And it is customary, when a new prime is installed, for that individual to reside at the palace for some period of time. It is not required," he added. "But it would be much appreciated by the king."

Zoe frowned. "It sounds awkward and uncomfortable. I am not accustomed to court ways, and I feel certain I would make dozens of social blunders."

"King Vernon very much wishes that you will take up residence in the palace," Darien said. His voice was still pleasant, but there was a *hunti* undertone that hinted of intransigence.

Zoe toyed with the idea of resisting, just to test her waywardness against his will, but she thought there would be many battles ahead between the two of them, and it might serve her better to conserve her energy. "What would be required of me?"

"You will join the wives for breakfast, the king and all his guests for dinner, and participate in whatever social activities occur during the duration of your stay. You will have your own apartments, with space for three or four servants, and you may come and go as you please. You would live at the palace merely to promote the notion that the kingdom is, indeed, one family, and that yours is a part of the king's."

"Will it be clear to King Vernon—and his wives—that I am no longer in contention to be one of his brides?"

Darien smiled. "It already was, the minute your aunt Sarone publicly named you prime."

She turned away and began pacing again. "And will you advise me if I seem to be on the verge of a solecism? For if I recall correctly, *you* maintain apartments at the palace as well."

"I do. And certainly, if I think you are about to make an error, I will try to guide your actions."

"When would I be expected to make my appearance at the palace?"

"I had hoped to bring you back with me when I leave your estate."

"Which will be?"

"Tomorrow or the following day."

"I am not sure I will be ready to leave so soon."

"Then I await your convenience."

She stopped abruptly and swung around to face him. "Let us travel down to the temple in town," she said. "Let us see if this arrangement you propose is, in fact, in my best interests."

His face was grave again. "Let us do so indeed," he said. "I am certain you will find that it is."

The temple in town was scarcely bigger than the *kierten* at Zoe's house in the village. It had the required five-walled shape, but room for only three benches, which made a triangle around a small covered table in the center of the space. There was no deep barrel here, filled with dozens of each blessing, just a pretty basket with a shallow layer of coins.

"My cousin Keeli tells me that there are only three of every blessing to be found in the basket," Zoe said with a slight smile. "So perhaps you will pull up something other than a *hunti* trait if you dip your hand in three times."

"Is that what you wish to do?" he asked. "Pull three blessings?"

"Let me see if I like the first one I draw," she said. She swirled her fingers through the flat metal disks and picked one. "Change," she said, showing it to him.

"Does that convince you?" he asked.

"Maybe," she said. "Let me try again."

Even she was a little unnerved when the second coin she pulled from the basket showed the exact same symbol. Darien said, "The message seems a little difficult to deny."

She kept both pieces in her fist and pointed at him. "Now you draw one. Let's see if even here you are showered with nothing but *hunti* blessings."

He nodded, his expression a bit sardonic, and swept his hand through the metal disks so quickly she was sure he didn't have the time to feel for any particular glyph. She had never seen him so surprised as when he glanced at the coin he had selected.

"What is it? Let me see," she demanded, and he wordlessly tilted his hand to show her.

Change.

A shiver went down her back. He was right; the message of the blessings seemed incontrovertible. Not only was her life scheduled for transformation, but Darien Serlast was an inescapable part of that future. The slightest laugh escaped her lips.

"I have to look," she said. "This won't take very long."

Handing her two coins to Darien, she carried the basket to a bench and dumped its contents in her lap. He sat on one of the other benches and watched her, idly turning the blessings over and over in his hand, as she sorted through every other coin in the basket. There were three symbols for triumph, three for talent, three for honor, three for loyalty, three for wealth—three for every single blessing on the list.

No other coin was stamped with the symbol for change. She and Darien Serlast had drawn the only ones.

FIFTEEN

Zoe supposed she should have expected it to be raining when she made her way down to the river flats. Here in the middle of Quinnasweela, the weather was still generally fine, but there was just enough chill in the air to remind everyone that colder, more miserable days were coming. She had to confess, she was glad she would not be camping on the Marisi when the truly wretched weather moved in.

She was not yet living in the palace, though she had been back in the city for two days. She had told Darien that she needed a little time to organize herself—assemble the rest of her wardrobe, for instance, and engage servants who would accompany her to the palace. Not at all to her surprise, Hoden had refused her invitation to come to Chialto. "I do not leave the house," he said. "None of us do."

"I suspected that," she said. "I will look for other people."

The people she had in mind were ensconced in their tent on the river flats, happily watching the rain dimpling the water. "Zoe!" Annova exclaimed when Zoe stuck her head through the flap. She rushed out into the wet weather to throw her arms around her visitor's neck. "Look at you! So finely dressed! Have you taken up with a wealthy man who showers you with gifts?"

Zoe laughed. "Oh, my tale is much stranger than that. Can we get in out of the rain? Calvin, how are you?"

Once they had exchanged greetings and settled on mats—quite close to each other in the cramped confines of the tent—Zoe told her story. Both of them made suitable exclamations of surprise, but she could tell neither was really astonished. People came down to the river flats for all sorts of reasons. She was not the first wealthy or well-connected person to hide herself among the squatters—indeed, nearly everyone who lived on the river had an interesting past. Even, she would guess, Annova and Calvin.

"So I will be living in the palace for perhaps a quintile," she finished up. "I am expected to bring attendants with me—and you are the only two people in Chialto I trust with my whole heart. Winter is coming. If you have nowhere else to go, and you're willing to play the parts of my servants, I would love to have you with me for the next season."

Calvin was tickled. "Me! Living in the palace! Wearing fine livery and ordering footmen to do my bidding!"

"It's a generous offer, and both of us have held such positions from time to time," Annova said, confirming a suspicion Zoe had had for a long time. "I would be happy to live out of the wet and the cold, and I don't mind acting as your maid, but I don't know that I'm fashionable enough to be of any benefit to you."

"My cousin Keeli will advise me on my clothes," Zoe said. "You would just be there to help me get *into* my clothes and make sure everything stays clean and mended. And Calvin would carry messages and run errands—and maybe lurk around palace doorways and listen to what the wives are saying about me," she added with a laugh.

"I suppose the two of us would need new clothes as well," Annova said thoughtfully.

"Yes. The Lalindar colors are predominantly blue with a touch of green. I thought we could get each of you some formal attire."

"Might get a little pricey for you," Calvin objected. "You realize we cannot afford to make such purchases ourselves."

Zoe laughed. "You have no idea how much money I control now! I can buy chocolates *every day* if I feel like it—and anything else I desire! And you realize, of course, that you will get salaries, as well as your bed and board."

Calvin thrust his hand out. "Then we're hired!"

"If you're certain we're the right ones to see you through this," Annova said doubtfully.

Zoe reached out to clasp Calvin's hand, and Annova laid hers on top of their interlaced fingers. For a moment, Zoe's blood reacted to the chemicals in theirs, busily decoding and defining; by now, she found the sensation soothing rather than strange. "You're the *only* ones," Zoe said. "I will feel so much better knowing that friends of the river are beside me."

Annova said, "Friends of the heart."

On her third day in the city, Zoe accepted an invitation to have lunch with Keeli and her mother, Christara's daughter Sarone. She had to ask directions to the house, a sprawling three-story building that had once been Christara's. Zoe's memories of it were much hazier than her memories of the house on the river; her parents had rarely brought her there and rarely stayed for long. But as she walked up the wide stone pathway from the street to the house, she was struck with a sudden mental image of racing across the yard, being chased by her cousins; the pathway, laid out from river rocks, was the secure zone where no harm could befall you. For a moment, on this chilly Quinnasweela day, she felt the humid air of high summer, the relentless overhead sun, her gasping breath tumbling against her rib cage as she collapsed within the margin of safety, one step ahead of Keeli. Then she blinked, and the sensations were gone.

Keeli answered the door. "Oooh, look at you, that dark blue is a very good color," she approved. "Come on in—it's just my mother and me, and she can't wait to see you."

Keeli tugged her impatiently through the house, but Zoe dragged her feet, glancing around, trying to take in as much detail as she could. Yes, she remembered *that* room, with its dark, heavy furniture and velvet curtains, but *that* room must have been completely redone. The arrangement of archways and doors was eerily familiar, as was the way a slant of sunlight threw a prism across one wall at just this hour of day. She heard a faraway splash and remembered that the house's grandest indulgence—an indoor water feature that resembled a woodland pool—was just down that corridor to her right.

But Zoe didn't recognize the small room Keeli eventually delivered her to, a cheerful place of many windows, blue-and-white furnishings, and a view of a busy city street. Sarone came forward to greet her, hands outstretched and face lit with a smile, much happier to see Zoe than her brother Broy had been. Sarone had that Lalindar look—golden, blue-eyed, full-bodied—though her face was warmer than Christara's had ever been.

"Zoe," she said, first clasping Zoe's hands and then dropping them to take her in an embrace. "I had given up all hope of ever seeing you again."

As soon as Sarone touched her, Zoe felt that shock of recognition in her blood, the quiver of acknowledgment that here was someone closely related to her. She felt herself involuntarily flinch against Sarone's hold, and then she raised her arms to cling. Sarone had enough of the look and feel and smell of Alieta that for a moment Zoe could imagine that she was hugging her own mother.

Sarone obviously had felt Zoe's strong reaction, because when she pulled back, she wore a quizzical look. "Do you have that ability, too?" she asked. "To identify a blood relative just by touch?"

Zoe was relieved to have such a thing spoken of aloud; it made the power seem so much less unnerving. "Yes—can you feel it, too?"

Sarone shook her head. "No, but my mother could. It was quite remarkable—even more so because it extended beyond her own family. She could go into a roomful of fifty women, all strangers to her, and discover which two were sisters, just by touching a hand to each of them in turn. She also used to claim she could hear the heartbeat of every person in the city, but *that* one was harder to prove."

"I can hear heartbeats, but only at the river house," Zoe said with a smile. "To tell you the truth, I am a little glad that ability hasn't followed me down the mountain."

"No, I imagine it would be very distracting."

"I think it would be *awful*," Keeli put in. "And then what if a heartbeat suddenly *stopped*? You'd know that person was dead!"

"Though I can imagine some situations in which that would be a useful skill," Sarone said. She had stepped back but was still studying Zoe, as if trying to match the new image to an old memory. "You look so much like your father," she said. "I remember you as small and dark and well-mannered until someone made you angry, and then you could throw a tantrum to bring down the house. Just from the outside, you don't look like you've changed much at all."

Zoe grinned. "I haven't had occasion to throw a tantrum in quite a long time, so I don't know about that part of it," she said. "I suppose I won't know until I'm actually incensed about something."

"Let's have lunch while you tell us everything about yourself," Sarone said, ushering them over to a broad table loaded down with a selection of delicacies. A fountain played nearby, the sound of running water soothing to *coru* sensibilities. They filled small plates with a variety of foods—breads and baked fish and roasted vegetables, which Zoe imagined were particularly expensive here out of season.

"Keeli tells me your father is dead," Sarone said as they settled in to eat. "I'm sorry for the grief that must have caused you."

Not, Zoe noticed, *I'm sorry he is dead.* "Soon it will be a year since he died," she said. "At times I still find it hard to believe he is no longer in the world."

"Yes, I've rarely met anyone with a stronger personality than Navarr Ardelay."

"You didn't like him," Zoe said outright.

Sarone hesitated. "He seemed to go out of his way to alienate the Lalindars," she said at last. "He was always arguing with someone. It didn't help that his politics and my mother's were so different. They both served as advisors to the king, and no matter what counsel my mother gave, Navarr was certain to contradict it. It infuriated her." She glanced at Zoe. "And perhaps it infuriated *him* that her views were so contrary."

Zoe smiled. "No, I think he enjoyed putting her in a temper."

"He must have been the only one in the kingdom," Keeli observed around a mouthful of food. "Everyone else was always so careful not to make her mad!"

"Except my sister," Sarone added. "Alieta and our mother had some bitter battles."

"I was never certain," Zoe said. "What was the final argument between Christara and my father? Because I know she's the one who spoke against him so strongly to the king."

Sarone lathered jam on a thick slice of bread. "Well, there was the public fight and the private one," she said thoughtfully. "Publicly, it was a dispute over a proposed marriage between the king and a girl from Soeche-Tas. One of the viceroy's daughters, I believe. Your father distrusted the Soechins for various reasons, but my mother favored the notion of a wedding. She rallied the Frothens and the Dochenzas and together they challenged your father. The Serlasts stayed neutral, though I believe Damon felt much as Navarr did. The king ultimately sided with the stronger coalition, though no marriage ever occurred."

"And the private argument?" Zoe asked.

Sarone gave her a level look. "Evidence had come to light of one of your father's infidelities. My mother was angry that he was unfaithful to Alieta, and she wanted to make him pay."

That widened Zoe's eyes. She vividly remembered arguments on that topic from the days her mother was still alive. *How can you think so little of me that you betray me with a woman like her?* And of course, even while they lived in exile, Navarr had indulged in dalliances. There had been at least three women in the village whose company he sought out on a regular basis, as well as women in nearby towns.

But. "My mother was dead at least a year before my father's fall from grace," she said. "He might have been seeing another woman, but at that point he could hardly have been considered unfaithful."

Sarone nodded. "I remember saying that very thing to her, but apparently—oh, it's been so long and the details escape me! Apparently she learned in some mysterious fashion that your father had been carrying on this liaison while my sister was still alive. My mother was *enraged*. She came stalking into the house—I will never forget it—*flinging* things in front of her, knocking pots and furniture to the ground. She was so furious that the water in the fountains all over the house started bubbling up over their basins. I'm not making this up. The pool overflowed. This room flooded. Her bedroom flooded. Water was dripping through the ceiling and ruining the floors and the rugs. And she just splashed through the halls shouting, 'How dare he? I will *ruin* him!' And she did."

Sarone fixed her gaze on Zoe. "She had disliked him long before this, of course. When my sister died, my mother offered to take you. Actually, that's not strong enough. She *demanded* that Navarr give you to her. She had already determined that you would be her heir, apparently, so she wanted to raise you in her house. But he refused to turn you over. I think one of the reasons she was so bent on ruining him," she added, "was that she believed the king would award her custody of you once Navarr was in disgrace. But he was too wily for her. The day before his assets were seized, he disappeared, taking you with him." She shrugged. "No one knew where you were. Until word came from Christara's house that you had reappeared, we didn't have the faintest idea where you could be found."

Zoe listened to all this with her head bowed in thought. Once Sarone finished speaking, she said, "I thank you for telling me that. I wondered, when I was younger, why none of my mother's family came to visit. It didn't occur to me that you simply didn't know where I was. My father's explanation was that you must not have cared about me after all."

Sarone made an exclamation of dismay. "That selfish bastard! I'm sorry, Zoe. I don't mean to speak unkindly of your father, but that was *cruel*! My mother looked for you for a long time. I'm not sure she ever stopped. My husband and I sometimes walked down through the southern slums, studying the street girls we thought would be about your age. But we never found you." She pressed her fingers to her mouth. "I try not to, but sometimes I hate your father."

Zoe shook her head, smiling sadly. "I loved him. He was— richness, excitement, brilliance, color—a man so alive I still cannot believe he is dead. But I am not surprised to learn of this new flaw. He had very many." She stretched out her hand across the table. "Feel free to hate him on my behalf, but don't expect me to feel the same. I am just glad I have found you again after all this time."

Over the next few days, Zoe spent a great deal of time replenishing her wardrobe, frequently accompanied by

Keeli. Her cousin had strong opinions on where they should buy overrobes and where they should look for accessories, but Zoe insisted that there was only one cobbler's shop where she would buy shoes.

A new girl was standing behind the counter when they strolled in—new to Zoe, anyway. She realized the girl could have been there for a quintile or more while Zoe was at her grandmother's house. The worker was dark-haired, a little chubby, cheerful, and she bounced right over to the newcomers.

"Are you interested in custom-made footwear or would you like to try one of the ready-made pairs that are suitable for the woman in a hurry?" she asked. "Are you looking for casual wear or something more formal?"

"I need several pairs, all of them formal," Zoe said. "But I think ready-made shoes will do."

The young woman ushered them to chairs and showed them a dozen of the latest styles. Even Keeli was impressed at the variety and the quality of the samples, all of them constructed of thin, delicate leather and gossamer-thin soles. Between them, they ended up choosing seven pairs.

The shopgirl approved of their choices. "A special discount applies when you buy more than two pairs," she told them. "Do you want to pay today or would you like to establish a line of credit? I can do that for you right now."

"Today, I think, though you've been quite helpful," Zoe said, handing over the appropriate number of gold pieces. "Would it be possible to talk to one of the owners and let them know how pleased I am at your service?"

The young woman looked over her shoulder, where—unless Ilene's habits had greatly changed—the shopkeeper was very likely hovering behind the hidden glass. "I think so," she said.

Almost on the words, Ilene came bustling out. She looked exactly the same: lean, fussy, a little dowdy, a little suspicious. "Good afternoon, we're very happy that you've stopped by our shop today," she rattled off in a businesslike tone. "Is there anything more we can do for you?" Her voice faltered a little as she met Zoe's gaze; her face showed a faint bewilderment.

Keeli said, "You know, Zoe, you might want a pair of gloves to match those little blue flats."

At the name, Ilene's gaze sharpened; she stared harder. "It can't be," she whispered.

Zoe smiled. "I wondered if you would recognize me."

"*Zoe?* But Barlow said—and you've been gone so long—but I thought you—and then you're a *Lalindar*? After all that?"

Keeli gave Zoe a quick sideways glance, clearly wondering what history lay between her cousin and the shopkeeper, but she didn't ask any questions. Zoe nodded at Ilene and said, "Yes, after all that. And not just a Lalindar, but the prime."

Ilene's mouth dropped open and she didn't attempt to say a word.

"I know. It was a surprise to me, too," Zoe said. "I'm still getting used to the notion." She glanced around the shop with its high shelves of shoes lining every wall. "I didn't know what was in store for me. I thought I was lucky to have a place like this where I could be safe." She smiled at Ilene again. "I still think I was lucky."

Ilene was shaking her head. "Melvin will never believe this. And Barlow! He'll love your story."

Zoe handed her a small silk bag, crusted with gold thread and closed with a tiny diamond clasp. She had bought it yesterday for a fabulous sum of money and refused to tell Keeli why she wanted it. "I have something of yours I need to return, thanking you humbly for the loan," she said.

Ilene took the bag, but her expression was bewildered. "I never lent you anything as expensive as this."

"You gave me what's inside—something worth far more to me at the time than this bag cost."

Ilene peeked inside, where the key to the shop lay prosaically in its silk cocoon. Now her face showed comprehension and the slightest blush. "It was a simple kindness," she said, her voice gruff.

"It was a great treasure," Zoe said. "I am glad to be in circumstances that allow me to repay it."

"Well, then," Ilene said, and tucked the bag in her pocket. She visibly regained her usual briskness, tinged with a certain calculation. Zoe could almost see what she was thinking: *I had no expectation that my small gesture would pay off so handsomely, for now one of the primes will be a patron of my shop.*

"Come back anytime." She nodded at Keeli. "Bring your friends. We'll always have special discounts available for you."

Zoe laughed and impulsively gave Ilene a hug, though she could tell the affection took Ilene wholly by surprise. "You can be sure I'll be back," she said. "I've missed you. I've missed everything about Chialto."

Z oe had hoped to move into the palace in a more or less unobtrusive manner, but that didn't appear to be possible. Two days later, Darien Serlast himself arrived at her fashionable inn, riding in a fancy smoker car, and oversaw the stowing of all her belongings into the back compartment. Calvin, strutting around in handsome new livery, enjoyed himself hugely as he directed footmen where to store each trunk and box.

"Careful with that, my boy!" he roared as one of the younger footmen dropped a box inches away from a puddle. "You don't want to ruin the prime's fine underthings by getting them all dirty, do you?"

Darien Serlast turned to give Zoe one expressive look—*You have hired a servant who discusses your undergarments with the hotel staff?*—but made no comment aloud. She smiled faintly and said nothing.

Eventually all the bundles were loaded to Calvin's satisfaction and the rest of them climbed in. Annova and Calvin crowded into the front compartment with the driver, while Darien and Zoe settled in back. She sat with her face turned slightly away from him so she could watch their progress. Here in the wealthy district at the foot of the mountain, the houses and multistory apartments were made of high-quality stone and marble, set on gracious avenues and surrounded by lush gardens, but the streets were still crowded and noisy, and travel was slow. The line between city and mountain was demarcated by a wide bridge over the northern loop of the canal; once on the other side, the road instantly began to climb. The ascent reminded Zoe a little of the trip to Christara's house—the gorgeous, solitary building ahead of them like a signal beacon, seeming by its very existence to pull them closer. Her eyes turned from the broad, turreted facade to the white water rushing down the mountain just behind it. It was the very same river that ran by Christara's house, a fact that she found comforting on this strange day. She had not, perhaps, traveled so far from familiar territory as it seemed.

"Surely you're not frightened."

Darien had been silent for so long that Zoe actually started at the sound of his voice. She glanced his way and then turned her attention back to the view. "Not frightened," she murmured. "But—uncertain. I don't know exactly what is expected of me in this particular role."

"Merely that you show yourself to be a loyal subject of the king."

She shrugged and did not answer.

As the road made its final twist, it delivered the *elaymotive* into a huge, well-maintained courtyard, paved with honey-yellow bricks very close in tone to the weathered stone of the palace itself. The courtyard was almost as busy as the Cinque, for it was filled with smoker cars, carts, horses, and people all threading their way around fountains and big stands of potted trees and shrubs. Horses whickered, grooms shouted, servants dashed between conveyances to deliver messages.

"Is this what it's always like?" Zoe asked.

"More or less. Except on changedays, when it is usually ten times as chaotic."

She glanced at him again. "I hope you don't plan to abandon me until you've seen me safely settled to my quarters."

He held her gaze. "I thought I made it plain that I don't intend to abandon you at all."

"While I'm at the palace, at any rate," she said.

He merely smiled and looked away.

The instant the driver brought the car to a stop, a footman ran over, bowing to Darien Serlast. "This is Zoe Ardelay Lalindar," Darien said. "These are her servants, and these are her possessions. See that they all are brought to her quarters with a minimum of fuss." The footman bowed again.

Zoe looked toward Annova, prepared to protest if she looked too bewildered, but Annova cheerfully waved her on. "We will get all of these things settled," she said. "Go on in."

Out of the car, across the courtyard, up the broad, shallow steps, and into a great hall. Zoe was not sure when Darien had taken her arm, but she was glad for the support. At first the hall seemed as big as the Plaza of Women. It was a round, echoing space, open for level after level all the way to a rotunda made of shaped glass. The floor was constructed of a rose-white stone cut in squares that were big enough for Zoe to lie down in. Directly across from the grand entrance, a huge bronze fountain was set into the wall; a collection of fanciful pipes and fluted pillars spumed with water that fell into the curved, scalloped bowl of a hammered metal basin. Zoe felt her heart clutch a moment. Her father had kept a small replica of this fountain in their house in the village.

She turned away from that memory to finish her inspection of the hall. Three great arching corridors opened off the circular bottom story; each higher level overlooked the atrium from terraced balconies lined with carved stone banisters. Right now, sunlight flooded in from overhead, but sconces dotted all the walls on the bottom story to illuminate the space at night.

It took Zoe a moment to realize that, except for the fountain, the huge space was empty of any furniture or ornamentation. It was a *kierten* sized for a king.

"I think I'm lost already," she said in a low voice.

"It *is* an impressive sight," Darien agreed. "Have you never been here before?"

"When I was a child," she said. "I rarely let go of my father's hand."

For a moment, his grip on her arm tightened in a gesture that seemed meant to be comforting. "Surely you're braver now."

"Surely I am."

He gestured to his right. "That wing is mostly reserved for the king, his prominent visitors, and the solitary men who have their quarters here." Next he indicated the hall opening off of his left. "That's the wing where the king's wives live and where you will stay. Other women of the court take up residence on that side of the palace. My aunt has quarters there as well. Ahead of us," he added, nodding toward the final hall a little to the left of the fountain, "are the public spaces—the throne room, a ballroom, several dining halls, and beyond them the kitchens and gardens. It is unlikely you will find occasion to go much beyond public spaces and the wives' wing."

"Then let's find where I will be staying."

They followed the left-hand corridor to a second, smaller atrium, clearly the *kierten* for the women's wing. Its central feature was a circular stairwell, one of the most beautiful architectural elements Zoe had ever seen. Each riser was constructed of a different kind of stone—white marble veined with purple, tumbled jasper in yellows and greens, rough red granite, lightless black onyx, lapis lazuli, and marble again, this time streaked with black.

"I suppose this answers any question I might have about how much wealth the king possesses," she said.

"Or the king who built this palace nearly three centuries ago," Darien replied, tugging her toward the first step. "The wives have their rooms on the second floor, but I'm afraid your suite is one level higher."

They climbed up sixty-three stairs, and Zoe never saw the same stone repeated. The stairwell circled on above them, but Darien guided Zoe down the third-story hallway that instantly put her in mind of Christara's house. One wall consisted largely of windows, the other wall of closed doors that most likely led to bedrooms. The hall windows overlooked the back of the palace, facing the mountain wall. She supposed that meant the view from the bedrooms must be magnificent.

"Yours is the place of honor, the fifth door down," Darien said. He escorted her there and handed her a key that was as long as her palm from fingertip to wrist and so heavy she almost dropped it. She thanked him gravely before saying, "I need a key for Annova and Calvin as well."

"There is a second one inside." He hesitated and then added, "You realize it is a courtesy only. The fact that two keys exist, and that I have had one for several days, means that there are likely to be copies, and that someone who wishes you ill could easily find a way into your suite. If there are jewels you do not want to lose or secrets you do not want to be found, they are best kept somewhere besides this room."

"Thank you for telling me that," she said. "Is one of the copies a key that you have retained for yourself?"

He watched her a long time without answering.

"I suppose it is," she said finally.

"Under normal circumstances, I would never enter your chambers without an invitation," he said. "But if there was an emergency—if you were missing, if there was cause for alarm—I would want to be able to check your rooms and ascertain that no harm had come to you."

"Do you have keys to the rooms of all the guests in this wing?" she asked. They were having this whole conversation outside in the hallway. The afternoon sun filtered in, murky and indirect, reflecting off the mountain and through the glass. "To the rooms of all the wives?"

He did not answer that question, either.

"I wonder what exactly it is about you that causes the king to trust you so much," she said.

"Probably the very same thing that makes you trust me not at all."

She almost laughed. "I think you're a man who gathers up power like a child gathers up wildflowers in the woods."

"Responsibility, maybe," he said. "Not necessarily power."

"Harder to gather handfuls of lake water or rain," she said.

"I know," he said. "I don't expect to be able to harvest you."

She smothered another laugh, turned the key in the door, stepped inside, and quickly looked around.

Her suite consisted of a small *kierten* and multiple interior rooms. A comfortably sized sitting room offered graceful furniture groupings and a wall of windows; doors to the right led to smallish rooms that were probably the servants' quarters. A much larger bedroom opened off the left. Zoe peeked inside to find it admirably furnished with fine materials in *coru* colors.

"I can only guess that this is a room where Lalindar women have stayed before me," Zoe said.

"If you look closely, you might find evidence of your grandmother's previous occupancy," Darien said.

She crossed the floor to gaze out the windows. The view was everything she'd hoped. From this height, she could look past the bustling courtyard to the green-and-brown contours of the mountain, ending in the variegated sprawl of the city. The joyful white froth of the waterfall was too far to the left for her to glimpse it from this angle, but she could see part of the serene blue pool that piled up here on this plateau before the river dove down once more to curl around the western edge of the city.

From here, she could see the colorful patchwork of the river flats tucked up against one last coil of the Marisi before it straightened itself and galloped south to the very edge of the world.

"You admire the scene now, but it is magical at night when all the lights come up," Darien said from behind her. "Sometimes I stand at my window for hours, just watching."

She pointed. "From the flats, you can see the palace," she said. "When night falls and the torches are lit, it is outlined in dozens of wavering lights. It seems to float against the mountain like an apparition from a dream. I don't know that I like the view *from* the palace any better than the view *of* the palace, but I will agree that each one is breathtaking."

"Surely the associated marvels of being *inside* the palace make this the better vantage point," he said.

She turned her back on the panorama and smiled at him. "I am not yet convinced that these are marvels that will completely win my heart."

"You will have to let me know once you have made up your mind."

"So!" she said. "What am I supposed to do now? Sit here with my hands folded until the king calls me down for dinner?"

"There *will* be a dinner tonight, and you *are* expected to attend, but in the interim there will be an intimate gathering in the smaller dining hall of this wing," he said. "The wives hope you will join them to become acquainted."

"And you?"

"I am not officially invited, but if you want to include me, I will be happy to join all of you."

"I think it might be easier if you were present."

"Then let us go downstairs."

SIXTEEN

It didn't take Zoe long to form opinions of the king's four wives. She supposed they had formed instant opinions of her as well, and none very favorable. She had planned to spend the whole reception saying little, listening closely, and betraying almost no emotion; but a few times she couldn't stop herself from making a pointed comment. Well, surely it was the ambiance that sparked her sharp replies. The king's wives all appeared to engage in a ceaseless, subtle war of words, often unkind and stuffed with hidden meaning. Surely anyone would occasionally respond with a barbed retort of her own.

They had gathered in a beautiful room that was painted in pale yellows and whites, and decorated with latticework along its windows and arched doorways. It was very much an *elay* sort of space, airy and light, and the colors were Dochenza. A reminder that the king's first wife was both Dochenza and *elay*.

The instant Zoe and Darien stepped inside, all four wives surged over to greet them. One put her hand on Darien's arm in an unconsciously possessive fashion.

"Darien! You have brought her straight to us! I'm so glad!" she exclaimed. Zoe remembered her from the parade, so she was sure this was Alys, but she took a moment to get a better look close up. The third queen was a small-boned, pale-complected woman whose dark red hair was her most striking feature. She wore silk trousers and an overrobe of the palest green; the scooped neckline was cut to perfectly frame a short copper necklace hung with three blessing charms. Intelligence, patience, resolve. Despite the fact that only one was a fire trait, the queen was obviously *sweela*.

As Darien introduced them, Alys turned her light green eyes on Zoe with sharp attention. "The missing Lalindar prime," she said. "We have been so eager to meet you. You must have very exciting stories to tell."

"Almost none, I'm afraid," Zoe said, smiling pleasantly. It was remarkable how instantly she disliked Alys, though she tried to keep a mask of civility on her face.

Alys offered a brittle laugh. "We'll tease them out of you."

Darien shook off Alys's hand and directed Zoe toward a second woman who had dark hair, white skin, blue eyes, and an engaging smile. She was short and a little plump, with a sort of puppy-dog friendliness that made Zoe like her on the spot. She could barely be twenty, whereas Alys appeared to be at least ten years older. "It is just that we already know all our own stories, and they're no longer interesting," the young woman said. "So we're wild with delight at the idea of meeting someone new. And someone from the Five Families at that! We have been waiting for you for *days*."

"I will try to be interesting," Zoe said. "But please don't expect too much."

"That's Romelle," Darien supplied. "The king's fourth and youngest wife."

Alys stroked Romelle's arm as she might caress a cat's fur. "Our little pet. We all adore her."

Romelle giggled and looked pleased. Zoe didn't have time to assess whether that was an act or not because Darien was already introducing her to a third woman. This one was taller than the rest, thin and fair-haired and attractive. "Seterre," he said. "The king's second wife."

Zoe thought Seterre looked crafty and curious, the kind of person who would pretend to be your friend just so she could find out your secrets and use them against you. Yet she was old for such adolescent games, probably in her late thirties. Zoe remembered that she had a daughter who was about fourteen. The king's oldest child and possibly his heir.

"Indeed, we are pleased to have you among us," Seterre said, and her voice was low-pitched and musical. "You look like your father."

"That's right," Alys said, as if she had just remembered. "You're Navarr Ardelay's daughter."

"Yes, I am."

"We were so sorry to hear of his death," Alys said. "We had always hoped he would be back in Vernon's good graces and we would have a chance to see him again."

"Alys," Romelle said in a shocked voice.

"Well, it's hardly a secret to Zoe that her father had fallen from favor."

"Indeed, that fact was the central tenet of my existence for ten years," Zoe said, displaying nothing but serenity. Inside, she had felt a small rip of grief, a spurt of anger—that a thing so huge, so awful, could be spoken of so casually—but she showed none of it on her face. "I am unlikely to have forgotten."

"He was such a proud man. Was he—was his exile difficult for him?" Seterre asked. Zoe supposed she spoke so awkwardly because, having brought up Navarr's name, she thought it would be rude to quickly turn the subject, and yet she could hardly think of what else to ask. *How did he die? Was there much suffering? Have you mastered your grief yet?*

"I never saw any bitterness in him," Zoe said, "no regrets. He remained, until he died, a vibrant and restless presence."

"That is good to hear," said the last woman in the room. "I, too, would have been glad to have one last conversation with Navarr Ardelay."

Zoe turned in her direction just as Darien said, "Let me present Elidon. The king's first wife."

Elidon was solid, full-bodied, and showing signs of her age, which must have been a little more than fifty. Her short hair was a mix of black and gray, and the skin around her gray eyes was rayed with wrinkles. She seemed sad, Zoe thought, but dignified, and touched with latent power. Zoe had the impression Elidon could be roused to attack if the incentive was strong enough, and that she could be merciless.

"Welcome to our home for however long you choose to stay

with us," Elidon said. She bowed her head in a great show of courtesy from the most powerful woman in the room. None of them extended a hand or came near enough to touch Zoe. She remembered that—among royalty and high-ranking families—physical contact was considered a privilege offered only to close friends.

Suddenly, frivolously, she remembered how Darien had taken her arm as they entered the castle. But that wasn't a sign of friendship; it was a mark of kindness.

"Thank you for opening your home to me," Zoe replied formally. "I am sure I will enjoy my time among you."

"Are we done with all the introductions and greetings?" Romelle asked plaintively. "Can't we sit and eat? I'm so hungry!"

A laugh rippled around the gathering, and Seterre linked her arm with Romelle's. "Yes, let us feed our child-bride," she said. "Oh, to be twenty years old again and eat whatever I want without turning into a fat old cow!"

"All her meals will catch up with her soon enough," Alys said. "As Elidon knows."

It was said in a playful manner, but it was definitely intended to be cruel, and Zoe waited for a reproof from one of the other women. But no one said anything, not even Elidon, who merely led the way to a lovely table situated in front of a wide window. The glass top of the table was laid over a filigreed metal base that echoed the whitewashed trellises both in the room and in the garden. Despite the lateness of the season, there were still plenty of green vines and bushes visible through the window, and a few hardy blossoms added splashes of desperate color.

"Sit by me," Romelle begged, so Zoe dropped into the seat beside her. Elidon settled at the head of the table, but everyone else took whatever chair was nearest to hand. Servants slipped in through side doors to pour fruited water into their glasses and bring out plates of bread and sweets. Romelle made a little purring noise of satisfaction and everyone else laughed.

Darien had seated himself directly across the table from Zoe, and Alys had instantly claimed the chair beside him. She gave him a teasing smile. "I cannot believe you have agreed to stay and visit with us so long!" she said. "You hardly ever join us anymore!"

"My services have been much in demand by Vernon," he said.

"Well, I can be very demanding, too," Alys said.

"I have not forgotten that," he said.

Romelle ignored them. "Isn't that good?" she asked as Zoe made appreciative sounds over a slice of some slim, sweet concoction that seemed to be nothing but honey and nuts.

"I've never tasted anything like it," Zoe said. "Clearly, I have lived away from society too long!"

She said it lightly, and to Romelle, but Alys was the one who jumped on her words. "Yes, and where exactly *did* you live when you were in exile with your father?"

"Alys," Elidon said.

Alys opened her green eyes very wide. "What? I am not supposed to even mention the fact that they were in exile?"

"You've already done so," Elidon said. "Perhaps you could keep from mentioning it every time you open your mouth."

Alys's pretty lips tightened in anger that she quickly concealed. *No love lost between these two,* Zoe thought. The red-haired queen spoke in exaggeratedly polite tones. "Where *did* you live while your father was alive?"

"In a very small town on the edge of the western provinces," Zoe said, holding on to her tranquility. "I imagine the entire village could have fit inside the *kierten* of the palace."

Romelle turned to her, aghast, and spoke around a mouthful of food. "No! But what did you *do*? Who did you talk to?"

"My father always talked enough for twenty people," Zoe said with a small smile. "My days were spent with him, and they were not empty."

"Still, even the most fascinating man palls from time to time, as all of us know," Seterre said, earning another light laugh from the company.

"You must have been so excited when Darien came to fetch you," Romelle said.

Zoe flicked a look at Darien; she didn't know how much of this story was widely known. Apparently, everyone in the palace and the Five Families had been aware that Zoe had been considered as the king's fifth bride. But did the wives know she had run away from Darien? Did they know she had lived on the river before she discovered her true inheritance? "Indeed, *everyone* in the village was excited when he arrived," was all she said.

Looking amused, Darien smoothly entered the conversation. "When I found Zoe Lalindar, she was deep in mourning for her father's passing and had a hard time grasping how greatly her fortunes had changed," he said. "Once Vernon and I realized she was Lalindar prime, we knew she could no longer be considered as a royal bride. I eventually decided to take her directly to her grandmother's house, where she could grow accustomed to her new position before she attempted to come to Chialto and hold her own against the likes of you."

Romelle widened her big blue eyes. "You say that as if she would have to defend herself against us!"

He laughed at her. "That is certainly how I view the situation."

Romelle turned back to Zoe. "Not at all! I am merely asking questions because I am *curious*."

Zoe smiled at her; Romelle seemed to be the most genuine of the lot. "All in all, I think the most astonishing part of Darien Serlast's appearance in my village was the kind of vehicle he arrived in. Until that time, I'd never seen one of the smoker cars, though my father had read about them in reports from Chialto."

"Yes, they're quite remarkable," Seterre said, speaking in a gushing voice. Her blond hair fell over her shoulder as she leaned forward. "And they've been such a boon to the Dochenzas! Turned around the family fortunes almost overnight."

That had been another dig at Elidon, Zoe thought, though the first wife didn't exhibit any visible signs of annoyance. Darien said, "The Serlasts should only hope to invent something so useful—and lucrative—someday!" which seemed to defuse any tension.

"So you have been staying at Christara's house for the past season," Alys said. "I have heard it is very beautiful."

"It is," Zoe said, adding innocently, "That is still how I think of it, too, as Christara's house. I keep forgetting that now it is actually mine."

By the way Alys's head snapped back, Zoe knew that her own barb had hit home. Any property these women might have owned had been forfeit to the crown upon their marriages. It was a subtle way to remind them all that Zoe herself—naïve as she might still be, outcast that she so recently had been—was not without certain power of her own. She saw Darien's faint smile, and in it she read approval.

It was possible she might quickly learn this game after all.

"Now that you are back in the city," Elidon said, "will you reclaim your other properties? I believe your grandmother owned at least one house in the fashionable district."

"No, my aunt Sarone inherited that one from Christara, and she seems happily ensconced there," Zoe said. "I might look around for something else to buy." She toyed with the stem of her water glass and watched Darien from under lowered eyelids. "Or I might petition the king to return to me the property that used to belong to my father."

Which Darien himself had told her was now occupied by Serlasts. He narrowed his eyes but showed no other reaction. Seterre was the first one to make the connection, and her face showed surprise and then a flash of indignation. Seterre was *hunti*, Zoe knew, but she couldn't remember if she was Serlast, too. "That property has been in other hands for ten years," Seterre said. "It seems cruel to take it away now."

"That's not a very good argument," Zoe said. "It belonged to Ardelays for seventy-five years."

Alys put it together next and looked maliciously pleased. "Isn't it—why, Darien, isn't it *your* family that lives in Navarr's old house?"

He nodded. "They like it very much," he said.

"I'm sure they do," Zoe said. "Of course, as Seterre says, it's been ten years since I was inside, but it was a lovely place when I lived there."

"I can't believe the king would dispossess any of Darien's family," Seterre said.

"I liked your original thought," Elidon said. "Perhaps you can buy a new place."

"And perhaps I just will not spend much time in Chialto," Zoe said. "I am already missing my grandmother's house."

"Oh, you can't go back so soon!" Romelle exclaimed. "We've hardly gotten to know you! How can we make you stay? What kinds of things do you enjoy doing?"

"I am easily entertained," Zoe said.

"We might find her a husband," Alys said. "*That* would be entertaining."

Since I am not to marry your *husband,* Zoe couldn't help thinking. She didn't dare look at Darien Serlast with the thought so clear in her head. "I rather think my life would be much simpler without one," she said.

The wives laughed. "Life is always simpler without a husband," Elidon said. "But there are some privileges—some status—a husband can bring that you might find welcome."

"I am just getting used to the status I have acquired on my own," Zoe said. "It seems grand enough already."

"What do you think, Darien?" Alys asked. "You know Zoe better than we do. What kind of man would appeal to her?"

For a moment, their eyes locked across the table. "I might have spent a little more time with her than you have," he corrected Alys, "but I am far from certain that I know Zoe Lalindar. I doubt I would presume to advise her on affairs of the heart."

"Darien can't even be troubled to find his *own* wife!" Romelle exclaimed. "I can't picture him matchmaking for other people."

Alys stroked Darien's arm with the same air of ownership she had showed earlier. "Darien is too busy for love," she said. "But someday he will wake up and find himself an old man—lonely, childless, and exhausted, having given himself wholly over to service to the crown. I think that will be a sad day."

He didn't look at Alys. Zoe couldn't tell how he felt about the queen's hand still resting on his arm. "I suppose I might have some regrets," he said. "But that day seems very far off."

"Indeed, we are all quite young and healthy now!" Seterre said. "Well—most of us. I mean—" She tittered unconvincingly; everyone avoided looking at Elidon. "*None* of us should be too worried about how we will feel during the dreary future. We have too many years ahead of us."

"Years spent enjoying each other's company," Elidon said icily. "Something to look forward to indeed."

Zoe didn't even try to fill the small silence that followed that exchange, but fortunately a distraction arrived in the form of a servant. "Would your majesties wish the princesses to be brought in now?" she asked. She spoke as if to the whole table, but it was clear she was asking Elidon.

The first wife nodded. "Indeed, this would be an excellent time."

Moments later a small parade of women entered the room from a side door—three servants, two young girls, and a child carried in the arms of one of the maids. Romelle cooed and jumped up to take her daughter from the maid, and then she began making sweet nonsense sounds into the little girl's ear. The princess looked to be about four quintiles old, beautiful and bad-tempered. Her dark eyes looked balefully at the room and she sucked her fingers with an air of dissatisfaction.

The other two girls went straight to Elidon's side and bowed. Elidon sat back in her chair and inspected them, motioning for them to turn around so she could judge them from the back as well. The oldest girl looked very like Seterre— thin, tall for her age, blue-eyed, with ashy blond hair in a long braid down her back—though she was not as pretty as her mother. Her face was also a little more set, a little more tense, as if she were continually braced for something bad to happen. The younger girl had Alys's red hair and smug manner, but her eyes were a woodland brown, huge and gorgeous. When the two princesses had turned to face Elidon again, the redhead kept cutting her eyes toward Zoe. The blonde kept her gaze on the queen.

"What did you learn in your classes today?" Elidon asked.

The blonde answered first. "I am still studying the history of Welce and the nations to the north, and the treaties that we signed after the War of Water."

The redhead grimaced. "I am studying mathematics *again*, because I cannot do my sums."

"It's important to know mathematics," Elidon said.

"I don't know why," the girl burst out. "My advisors will always tell me how much money I have and where I've spent it and why I don't have any left till changeday."

Seterre tittered again, though she pretended to try to muffle the sound. Zoe guessed the daughter resembled her mother in one other important attribute—an inability to curtail her spending.

Elidon maintained her serious expression. "Ah, but what if

your advisors are untrustworthy? What if they are *stealing* from you? You will only know that if you are able to read their accounts."

"If they are stealing from me, I will have them ruined," the girl said with zest. "All their property seized and turned over to *me*."

"That is a strategy that might work very well for a princess or a queen, but what if you are not sitting on the throne? What if you marry an ordinary man? You might not have the power to order people stripped of their assets. Indeed, you will have to pay much more attention to your own."

It was clear the little girl couldn't comprehend the idea that she might at some point be living in straitened circumstances. She frowned. Across the table from Zoe, Alys scowled as well.

"Really, Elidon, it is not as if you must prepare her for a life of penury," Alys said. "Even if she is not chosen as Vernon's heir, she will hardly be living on some windswept prairie, counting quint-coppers after a meager harvest."

"It is the wise woman who fortifies herself against an unexpected reversal of fortune," Elidon replied.

Everyone at the table looked at Zoe. Who said, serenely enough, "Indeed, I think it is a very good idea for *any* woman to know mathematics. And assorted other skills."

The redhead bounced in place. "Are you the missing Lalindar prime?"

Zoe wasn't sure if she was supposed to speak to a princess before being officially introduced, but Elidon quickly remedied that. "Corene, this is Zoe Lalindar, who has come to visit with us for a while."

"You don't look *anything* like I expected," Corene replied.

"Do I look like someone who can add and subtract?" Zoe asked. Everyone laughed softly at that, except Corene, who scowled again.

"*No.* I mean—I thought you would be—well, you don't look anything like Keeli."

"That's true. I favor my father—although even he was dark for an Ardelay."

"*Ardelay,*" the little girl said. "But none of them—" She closed her mouth and glanced quickly at her mother.

"They're not often seen here at the palace," Elidon supplied smoothly. She gestured at the blond girl. "Josetta, Zoe Lalindar."

Josetta bowed very properly, as Corene had not. "I welcome you to our house."

"I hope *you* don't find me disappointing," Zoe said.

"I did not form any expectations about you at all," the girl replied carefully.

Well, she's *having a difficult and stressful life,* Zoe thought. *Trying very hard not to make mistakes.* Aloud she said, "I have found that is the wisest way to meet any new person—or situation."

Elidon now indicated Romelle, still mincing around the room, singing quietly to her daughter. "And behind you is Princess Natalie—well-behaved, I assure you, only because she has just woken up. As a general rule, she is *quite* interested in making her needs and her opinions known."

"I don't believe I've ever known a child who could throw a tantrum that lasted quite so long," Seterre said.

"She *is* a handful," Romelle said, looking a little guilt-stricken. "But when she's happy—oh, she's just delightful."

Elidon must have made some kind of signal that released the other two princesses from waiting on her, for Josetta instantly went to stand by her mother, while Corene drifted toward Zoe. She moved in an indirect, catlike fashion, as if she were really interested in something that was on the wall behind Zoe, but pretty soon she was standing just behind the stranger. Zoe looked over her shoulder to meet the girl's eyes.

"What are your blessings?" Corene asked immediately. "Do you keep them on you?"

Zoe turned halfway around in her chair and extended her arm with its silver bracelet. "Beauty, love, and power," she said. "What about yours?"

Corene held out her hands, fingers spread, so Zoe could inspect her three rings. One was copper, one was silver, one was gold. Each was a wide, plain band in which a single blessing glyph had been carved to show the skin beneath. "Imagination, intelligence, courage," she recited.

Two *sweela,* one *hunti.* No reason to ask this question, since it was so obvious, but Zoe said, "And are you *sweela,* like your mother? Or *hunti* like the king?"

Everyone at the table answered at once. *"Sweela."*

Corene laughed. "But I try to remember that I have a *hunti* blessing, too, and that I must cultivate the strengths of wood as well as fire."

"Balance is everything," Darien said.

Zoe glanced at Josetta, standing stiffly behind her mother. "And you?" she asked. "What are your blessings?"

Josetta relaxed a little. Zoe thought she might have been afraid she would be overlooked—as perhaps she often was when the lively Corene was in the room. "Beauty, grace, and joy," she said.

"All *elay* traits!" Zoe responded. "But your mother is *hunti*, is she not?"

Seterre nodded. "Yes, but my mother was all *elay*, and Josetta is the same. More *practical* than most *elay* women, I am glad to say, but still with that sort of ethereal spirit."

"I, of course, am pleased to have a child of air and spirit in my house," Elidon said.

"And I'm not sure yet what Natalie will choose to be," Romelle said. "For I am *torz*, and the king is *hunti*, but her blessings are hope, surprise, and clarity. She could draw from any tradition."

"Maybe that's why she's always having a fit," Corene said. "She doesn't know who she's supposed to be."

Zoe heard Romelle's little *tsk* of irritation. "She isn't *always* having a fit."

"And it is good for a baby to have so many ways to grow," Elidon said in a gently reproving voice. "To choose for herself who she will be."

As if she could tell everyone in the room was discussing her, and she didn't like it, Natalie's sullen face reddened and she began to wail. Her small fists beat at Romelle's shoulders, and she choked out a few syllables that might have been *mama* or *mine*. Romelle bounced the girl in her arms and tried to quiet her, but Natalie's sobs just increased in volume.

"I *told* you she cries all the time," Corene said with satisfaction.

"I think she's hungry," Romelle said. "Let me take her into the other room—"

Elidon made a gesture, and two of the servants reentered.

So quietly did they move that Zoe hadn't noticed them leaving in the first place. "It is time for all three of the princesses to be gone," the first wife said.

"Not yet!" Corene exclaimed, but Josetta looked slightly relieved. She was already bowing and turning to join the maid while Corene was still protesting. "I thought we would stay until dinner, talking to Zoe Lalindar—"

"I don't know why you thought that," Elidon said calmly.

Darien was also standing up. "Don't worry, my princess, you won't miss anything," he said, turning a warm smile on her. "It is time for Zoe to leave as well. She has an appointment with the king this afternoon, and we do not want her to be too overwhelmed by all your attention."

Josetta had already disappeared, and the second servant still waited at the door, but Corene hadn't yet left Zoe's side. "Will you be back tomorrow? Will you be back every day?"

Zoe was trying to hide her immense relief at the news that she was about to quit the room, so she rose slowly from her chair, as if reluctant to go. "I don't know what my schedule holds," she told Corene. "But I am sure I will see you often." She reached the door and bowed at the group. "Thank you for your warm welcome. I look forward to getting to know all of you better."

SEVENTEEN

Zoe and Darien Serlast kept complete silence as they stepped out of the room, down the halls, and back to the *kierten* at the base of the multicolored steps. There he stopped and turned to face her.

"And you *still* see me as the villain," he said, as if resuming a conversation that had been interrupted by only a pause.

She smiled faintly. "Because I talked of dispossessing your family?"

"My father had nothing to do with Navarr's fall from grace. In fact, as I told you, my father fought hard to have Navarr reinstated."

"So you say. Yet Serlasts profited from his exile."

"Christara Lalindar was the one who spoke most strongly against your father."

She nodded. "That's who my father always blamed. And my aunt Sarone told me some of the reasons my grandmother hated my father. But I can't help thinking there is more to the story than a private feud between my relatives and a public disagreement about political treaties."

Darien's face instantly took on that alert and watchful expression that Zoe had decided meant he didn't want her to ask the next likely question. She did it anyway. "But you know, don't you?" she said slowly. "You know the real reason my father was banished?"

He was silent a long time, studying her with narrowed gray eyes. She merely stood there, showing no impatience, willing to wait until night fell or the river dried up or the world itself ended. "Essentially," he said at last.

"Will you tell me?"

He shook his head. "Not unless there turns out to be some reason it is important that you know."

"I *want* to know. That's important enough."

He shook his head again. "No, it isn't. Not for this."

"You promised you wouldn't lie to me."

"I'm hardly lying when I say I cannot tell you what you ask."

"Then you can't be surprised that I continue to think of you as a villain."

Now he smiled. "I do not think any of us has foresight enough to guess what kind of turmoil you are going to bring," he said.

She showed him an inquiring face. "I don't know what you mean. I have done nothing."

He gestured toward the room they'd just left. "Any audience with the king's wives is a grueling experience, for they can be jealous and spiteful and sometimes cruel. Even Elidon, who is not by nature unkind. Yet you handled yourself with poise, you did not allow yourself to be intimidated, and you displayed your strengths. I think if they try too hard to provoke you, you will grow tired of behaving with that assumed tranquility. You will be like a squall upon the waters, and none of us will be able to guess how much chaos you might churn up."

"Darien Serlast," she said in a mocking voice, "what a romantic turn of mind you have."

"I would be interested to hear your opinions of the king's wives."

Zoe answered readily. "Seterre is a schemer, but a cautious one—she would take petty measures to make someone else unhappy, all the while pretending to be her best friend. Romelle is still young enough, and likable enough, to believe the world likes her back. When she is hurt or disillusioned—as she inevitably will be—she will either become depressed and withdrawn or bitter and loud, though I don't see her as danger-ous. Alys is ambitious and determined—and smart enough to figure out how to get what she wants, no matter what it costs. Elidon—" Zoe shrugged. "Trying hard to be graceful, not al-ways succeeding. She could destroy Alys if she wanted—and she'll do it, if she ever needs to."

He was laughing softly. "All this from an hour in their com-pany! I'm impressed."

"I am *coru*," she said. "You think that means I am as will-ful as water, but it also means I am bound by blood. Since I have taken my place as Christara's heir, I have gained some insights into the human heart."

"And the princesses? What did you think of them?"

"Josetta is unhappy and Corene is unbridled," Zoe said promptly. "And Natalie probably really *is* a spoiled brat."

He was frowning. "Why do you think Josetta is unhappy?"

She gave him a scornful look. "Why would *you* think so? You yourself called a visit to the wives' wing grueling. She must *live* there, and she seems ill-equipped for the life. I imag-ine she is not particularly good at defending herself."

"Her mother is perfectly capable of fighting for her daugh-ter."

Zoe shrugged. "I doubt her mother is always nearby when the battle is joined."

He was still frowning. "Still. If she cannot protect herself when she must, that is a serious flaw. If Vernon were to name her his heir—if she were to become queen—she would need to be fierce on her own behalf. She would need to be strong enough to fight."

"Would she?" Zoe said, her voice very dry. "Doesn't the king surround himself with people who protect him? Help him make decisions? Smooth his way?"

Darien's face was instantly alert again. "He has advisors, certainly, who provide valuable counsel."

"The king cannot even choose what buckle to wear on his boots unless one of those advisors is by his side. I find myself wondering what other decisions he relies on other people to make."

It was comical to watch his face, to see him reconstruct-ing a visit to a cobbler's shop—two full quintiles ago!—

remembering how the king dithered over the purchase and how Darien had helped choose the leather, the color, the decorations. Then his expression became rueful.

"I had forgotten all about that day," he said. "I chose that shop to patronize because I knew you were working there."

"And here I thought I had been so lucky to be working in the back room when you arrived. I didn't realize you already knew I was there. But I found it very interesting to watch you oversee the king's purchase."

"I don't know what you think you learned, but—"

"What I *learned*," she interrupted, "is that you have a great deal of power in the royal household. What I *learned* is that the king doesn't even make very small decisions without your approval. What I *guess* is that the king's wives are consumed with trying to influence his choice of heir. They know that he listens to you, and that is why they fawn over you and flirt with you and show off their daughters for your approval. But they know better than to rely on one man and one potential avenue to the throne. Favorites come and go, after all—look at my father, once so dear to the king—they know the same fate might befall you as well. So they scheme and whisper and make alliances and vie for position. If one strategy fails, they are prepared to try another. And another, until the heir is chosen and the king is dead and a new monarch sits upon the throne."

She came a step closer to him, suffused with a fury she had not realized she had been holding back. "What I *don't* know is what you expect of *me*. Why do you want me in the palace? You say you never expected me to marry the king, but clearly you were eager to introduce me into this volatile company."

"I told you," he said stiffly. "Your father wanted you returned to Chialto and the king wanted balance in the palace. The Lalindar prime should be on excellent terms with royalty. My motives are no more sinister than those."

She shrugged. "You see? You're lying again. And *that* is why I continue to see you as a villain."

"Is that what I have earned myself by fetching you to the city?" he said, speaking with a little heat himself. "A woman who has set herself against me and my family? Is it now your goal to bring down the Serlasts?"

"Not at all," she said. "I would like to see *you* confounded, perhaps—not even discredited, not exiled, as my father was—just stripped for a moment of your arrogance and certainty and steel. You believe I will sweep a storm through these palace walls, but it will be a small one, I think. Only enough to knock you off your feet."

"I am *hunti*," he shot back. "Not easily overcome or thrown off course."

She gave him a savage smile. "I didn't say I expected it to be easy."

He was silent a long moment, watching her. When he spoke, his voice was calm. She didn't think he discounted anything she had said; he had simply braced himself to meet the chaos, whenever it might come. "When I traveled from Chialto to find you, I journeyed through a land parched with two years of drought," he said. "Yet when I made it to your village, the wells were full, the crops were watered, and there was no sign of privation. It was raining when I arrived, and rain followed us all the way home. For the next two quintiles, the city saw more rain than it had seen for three years. The river swelled back to its normal size, and farmers from the outlying territories reported that their springs and aquifers were once again flowing freely. The drought that had seared the kingdom for two years had ended. Because *you* ended it."

"I—"

He spoke over her. "Oh, you didn't do it on purpose. You didn't even know there *was* a drought—water followed you like a puppy follows a friendly master, and you never knew a day of thirst or worry. But *I* knew you were in the city and *I* knew you were in your grandmother's house, because of the way the rain and river responded. And now that you, too, have seen how water obeys when you call it, I think you will not be able to resist the temptation to speak its name. And you are surprised that I think you belong in the king's palace? Where else should such a woman reside? It seems like a very bad idea for anyone who cares about the kingdom to lose track of you."

She tilted her chin up; she was irritated again. "I am no danger to anyone."

"You have already threatened *me*," he pointed out.

"You deserved it."

"And who else, eventually, will deserve it—at least in your

opinion? Will Seterre make you angry? Will Corene? It is very difficult to refrain from using power once it comes into your hands. And you, Zoe Ardelay Lalindar, wear the symbol for power dangling from your wrist. I cannot think it is the sort of blessing you will cast off without exploring it to the fullest."

"Spoken like a *hunti* man," she said.

He shrugged. "There is no winning an argument with a *coru* woman," he said. "She redirects the conversation every time she finds herself in a channel she cannot control."

Zoe lifted her hands, as if in surrender. "And there is no ending an argument with a *hunti* man," she replied. "He takes a stand and will not yield it, even when the battle no longer rages. I am done quarreling, at least for the day. You said Vernon wanted to see me. Was that the truth, or merely an excuse to allow us to escape from the king's wives?"

The quick change of subject caught him off guard only momentarily. "I do sometimes speak the truth," he said coolly. "Yes, the king wants to meet with you. I know he is free at this time. Would you like to see him now, or have you found your last audience too harrowing?"

"Not at all," she said. "Lead me to him."

He offered her his arm again and she took it. She didn't need his support. She didn't need to feel, again, the precise chemical mixture of the blood racing through his veins, as distinct to her as the shape of his face and the particular weight of his body. She took his arm because he was the favorite of the king and anyone who encountered them in the hallways would see it as a mark of high esteem for Darien Serlast to allow the touch of Zoe Ardelay Lalindar. There was no other reason.

Z oe had not expected to like the king, but she did. He was awaiting them in a small study, though they must have passed a dozen rooms of mammoth size and smothering opulence. It was situated on the second floor, at the very westernmost tip of the men's wing, and it had a stunning view of the waterfall lashing its way down the mountain. When they entered, he was standing in front of the window, motionless, apparently absorbed in that magnificent sight. Zoe had the impression he had been standing there a very long time.

"Majesty," Darien said, and the king turned around. Zoe and Darien both bowed very low. "I have brought Navarr Ardelay's daughter to meet you."

"Oh, I am so glad," King Vernon said, immediately crossing the room. Unlike his wives, he took her hands in his and smiled at her, clearly trying to read her heritage in her face. Against her skin she felt the prickle of analysis as her body read the composition of his blood. She would know him again if she was blinded and he reached out for her. It was a peculiar thing to realize.

"You look very much like your father," he said.

She smiled. "So people have been telling me. What I'm unable to determine is if they mean that as a compliment."

He smiled and dropped her hands. He looked much as she remembered him from her clandestine spying in the cobbler's shop, although close up his face showed deeper lines and his skin was softer. His eyes were a lost blue. "I suppose that depends on how they felt about your father," he replied. "Since at times I admired him and at times I was furious with him, I suppose you might consider my opinion mixed. But of late I have been wishing I could meet with him one last time, and so I am pleased to see that you resemble him so nearly."

"Then I shall thank you for the words."

He ushered her and Darien toward an arrangement of chairs and indicated that she should take the one that faced the window. "I imagine that is a vista a Lalindar woman would never tire of seeing," he said as they all took their places.

"No, indeed. I just came back from the Lalindar estate up north, and I spent part of every day merely watching the river run. But no prospect from that house can compare to this view."

"There are other rooms that show the waterfall, of course, but none of them are as conducive to merely sitting and contemplating the scene. Whenever I need to think or rest, this is the room I choose."

"And yet your majesty is a *hunti* man," she said, her voice gently teasing. "Shouldn't you find your renewal by walking through a forest?"

He laughed heartily. "Or strolling through a mausoleum!" he added. "For the *hunti* are creatures of wood *and* bone, don't forget. Indeed, my father occasionally visited graves and cemeteries. He said he found the wisdom of the dead to be powerful and soothing. But I must confess I have never been at ease with skeletons." He glanced at his other guest, who had sat silent this whole time. "What about you, Darien? Do you find comfort in forests and gravesites?"

Darien smiled. "I rarely need comfort."

"Inspiration, then," Zoe said.

"There is a stretch of land on my aunt's estate," Darien said. "A grove of plum trees. I can walk through them in any season and feel my scattered thoughts cohere. The trees are most beautiful when they are in flower and most useful when their branches are hung with ripe fruit, but it does not matter to me. They offer wisdom when their limbs are bare except for snow and when every sense would tell you they are sleeping or dead. From this I have extrapolated the general principle that nothing can be discounted, even when it seems to have little value to offer."

"That is much more philosophical talk than I am used to hearing from Darien Serlast," Zoe said.

"I am merely providing conversation for my king."

"I am still surprised—but pleased—to learn that my king draws strength from watching water," Zoe said.

"Oh, but I was blessed with two *coru* traits," the king replied, "and so I am susceptible to water." At Zoe's questioning look, he readily supplied, "Flexibility and surprise. I must say, in general neither of them seems to have described my life, but I have always had an affinity for *coru* passions."

"The king particularly enjoys travel by water, though he has had few opportunities to indulge that pleasure," Darien said.

"But we are holding another regatta on Quinnelay changeday," the king said, showing real animation. "Will you join us?"

"If it is an event upon the water, I certainly will," Zoe said, "but what exactly are you planning?"

Darien answered. "In the mountains nearby, right before the Marisi rushes into its fall, there is a long stretch of water that is placid enough to navigate but rapid enough to present a challenge. Usually once a year, we organize races that cover about twenty miles. Dozens of people enter in a variety of watercraft. There are a few prizes for the winners, but the real draw is the competition itself, which is very spirited. *Coru* men have won for the past two years," he added, "but *hunti* and *elay* champions are determined to wrest the trophy away."

"It sounds delightful—but it also sounds as if it would be more delightful at a different time of year," Zoe said. "It must be chilly on the river right now."

"That's part of what makes it fun," Darien said with a laugh. "Knowing how sorry you will be if you go into the water."

"So you are one of the challengers?" she asked him.

"I am. I have a craft that carries four, all of whom are expected to paddle or steer. Would you like to be one of my crew?"

"Oh, that is something I would have to consider long and carefully!" she replied. "For my first time at the royal regatta, I might simply want to observe. Or take my place in a Lalindar boat, if any of my relatives are contenders."

"Your uncle Broy won the last race," the king said.

"Yes, *he* might be the one to back," Zoe said. She wasn't so sure he would welcome her aboard, but she did not voice the thought.

"Or you could take a place in my boat," the king added.

"You're one of the racers?"

"Yes, and sometimes the queens and the princesses take part as well."

"Alys and Seterre," Darien said with a grin. "Romelle's afraid of water and Elidon generally avoids competitions of any sort. Though they both come to cheer on his majesty, of course."

"Well, I will certainly watch, even if I don't participate," Zoe said. "But do you ever have events on the lake in front of the palace? It looks like it would be much less adventurous."

"The women sometimes go boating there during the summer," Darien said. "But the water is too serene to make those outings exciting."

She gave him a slanting smile. "Don't dismiss a lake so lightly," she said. "No body of water is truly serene."

He gave a soundless laugh. "I ask your pardon, Zoe Lalindar," he answered. "I did not mean to accuse *you* of tranquility."

"Your father won the very first race we staged," the king

said, unexpectedly bringing Navarr back into the conversation. "Your grandmother was annoyed because she had been convinced *she* would take home the prize. Maybe that was the start of the long animosity between them."

Zoe laughed. "I can believe it of both of them—to let something so small become so important."

Vernon's face clouded over. "I was sorry to hear of Navarr's death," he said. "I hope he—that is—sometimes a final illness can be very painful and sometimes it can be nothing more than a slipping away. I would hope his was the second kind."

She found herself in the odd position of wanting to comfort the man who had sent her father into exile. "It was not precisely an easy death, because my father never made anything easy," she said. "And he was *not* pleased to be leaving this world behind, so many arguments still to be won, so many books still to be discussed. But he did not suffer greatly, in the physical sense. His final days were more peaceful than painful. And he slept through his last day."

"I am glad to hear it," the king replied. He started to say something, hesitated, and then spoke in a strangely wistful voice. "I always wished I'd been able to tell him that I forgave him," he said. "I always wanted to know if he'd forgiven me."

Darien escorted Zoe all the way back to the *kierten* in the wives' wing before he dropped her hand. They had traversed the entire length of the palace in almost complete silence, if Zoe discounted the people who called out to Darien and whom he mostly ignored. At any rate, they didn't speak a word to each other until they were back at the base of the stairwell and Zoe once again prepared to ascend. She stood on the bottom step, the white marble one with its shadows of purple, and stared down at him.

He shook his head. He was trying not to laugh. "Don't even ask," he said.

"Do you *know* what he meant? I accept that you will not tell me, but is it a secret from you as well?"

"I can only guess."

"Then will you?"

"No."

"I thought, if I came to the palace with you, I might begin to find some answers about my father," she said. "Instead, all I am finding are more questions."

"I hope that is not the only reason you came," he said.

"What other reason might I have had?"

"To find out answers about you," he said. "I imagine those might be even more interesting."

She could not think of a response. Shaking her head, she laid her hand on the banister and slowly climbed all sixty-three multicolored steps. When she reached the third-floor landing, she peered over the coiled stairway to see if Darien Serlast was still standing there, watching her.

He was.

EIGHTEEN

It was quickly clear that Annova and Calvin were adapting to life in the palace more easily than Zoe. Calvin, in fact, was thriving. The food was so good, and so plentiful, that in two ninedays he had put at least ten pounds onto his scrawny frame, and his normally cheerful face now had an almost beatific glow. He had made friends with servants in every quarter of the palace, so he returned to Zoe's suite daily with gossip about visitors, members of the Five Families, and the king's wives. Alys had been seen buying a scarf from a street vendor in the Plaza; Elidon had gone to the blind sisters, either to share or ask for information. Kayle Dochenza was working on a new kind of motor that would power a watercraft, though it wouldn't be ready in time for the regatta. Mirti Serlast had gotten bad news about one of her overseas investments, though her personal fortune was still respectable.

"Anything you need to know, I can find it out," he boasted.

Zoe was not sure she had actually needed to know any of the bits of information he had uncovered so far, but she was convinced that someday his connections might come in handy.

Annova, by contrast, seemed to spend her time either inside Zoe's suites or outside of the palace altogether, but she, too, appeared utterly content. She was always returning with some new treasure picked up at the Plaza of Women—a ribbon for Zoe's hair, a bracelet made musical with dozens of hanging charms, a pot of rouge in a crisp new color.

"You should be buying things for *yourself*," Zoe told her as she tried a slinky silver scarf over a dark blue tunic. Yes, the contrast was perfect.

Annova waved a hand. "I have everything I need. I like finding special things for you. It's like having a daughter again." She came over to tie the new scarf in a complicated knot. "Anyway, as far as I can tell, you never had anyone who spoiled you. I like to do it."

"Well, I do appreciate it."

The other thing that had become clear almost immediately was that, despite the new wardrobe Keeli had helped her assemble, Zoe was woefully undersupplied with clothing. The second time she wore a particular set of trousers and overrobe to an audience with the wives, Seterre had giggled and said, "Oh, that must be your *favorite* outfit. It *is* awfully nice." That was when she realized that none of the wives ever wore the same thing twice—at least not within a couple of ninedays.

So she had to commission dozens of new robes and tunics and trousers to wear to an endless array of events.

Worst were the formal dinners, which occurred two or three times every nineday and often boasted more than a hundred attendees. The king, his wives, and eight honored guests always sat at the circular central table, which rested on an elevated platform in the middle of a very large room. Set up in spokes fanning out from that central location were tables of eight and sixteen and twenty-four, depending on how many were present for the night.

Zoe was almost never seated with anyone she knew. Her Lalindar relatives were only rarely in attendance, and, of course, Darien always took his place with the royal family. At one dinner, she was one of the exalted guests at the high table, right beside the king, and that was *worse*. She spent the whole meal aware that strangers were staring at her and the wives were resenting her and Darien Serlast was laughing at her. She hoped never to be granted such an honor again.

When she wasn't trying on new clothes or enduring interminable meals, Zoe often found herself engaged in small, private duels with the king's wives.

Seterre was the first one to invite Zoe to her suites on the second floor, "just for a little conversation to break up the monotony of the afternoon." Following Annova's instincts, Zoe dressed in a new overrobe and brought a handful of the decadently delicious candy drops that Calvin had picked up the day before. Sure enough, Seterre was wearing a long tunic and overrobe of heavily beaded silk, and she had ordered an impressive spread of fruit and nuts and baked delicacies.

"Oh! You look quite lovely!" Seterre greeted her with what Zoe thought might be a trace of disappointment. "Most people don't attempt to wear just that shade of coral, but it looks very good on you."

"Thank you. And thank you for the invitation to your rooms."

As she might have expected, Seterre's suite was sumptuously appointed. They dined in a room that was all warm wood, from the floors to the walls to the highly polished tables and chairs. Bright rugs and plush cushions softened both the look and the hardness of the furniture, but it was clearly a room designed to please a *hunti* woman.

"We've had so little time to sit and talk, just the two of us, and I feel certain we would enjoy each other's company," Seterre said in that honeyed voice that seemed so jarringly false to Zoe. "But it is difficult to be friendly and natural when Alys and Elidon are in the room."

"Sometimes you can't talk plainly unless you're speaking with just one other person," Zoe agreed.

"Exactly! Here—sit down—don't you love this table? Mirti Serlast had it made for me from wood grown on her property."

"I was admiring it from the minute I walked in."

As soon as they took their places, Zoe said, "I brought you a treat," and offered up the chocolates. Annova had further informed her that she couldn't just hand them over in a crumpled bag; she had to find a small box, perhaps of carved wood, and make a presentation to her hostess. "These are my favorites, so I thought you might like them, too."

"Oh, I do! How very thoughtful of you. And here, you must have some of these spiced orange slices—*such* a delicacy, particularly at this time of year, but I always say if it's something you love so much you can't stop thinking about it, then it is almost a sin to deprive yourself."

An interesting definition of sin, Zoe thought. "Oh, yes, those are *very* good."

They had a few moments of the most desultory conversation, trying the other foods and commenting on their deliciousness. Zoe watched Seterre closely, taking the same portions that Seterre did, toying with her food in the same way. She did not want to make mistakes.

"So, how do you find life at the palace?" Seterre asked finally, her voice artless. "I know it must be very different from what you're used to."

"Oh, when I was quite young, my father spent a great deal of time here, and I accompanied him now and then," Zoe said coolly. Implying, *I am not the bumpkin you think I am, even if my recent life has been very strange.* "I admit the woman finds the life more complicated than the child ever realized, but it is never less than fascinating."

"I could give you advice anytime you needed it," Seterre said. "Anytime things become too—complicated. Sometimes all it takes is a simple explanation from someone who understands how things work."

You are almost the last person I would turn to with questions. "Yes, I have often thought I needed a source of reliable information," Zoe replied.

Seterre ate another orange slice. "I wouldn't turn to Alys for guidance, if I were you," she said. "She can be—untruthful—at times. She might give you misinformation."

"Deliberately?"

"I hate to say it, but, yes, deliberately. She thinks it is amusing to see other people stumble or even humiliate themselves." Seterre shrugged delicately. "I can't imagine why. Perhaps she thinks it makes *her* appear more clever or elegant by contrast."

"I suppose."

"And Elidon—well. She would not misdirect you on purpose, but at times she is not—that is—she is so much older than the rest of us. She is out of step. She does not realize how things have changed."

This was particularly amusing coming from Seterre, who

was probably only ten years younger than the first wife. "Yes, I can see how that might have happened," Zoe said.

"And Romelle—so adorable!—but so childlike, as you may have noticed. We all love her very much but she is not the steadiest of creatures. She is still finding her way."

"And yet, she's *torz*. I would think she would be very levelheaded."

"Exactly! That's what you *would* think! But she can be as flighty as an *elay* girl and as unpredictable as a *coru* woman. Not," she added hastily, "that I would say a word against anyone of water and blood."

Zoe grinned. "It is hardly an insult to call *coru* women unpredictable. It is part of their charm."

"I am relieved to hear you say so! At any rate, I just wanted to let you know that I will be glad to help you if you need assistance, and I would never lead you astray."

"Thank you," Zoe said. "That is good to know."

They talked another twenty minutes on topics just as laced with hazards; Zoe was getting a headache from trying to be so careful. She was relieved when a bustle at the door drew their attention that way and Josetta stepped into the room.

"Hello, love," Seterre greeted her, with what seemed like the first genuine emotion she had shown all afternoon. Josetta gave her mother a quick kiss and Zoe a quick bow. "You remember Zoe Lalindar, don't you?"

"Yes."

"Why don't you sit with us for a few moments?" Seterre said. Then adding to Zoe, "You don't mind, do you?"

"Of course not. I was hoping to get a chance to spend more time with the princesses."

Josetta perched on one of the empty chairs. To Zoe's eyes, she still looked strained and anxious; this might be a girl who was always a little tense, no matter what the company. Zoe wasn't particularly skilled at putting other people at ease, but it seemed cruel, in this case, to not even try.

"Did you just come from lessons?" she asked with a smile.

Josetta nodded tightly. "Math and languages."

"You're learning a foreign language?" Zoe exclaimed. "Oh, I envy you! Which one?"

Josetta seemed to relax ever so slightly. "Soechin, which is what they speak in Soeche-Tas," she said. "It's very hard."

Zoe remembered that the king had once investigated the notion of marrying a girl from Soeche-Tas; it would be useful if *someone* in the household could communicate with her. But she knew better than to bring up the idea of a fifth wife. "That's brilliant," she said. "Isn't that a nation where your father wants to do more trade? You could become his minister of commerce and negotiate all the contracts. I'd think that would make you very important."

Josetta relaxed even more as a slight smile came to her face. A lock of her ashy hair had come loose from its precise styling, and she pushed it absently behind her ear. "That would be fun," she said.

"So, say something to me in Soechin," Zoe invited.

Josetta responded with a string of sounds and syllables that were impossible to decode. "I said that it was five in the afternoon on a sunny day," she translated. "I've spent a *lot* of time learning how to say things like numbers and days, and I know all the words for weather! So I hope it's raining or foggy or windy if I ever get a chance to talk to the Soeche-Tas viceroy."

"Wasn't he here not too long ago?" Zoe asked.

Seterre nodded. "Yes. There was a parade and all sorts of festivities. The food was so good while he was visiting that we wanted him to stay for a quintile!"

"My father says he might be back in Quinnelay," Josetta said. "So I'm hoping to be able to talk to him."

"I'm sure he'll appreciate that," Zoe said. "I'll look forward to the food and the excitement."

Seterre had another chocolate drop. "Oh, there will be more excitement much sooner than that," she said. "I'm sure you've heard about the regatta on changeday. It's all anyone can talk about."

"Oh yes! I believe the subject comes up five or six hundred times a day. Will you be a contestant?"

"Yes," mother and daughter answered simultaneously.

"Will you crew a boat together?" Zoe asked.

Seterre waved a hand. "No, there's one race for adults and one for children between the ages of ten and seventeen," she said. "I suppose there are usually about a dozen challengers in the youth race. Corene has one boat, Josetta another, and a few of the boys and girls from the Five Families."

"All by yourself in a boat on the Marisi River in midwinter?" Zoe said to Josetta. She couldn't quite keep her disapproval out of her voice. "That might be a little dangerous."

Josetta seemed pleased rather than offended that someone would bother to worry about her. "No, I have a crew. Corene and I each do—professional sailors who do all the rowing."

"Do you plan to compete?" Seterre asked. "It always seems a little unfair when a Lalindar is on the water, but now and then someone who is not *coru* does win."

"I don't plan to run my own boat, but I have been offered a place in a few others," Zoe said. "At the moment, I'm leaning toward watching the regatta from a safe, warm place onshore. But of course I'll attend. It sounds most delightful."

"I can't wait," Josetta said.

A few more exchanges and then a chiming bell announced the hour. Annova had discovered that afternoon visits like this were supposed to last precisely one hour, though the guest was expected to manufacture a reason for leaving. "Oh, I hope you'll excuse me—I need to send a note to my aunt before dinnertime," Zoe said, coming to her feet. "I enjoyed this chance to talk."

"I am certain we will become close friends," Seterre said. Not close enough to touch hands at the farewell, but that was fine with Zoe. She bowed and exited, extraordinarily relieved to be out of the room.

Similar invitations were extended in the next few days, and she knew she had to accept them all. She was certain the wives were comparing notes about her, discussing what she wore, what she ate, what she brought as an offering. It was exhausting to care about such myriad, petty details, so she didn't. She let Annova choose her clothing and her hostess gifts and tried to navigate through the charged conversations with as few mistakes as possible.

Alys had a roomful of young women in her suite when Zoe arrived. Their conversation was sharp and pointed, full of sneering remarks about absent friends and falsely sweet compliments to each other.

"But, Gildis! You haven't told us your news!" Alys said as they all munched on glazed and sugared fruit.

Gildis, a full-figured blond girl who looked all *elay*, instantly showed a wary expression. "My news?" she repeated.

Alys patted her own flat stomach. "When is the baby to be born?"

Gildis's pale face was instantly red with mortification. "I— no, I'm not—there is no baby—"

"Oh, my *apologies*!" Alys said with exaggerated remorse, while the other women pretended to try to hide their amusement. "How could I have been so gauche? Here, try one of these choco—or, well—would you like more water?"

A few moments later, Gildis left in tears, which even Zoe knew was a strategic defeat. "Silly thing," Alys said fondly once she was gone. "Who cares if she's fat? I'm sure that's not the reason her husband has lost interest in her."

Zoe deliberately took two more candies and ate them with great relish, smirking at Alys, daring her to make some comment. But Alys merely smiled at her and turned her attention to someone else. It was a decided relief when the hour was over.

During Zoe's obligatory visit to Romelle's room, the queen chased after Natalie the entire hour, carrying on such a distracted and disjointed discussion that it hardly taxed Zoe's conversational abilities at all. They had only one exchange of any interest, when Romelle said, in a scandalized voice, "Did you hear that Gildis Fairley has prevailed on her husband to take her back to the family's country estates?"

"I don't know who they are," Zoe replied. "Oh, wait—I think I met Gildis the other day in Alys's rooms."

"Very likely. Alys hates her."

"Why?"

"Who knows why Alys hates anybody? I always thought Gildis was a very likable girl, though her husband is so stern and surly. Natalie, put that down! Put it down *now*! There was some thought she would marry Wald Dochenza two or three years ago, and I *hear* that the two of them have been seen together whenever he's in the city. Perhaps she's been wishing she had married him instead. *I* would be, even though Wald is so peculiar."

"Why is she going home?"

"She said it was because her mother was sick, but everyone knows it's because Alys made fun of her in front of all their friends. Natalie! Don't eat that!"

"That's the morning I met her."

"You only saw it happen once, but I've seen Alys mock her a dozen times. I suppose Gildis couldn't stand it anymore."

"Doesn't anyone ever put Alys in her place? Say something mean right back to her?"

Romelle looked shocked. "She's a *queen*," she said. "No one can insult royalty."

Zoe didn't speak the thought in her head. *I think I could.*

When she was invited to Elidon's rooms, Zoe found Mirti Serlast there before her—a surprise, but not precisely an unwelcome one. She hadn't spent enough time with Mirti to form a clear opinion of Darien's aunt, other than to note that the older woman had strong opinions, an outspoken style, and a no-nonsense manner.

"I thought the two of you might enjoy a chance to get to know each other in a somewhat more intimate venue," Elidon said. Her private rooms were filled with sunlight and gauzy curtains and streamers hanging from the ceiling that swayed with the gentle currents of the air. Birds twittered and chirped in a large cage made of slim, bent wood. All the birds were yellow or white, *elay* colors, and most of them were tiny.

"Exactly so," Mirti said, touching her fingers very briefly to Zoe's. It was enough; Zoe could read in her blood the same chemicals, the same coded patterns, that she could identify in Darien's. She looked a little like Darien, too, with the familiar narrow face and smoky eyes, though her hair was longer, grayer, and more unruly. Her skin showed every one of her years, Zoe thought, and she obviously didn't have the patience to put much effort into beautifying her appearance. *This is who I am, stark and unyielding,* she might have been saying. *Love me or hate me, I will not change for you.* It was an attitude that inclined Zoe to like her.

"I appreciate the invitation," Zoe said.

They sat at a small table covered with a lacy cloth and fragile china painted with butterflies and songbirds. Although the frilly setting didn't suit Mirti at all, she looked comfortable as she leaned back in her chair and crossed her ankles before her. "So I assume all the other wives have been having you over, filling your head with nonsense," she said.

"Telling you who to trust and who to avoid and offering to be your best friend," Elidon added. She poured fruited water into tall glasses and handed them around the table.

Zoe didn't plan to get tripped up by honesty any more than by intrigue. She was not about to assume she was safe just because these women were refreshingly plainspoken. "Indeed, I have had a chance to spend time with each of them," Zoe said. "Each visit enjoyable in its own way."

Mirti grunted. Elidon merely smiled. "It can be tricky for an outsider to understand all the undercurrents at the palace," Elidon said. "But from what I've observed so far, you've managed the task gracefully enough."

Zoe sipped at the water, identifying hints of citrus and something a little sweeter. "I wouldn't have been an outsider if my father had not lost the king's trust," she said in a mild voice.

Mirti flung her head back; Elidon's eyes narrowed. But Zoe had put no accusation in her voice, so neither could take offense. She went on, still in that light voice, "Or if things had been different between my father and my grandmother. But if I've learned anything, it's that there's no changing the past, only embracing the future. There is only going forward."

"A *coru* attitude, that's for certain," Elidon said, smiling again.

"Well, it is good to have the Lalindar prime back in the city," Mirti said. "I can already feel the balance righting."

"All this rain," Elidon said. "It's been wonderful."

Mirti waved a hand. "Yes, that's been welcome, but more than that. There's a sense that things are falling in place. Lining up as they should. That's a feeling that's been missing ever since Christara died."

Elidon nibbled at a piece of fruit completely lost in a heavy coating of chocolate. "And yet not entirely in balance yet," she said, "while the Ardelays are still in exile."

Though she was able to keep her face absolutely guileless, Zoe felt her body string with tension. This conversation, she sensed, was the reason she had been invited here today. "Exile?" she repeated. "I thought my uncle and some of my cousins still lived in the city."

"They are here, but they are out of favor," Mirti said bluntly. "They need someone to bring them back into fashion."

"Have you tried one of these? They're marvelous," Elidon said, offering a plate of the candy-coated fruit to each of her guests.

Mirti helped herself to two sizable pieces. "I bought some down at the Plaza the other day," she said. "Never tasted anything so good."

Zoe kept her hands in her lap. "Am I to understand," she said slowly, "that it is up to *me* to restore the Ardelays to their place?"

Elidon made an equivocal motion with her hands. "It is not something you could do all on your own," she said. "But you could start the process. You could invite your uncle and his sons to your rooms for a meal. Everyone would see that they were welcome at the palace again."

"Welcomed by the *Lalindars*," Mirti emphasized. "Since Christara was the one who ostracized them, Christara's heir is the one who should make reparation."

"The one who should show them affection," Elidon added.

"I scarcely know them," Zoe said. "I haven't seen any of my father's relatives for ten years."

"Immaterial," Mirti said.

"You may not be aware of how closely everyone is watching you," Elidon said. "What you do will be imitated."

"Unless what I do is disastrous," Zoe said flatly.

Mirti actually grinned. "We're not setting a trap for you," she said cheerfully, "though I don't blame you for wondering. We are giving you very good advice. It is time the rift with the Ardelays was mended, and you can do much to mend it." She slipped one of the chocolate fruits in her mouth, and then spoke around it. "Unless you can't stand your uncle and his sons, that is. They're talkers and charmers, like all *sweela* men, and I know a few people who can't abide them. But I rather like the lot of them."

Elidon gave her a quick smile. "But then, your taste in people is notoriously unreliable."

Mirti snorted again. "Bad, you mean. Not so. I have plenty of upstanding citizens among my ranks of friends."

Elidon laughed softly. Zoe had the sense they were sharing a private joke, perhaps an intimate one, certainly one she would not be allowed to share. "I will get in touch with my uncle, then," she said.

Elidon nodded, satisfied. "Good." She touched her fingers briefly to the back of Zoe's wrist, a mark of high approval. "You learn quickly, I think. And I like that you are so agreeable and accommodating."

But Mirti was appraising her with those disconcertingly direct gray eyes. "I don't think so," said the Serlast prime. "Or, at least, only when it suits her."

Zoe smiled and ducked her head in an approximation of a bow. "How could it not suit me to be agreeable to the first wife?"

Now Mirti was laughing out loud. "Exactly so."

Elidon passed another tray of treats, flat, crunchy breads sprinkled with colorful salts. "Try these," she said. "You'll love them."

NINETEEN

E arly the following morning, Zoe met Darien Serlast in the *kierten* of the palace, which was bustling with activity even at that hour. She had sent Calvin to him with an urgent message the instant she returned from Elidon's suite, and this was the meeting place he suggested. Almost immediately, they slipped outside to stroll along one edge of the river, so placid here it masqueraded as a lake. The weather was so cold that a rime of ice had formed all along the shallow shore, but there was enough of a current to keep most of the water fluid. Zoe had wrapped herself in her heaviest overrobe and pulled on a delicate pair of painted leather gloves. She was chilly, but the brisk air was refreshing, and she found it deeply soothing to be this close to flowing water. If Darien minded the temperature, he didn't mention it.

"I wasn't sure of the best way to get in touch with you," she said. "Should I have written a note? Stopped you in the hallway?"

"Sending Calvin was the best choice," he said. "And it's always preferable to send a verbal message. Put nothing in writing. You never know how words might be misinterpreted."

She sighed. "Just living here makes me tired."

He laughed. "No, no, it should invigorate you with its constant challenges."

She ostentatiously cast a glance all around them. They were highly visible to anyone who might glance out of a palace window, because there was very little ground cover near the shoreline. On the other hand, there was no convenient hiding spot where spies could lurk to eavesdrop on their conversation.

"Are we safe even here?" she asked, her voice derisive. "Should we cross the bridge to the halfway point and whisper to each other over the murmurs of the water?"

"I think we may speak freely," he answered, grinning. "I suppose you have come to seek my opinion on some finer point of palace etiquette."

"Just so. Even though I know you will lie to me when you like," she said dryly, "you don't seem to want me to stumble. So I trust you to warn me away from behaviors with catastrophic consequences."

"I am relieved to think you trust me even that far," he said.

"I received some advice from Elidon and your aunt Mirti, and I'm not sure it's sound," she said. "I'm not accusing them of trying to cause me trouble, but—"

He laughed again. "Oh, but they are both wily women who have complex agendas," he said. "You are wise to wonder if they have your best interests at heart."

She said bluntly, "They told me I should bring the Ardelays back in favor."

Darien's eyebrows shot up, and then his face assumed a thoughtful expression. "That would be an interesting step for you to take," he said slowly. "The king has been debating the best way to mend the rift with Nelson Ardelay. He had considered inviting Nelson and his sons to one of the formal dinners, but this is better. It gives you a chance to demonstrate your own strength and prove your commitment to blood—your father's as well as your grandmother's. And it means that Nelson will already be somewhat reestablished before Vernon issues an invitation."

"So I wouldn't be condemned and banished if I brought my uncle to the palace."

He glanced at her. "Is that what you were afraid of?"

She grinned. "It's what I *hoped* for. I find court life wearisome in the extreme. What grave error can I commit that will get me flung off the mountain?"

"I have to believe you're joking."

"Only a little."

He shrugged. "So what stops you from simply walking down the stairs and out the doors?"

"I don't know—the thought that you might go hunting for me and drag me back?"

"I might go to some effort to make sure you were established in reasonable new accommodations, but I would not force you to return against your will. Though I do think you betray your family if you do not play the role it has fallen on you to play. Like it or not, you are their representative, their advocate with the king. If you abandon the palace, you abandon them."

"I have had some experience with abandonment," she said. "It is not as bad as everyone thinks."

"I would wager your father did not agree."

"No, probably not." She kicked at a stone that lay in her path, and it bounced down the shoreline to plop into the water. She was wearing the sturdiest of her new shoes, the ones that could survive hard usage like walking outside. They were also roomy enough to accommodate socks; even so, her toes were starting to turn to ice. "Then I shall have my uncle in for a visit as soon as I can arrange it."

"Good," he said. He smiled. "Do you have any more questions? Any other matters on which you would like to consult my wise counsel?"

"I'm too cold to think of any," she said. "Let's just go back inside."

She turned toward the palace, but he stopped her with a hand on her arm. His expression was serious. "If you *did* leave," he said. "If you did simply walk out the doors and stroll down the mountain, leaving behind no word of where you were going or why, I *would* come looking for you. I would never stop looking for you. I would find you, too."

She gazed up at him, her own expression neutral. "Just because you found me the last time I ran away from you doesn't mean you would be so successful a second time."

"Ah, but I know you much better now. And I know where you are likely to run. I could find you even more quickly."

"There are always new places," she said.

"Even for a *coru* woman," he said, "there are finite places to go."

She shrugged. "Why? Why not let me go? Why come after me at all, if I choose to leave?"

He was silent a moment. "Because I said I would," he said. "Word of a *hunti* man."

Everyone knew what that meant: solid as wood, unyielding as bone. She nodded but made no answer, and they finished the rest of the walk in silence.

Calvin took the formal message to Nelson Ardelay, inviting the prime and his two sons to a private luncheon in the quarters Zoe Ardelay Lalindar enjoyed at the palace. Zoe instructed Calvin to deliver the message in person so that he would know what Nelson looked like, and he could be waiting in the *kierten* when the Ardelays arrived at the palace two days later. Nelson would not have to humble himself to ask a servant to announce him; he would not have to endure stares and whispers. Calvin would already be there, bowing and leading the way.

Annova and Zoe had gone to some trouble to decorate Zoe's sitting room to honor her conflicting heritage. On the day of the visit, they placed tall girandoles in the four corners of the room and fitted them with slow-burning tapers. They set a small fountain before the window and filled its bubbling waters with tiny golden fish. For the table, they made a centerpiece of a flat, transparent bowl of water; on its surface floated lit candles shaped like birds and flowers. Water and fire coexisting. *Sweela* and *coru* at peace.

Zoe dressed herself carefully in a sea-blue overrobe and trousers heavily stitched with gold embroidery in a flamelike pattern. She stood motionless beside the table, so still that none of the charms on her bracelet rattled. She was listening intently to the sounds in the palace corridors, trying to convince herself that she could identify her uncle's heartbeat as he climbed the multicolored staircase. But she was still startled enough—or nervous enough—to catch her breath when Calvin stepped through the door, visitors at his heels.

"Zoe Ardelay Lalindar," he said importantly. "I present Nelson Ardelay and his sons, Kurtis and Rhan."

"Uncle," Zoe said, bowing deeply. "Cousins. I am delighted to see you again."

"Niece," Nelson replied. He performed an offhand, hasty bow, then snapped back to an upright position and studied her with great curiosity.

She inspected him in return. He did not look much like Navarr, his younger brother, who had inherited his dark eyes and hair from his *hunti* mother. Nelson Ardelay was all *sweela*, with brushy red hair and a ruddy complexion, though the hair was heavily grayed and the skin was creased with wrinkles. Although she guessed him to be in his mid-sixties, the essential force of his personality didn't seem to have banked down at all. He kept a neutral expression on his face, but it was clear he was a passionate man, quick to anger, quick to laugh. She had a sudden, swift, visceral memory of boisterous conversations at his house, loud arguments and outbursts of gusty merriment.

"Oh, surely we're not all just going to stand around and stare at each other for an hour," one of her cousins said, and her attention was drawn to Rhan. He was the younger of the two, burlier than his father, with a wild mane of curly red hair and a wicked smile. "I remember you, Zoe! But you were a skinny little thing with big eyes and no meat to you. Look at you now!"

He strode across the room to envelop her in a crushing hug. For a moment she was assaulted by sensations—not just the sheer physical impact of body to bone, but the electrifying leap of blood as her own sparked in recognition of his. *Mine. Family. Mine.* The thoughts were inchoate but powerful. She smothered a gasp and hugged him back.

"Well, if that's how we're greeting cousins these days," Kurtis said, and pushed his brother aside. He was taller and slimmer than Rhan, with more orderly hair of the same bright color. When he took Zoe a bit more sedately in his arms, she felt that response in her blood again, that jolting excitement. Again, she returned the embrace with enthusiasm.

"I would apologize for my sons, but you do not seem to mind their mauling," Nelson said, once Kurtis had released her. "Let me greet you with a bit more restraint, but just as much heartfelt happiness." And he took both of her hands in his, squeezing them tightly and smiling down at her. There it was, even stronger this time. *Mine. Mine. Blood of my blood . . .*

A little dizzy, but teetering on euphoria, Zoe laughed and pulled her hands free. "I didn't expect quite so much fervor! Everyone else has been so measured and cautious that I have forgotten what it is like to be engulfed by visitors."

"Measured and cautious are not words that are often used to describe Ardelays," Rhan said with a grin.

"Though we have spent some years struggling to achieve thoughtfulness and wisdom," Nelson said with a sigh. "It has not come easily."

Zoe gestured at the table. "Sit! Please! We'll eat while I regain my balance and you catch me up on everything that has happened to my father's family while I was in exile."

Nelson was instantly grave. "I was very sorry to hear about my brother's death," he said as the three men settled around the table. "We corresponded frequently while he was out of favor, but I only saw him once every year or so, and that loss cut into me deeply. I missed him."

Zoe was pouring water into their goblets, so she was able to pretend that all her attention was on this task. Her father had met with Nelson almost every year? Had those visits been part of his infrequent pilgrimages to nearby towns during the times Zoe was not permitted to accompany him? As she had gotten older, she had assumed those journeys involved visits to accommodating women. It had not occurred to her that he had maintained his connection to his family—to Zoe's family—and had not invited her along.

"I miss him still," she said, her voice steady. "And yet he was not a perfect man."

"Far from it," Nelson agreed. "But then, that describes every Ardelay."

She smiled at him as she took her seat. "So tell me about the Ardelays," she invited. "It seems their fortunes ebbed when my father fell into disgrace."

"They did," Nelson said. "Though I blame that bitch Christara—"

"Remember your audience," Kurtis interposed.

"Sorry, Zoe—I blame your grandmother for most of our

downfall. She set out to ruin your father, and she did so, but she didn't care that we came tumbling down after him."

"You make us sound pathetic and helpless!" Rhan exclaimed. "It is true we lost some properties. And some trade deals. And some allies. But we have not done so badly after all."

"So? How have you been propping up your fortunes?" Zoe asked as she handed around the first platters.

"Mostly, we invested in land down by the southern coast," Kurtis answered. "It was land that was bad for farming, bad for mining, bad for *anything*, it seemed, and nobody wanted it. But we've built a couple of huge factories there and made a small fortune on manufacturing. We're so close to the coast we can buy raw materials cheap—and ship out finished products straight from the warehouse."

"What are you manufacturing?" Zoe asked, nibbling on a crumbling sweetcake.

"Mostly parts for other factories," Kurtis said with a laugh, taking two small sandwiches. "But the real money is going to be in transportation."

"Smoker cars," Rhan said when Zoe looked confused. "We've entered into a deal with the Dochenzas—"

"*Very* quietly," Kurtis interrupted.

"To produce the *elaymotives* that run on their compressed gas. So far, there have only been a couple hundred put together by hand. We can make a thousand in a *year*. It'll change the way everyone travels."

"It'll change the whole economy," Nelson said. "We're poised to become very rich."

"How nice to hear!" Zoe said. "I suppose you don't need me, then!"

Rhan reached across the table to lay his hand on hers. Again, she felt that recognition singing in her pulse. She liked the sensation so much she didn't pull away. "Oh, but we *want* you," he said. "Little cousin Zoe, returned to us at last! Even if you couldn't haul us back into the king's good graces, we would be delighted to find you again."

"But I for one would like to be back in the king's good graces," Kurtis said honestly. "If you can figure out a way to make that happen, I would be everlastingly grateful."

She looked at Nelson, her brows lifted in a question. He

shrugged and swallowed a mouthful of food. "I'm getting older," he said. "I used to relish the battles, even the ones that didn't result in victory. I just enjoyed the fight. These days it doesn't matter to me so much who is in power and who has been kicked down the mountain, and arguing takes too much energy. But I would like to see my sons reinstated, and I will do what I can to make that happen."

She glanced at Kurtis. "Are you next in line to be prime, then?"

"Yes, though I rarely make a decision without Rhan's input."

"And do you have families of your own?"

"I have a wife—a *sweela* girl who was not embarrassed to marry a man who is unwelcome at court!—and ten-year-old twins," Kurtis replied. "Rhan has so far proved impossible to satisfy."

"Impossible to tame," his brother said with a grin.

"That's how you can help us out," Kurtis said. "Arrange a political marriage for Rhan! Someone from the best family, of course—maybe even one of the princesses—"

"I think they're all a little young for him," she said, amused. She thought Kurtis might be in his mid-thirties, Rhan a year or two younger.

"I'm willing to wait. I'm *happy* to wait," Rhan said. "I'm not so sure that married life is for me."

"A common Ardelay failing," Nelson said dryly.

Zoe tilted her head to one side. "What kind of girl do you think you would like?" she asked. "*Hunti?* Fire burns wood, but wood sustains fire—*hunti* matches are always good for Ardelays, aren't they? I think a *torz* girl would be too dull for you altogether."

"Earth smothers fire," Rhan agreed. "Fire irritates earth."

"Perhaps a *coru* woman," Nelson suggested. "Fire and water are a powerful combination."

Kurtis snorted. "Even with Christara dead, I don't think Lalindars are ready to start marrying their daughters off to Ardelays again."

Zoe laughed. "And I am hardly in a position to begin matchmaking," she said. "I will certainly look around and see if any likely candidates present themselves. But first we will consider how respectable we can make you."

"Yes, let us talk about how to rehabilitate the Ardelays," Kurtis said.

"Well, you're here. That's the first step, as I understand it," Zoe said.

"Yes, we're here, and we hope you will join us for dinner on the next firstday," Kurtis said. "We'll have a few other friends there—a small gathering—I admit it might not be much fun for you, but it *will* be important for us to show you off. If you will come."

"I will," she said.

Rhan hastily swallowed a large bite of curried meat. "Oh, but I know!" he exclaimed. "She can crew the boat with us! For the regatta! *That* would be a mark of high favor, to have the Lalindar prime actually with us *on the water*!"

"Excellent idea!" Kurtis approved. "That is—Zoe—if you will?"

"Can you believe that this is the third time I've been asked to sit in someone's boat?" she asked.

"Of course I'd believe it!" Kurtis replied. "I would think you would be a lucky talisman. Anyone would be glad to have you."

"Can you actually row?" Rhan demanded. "Or will you be a liability?"

His father and brother exclaimed aloud and demanded he apologize, but Zoe laughed and threw a baked roll at him. "The water loves me," she said. "I might not be a good oarsman, but I don't think you'd find my presence a hindrance. Far from it."

Rhan placed his hand over hers again. He was clearly a flirt, whether the nearest woman was a stranger or a blood relation, but it was rather delightful to be flirted with, Zoe thought. "Then the Ardelays claim you," he said with a smile. "You can't turn us away now."

Darien Serlast approved the notion of Zoe taking her place in the Ardelay boat when she had a chance to ask him about it the next day. "Though it is a bold step," he added. "It might raise some eyebrows. But I don't think it will harm you."

"I am less worried about harming my own reputation than failing to do the Ardelays any good," she told him. "I care very little how I am perceived."

"That's because there is a natural contrariness to you that seems to have been designed specifically to drive me mad," Darien replied.

She laughed out loud. "Oh, no, I don't think of you at all when I am trying to determine my next course of behavior."

He smiled in return. "I find that I do not believe you," he replied. "I am convinced you think of me a great deal of the time."

It annoyed her that this was true, so she snapped, "Only when I'm feeling spiteful."

His smile widened. "As I said. For I am certain you are feeling spiteful more days than not."

He made her want to laugh; he made her want to scowl and stomp from the room. Instead, she threw her hands in the air and shook her head and did not reply.

It was easy to forget about Darien Serlast a few days later during the rather rambunctious party she attended at her uncle's house. There were at least a hundred guests present, half of them related to her, all of them loud and outspoken and vying for attention. She couldn't keep track of the second cousins and third cousins and relations once removed, but every time she touched a hand or submitted to an embrace, she could tell which ones she shared a bloodline with and which ones were tied to the Ardelays by marriage or friendship. She came away from the event feeling suffused with warmth; her cheeks were heated and her blood seemed to pulse with an added exuberance. She was not sure how often she would be able to survive such outings, but she had certainly enjoyed this one.

Seven days after the party, the seasons changed, the year turned over, and the world prepared to celebrate Quinnelay changeday. Zoe couldn't help thinking about the same holiday last year. Her father had been well enough to observe it with traditional songs and spoken remembrances, though his voice had been weak and his memories had focused on long-ago days. She was just as glad that, for this changeday, she would not have time for the conventional hours of contemplation and review. She would be too busy crewing down the Marisi in the king's grand regatta.

TWENTY

The day of the race dawned very chilly but absolutely clear. Zoe joined the large group of palace residents who were transported to the launch site in a series of *elaymotives*. Over the last nineday, so she had been told, all the racing boats had been hauled to the river's edge and set in the water. At the same time, pavilions had been constructed along the coast at the end of the course—the wide, turbulent pool where the river gathered its strength for its headlong leap down the face of the mountain. Here, spectators—like Elidon and Romelle and Mirti Serlast—would gather in comfort to cheer on their favorites and award prizes to the winners. As Zoe understood it, audience members outnumbered contestants by about three to one, and the racing field was by no means small. Last year's event had included twenty-five boats, most of them crewed by three or four people.

Once she arrived at the launch site, she picked her way through the chaos on the riverbank, searching for the boat she would share with Kurtis, Rhan, and Nelson. She was staring the whole time. On this relatively calm, relatively narrow stretch of the Marisi, an entire flotilla lined the southern bank. Most of the vessels were small, efficient, and unadorned, with narrow pointed bows designed to cut cleanly through the water. A few were larger and more elaborate, painted with bright colors and boasting short poles hung with snapping pennants. These, Zoe assumed, were the boats that would carry members of the royal family—as well as trained rivermen to guide the boats through the water.

Despite the raw air and whipping wind, the atmosphere was one of carnival excitement as the participants shouted to each other, readied their craft for racing, and listened to the officials bawling out the final rules: No launching of any craft before the signal was given. No deliberately trying to ram or overturn a competitor's boat. The winning crew must row *past* the queens' pavilion. All boats must come to shore on the southern edge of the river, where the water was calmer and workers were in place to help contestants secure their craft. All crew members should know their designated number and be prepared to present it to the judges at the completion of the race.

"There you are," Rhan said when Zoe finally found the Ardelays, as they were doing a last-minute inspection of their boat. It was small and agile, little more than a metal hull and four benches bolted inside to accommodate passengers. He handed her a white silk vest with a huge numeral embroidered on it in black thread. "We're lucky number eight. Slip this on so that everyone will be able to recognize us as we cross the finish line."

"Why do I have to be the one to wear it?" she said, though she quickly tied the strings around her waist.

"Because you are the one who is least likely to have fallen into the water before the race is half over."

"When do we start?" she asked.

Kurtis nodded toward the riverbank, where the king and four men who looked like professional athletes climbed into the largest of the painted boats. A dark-haired sailor wore a thin vest sporting the numeral one. "Very soon. The king is always the first to board, and then the rest of us follow. After everyone is in the water, we will be signaled to begin."

There was a short delay while the rest of the racers waited for Seterre, Alys, Josetta, and Corene to settle into their boats, accompanied by more hired men. Once the royal family members were aboard, all the other participants surged toward the riverbank. Zoe clambered aboard her own neat craft, squealing as Nelson's weight rocked the boat so hard that she thought she would pitch into the water. But quickly enough they were all in place, Rhan in the front, Zoe behind him, and Nelson and Kurtis on the back two benches. The men paddled the boat into the middle of the river, lining up as best they could with the other contestants, using oars and oaths to try to keep in place against the insistent current.

"All contestants not in place at this instant are hereby disqualified!" one of the officials bellowed from the shore. "On the word *now*, you may all begin the race! And I give you—that—word—*now*!"

There was a muffled roar of enthusiasm, followed by dozens of tiny splashes as a hundred oars hit the water simultaneously. Zoe felt her heart hammer with excitement as the craft leapt forward. It was even colder on the river than it had been on land, and the oars kicked up a constant fine spray that had them all damp within five strokes. Rhan had lent her a pair of thick boots, for which she was immensely grateful, since about an inch of water already sloshed along the bottom of the boat. She was equally thankful for her own heavy overrobe, which provided some protection from the cold. But none of these discomforts really weighed with her. She clung to the sides of the boat and laughed with sheer delight.

She could feel the river coiling and uncoiling below her, a joyous, eager, raw, and unpredictable presence. Like a horse that lived for the flat-out gallop, the Marisi loved a race; she could practically sense its own excitement reflecting and intensifying the emotions of all those riding on its back. It was almost as if the water ran even faster this morning than it did on an ordinary day, just to show off, just to thrill these creatures who had chosen to hurl themselves across its lashing surface. Zoe felt it lift and strain within its banks, flinging itself with a lunatic exuberance toward the crashing abandon of the falls. Behind her, before her, she could feel the Ardelay men plunging their oars into the swift water, powering the boat forward with strength and skill, but she knew it wasn't their efforts that sent them skimming down the river. It was the Marisi itself, catching them up in its foaming arms and dancing madly down the channel.

A whoop of victory jerked her attention from the water

below her to the race all around her. "We're in the lead!" Rhan shouted, his words ripped out of his mouth by the driving wind. "We just passed Broy Lalindar! No one else will be able to catch us!"

"Don't gloat too early!" Nelson shouted back a little breathlessly. "If anyone can beat us, it's Broy!"

"The king isn't too far back, either," Kurtis called out. "And his paid sailors know tricks we'll never learn!"

Zoe didn't say anything, but she had the sense that the river wouldn't allow anyone to outrace the boat carrying the Lalindar prime. She crouched down a little lower, partly to shield her face from the wet wind, and partly to make herself too small to create any kind of resistance. *Faster,* she thought, imagining the choppy waters smoothing out and plunging forward at her behest. *Even faster.*

The landscape on either bank started to blur as their pace increased; she could see nothing but a streaming impression of bare trees, rocky banks, and crystalline blue sky. It felt as if they were skating along the top of a river grown glass-smooth and steeply canted—as if their speed increased again, and *again,* almost as if they were careening down a hill. The water broke against the sides of the boat with frantic energy, dousing Zoe's icy fingers for the hundredth time. She was almost hypnotized by the sensation of dizzying speed. *Faster,* she thought, and felt the boat respond.

She was scarcely aware of sudden shapes bulking up on the right edge of the river—colorful canvas structures swaying in the steady wind. She could hear, but paid no attention to, a rushing, roaring, cavernous sound that grew louder with ominous swiftness. There were other noises she ignored—shouts from the shoreline, a clanging bell, something that sounded like a cannon shot, loud and cautionary. All she could think about was the accelerating forward motion. *Faster. Faster.*

Suddenly, someone was shaking her from behind and her uncle Nelson's voice shouted urgently in her ear. "Zoe! Zoe! We can't slow the boat and we're going to crash over the falls! Zoe! *Let the boat go!*"

With a start, she came to, as if shocked out of a fevered, hallucinogenic dream. She could see Rhan in front of her, desperately rowing backward, trying to abort from their disastrous course toward the frothing waters of the falls. Behind her she could sense the terrific strain from Nelson and Kurtis as they did the same. All of them were shouting her name, and Nelson shook her once more by the shoulder. "*Zoe!* Stop the boat!"

She flung her arms out over both sides with her fingers splayed, and cut her connection to the Marisi. Instantly, the little craft started spinning in the water, caught between the ordinary current and the strokes of the three men. She heard Kurtis's nervous laugh as the Ardelays quickly got the boat back under their control, and in a few moments they were cutting across the water toward the southern shore where a harbor of sorts had been set up. No other vessels were docked there yet, though about a dozen rough-looking men were lined up with ropes and other gear, ready to secure them to shore. Three brightly draped pavilions stood on the land just up from the harbor, filled with spectators, and more people crowded on the shore, watching and waving.

"Are we the first?" she asked, glancing up the river to locate their nearest competitors. She could make out dozens of shapes skipping along the water; none of them seemed too close.

Rhan laughed, though the sound was shaky. "The *first*? By a good twenty minutes, I'd guess! No one will ever beat our time. It was impossible that *we* covered the distance so fast! What did you *do*?"

"I didn't do anything," she said a little nervously. What *had* happened back on open water? "At least, not on purpose. I was just thinking that I wanted us to go fast. Really fast. I didn't—I mean, it wasn't like I thought I could do anything to make that happen."

"You seemed to be in some kind of trance," Rhan said, "and the waterfall kept getting closer and closer."

"Sorry," she said. "I didn't mean to do—whatever I did. I don't think I can explain it."

Nelson patted her on the back. "I understand it, but I can't explain it, either," he said. "Fire takes me that way, too, sometimes, and I've more than one burn scar to prove it. You can't let it master you, though—that's the trick."

"Especially when your cousins are about to be swept away with you," Kurtis added.

"I am truly sorry."

Rhan laughed. "I'm not! We won the purse. And what a ride!"

By this time, they had made it to the bank, and a few of the dockmen splashed out into the shallows to haul them up to the makeshift piers. Zoe took off her embroidered vest and handed it to the official-looking man who was clearly acting on the judges' behalf. But the instant she clambered out of the boat, she staggered. She felt so *heavy*; she could not accustom herself to the stubborn, unmoving solidity of land. She was also freezing and wet and sore all over from bracing herself against the tumultuous journey downriver.

Nelson seemed to have anticipated her reaction, though Zoe had not. He caught her arm and guided her toward the smallest of the pavilions, which was invitingly lit and filled with a handful of people. While it had a sturdy wooden floor, and a roof and three walls constructed of heavy canvas, one whole side was open to give spectators a clear view of the Marisi. Inside, Zoe could see braziers for heat and heaps of pillows and blankets for comfort.

"You'll be welcome inside the queens' pavilion," Nelson said softly as he led her there. "That's where the winners traditionally watch the end of the race."

"You, too," she said, "and Kurtis and Rhan."

"We'll see."

But as they stepped off the dock and toward the tentlike structure, Elidon herself came forward, hands outstretched, a smile on her face. Mirti Serlast hovered behind her, grinning. "Zoe!" Elidon exclaimed, briefly taking Zoe's hand and letting it fall. "Once I heard you were in the race, I was sure you would win it, but by such a margin! How in the world did you manage such a feat?"

"Ask my cousins and my uncle," she said.

Elidon turned to Nelson, that smile still in place, and touched him on the shoulder, a mark of high favor. "Nelson Ardelay," she said. "How clever of you to make the Lalindar prime one of your crew."

He smiled back, all *sweela* warmth, holding no grudges for past slights. "No, no, I brought her aboard only because she is my brother's daughter," he replied. "The Lalindar heritage was an unexpected benefit."

Mirti snorted and clapped him heartily on the back. "I'll believe that when the soil itself shoots up out of the ground and smothers the river in its channel," she said. "Well, come inside, you and your sons, too! We have brought all sorts of food and drink to sustain the winners as we watch the end of the race."

"I'm concerned about Zoe," Nelson said. "She's starting to shiver, and I don't think she realized how much energy the whole event took out of her."

"I'm fine," Zoe said, though that was a lie.

Mirti gave her one quick assessment, and nodded. Another prime; someone else who understood how deeply and foolishly a person could be absorbed by the elements. "Here. Sit by the fire," she said, leading Zoe to a pile of pillows arrayed before one of the braziers. "I'll bring you something warm to drink. Are you hungry?"

"I don't think so," Zoe replied.

"Hmm. You'd better have something to eat."

A few moments later, Zoe was sitting as close to the brazier as possible, sipping some sweet and steaming drink and munching on toasted bread. Mirti turned out to be right; Zoe was starving. Her Ardelay relatives were standing with Mirti and the king's wives, holding their own refreshments and recounting, with a great deal of animation, their race down the river. Rhan was flirting with Romelle, who seemed to have left Natalie back at the palace, while Mirti and Elidon appeared to be holding a more businesslike conversation with Nelson and Kurtis. Servants glided noiselessly among them, replenishing drinks and offering more food. Zoe accepted a bowl of some kind of thick soup and practically gulped it down. Her toes and fingers were starting to regain some feeling, but she couldn't say she actually felt warm. And she hated to think how her hair must look—a hank of wet, tangled disaster, she supposed. As soon as she was done eating she might see if there was a private corner of the pavilion where she could put herself back together.

Cheers and light applause drew her attention to the open wall of the pavilion, and she gazed out in time to see three boats cross the boundary in quick succession. The smallest, most agile craft belonged to Broy, Zoe thought, while the larger, brighter one was crewed by the king's paid sailors. From this distance, she couldn't tell who was in the third boat, which had clearly attempted to beat the king to the finish line. While she watched, several more vessels drifted past at an appreciably slower pace. No need to strain against the oars any longer now that the top three winners were determined.

Nelson turned to Kurtis. "Have any of the children's boats showed up yet?" he asked. "I wonder who's in the lead."

Which was when Zoe remembered that there *was* a separate race for younger contestants. "Do you have someone in that race?" Mirti asked him.

"My wife's nephew is participating for the first time this year," Nelson replied. "He spent several ninedays practicing his rowing skills over the summer, so I hope he acquits himself well."

"How old is he?" Elidon asked.

"Thirteen. Skinny and awkward." He smiled in Elidon's direction. "All *elay*, I'm afraid. I don't think he'll have much chance to win a *coru* event, but I have high hopes of him in many other fields. He's much smarter and far more charming than he realizes."

She smiled back. "Adolescence does not tend to be kind to *elay* boys, but I am certain better days await him."

"Well, I hope he doesn't have his heart set on winning this race," Mirti said in her astringent way. "Josetta and Corene each have their own boats, with professional crews, and I doubt any amateurs will beat them." She glanced in Zoe's direction. "Even *coru* amateurs."

"I think what he hopes for is to not drown," Kurtis said. "And, if he could be said to have a higher aspiration, it would be to not fall into the water at all."

Romelle had wandered closer to the open wall, leaning over a little to look out. The makeshift harbor had grown crowded with boats, though no more contestants had come laughing and shivering into the queens' pavilion. Zoe supposed most of the other participants had headed to the larger, public tents, though she thought the king would join Elidon and Romelle—and so would Darien Serlast, if he had docked by now. Perhaps both of them were waiting on the pier for the king's other wives to arrive.

"About fifteen boats are already in," Romelle reported. "And I can see two—three—four boats up the river, coming pretty fast." She glanced back at Nelson with a grin. "The one in the lead is flying royal colors. Mirti's right. Either Josetta or Corene is going to win."

"As they should," he replied gallantly. "Who would want to outrace a princess?"

But he had lost Romelle's attention. She had straightened up and started waving; Zoe could see only the profile of her face, but she appeared to be suddenly lit with happiness. "Well-done!" she called. "A very good race!"

Darien Serlast stepped into the tent.

Zoe felt her stomach contract as if absorbing a heavy blow. *Darien Serlast? Her smile is for Darien Serlast?* But Romelle was looking past him, still waving, as Darien came deeper into the pavilion and started wiping river mist off his overrobe.

"Fourth place," his aunt Mirti said to him with a grin.

"But I had money on the winner," he replied, grinning back. "So I don't mind too much."

"I'll wager you didn't expect the Ardelays to get down the river in *quite* such a speedy manner."

He had glanced once around the tent, apparently looking for someone, and his gaze had snagged on Zoe. She kept her eyes focused on the brazier, as if dreamily fascinated by some pattern in the glowing coals; but, in fact, she was aware of every gesture he made, every detail that caught his attention. "I never know quite what to expect of the Lalindar prime," he said softly, though Zoe caught the words. "I wasn't surprised at all."

There was a burst of color and motion at the open wall of the pavilion, and Alys and Seterre stepped inside, King Vernon between them. They were surrounded by servants who must have met them on the dock, for they were already wrapped in warm robes and carrying mugs of hot liquid. Seterre nursed hers against her cheek as if trying to absorb its heat through her skin.

"I wanted to wait on the shore until the children's race was run, but it was so *cold*," Seterre announced, shivering where she stood. "I'm sure my toes have turned to ice by now."

"Oh, I love running the river in this kind of weather!" Alys exclaimed. Indeed, her face was becomingly flushed, either with cold or excitement, and she threw off her outer robe as she strode inside. It was clear she was trying, by her own vigor, to make Seterre look wan and pathetic. "It makes me feel so alive! I could go twice as far and still feel this—elation."

Rhan looked over at her with his ready smile. "A *sweela* woman rarely feels the cold," he said in an approving voice.

Alys laughed and sauntered in his direction. "Warmed by internal fires," she agreed, tossing her red hair. "The best of the elemental gifts, I think."

"*I* think so," he said, "but, of course, an Ardelay would be biased."

She was standing very close to him, smiling with an unmistakable wickedness. If Zoe hadn't been certain that Rhan knew all about handling dangerous, combustible women, she would have drawn him aside and warned him against attempting even the most casual friendship with the king's third wife. "Rhan Ardelay," Alys said. "It has been far too long since we have seen you at any of the palace functions."

He bowed with a great deal of flourish. "My very dear majesty," he said, "I am so glad you noticed."

Practically everyone else in the tent noticed, too; Zoe saw Elidon, Mirti, Darien, and Kurtis all watching this little flirtation with varying degrees of disapproval. The only people who paid no attention were Romelle and Vernon, who had moved to a comfortable bench in the back of the pavilion while servants brought him more blankets and hot food. Zoe thought it was a little sad that only one of the king's wives bothered to sit beside him and listen to him recite the details of his race, but Vernon seemed content to pour his tale into Romelle's ears. The fourth queen did little besides smile and nod, but he seemed happy enough with her company.

One other person barely bothered to give Alys more than a reproving glance—Seterre, still standing at the wide doorway, looking unhappy and uncertain. It was clear she wanted to be part of the lively conversation inside the tent, but something outside claimed more of her anxious attention.

Zoe watched as Darien excused himself from his conversation and stepped over to Seterre. "Is something wrong?" he asked.

"Oh, I just—Corene has won the children's race already and she's coming up the shore, and five or six of the other boats have docked, but Josetta hasn't arrived yet."

Darien's eyebrows rose. He peered outside, craning his neck so he could look upriver. "Maybe her craft went aground upstream."

"Maybe," Seterre said doubtfully. "But she had hired men with her—I wouldn't think they would encounter any trouble—"

Darien smiled. "Oh, I'd wager every *coru* man in the country would tell you that an affinity for water does not guarantee that your boat will never go awry," he said. "They could have come across any number of hazards. Have all the other boats arrived?"

"I'm not sure," Seterre said. "I don't know how many were racing."

Nelson had stepped over, his bluff and solid shape seeming to offer Seterre a certain reassurance. "Twenty-six," he said, "and ten of those in the children's race."

"Well—" Darien said. Zoe saw him adjust his stance and narrow his eyes. She guessed he had started to count the vessels already tied up at the dock.

At that moment, Corene came charging into the pavilion, almost pushing Seterre aside in her eagerness to enter. "Did you see? Did you see? I won the race! We were so far ahead!" Like her mother, she seemed to have been made more vibrant and alive by the challenge of the regatta. Her color was high and her eyes sparkled with excitement. "I knew no one would be able to catch us."

"How far back was Josetta? Do you remember?" Seterre asked her.

Corene shrugged away the question. "I wasn't paying attention to anyone else. Mama, did you hear? I won!" she cried, and hurried over to where Alys and Rhan were still laughing together.

"I knew you would, my pet," Alys said, giving her a perfunctory kiss. "Now get yourself something to eat. Are you cold?"

"No," Corene said scornfully.

"This must be your daughter," Rhan said. "Never did a princess look so much like a queen—or talk like one."

There was probably more along this line, but Zoe transferred her attention back to the small, sober crowd at the doorway. "I count twenty-five boats," Darien said, his voice concerned. "Maybe I should grab a few men and row back up the river to look for her."

"I'll come," Nelson said instantly. "And so will my boys. You want our boat?"

Kurtis had caught the serious tone of the conversation and joined them. "It'll be hard to fight that current," he said. "We might be better off taking one of the smoker cars and driving along the shoreline, looking."

Darien was shaking his head. "There are a few stretches of land where you can't get close to the shoreline. But you might be right. Maybe we send a car up to the embarkation point and then send a boat all the way down the river—"

Before he could finish speaking, Seterre screamed.

Everyone in the pavilion froze, or swung around to stare, or dropped whatever they had been holding in their hands. "Seterre, what—" Elidon began, but Seterre screamed again and again, her voice fading as she leapt off the low floor of the pavilion and scrambled down the bank toward the Marisi.

"Majesty!" Nelson shouted and went after her. Darien was a split second behind them, and everyone else in the tent rushed for the door. Zoe pushed impatiently through the gawking crowd to see what terror was unfolding outside.

A single small boat was spinning down the river, its jaunty colors and cheerful flag bouncing gaily over the water. It moved like a piece of river trash, rudderless, directionless, and it was headed, in a wayward fashion, toward the sudden, murderous drop-off of the falls.

A single figure huddled inside, clinging to the edges, blond hair whipping around her face as the craft swooped through another curl of water and practically dumped her overboard.

Within another few tumultuous yards, her boat would tip over the lip of the falls into an unsurvivable dive.

Nelson, Kurtis, and Darien were already untying a boat from the makeshift harbor, clambering in, pushing off, but there was too much distance to cross and the current was too strong. It was not possible for them to reach Josetta before the river flung her off the edge of the world.

Almost without conscious intent, Zoe stepped outside of the pavilion, stretched her hands toward the river, and whispered a single word.

Stop.

Everything came to a halt, or perhaps everything else simply stopped registering on her senses. Noise fell away, cold ceased to matter, there was no such thing as time. As if she had plunged her fingertips into the river, she felt water rising up her arms, silken and cold, covering her palms, swirling around her wrists, inching up her forearms, past her elbows.

Stop, she told it again, having no idea why she was convinced it would obey. She felt a series of splashes—her shoulders were wet with a few drops—but then the water subsided, sloshing around her elbows with a gradually quieter motion.

Below her, the river ceased tumbling over the rocks at the head of the falls. It collected, tame and content, in the wide basin where the racers had come to shore, an eerie silence replacing the roar of the cascading water. But still the unrelenting currents flowed from farther upstream, rippling through the calm pool with visible shivers. And more water poured in, steady and inexorable. *Stay,* Zoe told it. *Go no farther.*

It obeyed, but fresh water still kept coming. Slowly, the river began to rise along both shorelines. The boats at the harbor started to lift above the dock, their loosely knotted ropes drifting free of the gradually submerging poles. Close to three hundred people gathered on the southern shore, watching in stupefaction as the water crept up the slanted bank, and still it kept rising.

Zoe heard, as if from miles away, murmurs of alarm and fear; she caught the small, unimportant sounds of rocks falling and feet skidding as spectators scrambled for higher ground. A voice called one word over and over—was it her name?—but she paid no attention. Someone laid a hand on her wrist but she could barely feel it through the sensation of frigid water swirling around her skin. The river climbed higher.

Out on the still, calm surface of the Marisi, buffeted only slightly by the continuously incoming water, Josetta's boat bobbed as if at anchor a mere three feet from the waterfall's edge. The girl sat motionless on her bench, eyes wide with countless varieties of terror, looking as if she was afraid to draw a breath for fear the extra weight would send her over the rocks.

The boat carrying Nelson and Kurtis and Darien pulled closer and closer, powered by three sets of manic oars. Zoe could see the strain on their faces, in their laboring arms. She couldn't hear what Darien shouted to the stranded princess, but she saw his mouth work, saw him call out words of instruction or reassurance.

Zoe's feet were suddenly engulfed in ice; the ground below her became unexpectedly treacherous. She slipped, stumbling to her knees, bewildered to find herself drenched to the waist in freezing water.

"*Zoe.*" That was Rhan's voice; those were Rhan's hands, under her elbows, forcing her to her feet. Her wet clothing clung to her skin down the length of her body. "Zoe, you have to move up the bank. The water's coming too fast. You have to move away from here."

She shook her head, all her attention fixed on the scene below. Darien was standing precariously in the center of Nelson's boat, reaching for Josetta, trying to convince her to release her death grip and allow him to pull her to safety. It was a tricky maneuver at the best of times; nearly impossible when the person to be rescued was too terrified to move. Zoe had to keep the water as calm as possible. She had to keep it soothed and tranquil under the chilly sun . . .

"*Zoe.* You don't have to stop what you're doing, but you have to *move.* I'm going to pick you up, do you hear me? I'm going to carry you up the bank. Don't fight me. If I don't get you away from here, you're going to drown. We both are."

She shook her head again as if trying to dislodge a troublesome insect, but she didn't resist when his arms closed around her and he lifted her in his arms. Just for a moment, she was just enough disoriented that her control faltered; there was a sudden powerful thrust of current and Josetta's boat rocked crazily in the water. The princess had come shakily to her feet, arms outstretched. The fresh wave knocked her vessel to one side and she lost her balance, screaming.

Darien snatched her as she fell, hauling her into his boat. "Go! Go!" he shouted, and Zoe heard his voice all the way across the water. Kurtis and Nelson bent feverishly to the oars, desperately making for the disappearing shoreline. Zoe felt as if she, too, were bobbing on the water, as if the motion of Rhan's climb mimicked the sensation of perilous floating. She twisted in his arms, keeping all of her attention on the river, her hands still outstretched. She could hear Rhan cursing, felt his feet slip now and then as he splashed up the side of the inundated bank, followed implacably by the encroaching water.

And there. They were safe. Dozens of men met Nelson's boat at the ever-changing waterline; dozens of hands reached out to haul the precious cargo to safety. Josetta was passed from Darien to a servant in royal livery, her body limp but her eyes wide open.

Zoe took a sharp breath and let her arms fall. Her head collapsed against Rhan's shoulder.

There was a shout from the men still climbing out of Nelson's boat and a hurried commotion as they jumped into the fast-receding water, aiming for land. With a giant *whoosh* of explosive sound, the swollen river broke wildly for the freedom of the falls. Noise echoed from every direction as men yelled, boulders rolled, and the plummeting water sucked dirt and plants and stones behind it in a swift, disordered tide. Josetta's boat was the first thing over the rocks and down the glittering side of the mountain.

That was the last thing Zoe saw before she fainted in her cousin's arms.

TWENTY-ONE

"More flowers," Annova said, bearing in an enormous vase filled with yellow blossoms, each one as big as a grown man's hand. It was the twelfth bouquet that had arrived in Zoe's suite that morning, though Zoe had slept through the delivery of the first five. "Where are they getting flowers at this time of year? But they smell wonderful."

She held the vase down so Zoe could sniff the blooms and agree that they were particularly fragrant. Zoe was sitting up in bed, propped against a ridiculous pile of pillows, feeling much too weak to move around the bedroom or get dressed or even get out of bed. It was now a little past noon on the firstday of Quinnelay. She had slept all afternoon, all night, and most of the morning, waking up only briefly several times before subsiding again into exhausted slumber.

Since the remarkable events the day before, she had talked to no one except Annova, although Calvin apparently had been very busy gathering gossip for her. It was Annova who had made the decision not to admit anyone to Zoe's room—not the king, not any of the queens, not her Ardelay or Lalindar relatives—for which Zoe was profoundly grateful. Despite the sleep, despite the bouquets from grateful admirers, she still felt shaky and uncertain and confused.

What had actually happened yesterday on the Marisi? How had she been able to bend the river to her command?

"I'm sure there must be greenhouses somewhere in the city where the wealthy can buy flowers year-round," Zoe said in a faint voice. "Who sent these?"

"Elidon," Annova answered.

Which made sense, since yellow was an *elay* color. The first to arrive—so Annova had told her—had been Seterre's thank-you, a small flowering tree massed with tiny purple blossoms. Seterre had brought it herself, begging for a chance to thank Zoe in person for saving her daughter's life.

"She's sleeping," Annova had said firmly. She had repeated the conversation to Zoe with a great deal of relish. "She was drained almost to the point of death by yesterday's efforts."

"I will never be able to express my gratitude to her—anything she wants from me, I will gladly give it—"

"Thank you, but Zoe Lalindar has everything she needs."

In rapid succession, more tributes had arrived—showy red flowers from Alys, a spray of orange lilies from Romelle, a gigantic vase of multicolored blossoms from King Vernon himself, and smaller remembrances from Mirti Serlast, the Ardelays, and a handful of others.

Zoe was a little surprised, after Annova reeled off the names, to learn that Darien was not among them. Not put out, of course—she had not expected *anyone* except Seterre and perhaps the king to offer thanks. But she had thought Darien might send a note or stop by the room or, in some fashion, express concern for her well-being after such a dramatic day.

Not, of course, that it mattered to her that he had not.

"What has everyone been saying?" Zoe asked Annova as the older woman found a place for the yellow flowers. "What happened yesterday? Why was Josetta alone in the boat?"

"Have a meal first, and then Calvin will tell you everything he knows."

It was the third time Annova had insisted Zoe eat something. Every time Zoe had opened her eyes during the past twelve hours, Annova had fed her small, quick meals before allowing her to fall asleep again. Zoe suspected that this was the reason she didn't feel even worse, though she was wretched enough—sore, exhausted, every muscle stretched and pummeled. She had been surprised, when she checked her skin, to find not a single mark or bruise. She would have sworn her body had been slammed against a wall or rolled down a rocky hill. Her arms and shoulders felt the most abused, aching from the strain of being extended for so long.

As Zoe held back the waters with her own two hands.

How was such a thing possible?

She shivered a little in the bed.

"Have a *hot* meal first," Annova amended. "Would you like another blanket? Should I build up the fire?"

"No—just—I want to hear what Calvin has to say. Please."

Annova relented. "All right. But you must eat while he's talking."

Five minutes later, Zoe was sitting with a tray across her lap, picking at the soup, the bread, the cheese, and the sweets that Annova had provided. Calvin had settled his thin body into a chair at the foot of the bed, as if prepared to stay for a long, entertaining conversation. He was dressed in his usual bright colors, and his face was alight with excitement. Annova leaned against the wall, willing to listen, but mostly focused on making sure Zoe kept eating.

"*What* happened? And what is everybody saying?" Zoe demanded.

"The young princess was too hysterical to talk much yesterday afternoon, so we did not hear her story until this morning," Calvin related in his raspy voice. "But she says that her hired sailors seemed to have trouble from the minute they cast off."

"How many men were in the boat with her?" Zoe asked.

"Two. Apparently it is common for those who hire outside crews to hire them in pairs."

"And what kind of trouble did they have?"

"One dropped his oar, the other steered them into a sandbar, so that before the race was even ten minutes old, they had fallen behind. She was very angry, she says, telling them that they would never be hired by anyone at the palace again and they might not be paid for this day's work."

"I imagine that made them angry as well."

"Maybe," Calvin said. "Once they got free of the sandbar, she says, they made some effort to get back in the race. They rowed hard until they were in a stretch where the river runs very fast and the boat was tossing on the water. Both of the men were on their feet when they got rocked by a rough current. One fell in and the other leapt in to try to save him." Calvin paused for dramatic effect. "Josetta saw both of them get swept away by the river. She thinks they might have drowned. But *she* was carried forward by the motion of the water, unable to help them—or help herself."

There was a short silence while the three of them thought this over. "It seems unlikely," Annova said, "that two professional men would *both* be lost. In such a manner. On a course that is not particularly dangerous."

Zoe nodded. It was exactly what she was thinking. Most men who chose lives at sea had at least some *coru* blood in them, and even though few of them would have the affinity for water that *she* had, not one in a thousand would lose his life under the conditions that had governed yesterday's regatta. "Who hired these men?" she asked. "Her mother?"

Calvin waggled his head in an equivocal manner. "A footman employed by her mother. A *hunti* man who has worked for Seterre's father his entire life."

"So probably he did not betray her," Zoe mused. "Then someone else bribed the sailors to abandon Josetta in the river."

Calvin nodded. "That is what everyone in the palace is whispering this morning."

Annova stirred, stepping away from the wall, her face full of disbelief and perturbation. "But—to desert the princess that way—in wild water—I mean, how could they know you would be able to save her?"

Zoe offered her the ghost of a smile. "They didn't. They expected her to die."

Annova stared at Zoe. Her eyes were a shocked hazel against her dark face. "Someone wanted to murder the princess?"

Calvin was nodding. "Of course, no one is saying so aloud. And it was cleverly done. The queen sent her own man to hire the sailors. They did not boldly leap overboard and swim for shore, but appeared to fall victim to a sad disaster. It *could* all have been a series of mishaps—tragic, of course, but hardly sinister."

"And yet no one believes that," Zoe said.

"No," he said. "Everyone believes someone wanted Josetta to drown."

"But why?" Annova demanded. "And who?"

"Someone who wants to eliminate her as a potential heir to the throne," Zoe said. "Someone who wants to see her own daughter named heir instead."

"Alys or Romelle," Calvin said.

"Alys," Annova and Zoe said at the same time.

Zoe added, "But if *we* think that, and we are practically strangers here, everyone else would also think it."

"They do," Calvin said. "I've heard her name a hundred times today—whispered so softly that you cannot tell who has said it."

"So it might not be Alys after all," Zoe said. "Because whatever else she might be, Alys isn't clumsy. She isn't obvious. She isn't *stupid*."

"Then—someone who wants to make it look like Alys tried to murder Josetta?" Annova guessed.

"I've heard that suspicion, too," Calvin said, almost happily. Zoe knew that he simply loved court intrigue—and the fact that no one had died during this particular bout of scheming made it possible for him to enjoy the situation to the fullest.

"Then Romelle?" Annova said.

Zoe shook her head. "I suppose it's possible, but she's so—*maternal*. You've seen her with Natalie. I can't imagine her harming a child. *Anybody's* child."

"And yet you scarcely know her," Annova said. "Perhaps she would risk anything to give her daughter a better opportunity."

Zoe sighed and nodded. "So what happens next?" she asked Calvin. "What is the king going to do? If everyone in the palace suspects attempted murder, surely there will be an investigation?"

"Oh yes," Calvin said. "And Darien Serlast is the one running it."

"Oh," Zoe said. So perhaps that was why he had no time to come checking on exhausted heroines. He was tracking down would-be killers.

"But no one expects him to discover anything," Calvin

added. "Even if he finds out who the sailors were. Even if they're still alive, they've surely fled Chialto by now. And if no one admits to bribing them, and there is no evidence—" He shrugged. "What can he find out?"

"Maybe nothing," Zoe said. "But maybe that wouldn't be the point. Maybe the point would be for Alys—or Romelle—or whoever did this, to be afraid to try again, because they know everyone is watching. That would at least be enough to keep Josetta safe."

"Josetta *and* Corene," Annova said. When Zoe looked at her, she added, "In case it was Romelle."

"You're right," Zoe said. "Both princesses could be in danger."

"All of them," Calvin said. "In case it wasn't any of the queens. In case it was merely someone who hates the king."

"In which case," Zoe said softly, "none of the princesses will be safe no matter what."

"But the princesses are only part of yesterday's story," Calvin said. "Everyone is talking about *you* as well."

"I'm not surprised," Annova said. "If the description I've heard is anything like the truth—"

"What are they saying?" Zoe interrupted.

Calvin waved his hands in the air. "The Lalindar prime has unimaginable powers! She can stop the river merely by willing it! The Lalindar prime is the one who has ended the drought that has strained the country for the past few years!"

"Is that true?" Annova demanded.

Zoe shrugged. "I don't know. It's true that there was never drought where I lived. But the rain just seemed to follow me. I never consciously called it."

"Well, you consciously stopped the river yesterday," Annova said. "Didn't you?"

"I don't know how to answer that," Zoe said. "I *wanted* the river to stop. I whispered the word. But I didn't think—and it hadn't occurred to me—it seemed impossible that it would do what I said."

"Well, it did," Calvin said, leaning forward. "And everyone is impressed, but everyone is a little uneasy, too. Is it safe for someone to have that kind of power? Some people are afraid."

"I don't know why they'd be afraid of *me*," Zoe said a little petulantly. "From what I've heard, Christara had some power over water as well. And if *I* can do such spectacular tricks, wouldn't you think the other primes have some abilities as well? Maybe Kayle Dochenza can call up the wind, if he likes, and Mirti Serlast can split the trunk of a tree merely by laying a hand upon it."

"I think it is the scale of your power that frightens them," Calvin said. "Stopping a river in its banks? Christara Lalindar never did that."

"Maybe she did, just never in front of anybody," Zoe argued.

"It works out to the same thing," Calvin said.

Zoe shrugged. "So? What do they want? These people who whisper about me. Do they want me to leave the palace? Gladly! Go live in exile? Not a hardship."

"It doesn't matter what they want, does it?" Annova asked. "Aren't you here because the king desires your presence? Then I think you must stay until he asks you to leave."

Zoe sighed and flopped back against the pillows. Impossible to believe, but she wanted to sleep again. Annova hurried forward to snatch up the tray of half-eaten food before it slid off of Zoe's lap. "Well, I don't suppose I have to leave this instant, at any rate," she said. "I suppose I at least will wait to hear what the king thinks about me now."

Or what Darien tells the king to think, she thought drowsily. The smile was still on her lips as she fell back asleep.

King Vernon was the first visitor to her room the following morning. He had sent a note warning them of his impending arrival, so Zoe was up, washed, dressed, and styled before he arrived at her door. She was feeling much better today—ravenous, which Annova took as a good sign, and unexpectedly cheerful. Almost exuberant. The aftereffects of power, she thought. Her father had sometimes claimed that fire acted upon him like alcohol; he could be drunk with sensation if he sat too close to the hearth. She suspected this was her reaction to the demonstration two days ago. Yesterday she had merely been too tired to feel it.

"Majesty," she said, bowing very low when he stepped into

the room. She spotted a contingent of guards in the hallway behind him, though none of them came in with him. None of them was Darien Serlast, either.

"Zoe," he replied, coming close enough to take her hand in both of his. She felt the sudden warm pulse of his blood, familiar from that last time that he had touched her. "I don't believe I can express how deeply grateful I am that you were there to save the princess's life. Josetta is very dear to me. I cannot imagine a world without her in it. By what token will you allow me to express my thanks?"

She shook her head. "I need nothing."

"I have land—beautiful properties in provinces throughout the kingdom—"

She shook her head again. "I am scarcely equipped to manage the Lalindar property that has come into my possession," she said. "I certainly would be a poor landowner for any other estate."

"Money, then—jewels."

"Majesty, I have more than enough of both of those."

"Status," he said, "political power. I could arrange a marriage that would raise you to a position even higher than it is now."

She couldn't help wondering what potential husbands might wield such political clout; surely Darien Serlast was among them? It would be interesting to see how he reacted to the notion that the king regarded him as a prize to be awarded for exceptional service to the crown. But she refused again. "I am not prepared to marry, certainly not for such a reason," she said. "But I do have a suggestion."

"Tell me."

"Take whatever gold you would give me and build a fountain on the west side of the city, where it is difficult to find clean water, because it is so far from the river. Put my name on it, or Josetta's. That would make me happy."

Vernon stared at her for a moment with his sad blue eyes. She thought he might exclaim, *Zoe Lalindar, you are the strangest girl.* It was what any of his wives might say. "I will do it," he said at last, "and gladly."

"Then I am rewarded," she said.

. . .

The king had not been gone more than ten minutes when other visitors began to show up at her door, staying only a few moments, never overlapping. Zoe supposed they all had spies in the corridors, gauging the flow of traffic to her room.

The queens were first, arriving in order. Elidon was elegant and gracious, praising Zoe's strength and steadfastness. "Your grandmother would have been so proud of you," she said softly. "I can offer no higher tribute."

Seterre was fighting back tears, though she instantly lost the battle. "What can I say?" she sobbed, and actually flung herself into Zoe's arms. Zoe murmured comforting phrases, awkwardly patting Seterre's shoulder, but the whole time she was automatically cataloguing the precise composition of the queen's blood. She might never have another chance to touch the fastidious *hunti* woman. "I owe you my daughter's life—I owe you everything—"

"I am only glad I was able to summon such ability."

Seterre pulled back and tried to regain her poise. "Thanks are inadequate," she said. "I must do something to show my appreciation."

She told Seterre about the request she had made of the king. Seterre liked the idea, Zoe could see; the *hunti* were nothing if not practical. "I will have an orchard planted around the fountain," she decided, "and anyone can pick fruit from the trees."

"That would be generous. That would please me," Zoe said.

"Then I will do it."

Alys came flouncing into Zoe's suite, glancing around quickly to assess the furnishings, clearly trying to gauge Zoe's wealth as well as her taste. "You are quite the marvel," she said, not bothering to sit for what was clearly going to be a brief visit. "Everyone is talking about you."

"Not an honor I aspire to," Zoe said gravely.

Alys gave her that rogue's smile. "There is so little *sweela* in you, isn't there?" she said. "Your father or your cousin would be basking in the court's attention, but you just sit in your room and pretend you have a headache."

"I do have a headache," Zoe said. "I developed it just as you walked in."

Alys flicked a spiteful look at her, interpreting that remark exactly as it had been intended. "Let me give you some advice," she said. "*None* of us gets more than one or two grand opportunities in our lives. Chances to remake ourselves, to accumulate prestige and other assets. You'll be sorry if you let this one slip away from you without making it pay off in some spectacular manner."

Zoe wanted to laugh. By Alys's reckoning, that really *was* good advice, and most generously offered. "I will bear that in mind," she said.

Alys laughed and headed for the door. "You won't," she said. "A year from now, you will be gone and no one will remember your name."

Romelle was distracted throughout her short visit, chasing after Natalie the whole time, trying to keep the princess from knocking over pieces of décor. "I'm so sorry!" she exclaimed breathlessly. "I just wanted to tell you in person—Natalie, stop that!—how very wonderful it was that you were able to save Josetta's life. All I could think about was how awful it would have been for me to see *Natalie* in such a terrible situation, and how grateful I would be if you had saved *her*."

Once again, Zoe thought it was utterly impossible that Romelle would willingly put anyone else's child at risk. Alys, she realized, had not said anything along these lines. *I hope you would have saved Corene if she had been the one in danger.* But the first thing Romelle had thought of was her own child.

Natalie knocked a metal vase to the floor, where it spilled water and blossoms in all directions. The little girl started wailing. "I'm so sorry—we'll leave right now," Romelle said. "But—thank you. It was an incredible thing to see."

After the last queen had departed, other visitors began knocking on Zoe's door. Mirti Serlast, Keeli and Sarone, a half dozen others, everyone eager to be associated with the most celebrated woman in the city. Rhan and Kurtis arrived together, Rhan catching her up in a hug and spinning her around, Kurtis more soberly clasping her hands.

"That was an astonishing thing to witness," Kurtis said. "Until my life ends I will not forget the sight of the river refusing to flow because Zoe Lalindar ordered it to pause."

"*I* will not forget trying to persuade Zoe Lalindar herself to climb out of harm's way," Rhan exclaimed. "Did you know she almost *drowned* because the Marisi was rising so fast but she refused to move?"

She laughed. "I don't think it would have harmed me," she said. "Even if I had been swept off the bank, I think I would have survived." She patted his cheek. "But I am very grateful that you watched out for me when I was too absorbed to watch out for myself."

"And we must do more than commend you on your strength and power," Kurtis said with a grin. "We must thank you for most dramatically bringing us back into fashion, since you were in our boat when we won the race."

She smiled. "I'm glad to hear you are popular again, but I'm sure it's because you and your father were in the boat that rescued the princess," she said. "*That* would have rehabilitated you even if I had never reclaimed my Ardelay relatives."

"Perhaps," Kurtis agreed. "And yet, I can honestly say that was not the thought foremost in my mind when I followed Darien Serlast down the riverbank. All I could think about was saving that little girl."

"And that," she said, "is the reason you deserve your new-found respectability."

Well after sunset, at least an hour past the time Zoe had decided that she would see no more visitors for the day, there was a timid knock on the door. Zoe had just sunk to a chair at the dining table, wearied by all the attention, while Annova prepared to serve dinner for the three of them. It would be moderately scandalous for Zoe to be caught sharing a meal with her servants.

"Shall I answer it?" Annova said, her voice barely above a whisper. "Or pretend we didn't hear it?"

Indeed, the knock had been so soft that Zoe suspected the visitor half hoped that no one was home. Which made her curious. "Let's see who's on the other side," she said.

Calvin whisked the plates out of view, while Zoe came to her feet and assumed an expression of saintliness. Annova opened the door.

"Is Zoe Lalindar still receiving visitors?" someone asked in a quiet voice. A girl. "I know it is very late."

Annova stepped aside. "She is. Please come in."

Josetta stepped through the door. Today she looked even more fragile and tense than she usually did—not surprising, Zoe thought, given her harrowing adventure. Her ashy hair was piled sloppily on top of her head and her clothes were decidedly casual. She might almost have spent the entire day sleeping, drugged by exhaustion or some more potent medicine, and just now climbed out of bed to come thank her rescuer.

Calvin and Annova disappeared into their room, though it didn't matter; Josetta had eyes only for Zoe. The princess crossed the room slowly, as if she had just recently relearned how to walk. Her face was pale, completely innocent of cosmetics; her eyes were huge and haunted.

"I just wanted to say thank you," the girl said in a raw voice barely above a whisper. Zoe wondered if she had screamed herself hoarse two days ago as she careened down the river. "I was certain I was going to die. I was so afraid. I could not imagine how anyone could save me. And then when the river stopped flowing—I didn't understand. I didn't know how it had happened. But *you* did it. *You* took the water into your own hands. For me. I can't—I have no words. Except thank you."

Zoe was so touched that she wanted to take the girl in a comforting embrace, but she wasn't sure the extremely breakable Josetta would welcome the gesture. Instead she said solemnly, "I was glad to discover that I had the power to still the Marisi. But others worked to rescue you from the river—three brave men who went into the water to snatch you back from the falls."

"I have thanked them and will thank them again," Josetta said, still in that half whisper. "But it was you who gave them the chance to save my life." The princess extended her arms, thin and shaking. "Please allow me to express my gratitude, once more, with all my heart."

"And with all my heart, I can only say, again, I was glad to be able to play a part," Zoe said. She reached out and took both of Josetta's hands in hers.

Then stood there, stunned immobile, as Josetta bent her head to press her lips to Zoe's fingers.

It wasn't that humble kiss that unnerved her, that sent flame, then shock, then fury through her veins. It wasn't Josetta's mumbled repeat of her thanks that left her completely speechless. It wasn't the princess's quick glance over her shoulder toward some noise in the hallway, her low exclamation of "I must go!" that made Zoe nod dumbly and pull her hands free and stare after the girl as Josetta dashed for the door and vanished.

No—it was the fact that Zoe recognized the blood in Josetta's body. *Sweela* blood, fiery and familiar. Ardelay blood, even closer to Zoe's own than that of Rhan or Kurtis.

Josetta was Navarr Ardelay's daughter.

TWENTY-TWO

It was barely light when Zoe headed down the mountain in a horse-drawn cart that Calvin had coaxed from a royal groom by the payment of a couple quint-golds. She had wanted to leave last night, but it was full dark, she was exhausted, and Annova flatly refused to let her out of the room "no matter what that girl told you that's got you so upset." Zoe didn't confide in her friends; she couldn't bring herself to speak the words out loud. She did consent to eat the meal and stay the night, since Annova made it clear she had no choice, but Zoe made it equally clear that she was leaving the palace the minute she could get free in the morning.

Calvin drove her toward the city down the well-used track that saw a surprising amount of traffic at this unholy hour of the day. Most of it, of course, was headed toward the palace instead of away from it. He didn't bother attempting to make conversation. He merely took her directly to the high-priced hotel she had patronized before she had taken up residence at the palace.

"When do you want me to come back for you?" he asked. He hauled down the single well-stuffed bag she had filled with a few changes of clothes and set it down on the street. She stood beside him, shivering in the cold.

"I don't know. I might not want you to *ever* come back for me."

His wide grin displayed the gap between his front teeth. He had been, on the whole, less anxious than Annova at her sudden and mysterious distress; obviously he believed whatever had unnerved her would eventually be set to rights. "Well, I don't know how long they'll let Annova and me stay in your suite without you, but we'll enjoy it while they do. Then it's back to the river for us!"

"I might—I don't know—it could be time for me to find my own place—here in the city," Zoe said, her speech jerky. "Of course, I will need you both to help me—set up my own household."

He tilted his head, considering her. "I don't think you have any idea *what* you want," he said, his voice so genial it was impossible to take offense. "But we'll be ready when you figure it out."

The excellent hotel servants had already stepped out of the wide glass door to welcome Zoe, bowing low, snatching up her luggage, gesturing for her to come inside. She turned to follow them and then pivoted back to Calvin. "Don't tell anyone where I've gone," she ordered. "Unless—I mean—if someone were to *interrogate* you about my whereabouts, you should not put yourself at risk—"

He gave her a real hug, holding her tightly against his thin chest for long enough that her racing thoughts started, just a little, to slow down. "Don't worry," he murmured. "Whatever it is, worse things have happened."

He made her laugh, and that gave her the strength to draw back and somewhat pull herself together. "Perhaps they have," she said. "I'll have to think that over."

She followed the servants to the *kierten*, a huge echoing space of icy marble and luscious malachite. Twenty minutes later, she was ensconced in a luxurious room decorated all in white. She flung herself onto the bed, which was so plush that she thought she might suffocate. She had lain awake most of last night; a nap now might help her develop perspective on her new reality.

But, of course, she couldn't sleep. She couldn't stop thinking. She couldn't stop picturing her father's smiling face, hearing his deep laugh. He had been so *alive*, so overflowing with vitality; the few times he had been confined to a place for too long, by illness or winter or unavoidable circumstance, he had become so restless he had seemed capable of bringing down the walls by his sheer longing to be free. "Do you know why people dislike you sometimes?" Alieta had said to him once, very dryly. "Because you're uncontainable."

Oh, but there had been other reasons Alieta had disliked her husband—or, at least, had been so furious with him she didn't care if a child could overhear their arguments. *Another one, Navarr? Another lovely* sweela *girl with flashing eyes and racing blood? Why didn't you marry a girl of fire and mind, then, if you were going to spend the rest of your life chasing after them, panting with infatuation?*

Her father's reply: *No* sweela *girl can satisfy me like my beautiful* coru *bride. They mean nothing to me. They are moments of passion and desire. It is you I live for, you I love, you I cannot exist without . . .*

Of course, he had existed without her for twelve long years. It had been hard to tell, because so many other factors might have broken his spirit during his decade of exile, but Zoe had always believed that her mother's death had struck her father to the core. He still laughed at the slightest provocation, talked whether or not anyone was listening, ate heartily, read voraciously, argued enthusiastically, and entertained lovers with little attempt at discretion. But some of that *sweela* fire had gone out of him. He was not entirely whole once his *coru* wife was gone.

Zoe lay on the white bed, practically buried in its dense lushness, and stared at the smooth, featureless ivory ceiling.

It was clear to her now exactly why her grandmother had worked to have Navarr Ardelay banished from the royal court. Sarone had described Christara's fury at learning about one of Navarr's past infidelities. At the time, Zoe had wondered how Christara could have discovered such a thing and why she would have cared once Alieta was dead. But now she understood. At some point, Christara must have touched Josetta's hand or brushed her fingers across the princess's face. Like Zoe, Christara would have automatically assessed and identified the components of Josetta's blood. Like Zoe, Christara would have instantly realized what that blood betrayed.

How long had Seterre been her father's lover?

That was probably not the right question, Zoe realized. More important to know was: Had Alieta still been alive when Navarr took the queen to his bed? Zoe closed her eyes and tried to work out the math. If Josetta was fourteen, going on fifteen, and Alieta had died twelve years ago—no, almost thirteen years by now—

Zoe opened her eyes again. Yes. Her mother had been alive when Josetta was conceived.

And yet, she might not have known the princess was her husband's child. She might not even have known about the affair. Christara, at least, seemed not to have learned of it for nearly three years, though it was possible Alieta wouldn't have confided in her mother anyway, guessing how angry Christara would become. But whether or not Alieta had discovered the affair didn't change the fact that Navarr had betrayed her.

Who else knew the truth?

Seterre, of course, unless she had taken more than one lover during that period of time. Zoe supposed that Seterre might think it just as likely that the king had sired Josetta.

Unless she had not had conjugal relations with her husband at the right time to conceive the child. Unless the king was impotent, and Seterre knew it.

Zoe's mind went back to that first sweet, almost rueful conversation she had had with the king shortly after she arrived at the palace. They had talked, toward the end, about Navarr Ardelay, and Vernon had made that odd comment. *I always wish I'd been able to tell him that I forgave him. I always wanted to know if he'd forgiven me.* It seemed obvious he hoped Navarr had forgiven him for the banishment, but for what act had Vernon forgiven Navarr? Taking his wife as a lover and getting her with child?

"Vernon knows," Zoe whispered.

It would be awfully hard for a king to forgive the man who had made him a cuckold—unless the king desperately wanted an heir and could not sire one himself.

Zoe turned on her side and sank into the thick, pillowy folds of the comforter. She stuffed the material under her cheek and strained to think this through. If the king needed another man to impregnate his queen, he might have explicitly invited Navarr into Seterre's bedroom. But if that was the case, why had he allowed himself to be turned against Navarr, who had, by a certain kind of reasoning, done the king a tremendous favor?

If the king was impotent, who had Alys and Romelle taken as lovers to produce Corene and Natalie?

And who else knew?

"Darien Serlast," Zoe said aloud.

She considered that for a moment. Darien had claimed he had no idea what the king meant by his obscure talk about forgiveness, but Darien was as likely to speak a falsehood as the truth, so Zoe brushed that aside. Darien was constantly at the king's side; he provided counsel on matters as unimportant as which buckle the king should choose for his boots. Darien almost certainly was aware of the king's problems in the bedroom—perhaps he even helped orchestrate the queens' visitors in the middle of the night. It could not be an entirely easy thing to slip men into and out of the women's wing—or arrange for the queens to make nocturnal visits to other bedrooms.

Zoe closed her eyes again. She didn't want to think about the king's difficulties in the bedroom and what his closest advisors might do to alleviate them. She didn't want to picture her father as Seterre's lover. She didn't want to know that shy, uneasy, anxious Josetta was her half sister. She didn't want any of this in her head. She wanted to sleep, and she wanted to wake up with her mind completely empty.

But she didn't sleep and her mind kept filling and refilling with the images she could not keep away.

Sighing, she finally pushed herself to a sitting position and then struggled to stand, barely able to fight free of the deep mattress. It was a crisp, cold Quinnelay day. She would distract herself with a visit to the Plaza of Women.

Accordingly she dressed in some of her heaviest garments and her sturdiest shoes, wrapping a scarf around her head and draping a wool overrobe around her shoulders. She felt better almost as soon as she stepped outside into the breezy sunshine. The walk to the Plaza of Women was longer from this direction than from the riverfront, but Zoe didn't mind. It felt good to move her body toward a productive end; living in the palace, she had lost all incentive to exercise. When the wind blew, she drew her scarf more tightly around her face to keep out the chill, and she strode a little faster.

The blind sisters were not particularly busy this morning. Zoe had to wait only a few moments until one of them was free, and then she settled herself in front of the large, serene woman.

"I have a question," she said and handed over a gold piece.

The seer fingered it to verify its authenticity, and even her composed face showed astonishment. "Something worth this much to you is something I might not know."

"I realize that," Zoe said. "But I will pose the question anyway."

"Go ahead."

Even so, she hesitated a moment, uncertain of what to ask or how to phrase it. Finally she said, the words halting, "King Vernon has four wives and only three children. Is there some thought—has anyone ever said—might it be possible that those daughters are not his own?"

The blind sister held out her hand and Zoe dropped another gold coin in the palm. A ridiculous sum to pay for a question she could answer for herself, but she was curious to learn if anyone else in the city knew the truth. "Now and then, over the past fifteen years, there have been whispers," the seer said, speaking so quietly that her own voice might have been a whisper. "Questions. Why aren't there dozens of royal heirs running through the palace? Is the king unable to sire children? If so, who fathered those three girls?" She shook her head. "Nobody knows for certain."

Zoe frowned. "Not much information for my two gold pieces."

The seer leaned forward. "Eleven years ago—almost twelve years by now. A man came to me. He was drunk. He was giddy. He claimed that his daughter had just been born, and that she had been endowed with the blessings of imagination, intelligence, and courage." The blind sister paused to let this information sink in, but it was not hard to put those pieces together. Those were the blessings claimed by Corene. "He said that the girl's mother was married to another man—a powerful man—and that he would never be able to claim his daughter as his own."

"Did he tell you his name?"

"No. But he had the shape and scent of an *elay* man."

"Was he telling the truth?"

The seer shrugged. "Insofar as I could determine, he was telling me something that he believed. That might not mean that it was true."

Zoe nodded. "And the king's other two daughters? Has anyone else claimed to be their fathers?"

"No," the sister replied. "There have been questions raised about them, but never any answers."

It was paltry, insufficient, and frustrating information, but Zoe spoke her thanks anyway and rose to her feet. Well, she hardly knew *more* than she had before, but she thought her suspicions had been corroborated. The king probably had not fathered any of his daughters, and a few of his subjects guessed as much, but there was no proof and no absolute knowledge. Therefore, the world went on as it had before. Only Zoe's world had changed—again.

She wandered around the Plaza for another hour, merely to give her mind something to focus on, trying on shoes and robes and bracelets and deciding none of them suited her. She ate the entire contents of a bag of lemon candy, which unfortunately neither improved her mood nor settled her mind. Neither did the purchase of a bright red scarf or a pair of brown leather gloves. She was out of balance; she needed a calm place where she could think.

Or not think.

This realization reached, she wandered with a little more purpose, searching for the elegant temple located in this district, though she tried three wrong cross streets before she found it. The instant she stepped into its scented warmth, out of the nasty wind, she felt a tranquility settle across her like a shawl draped over her shoulders. She paid the tithe at the door and then moved as quietly as possible to sit on the blue bench before the *coru* glyph.

About ten other people were inside the temple at this hour, three of them grouped on the white *elay* bench, three of them pulling blessings from the central barrel, and the rest scattered about on the other seats. An acolyte moved soundlessly around the perimeter, extinguishing guttering candles and lighting new ones, radiating an air of contentment and peace.

Gradually Zoe felt her muscles relax, her hurt and confusion start to drain away. In the temple, this was the gift of *coru*; it washed you clean of worries. Your troubles were carried away in the river's insistent hands.

She passed next to the *elay* bench, now conveniently deserted as the other congregants moved on. This was always the element that spoke to Zoe the least, conveying as it did a sense of spirituality, occasionally even visions; she did not seem prone to such things. But *elay* also equated with hope, a renewed belief that the world could be restructured or at least comprehended, and Zoe let these thoughts rise to the forefront of her mind while she sat perfectly still, inhaling the spiced air. Yes—of course—she was puzzled now, a little lost, but eventually the world would make sense again. She had been lost a time or two before in her life, and she had always found her way.

The *hunti* pew, which she chose next, was painted a handsome ebony and seemed to be so solidly bolted to the floor that no catastrophe could budge it by so much as an inch. Zoe felt herself grow stronger, surer, as she sat before the sigil for wood and bone. Her spine stiffened; she drew herself up taller. She had survived so much already. How could she allow herself to be knocked askew by a piece of old knowledge, a fact that scarcely mattered, and that certainly changed nothing? She would not.

Four other congregants were sitting on the green *torz* bench when Zoe made her way across the temple floor, but they slid aside to give her room. It was always the way when you sat and contemplated the symbol for flesh and earth, her father would say, heartily complaining. You were squashed up against a half dozen other visitors, begging each other's pardon, trying to hold your arms tightly to your body so you didn't brush against anyone else. But that was the *torz* gift—connection to humanity, connection to the world. You might apologize for bumping into your neighbor, but then you would smile, you would whisper a comment about the weather. You would feel human again, part of the great, messy pageant of life. You would cease to feel so alone.

Zoe remained for a long time in the *torz* section, trying to muster the resolve to move on to *sweela*.

Where her father would linger, if his spirit were ever to make its way to a temple.

The other congregants shifted and re-formed around her; some left, new ones came in, and yet Zoe stayed where she was, staring at the red pew just a few feet away. She was not startled to feel a touch on her arm—there were, after all, six people currently crowded beside her—but she was a little surprised to find that the woman next to her was smiling in a knowing, encouraging fashion.

"I'll walk over and sit with you, shall I?" the woman whispered. She might have been in her eighties, a frail, tiny thing bundled in so many scarves and overrobes that her clothing probably outweighed her body. "It will be easier then."

"It's not that I'm afraid of fire," Zoe whispered back. "It's that someone—my father—"

"My father was *sweela* as well," the old woman replied. "And I always prefer to take a friend when I go to sit on the red bench."

The kindness was irresistible. Zoe found herself smiling. She held out her hand, and the tiny old woman took it in a comforting grasp. Zoe felt the thin, shredded journey of blood in her veins, a complex mix of heritage and experience. "Then let us go together to confront our fathers," she said.

They had the *sweela* seat to themselves; it tended to be a place where only certain people paused for long. Despite her new friend's reassuring presence, Zoe felt some of her tension return as she sat before the slashing sign for fire. *Sweela* was not a restful element at the best of times. It exhorted you to feel, to care, to think, to love, even to remember. Zoe closed her eyes and unlocked her heart and let her mind flood with images of her father. Laughing. Arguing. Dancing with her mother. Flirting with a strange woman. Reading by candlelight. Listening to music. Meditating. Sleeping.

Coughing. Suffering.

Dying.

It was impossible, but that great fiery soul had been extinguished, and now all that was left of him were Zoe's memories—and Navarr's two very different daughters.

But *she* was alive, filled with her own flickering light, her own restless desires. She was not all *coru*, as she had pretended these last few ninedays. Her own heart could be reckless; her own mind could be clouded by emotions. That did not just mean she was her father's daughter; that meant she was alive.

Beside her, the tiny woman sighed and released Zoe's hand. "Not so bad after all, is it?" she whispered. "I always feel a little more *energetic* once I've faced down the mind and the fire."

Zoe laughed softly. "That's why we visit the temple," she replied. "To put ourselves back in balance."

"Have you pulled your blessings yet?" the woman asked, coming to her feet.

"No, have you?" Zoe said, standing alongside her.

"Let us do that together as well."

They waited until a heavyset young man finished tossing through the coins, obviously seeking specific ones, and then they approached the barrel. The woman was so diminutive she looked as if she could comfortably fit inside it.

"Would you choose my blessings for me?" she asked Zoe. "I find my life is much more interesting when someone else makes the selections."

"Gladly," Zoe said, and quickly pulled out three pieces.

Her new friend looked inordinately pleased. "Joy, charm, and time," she said. "I do not believe I have ever been more felicitously blessed. What happy traits to take out with me into the world!"

"Forgive me if I do not ask your intercession in return," Zoe said. "My life has been so complicated lately that I am not eager to give over to a stranger even the smallest detail."

"I felt much the same way when I was your age," the woman replied. "Shall I leave now or do you want me to stay and support you?"

Zoe laughed softly. "I don't think I need support any longer, but you may certainly stay and watch."

Zoe dipped into the cool pile of metal and let the disks slide through her fingers until her hand, almost of its own volition, closed over a coin. She pulled it up and showed it to her companion.

"Surprise," the old woman said.

"Accurate as always," Zoe replied in a dry voice. She dug through the heap of coins again, and pulled a second *coru* trait. Resilience. "Well," she said on an exhaled breath, "I hope that is true."

The third blessing was change. "Am I right in guessing you are *coru*?" the old woman asked.

"Yes," Zoe answered, "though usually my blessings are a little more evenly distributed."

"Try again. Three more."

But the next three were *coru* traits again—and the next three—and the next. Zoe felt herself shivering a little even in the warm, aromatic air of the temple.

"I thought I had brought myself back into balance," she said in a low voice. "Perhaps I need to meditate again before each element."

"Perhaps you have, after all, achieved balance," the old woman suggested. "But your destiny still lies with water."

Zoe glanced down at the twelve coins in her hand. "Or with blood."

Her new friend waved off Zoe's offer to see her safely home—in fact, there was a carriage awaiting her outside the temple and a concerned coachman to help her inside it. Just as Zoe had suspected; a woman of some wealth, possibly even from one of the Five Families, though Zoe had not recognized the composition of her blood. She grinned to herself as she waved goodbye. It would have been entertaining to realize she had struck up a friendship with, say, Seterre's mother or Mirti Serlast's aunt. She thought it was better for their acquaintanceship to end in anonymity.

The temperature had dropped at the urging of a northern wind, and Zoe made the return trip to the hotel at a walk so brisk it barely avoided being a run. Night was not far off. She began considering what she might do for an evening meal, since the lemon candies had been tasty rather than filling. The hotel might have a place to recommend; otherwise, she would have to find warmer clothes and go out exploring.

But it was clear as soon as she stepped into the *kierten* that she would not be foraging for dinner on her own. Darien Serlast stood in the empty high-ceilinged room, his arms crossed, his expression forbidding. It looked like her main course for dinner would be an argument.

TWENTY-THREE

Zoe did not attempt to speak first. She just came to a halt in front of Darien and waited for him to berate her.

"I thought I made it clear," he said, his voice clipped and his arms still pressed to his chest, "that I would *appreciate* it if you would not relocate from the palace without first apprising me of your intention. I thought I made it clear that the king himself desires your ongoing presence in his life. I know you consider your restrictions chafing but your duties have not been onerous, so I am mystified as to why you suddenly find yourself anxious to slip away, in secrecy, without a word to anyone."

She was pleased that her own voice sounded calm—that, in fact, she remained composed, unmoved by his anger. "And I thought I made it perfectly clear," she replied, "that I am not particularly interested in being governed by your wishes. *Or* the king's. As long as it suits me to stay at the palace, I will. When it does not, I will leave."

"As you *have* left?" he demanded pointedly.

"I have not moved here permanently. Most of my belongings remain in my suite at the palace. Surely your spies verified that before they sent you chasing after me."

"Your servants are still in place, it is true," he said stiffly.

"But they seemed singularly ill-informed about your future plans."

Zoe found herself wondering if Darien had interviewed Calvin and Annova himself. She hoped so. Calvin would have enjoyed the experience hugely, while Annova would have been fascinated to observe Darien's strangely possessive attitude toward Zoe. *There* was a conversation Annova would certainly want to have someday soon.

"My future plans depend to a large extent on you," she said. "Or, more precisely, the answers you give me to a few key questions."

He jerked his head back; she saw wariness cover his face like a mask. "What questions?" he asked.

She glanced around the *kierten*. There were maybe a dozen people inside, hovering near one of the tall glass doors or crossing the polished marble floor, hurrying in or dashing out. "Are you certain that this is the venue to discuss sensitive matters?" she inquired in a provocative voice. "*I* have no secrets, of course, but *you* might."

Alarm briefly changed his expression, though it quickly settled back to guarded neutrality. "We shall go to my lodgings," he said. "We may speak there in perfect privacy."

"Gladly," she said. "I admit to some curiosity about the sort of place *you* would consider home."

He offered her his arm and she took it, shallowly pleased that, despite his anger, he was still willing to extend the courtesy. In a few moments, they were settled into his *elaymotive*, which he drove himself. She was grateful to discover that the vehicle had an internal heating system that negated the power of the rising wind—and surprised to see how far they had to travel. Darien Serlast did not keep lodgings in the elite section of town where Zoe's hotel was located and where the Five Families had their homes. Instead, it turned out he owned a tall, narrow house, on a street of tall, narrow houses, in a far western section of town that crowded between the boundaries of the Cinque and the canal. The buildings were similar in size and structure, yet appealingly idiosyncratic—some built of wide, sleek slabs of patterned stone, some constructed of brick and roofed with clay, some graced with whimsical statuary at the eaves, some covered with vines, some stark, some ornate.

Darien Serlast's house was made of wood painted in rich red earth tones. The scrap of yard between the street and the front steps was not large enough to sustain a tree, but he had planted the whole expanse with hardy shrubs whose thin, tough limbs had woven into an impassable tangle. Zoe suspected it took a gardener the better part of an hour every day to keep a passage cleared from the street to the door.

"The house of a *hunti* man," she said as he helped her out of the smoker car. He did not bother to answer.

The small *kierten* featured wood parquet flooring and walls covered with stained oak paneling. Darien did not offer to give her a tour of the house, just escorted her through one of the three doors that led off the *kierten*. It opened into a comfortable room filled with bookcases and worn furniture.

"Sit down," he said. "I'll build a fire."

She sank into a deep leather chair near the hearth. It was chilly enough in the room that she could see the exhalation of her breath.

"You don't keep servants here?"

"Someone comes by every day to make sure all is in order, but no, most of the time the house stands empty," he said. He was kneeling on the floor, not seeming to care that he was getting dirt on his silken trousers, and building a fire with as much speed as any *sweela* man. "Normally I give my housekeeper some notice if I am planning to spend any time here, so the place has a more welcoming air."

"How much time *do* you spend here?"

The fire caught quickly and began arcing with its usual joy over the carefully laid fuel. Even so, Zoe couldn't imagine the room would warm up soon. She edged her chair closer to the blaze.

Darien sat back on his heels. "Not as much as I'd like," he admitted. "Someday, when my responsibilities at the palace take less of my time . . ." His voice trailed off and he shrugged. "But for now, I like to remain within easy reach of the king whenever I can."

"So there's no food in the house," Zoe guessed.

He laughed, his gray eyes snapping with amusement. "Are you hungry? You should have told me to stop for a meal."

"Maybe our conversation will go so quickly that you will return me to my hotel before the dinner hour."

"I doubt that somehow." He stood up. "There's likely to be bread and fruit in the kitchen. Shall I go hunting?"

"Let's talk first," she said.

He dropped into another chair set before the fire, turned at a friendly angle toward hers. "Why did you run away?"

She leaned back, pretending to be at ease, but every nerve was taut as if braced for some trauma she couldn't quite identify. "Why did you make me do something so drastic merely to catch your attention?"

He looked briefly thunderstruck before quickly wiping his face clear. "If you wanted to talk to me, you merely had to send a message."

"Everyone else in the entire palace, in the entire *city*, came to my door yesterday," she said, exaggerating only slightly. "To express astonishment at my powers and offer thanks for my actions. But there was no word from you."

"You can hardly think that means I place no value on what you did," he answered sharply.

"Or that you feel no worry about how well I recovered from such an immense outlay of energy."

His eyes were narrowed, intense, as he weighed the meaning behind her words. "What is it that you want from me?" he said bluntly. "Praise? Adulation? Concern? Only let me know, and I will try to produce the proper emotion."

She leaned forward, unable to feign serenity much longer. "You watch me night and day. You probably knew within the hour that I had moved from the palace to the city. You have made yourself my guide and, to some extent, my friend. And yet, when we both participate in a dramatic and potentially catastrophic event, you do not turn to me to share your reactions, to admit your own relief and terror, to inquire after mine. You vanish. You stay away."

"I am surprised to learn you consider me a friend," Darien said, but she ignored him, since it was obvious he was trying to divert her from her central point. Her fingers tightened on the worn leather armrests of the chair.

"What question do you not want me to ask you about Josetta's terrible ordeal on the river?" she demanded.

He answered with silence and another glare.

"'Who tried to kill the princess?'" she asked. "Because both of us know that it was most definitely an attempt at murder."

"That's it, of course," he said. "The question I do not want you to ask."

"You don't deny someone wants her dead."

He shook his head. "It's possible that it is not the first time someone has tried to kill Josetta."

Zoe felt her stomach clench. "What? No one else has mentioned—"

He waved a hand. "There was an accident. A year ago. She was riding in a smoker car, and its gas canister exploded. The driver was badly burned, and Josetta badly frightened, but she was not injured. At the time I was suspicious and I made pointed inquiries. But I could discover nothing particularly damning, and I did not voice my suspicions to anyone."

"Have Corene and Natalie ever been in danger?"

"Not that I am aware of."

"Then why Josetta? And who would want to harm her?"

Darien shook his head again. "I have a dozen men scouring the docks at the southern port where her crew members were hired. So far, I have turned up nothing. Of the two men who abandoned Josetta in her boat, one has a sister. Though she claims she has not seen her brother in a couple of quintiles. The other appears to have no family in the area, and his three closest friends shipped out a nineday ago on a trading vessel. I will keep searching."

"Who would want Josetta dead?" Zoe repeated.

He gazed back at her. "Someone who does not want her to inherit her father's throne."

"Alys," Zoe said flatly.

She had thought he would protest or at least manufacture some outrage, so his answer surprised her. "She would be the obvious choice, but public assassination is not her style. Poison, maybe. Suffocation. I would not put it past her to harry Josetta into killing herself, but to murder her before an audience of hundreds? Alys is too clever to take such chances."

Zoe laughed softly. "I did not realize you disliked her as much as I do."

"Even more," he said with a certain grimness. "And I say that without even knowing how deep your animosity runs."

"Then if not Alys, who?"

"If I knew that, I would have brought the scoundrel to justice and you would not have had to flee the palace to ask me uncomfortable questions."

She smiled a little and dropped back into the chair. "I am glad you realize I have more than one question."

"I was sure you would. I am nerving myself for the possibility that each one is worse than the last."

"That may very well be," she said. "My second question is: How many people know who Josetta's father is?"

Staring at her, Darien was so completely silent for so long that she could hear the occasional bright *pop* of the fire over the continuous low ruffle of flame. Finally, to prod him into speaking, she added, "I presume *you* know?"

"Why would you have any reason to suspect it is not Vernon?"

"The man has four wives and three children," she said. "It takes no great leap of imagination to deduce that he either has no desire for women—or little ability with them."

"Even so—I'm not sure why you think—"

She extended her right hand, fingers spread, and turned it this way and that as if examining it for blemishes. She was still cold; her rings were loose around her icy fingers. "Something I learned once I became prime of Lalindar," she said in a conversational voice. "Something perhaps Christara would have told me if she had had a chance to prepare me for my role." She leaned forward suddenly and placed her hand across his arm where it lay, tense and immobile, on the armrest of his chair. Through his silk and wool she could feel his *hunti* bones and his *coru* pulse. He did not move so much as an inch. "I can touch every man and woman in the city—*every* man and woman—and tell you something about their blood. I can identify them. I can sort them into families."

She tightened her fingers around his wrist. Even if she hadn't been able to tell it by the expression on his face, his clamoring heartbeat would have told her he was horrified. "Josetta came to my room last night and took my hand," Zoe said, her voice almost a whisper. "And I knew instantly that she was Navarr Ardelay's daughter."

"Ahhhhhhhhh—" he breathed, and dropped his head heavily against the back of his chair. Otherwise, he sat unmoving; he did not try to pull his hand away. "I knew that was how Christara had learned the truth, but it had not even occurred to me that you—" He seemed unable to finish.

She was relieved that he did not try to deny it. She did not blame him—much—for trying to conceal the truth from her, but she would have been bitterly disappointed if he had kept trying to pretend at this juncture. "I have made some strange discoveries since I became prime," she said. "I hope this one is the most astonishing—but I entertain fears that something worse will reveal itself at a not too distant date."

He opened his eyes and fixed his gaze on her again. "And do you, like Christara, now despise Navarr for what you have learned about his royal infidelity?"

"A little," she admitted. She released him and settled back against the cushions of her chair. "I am furious with him for so many reasons, and more reasons accrue almost every day! He lied to me on so many fronts, on matters great and petty, that I am beginning to think I did not know him at all. I can understand why he did not want to discuss with me his liaison with the king's wife and the child it produced—but I am not sure how quickly I will be able to forgive him for thinking it was acceptable to have such a liaison in the first place."

"Which I think is exactly where Christara came in," Darien murmured. "And she did *not* forgive him. She destroyed him. But you do not have that option."

"If he was alive, I might have abandoned him at this point, tired of one too many betrayals," she said. "But I do not have that luxury now. I must understand him and accept him, or lose even my memories of him. And I am not prepared to do that—not now. Not yet. Perhaps not ever."

"I do not think," Darien said, "you should consider it a weakness if you still love him. But I am sorry you had to learn something about your father so greatly to his discredit."

"Which brings me again to the question you have not answered," Zoe said. "How many people know the truth?"

He hesitated a moment, as if thinking even now he might avoid answering her, and then shrugged and capitulated. "It might be no more than five still living," he said. "The king, Seterre, Elidon, me—and now you."

"It is obvious why the king and Seterre know," she said. "But I am not certain why you were included in the knowledge. Or even Elidon."

He rubbed a fist against his forehead, as though his head hurt. She wouldn't be surprised if it did; she wouldn't even be sorry. "It's complicated," he said.

"Let me tell you what I have surmised," she said. "At some point—whether during his first marriage or his second—the king comes to realize that *he* is the one who is sterile, not his brides. But he wants children—he wants his subjects to perceive him as a virile, vital man. So he enlists the aid of a trusted advisor to act as his substitute in the marriage bed. It would not have been difficult to gain my father's consent to such a project. Quickly enough, the queen becomes pregnant. Elidon's status as barren wife is cemented, while Seterre and Vernon celebrate their fertility. Josetta is born and all seems well. Until Christara discovers the truth and threatens to publish it. The king appeases her by banishing Navarr."

"That outline is generally correct," Darien replied.

"But it doesn't make *sense*," Zoe said. "If the king was complicit in the affair, he would have found a way to protect my father. He would have found a way to silence Christara. If nothing else, by telling her the truth!"

He eyed her soberly. "What you don't realize is that the truth would not have mattered to Christara. Navarr Ardelay had been unfaithful to her daughter—one last time—and her daughter was dead. She could not forgive that, and the urgent necessity behind the infidelity was lost on her. The queen needed a lover to produce a child? Very well, there were any number of men in the city who could have fulfilled that role, men who were *not* married to Alieta Lalindar. Christara was filled with spite and rage, and she was determined to bring Navarr down. She began to criticize him publicly and privately—she opposed his every political proposal; she cast doubt on his character. But it wasn't until she began whispering of treason that the king was forced to act."

Zoe stared at him. "*Treason? My father?*"

He nodded. "The king's only child was in fact Navarr Ardelay's daughter. What if he made a bid for power? Tried to depose the king, set himself up as regent? It wasn't so far-fetched. At first, Christara whispered these accusations only to Vernon and Elidon. But as her whispers grew louder—and she threatened to reveal the truth about Josetta to the rest of the court—Vernon finally had no choice but to send Navarr away."

"I'm surprised no one thought my father would strike back by revealing the truth about Josetta anyway."

"It was a risk," Darien admitted. "But everyone knows a discredited man is liable to lie, and Seterre had no incentive to corroborate him. No, it seemed safe enough to banish him, despite the great service he had rendered his king."

Zoe drew a long breath. She felt as if her mind had been shattered into fragments that would not be reassembled any-time soon, and once they were, the images in her head would bear little relation to the ones she had carried with her since childhood. Everything was changed; every*one* was changed.

"Given all the trouble it caused him to sire Josetta," she said, "why would the king go through it all again to give Alys a child? And then Romelle?"

The look on his face was almost comically alarmed. "Have you made any discoveries regarding Corene and Natalie?" he demanded.

"No," she said, and was annoyed to see him relax as if he had been reprieved from death. "But I cannot imagine that *they* are Vernon's any more than Josetta is. So, after all the trouble surrounding my father's disgrace, why did the king again take the risk of finding lovers for his wives?"

"That was Elidon's influence, I think," Darien replied. "She didn't like the idea that Seterre would be the only queen to bear an heir. She also didn't like the thought that Navarr might tell his brother the truth, and Nelson would try to force concessions for the Ardelays. Elidon has always been very interested in maintaining a balance of power, and she did not want Seterre—or the Ardelays—to wield too much."

"It still surprises me that Elidon was included in this conversation at all."

"Elidon has always been the king's closest confidante," Darien replied. "I think it is she who urged him to share his queens with proxies in the first place."

"Did she also pick the proxies?" Zoe asked. "Who were the others? Don't tell me you don't know."

Again he was silent a moment, as if he wanted to disclaim any knowledge, and then he made a tiny gesture of surrender. "In fact, I am not certain, but I can tell you the likeliest candidates," he said. "I have always thought Wald Dochenza might be Corene's father. He was much at court during that time, and clearly infatuated with Alys. Shortly after Corene was born, the Dochenzas entered a period of unparalleled prosperity. The king extended for another hundred years their property rights to a stretch of land where they mine their compressed gas—which has made the Dochenzas extraordinarily wealthy."

If Wald had been Alys's lover, it explained why the queen had so much hatred for poor Gildis Fairley, whose only crime had been a rumored liaison with the Dochenza man. But at the moment, Zoe had little interest in Alys or sympathy for her victims. She could think only of her father and the injustice done to him. She could not keep the bitter tone from her voice when she said, "So *this* time, the man who is presumed to have bedded the queen is considered to have rendered a valuable service to the crown," Zoe said. "*This* time his family is rewarded, not banished."

"It is very unfair, I know. If it mollifies you at all, the king was very grateful to your father until Christara took a hand."

She shook her head, as if to say it didn't matter, though it did. "Who is Wald Dochenza?" she asked. "Kayle's son?"

"His nephew. A dreamy young romantic who didn't realize that Alys would discard him once she had achieved her purpose."

"I don't think I've met him in Chialto."

"Perhaps not. He comes to the city only rarely. Alys claims she never sees him, but, of course, I always assume everything she says is a lie, so who knows?"

"What about Princess Natalie?" Zoe asked. "Who is *her* father?"

"I don't even have a good guess for her," Darien said. "But I have always thought it was a man picked out by Taro Frothen.

If you want to make sure someone conceives a child with a minimum of fuss, you could hardly do better than ask the *torz* prime to find her the right partner."

"It makes sense," Zoe said. "Since Seterre is *hunti* and my father and Alys are *sweela*—this would be a very good time to bring *elay* and *torz* men into the mix."

"Yes, I have always thought that was Elidon's reasoning," he replied. "If she indeed had a say in determining the queens' lovers. I find it hard to believe Alys, at least, would bed any man on Elidon's recommendation. In fact, I heard whispers that Alys enjoyed her extramarital relations a little *too* much, not confining herself to one man."

"Then no one can be certain Wald Dochenza is truly Corene's father."

Darien studied her a moment in silence. "I beg you will not take it upon yourself to discover the truth one way or another. As Corene cannot possibly be your father's child—and neither can Natalie—I do not see that it can matter to you at all."

She almost smiled. "I have an affinity for blood, which gives me an interest in bloodlines," she said. "But Corene is even less open to casual contact than Josetta, so I do not imagine she will be allowing me to touch her hand anytime soon. And I have no interest in holding Natalie, who is always throwing a tantrum."

"I wish I could say that put me at ease."

Now she did laugh, very slightly. She was feeling so crushed it was hard to allow herself to expand to humor. "One thing I still don't understand," she said. "Why are *you* among the ones who knows the truth about Josetta?"

"Because my father knew," he said wearily. "He helped set up the assignations in the palace. Your father would arrive on the pretext of visiting mine." He shrugged. "I was a young idealist then—barely eighteen—and I believed that our secret work was essential to the preservation of the crown. Who knows? Maybe it was. But I would not be so eager to pursue such activities now."

"Another thing surprises me, at least a little," she said. "Seterre does not behave oddly around me at all. Oh, she pretends to want to be my friend, and she brings up my father's name now and then, but she does not seem—*self-conscious*, I suppose I mean. If *I* was trying to make idle conversation with my former lover's daughter, I think I would be nervous and strange. And if I had truly loved him, I would be affectionate and emotional. But that is not the sense I get from her at all."

"As to that—" He hesitated, then spread his hands in a gesture of uncertainty. "As to that, it is possible she does not know that Navarr Ardelay was the man in her bed," he said.

"But surely—"

"My father said that Navarr was brought to her in a great deal of stealth and that Elidon impressed on both of them the value of secrecy. He said that Seterre played along, agreeing to wear a blindfold and never ask her lover's name, but— well—no one was in the room with them when they . . . when they carried out their task." He risked a quick look at her; she was surprised to see him blushing, embarrassed by the specifics of the conversation. "I don't know if Navarr was the kind of man who would enter into the spirit of such intrigue—"

"Oh, he was *exactly* that kind of man!" Zoe exclaimed. She knotted her hands to keep from clasping and unclasping them; she had grown a little calmer as they discussed the role of other people in that bedroom farce, but once they were focused on her father again she found it difficult to sit still. "He loved secrets and disguises and puzzles and tricks. It would not surprise me at all to learn he entered the room wearing a mask and speaking in an assumed accent! He would be *delighted* with such a part! And then, the following day, to sit beside her at a formal dinner and speak casually of inconsequential things—nothing could have entertained him more."

Darien nodded. "So. It is possible that Seterre is not dissembling when she treats you as the daughter of a man she liked, but did not know particularly well. Your next conversation with Seterre may well be strange to *you*, but she will not know why you are suddenly ill at ease."

She knew what he would say, but she could not resist the temptation to bait him. "So then you think I shouldn't mention to her that I have discovered her secret?"

He sat up so suddenly that his chair rocked; she thought it might turn over. "Of course you shouldn't!" he exclaimed. "Why would you—"

"I never liked being an only child," she said, still deliberately provoking him. "And now to discover that I have a half sister—"

"You cannot claim her," he said. "You can befriend her, if you like, if your attentions do not seem too singular, but you cannot expose her. Zoe, you cannot."

"Why not? Where is the danger? Where is the harm?" She made an indecisive motion. "In fact, perhaps such an announcement would *avoid* harm. If it was revealed that Josetta was not the king's daughter, perhaps she would no longer be in danger. Perhaps she would be removed from the succession. She would be safe. Although, the corollary questions would soon arise—and I imagine life at the palace would get *very* interesting for all the wives—"

He leaned forward now, elbows on his legs, linked hands between his knees. "You're joking," he said, keeping his voice steady with what seemed to be an effort. "You're just tormenting me. You wouldn't do anything so catastrophic."

She tilted her head. "You ascribe to me more kindness than I might possess. I have been exiled from society too long to care about other people's scandals."

"You have suffered too much for your father's actions to want to see other girls put through a similar kind of disgrace," he said sharply.

She shrugged and flopped back against the chair. Suddenly she was so tired. It was amazing how much energy it took to juggle rage and humiliation and astonishment, particularly for someone who hadn't slept very well. "The truth is, I don't care about this knowledge within the context of the palace walls," she said. "I don't care who is king and I don't care who is heir. I don't care what families are in favor and what families are banned from court. I am angry at my father and curious about my sister, and none of the rest of it matters to me."

"Then will you promise—"

"No," she cut him off. "I won't promise anything. It wouldn't matter to me if you were to lie awake every night wondering what I might do or say next. But I see no *value* in rearranging the lives of every child living at the court or exposing the lies of the king and his women. If I ever do, you can be certain that I will speak up, no matter who bids me keep silence."

Darien said nothing for a moment, as if she had proposed a deal and he was considering its terms. Finally he nodded. "I suppose that is the best I can expect you to offer."

"I suppose it is."

"Is there anything you would ask of me in return?"

Zoe watched him a long moment. That narrow face did not look so arrogant now; she could not think *he* had had an easy time of it these past few days, either. He had been one of those frantic men on the boat, rowing desperately to Josetta's rescue, and he must have spent hours questioning anyone who could have been implicated in the attempted murder. No wonder he had been short-tempered when he confronted her after her sudden disappearance. And her revelations tonight had unquestionably added to his mound of worries.

She didn't feel sorry for him, though. He could choose to trust her. He could choose to confide in her. He could choose to tell her secrets that, even now, she was sure he kept. He would find any *coru* woman much more manageable if he worked with her instead of attempting to block her at every turn.

"Is there anything I would ask of you?" she repeated. "How about dinner?"

The transformation of his face was amazing to see. The weariness dropped away, making him appear much younger; the laughter warmed his gray eyes, softened his stern mouth. "Dinner I will be happy to provide," he said. He came to his feet and extended his hand. "Come. I know just the place to take you."

She allowed him to pull her up, but he did not immediately drop her hand. For a moment, they stood unexpectedly close, hemmed in together by the placement of the chairs before the fire. It was the first time all night that Zoe had felt warm.

"I *was* moved and astounded by your ability to control the Marisi on changeday," Darien murmured. "I was never so afraid for anyone in my life as I was for Josetta when I saw her floating down the river. I knew she would die. I knew there was no saving her. And then you—" He shook his head, apparently unable to find words. "I would have come to you the next morning—before you were awake, even!—to express my gratitude and amazement, but I had already left the palace. I headed straight to the southern harbors, and I didn't get back until a few hours ago."

Only to find that Zoe had fled the palace. She began to feel a *little* sorry for giving him something else to worry about. Another detail to take care of, when it was clear he was responsible for so many.

"I would have asked, as soon as I saw you, how you had recovered from the ordeal, for I saw you carried away in your cousin's arms. I knew such an immense effort had drained all the strength from your body. I would have come to you, anxious and frantic. I just didn't have the time."

He lifted his free hand to brush her cheek with the very tips of his fingers. She felt the blood leap to her skin, right where he had touched her, eager to be touched again. "I am hopeful that your impressive act of bravery did not permanently damage your body or your power. But here you are. Scheming to enrage me and making me chase you all over the city. I cannot think you suffered any lasting harm."

She had to laugh. "Bank the fire," she said, freeing her hand and pulling away from him. "I am still making up for all that energy so recklessly expended, and I am very, very hungry."

TWENTY-FOUR

Zoe was back at the palace a nineday before she had an opportunity to speak to Josetta alone. In truth, she barely spoke to *anyone* alone for that period of time, for she was still being honored and feted to a degree that was almost tedious. She was included at the king's table every night, except the one when she pretended to feel too ill to partake in the meal. She was invited to breakfasts with the queens, lunches with members of the Five Families, excursions with anyone who set foot outside the palace. Keeli begged her to attend a "small get-together" at Sarone's house, where nearly two hundred guests were in attendance—and Zoe was obviously the one they had all come to see. Two days later, Kurtis repeated the invitation, almost down to the wording. Zoe did not mind spreading whatever cachet she had over her cousins on both sides, but the rest of it wore her down. She wanted to burrow inside her suite and refuse to come out, or run to the city and camp by the river where no one could find her.

Well, no doubt Darien Serlast could find her. If he had time to look. After their extraordinary conversation at his house, he had made no effort to seek her out. He was present at many of the events, of course, sometimes meeting her gaze and grin-

ning a little; he knew this degree of polite socializing did not
come easily to her. But he did not rescue her or try to smooth
her way.

Zoe kept mulling over how to seek out Josetta without ap-
pearing too forward or too peculiar but, in fact, the princess
herself solved that problem by showing up at Zoe's door one
morning. It was still early in Quinnelay, but the day, though
cold, bid fair to be gorgeous; the air already appeared to sparkle behind a flirtatious sun.

As always, Josetta seemed to feel awkward, but determined
to play the correct part. "My mother told me that the two of
you discussed the proper way to memorialize my recent accident," she said formally. "And I wondered if you might like to
see the park where my father will build a fountain and my
mother will plant trees."

"I most certainly would," Zoe said. "When would you like
to go?"

"I am free now if you are."

"Free" apparently did not mean "unaccompanied," for a
maid and two guards awaited the princess in the hall and fell
behind her, once she and Zoe emerged. Although Josetta did
not pause to speak to her retinue, Zoe was pleased to notice
that she didn't treat them as if they were invisible, either. She
nodded at them all and said, "I have a car waiting downstairs."

The *elaymotive* was big enough to seat eight or ten and
roomy for the five of them. Unexpectedly, it *did* offer a little
privacy, for the car featured two chambers separated by a thick
glass wall. Zoe and the princess sat in what was obviously the
more luxurious compartment.

"Have you recovered from your adventure?" Zoe asked.
"Or do you still have nightmares about almost drowning?"

Josetta gave her a sharp look. "How did you know about
the nightmares?"

Zoe smiled. "I have had an adventure or two myself. I find
I relive them for a long time in my dreams."

"They haven't been so bad the past few nights," Josetta said.
"But I am certain of one thing. I'm never getting in a boat
again!"

"Oh, now, that's exactly the wrong thing to decide," Zoe
said. "You should arrange for outings in dozens of boats! On

lakes and on rivers, in still water and wild. You should swim every day—do you know how to swim?"

Josetta shook her head. Her blue eyes were huge.

"You should learn. If you master the water, you will never fear it again. And the nightmares will almost certainly go away."

"Even if I could swim," Josetta said, "*nobody* could have survived a fall over the mountain. Could they? Even a *coru* woman like you?"

"Well, I would have jumped out and made for shore long before I pulled too close to the waterfall!" Zoe exclaimed. "I know the river is rough along that whole stretch, but there are places a strong swimmer can leave a boat and make it to safety."

Josetta was silent for a moment. "Like *they* did," she said, her voice subdued. "Jem and Nic."

"Who?"

"Those were their names. They *said* those were their names," Josetta amended. "The sailors on the boat with me."

Zoe was impressed that Josetta knew that particular detail. She was willing to bet Corene, Seterre, and Alys had not bothered to inquire into the identities of their own hired rowers.

"You think they jumped out and abandoned you on purpose?" Zoe asked quietly.

Josetta nodded. "I didn't. Not at first. But then I heard people whispering—talking—saying what must have happened, and I realized they were right. Alys said—"

When Josetta abruptly fell silent, Zoe prodded, "What did she say?"

"She said people had wanted me dead since the day I was born."

It was in moments like this one that Zoe was most aware of her *sweela* heritage. Her rage was so sudden and hot that if the redheaded queen had been anywhere in her vicinity, Zoe would have slapped her until Alys was dizzy. "I hope you realized she didn't mean they wanted *you* dead," Zoe said, her voice as gentle as she could make it around the angry singing of her blood. "She meant that *every* princess—and every queen, and every king, too—is always somewhat at risk. There are always malcontents who think the world would be a better place if someone else was in charge. So they try to get rid of the people who are already in power."

Josetta absorbed that new thought for a moment. "So then, someday people might try to hurt Corene? Or Natalie? Just because they're princesses and not because—not because they don't *like* them?"

"That's exactly what I mean," Zoe said briskly. "It's scary, I know. But that's why you have guards." She nodded at the men sitting on the other side of the glass. "And that's why you need to learn useful skills so people find it harder to hurt you. If you can swim, you won't drown if someone throws you in a river. If you can build a fire, you won't die if someone abandons you in the wilderness. You might even enjoy learning such things."

"I've always been a little afraid of the water," Josetta said thoughtfully. "But if I could swim—I suppose I could practice in the lake by the castle. Oh, but people would see me and make fun of me. And the water's always so cold, even in summer."

Zoe grinned. "You need to learn inside a heated room, in private, where no one can watch you."

"I don't know any place like that!"

"I do." She tapped her chest. "*Coru*, remember? My aunt Sarone has a pool in her house right here in the city. You can learn there."

"Will she mind?"

"Will she mind doing a favor for a princess of the realm?" Zoe demanded in such an incredulous voice that Josetta laughed. "She'll be thrilled!"

"And will she teach me to swim, do you think?"

"No," Zoe said, "*I* will."

The park where the new fountain was under construction was—as Zoe had requested—in a seedy part of town where such amenities were rare and would be desperately welcome. However, that didn't mean she wanted Josetta to get out of the smoker car and stroll around the site, muddying her fine shoes and exposing herself to the dangerous-looking characters lurking nearby. So they instructed the driver to circle slowly three times, while Josetta described the design of the fountain and the planned layout of the orchard.

"And because the fruit won't be ready this year, my mother and I will deliver baskets of oranges and apples and pears every nineday during Quinnahunti and Quinnatorz," Josetta added as they signaled the driver to be on his way.

"That's generous," Zoe said.

Josetta glowed. "Do you think so? It was my idea. My mother said I could do whatever I wanted."

"I think you will bring great good to people who can use it most."

There was no way of knowing if Sarone would welcome visitors at this particular hour, but they decided to go by the Lalindar town house just in case Sarone was home and bored. Admonishing Josetta not to be disappointed if they couldn't go swimming this time, Zoe left the princess in the car with the guards and approached the door by herself. Servants hastily summoned her aunt, who stepped onto the porch and gazed with great curiosity toward the car.

"Really? You've brought Josetta *here*? But, Zoe, how delightful! Of course she can come in! I just had the water cleaned yesterday and I was thinking about taking a dip this afternoon, but it's not nearly as much fun to be there by myself and Keeli's gone for the afternoon. She'll be so jealous when she learns who came by to visit."

"Well, if Josetta really sets her heart on learning to swim, Keeli will have plenty of opportunities to get to know her," Zoe said. "Excellent! I'll bring her in."

The water feature at the Lalindar house was magnificent, and Zoe was not surprised that Josetta stared at it in wonderment. It had been designed to resemble a lush, unspoiled mountain pool surrounded by scented shrubs and grasses speckled with wildflowers. The clear surface of the water revealed a stone floor painted to look like river rocks, and the pool itself was fed by an artificial stream that bubbled over a fall of mossy boulders. No matter what the outdoor weather was like, inside this room it was steamy and warm; a combination of condensation and plant growth obscured every inch of the glass panels that enclosed the space.

Josetta stood wide-eyed and openmouthed, taking it all in. "I've never seen a place like this," she said at last.

Sarone laughed merrily. "No, it's a little outrageous, isn't it? My grandmother commissioned it before I was born. We've all added our own touches—do you see the little birds, way up high in the branches? I brought those in. Once they're used to us being here, they'll start chirping. I find it very soothing to swim to birdsong."

"It must cost a fortune to keep the place warm in the winter," Zoe said.

Sarone nodded vigorously. "Oh, it does! But I've found that heating it with Dochenza compressed gas is much cheaper than heating it with wood. It's an indulgence, of course—but such a *lovely* one."

Josetta glanced down at her clothes, which Zoe guessed probably cost more than a quintile of heating the pool. "What do I wear in the water?" she asked.

"When I am alone, I sometimes swim in the nude, but I would certainly not expect you to do so," Sarone said. "I have plenty of swim clothes on hand—I keep them in all sizes to fit unexpected guests."

Josetta glanced behind her, where her attendants waited on the other side of the glass door that separated the pool from the house. "Do you have clothes they can wear, too?"

"Your guards?" Sarone asked, a little startled. "I assure you, you are quite safe in my home—"

"Oh, I'm not afraid," Josetta said swiftly. "I just thought they would enjoy it." She glanced back at the water, rippling faintly from the constant flow of the stream. "It looks like there would be enough room."

Sarone glanced at Zoe, her eyebrows lifted slightly. Zoe thought she could read her aunt's expression. *A princess who cares about her common subjects. That's a rare creature.* "Indeed," Sarone said briskly, "there is water enough for all."

It turned out to be the most enjoyable hour Zoe had spent since she had returned to Chialto. The maid and one of the guards declined the offer of changing into swimming attire, but they did roll up the hems of their trousers and sit on the banks of the pool, kicking their feet in the heated water. Sarone, Zoe, Josetta, and the other guard—Foley, who, as it happened, already knew how to swim—changed into outfits that modestly covered them from neck to midthigh while leaving their arms and legs free. All of these ensembles tied at the waist and seemed to repel water with some efficiency, but Zoe couldn't say they were particularly flattering.

Josetta had been alarmed to learn there was no part of the pool shallow enough to stand in, but Zoe and Sarone eased her into the water, one on either side of her, and showed her how to kick and how to breathe.

"This pool is so small that you can't get far enough away from me to drown," Sarone told Josetta cheerfully. "If you feel yourself going under, don't panic. Zoe or I will be at your side in seconds."

"Or I will," Foley said.

Zoe glanced at him. He was keeping a respectful distance away, treading water in the center of the pool, but she guessed he could reach the princess with a few quick strokes. The arms revealed by his borrowed suit were impressively well-defined. "I wouldn't have taken you for a *coru* man," she said, "but you look awfully comfortable in the water."

"*Torz*," he said. He didn't grin; he didn't look like a generally lighthearted man. He looked serious and practical. At some point in his life, it must have seemed to him practical to learn this particular skill, so he had studied it till he mastered it. That life hadn't been overlong, Zoe judged. She thought he might be eighteen or nineteen years old.

"Too bad you weren't in the boat with the princess during the regatta," she said.

Foley pressed his lips together and didn't answer, but Josetta spoke up. Her blond hair was plastered back from her face, making her look even younger than her age and more vulnerable than usual. "I wanted him to be," she said. "He was last year."

Last year, when the princess *didn't* almost drown. "So why not this year?"

"My mother had already hired the sailors, and there was only room for three," Josetta said. "She thought I had a better chance of winning if both rowers were professionals."

"I suppose she's learned there are some things more important than winning," Zoe said.

"I suppose," Josetta said. She had been holding on to the lip of the pool, but now she ducked her head under the water, moving her arms and legs in practice strokes before surfacing again. "Let me see if I can make it to the other side by myself."

"I'll swim alongside you," Zoe said.

"Go past me," Foley said. "I can help you if you're in trouble."

Josetta dipped her head in the water again, as if trying to wet her hair enough to keep it out of her way. "All right. Watch me."

The princess splashed a lot, and her kicks were erratic, but she made it across the water without needing help from her instructors. "Excellent! Very smoothly done!" Sarone called, clapping her hands. "Now back to me."

But Josetta had to pause a moment to celebrate. "I did it!" she exclaimed, clinging to the stone border on the other side. "I didn't think I could! It's always so hard for me to learn new things but—I like this! This is easy!"

Lazily kicking her feet to keep herself afloat, Zoe smiled at the princess. "I'm glad you're enjoying this. You must always respect the water, of course—always, even in a controlled environment like this one—but if you do, it can be a powerful friend."

Josetta nodded, listening, but her eyes were already on Sarone, measuring the distance between them. "Come back to me!" Sarone called again. "We'll have you cross the pool a few more times, until you start getting tired."

Josetta laughed, a small, happy sound that Zoe didn't remember hearing before. "Oh, I don't think I'm going to get tired of this for a long time."

O f course, the princess found herself immensely weary when she pulled herself out onto one of the artfully placed boulders some time later. "It's the water," Sarone explained, bringing over a towel to start drying Josetta's hair. "It takes your weight for you. You always feel dreadful when you first get out, but you'll feel better soon enough. In fact, the more often you swim, the stronger you'll feel in general."

"I'm so hungry," the princess exclaimed, and then looked mortified. "I'm sorry! I'm not asking you to feed me—"

But Sarone was laughing. "Swimming always leaves me ravenous," she confided. "I would have been astonished if you *hadn't* been hungry. Food is on its way."

"How can I thank you for giving me such an enjoyable afternoon?" Josetta asked.

"By coming back, of course," Sarone said promptly. It was clear she had gauged the princess correctly; Josetta could not bear to push herself where she was not welcome. "I will be offended if you don't!" She gestured at the royal retinue. "All of you. Come anytime. I will leave orders that you are to be admitted even if I am not here." She bent a stern look on Josetta. "But you are not to climb into the pool without me or Zoe or Foley with you. Not until I decide you are skilled enough to swim on your own."

"Oh, I wouldn't *think* of trying it by myself," Josetta said earnestly.

"Good. Then you may come whenever you like."

As soon as they had blunted their hunger on Sarone's excellent selection of breads and cheeses, they redonned their formal clothes. Zoe just let her damp hair hang down her back to dry as it liked, combing it out once with her hand. But Josetta's blond locks twisted into messy curls as they started to dry, and the maid had quite a time trying to tame them into something more presentable.

"Start wearing your hair in a braid coiled into a knot on the back of your head," Sarone suggested. "Very practical for a swimmer."

"*Not* practical for a girl who's nearly fifteen and who must present a certain appearance at court," Zoe said firmly. "So make sure you don't go swimming on days it matters what you look like."

Finally, they had restored themselves as best they could and were back in the car, heading up the mountain. Josetta chattered for the whole ride back, as animated as Zoe had ever seen her.

"I liked your aunt so much! She seems like such a warm person. Is she always like that? Or was she just being nice to me because I'm a princess?"

Zoe had to smile. "I think that is who she genuinely is, but I'm sure she never forgot for an instant that you're a princess. I'm afraid that's the way things will always be for you. You'll find it difficult to know who is being kind to you because kindness is in their hearts or because they think it will win them favor."

Josetta thought this over a moment, some of her exuberance fading. "So are you saying I cannot trust her? I thought, since she is *your* aunt—"

Zoe leaned forward, catching Josetta's hands in hers. For a moment, she was almost overcome with the implications of that touch, the familiar rhythm of the blood dancing through Josetta's veins. "I have not been at court long enough to know who *I* can trust," she said quietly. "I have led a strange life, much of that time isolated from my own family, and it is hard for me to tell sometimes who wishes *me* well. I would not want you to trust anybody merely because they are related to me, or because you met them in my company. I do not know enough to be able to guarantee that *anybody* is safe for you."

Josetta absorbed this in silence, her face very sober. She made no move to pull her hands from Zoe's grasp. "Can I trust *you*?" she asked at last.

Zoe's breath caught so hard that for a moment, her ribs hurt. "Yes," she said, when she could trust herself to speak. "To never offer you harm and to keep you from harm if it comes from someone else and I have any power in my body to shield you. I will swear that before the booth of promises in the Plaza of Men, if you like."

But Josetta's face had relaxed into a smile. She leaned back into the plush cushions of the carriage. "I believe you," she said. "I don't require any vows."

Zoe released her and settled more deeply into her own cushions. This city car was nearly as comfortable as Darien Serlast's opulent travel vehicle. "Judging by what I saw today, you can trust Foley, too," she said.

Josetta nodded. "Yes. I always feel safe when he's nearby. I never leave the palace without Foley."

Zoe was certain she should offer some kind of sisterly advice at this juncture. *Be careful about how much you come to rely on one particular man,* perhaps, or *Do not lose your heart*

to a lowly soldier who has clearly already lost his heart to you.
But she did not speak the words. If someone in the city wanted
the princess dead, Josetta's best defender would be a besotted
guard who would give his life to protect her.

And if, a few years from now, Josetta gave him her affection in return, well, Zoe was hardly one to be outraged by that.
She knew, as few others did, how impure the royal bloodline
already was, and she had little reverence for societal conven-
tions. Princess or no, queen or no, let the girl love where she
would. When Zoe got a chance, she would tell her sister exactly that.

During the following few ninedays, Josetta and Zoe made
a half dozen trips to Sarone's house. After that first visit,
Keeli made sure she was always present, and she quickly became a favorite with the shy princess. Zoe had to smile to
watch them together. Keeli loved fashion and beauty, and she
took it upon herself to recommend colors, clothes, and hair-
styles to Josetta that the more conventional advisors at the
palace never would have suggested. Keeli even collected products that would smooth Josetta's hair once it came drenched
out of the pool, and glittering accessories that would pin the
recalcitrant curls in place. Eventually, Josetta looked better
after their swims than before them, and all due to Keeli's ministrations.

"I like that little sparkly hair thing you got for Josetta," Zoe
said one afternoon as they all freshened up after a swim. "She
can wear it tonight at the dinner. It's going to be very fancy."

Visitors from Soeche-Tas had arrived the day before—not
the viceroy himself, but two of his top advisors and their
wives. From what Zoe could determine, they would be entertained for every minute of the next nineday while they were in
Chialto. She was very annoyed about it, since she was expected
to attend most of the planned events.

"I'm so jealous that you get to go!" Keeli exclaimed. "My
mother and I have been invited to the luncheon the day after
tomorrow, but it won't be as exciting as tonight's meal. What
are you planning to wear?"

"I don't know yet. I haven't had time to buy something new,

so Annova is trying to pull together an outfit from older pieces that I have never worn together."

Keeli was horrified. "You can't do that! It has to be something no one has ever seen!"

"Well, no one from Soeche-Tas has ever seen me in *anything*, so I don't suppose it matters."

Keeli was shaking her head. "No, no, no. It matters. Trust me. But I have just the thing for you to borrow—I bought it because it was so beautiful, but it doesn't fit me, so it's never been worn. You can have it."

Zoe laughed. "All right. But only if you let me buy you an outfit next time we go shopping. And only if I like the one you're foisting off on me."

She loved it, of course. Keeli's taste was unerring. This ensemble was cut from a shimmering cloth woven of metallic threads in shades of emerald, sapphire, and gold. If the light hit from one direction, it appeared to be printed with a motif of twisting vines. If the light hit it another way, the cloth showed a pattern of flowers and birds. There was no other ornamentation. The cut of the overrobe was severe—very straight lines down the front, down the arms, and along the hem, which fell to Zoe's knees.

"Oh, I'm going to have to break some fashion rules and wear this more than once," Zoe said as she gazed over her shoulder at her reflection, moving just enough to cause the design to shift from vines to blossoms.

Keeli's voice was smug. "I thought you would like it. You'll look perfect tonight."

TWENTY-FIVE

It was hovering near dark as Zoe and Josetta left Sarone's house and arrived back at the palace, which was cutting it close. Both of them knew that consequences would be dire if they missed the dinner with the Soechin guests. Elidon had made that clear over breakfast when the queens discussed how they would entertain the ambassadors' wives.

"If they have any notion of fashion, we can take them to the shop district," Alys had said.

Romelle was leaning over the table, resting her forehead on her hand. "I'm not taking them anywhere unless I feel better tomorrow," she said.

"I was sick two days ago!" Seterre exclaimed. "It was horrible. But it passes quickly."

Elidon had fixed Romelle with a cold gaze. "You will be well enough to join our guests for dinner tonight," she said. She had lifted her eyes to stare at each of the wives and princesses in turn. All of them were gathered around the breakfast table, but none of them was feeling too sorry for Romelle, who was always complaining about some headache or stomach disorder. "Every one of the king's wives and daughters will attend, dressed for the occasion and looking their best. No excuses are acceptable."

Next, Elidon pinned Zoe with that icy stare. "*You* must be

present as well," she added. "All the primes will be at the dinner and introduced to the envoys. Kayle Dochenza has traveled in from the southern ports merely to be at this dinner. Taro Frothen arrived last night."

Zoe raised her eyebrows. "And Nelson Ardelay?" she asked.

Elidon's expression was unreadable. "To be seated at the table next to the king's."

Well. This *was* a critical occasion, then, if the Ardelays were to be treated like honored citizens. "Then I'll be there," Zoe said.

And, thanks to Keeli, she would be impeccably dressed.

Once the royal car arrived at the palace, Zoe and Josetta hurried through the crowded *kierten* at a pace scarcely slower than a lope. Foley was a step ahead of them, clearing people out of their way; a second guard and the maid hurried to keep up.

"At least your hair is already done," Zoe said on a breathless laugh.

"It will take me an hour to get dressed. My tunic has all these buttons and laces."

Zoe grabbed her hand and squeezed it. Partly because she had learned Josetta liked physical reassurance, though the princess would never say so aloud. Partly because she still got a shock of satisfaction at feeling that familiar blood pulse for a moment against her skin. "You'll manage. Try to enjoy the evening. Maybe you'll get a chance to speak Soechin to one of the ambassadors."

"I know! That's what I'm hoping."

They parted on the broad stairwell in the women's quarters, Josetta and her entourage heading down the corridor on the second floor, Zoe continuing up another flight. Annova would be scolding her the minute she opened the door, since Annova put far more effort into Zoe's appearance than Zoe did.

"I'm sorry!" she was saying as she stepped into the suite. "We swam for a little longer than we planned, and then—"

Her voice trailed off the minute she saw Annova's face, drawn into a curious expression of rage and apprehension.

"What's wrong?" Zoe demanded.

"I was only gone an hour and when I got back—"

"What? What happened?"

"Your clothes—all of them—someone's been in your suite—"

Zoe tossed her bundle impatiently to a chair and strode past Annova into her bedroom.

Which now resembled the scrap room of some very busy tailor.

The bed, the floor, the side tables, the chairs—every surface was covered with bits of shredded cloth, the frayed edges glittering with gold thread, dangling sequins, and knots of dyed embroidery. Every tunic, every pair of trousers, every overrobe from Zoe's closet appeared to have been slashed and reslashed, hacked into ribbons of fabric, then churned together in a muddled heap. Some piles on the floor were five and six inches deep.

Zoe's first thought was that she could hardly believe she owned so many clothes. Her second thought was that someone had deeply misjudged how much she cared about material possessions.

"Everything, I'm guessing?" she said in a faint voice.

Annova nodded. "Except your shoes. I don't know why they were left untouched."

"I suppose whoever did this thought it might be amusing if I came to the dinner naked, but wearing expensive footwear."

"It's not funny!" Annova exclaimed. It was sometimes hard to read emotion on Annova's dark face, but the anger was perfectly visible right now. "Someone has targeted you—sabotaged you—"

"Tried to make sure I couldn't go to the dinner," Zoe agreed. She knew she was supposed to be more upset, but she couldn't see this as a catastrophe; it hadn't hurt her in any way that mattered to her. "Apparently, to not attend tonight is tantamount to insulting the king and his very important guests. And if I have no clothes—"

"Oh, you'll have clothes," Annova said. "I sent Calvin to the Plaza with strict instructions on what to buy. It won't be fancy, it won't be fashionable, but it will be *something*."

Zoe couldn't help but be amused. "What, you wouldn't let me borrow something of yours? I like that gold overrobe with the river embroidered on the back."

"Ripped in half," Annova said shortly. "And everything else in my wardrobe."

Now Zoe did feel a spurt of rage. "Everything *you* own as well? That's thorough!"

"That's spiteful, that's dangerous," Annova said impatiently. "Someone hates you. Which worries me more than a little. How did they get in? I know the door was locked."

"There are extra keys. Darien Serlast told me that the day we arrived. And—" She shrugged. "There are people who are not defeated by a lock."

"Well, I am not defeated by malice," Annova said briskly. "Sit down and let me start on your hair. We'll do what we can before Calvin gets back."

Now Zoe started laughing. It was too ridiculous. It was too petty. Surely one of the wives had ransacked her room, hoping to keep her from the banquet and perhaps spark a minor scandal. The Lalindar prime absent when all other primes were present to greet the envoys! Probably not sufficient to get her exiled from court, but certainly enough to cause a buzz of unfavorable gossip. But her adversary had made two mistakes.

First, today of all days, Zoe had an alternative to wear to the banquet—something lovelier than anything she already owned.

And second, Zoe didn't care. About the clothes, the dinner, the ambassadors, her social standing. Any of it. She could leave it all behind right now and feel light of heart.

"You don't have to worry," she said, speaking through her mirth. "My cousin lent me an outfit to wear to the dinner. *Much* nicer than anything Calvin will be able to find, though I greatly appreciate his effort. I just wish whoever did this hadn't ripped up all of *your* clothes as well."

Annova sank onto the bed, sending a colorful dusting of decorative beads into the air. "You know that I never buy anything I love too much to lose," she said. It was true; too much loss and too little acquisitiveness had made Annova notoriously careless about possessions. She fretted far more over Zoe's things than her own.

"So we'll survive this disaster with our self-worth intact," Zoe said, flopping down on the bed next to Annova. Instantly she was covered with bits of thread and a few jagged shreds of a green overrobe. "But now the question is: Who did this? And why? Was this just spite, or a real attempt to harm me and my standing at court?"

"I'll have Calvin ask around," Annova said. "But—"

"But anyone who would plan something like this would probably be too careful to leave clues," Zoe said.

"That's what I was thinking."

Zoe toed a pile of diaphanous cloth swirling around her ankles. "I suppose my old beaded shawl is somewhere in this whole mess," she said with a sigh. That would be an actual loss; there were still a couple dozen gold and silver coins sewed into the border. Not that she needed the money these days, of course, but it made her feel safer to know she had a secret cache of funds that she could draw on during an emergency.

Annova tilted her head, thinking. "I'm not sure," she said. Jumping up, she went to a chest where Zoe's underthings and sleeping shirts were stored. "I didn't keep it with your fancy robes and tunics, because it's not something you'd ever wear at court, but—ha!" She turned back to face Zoe, her face triumphant, the sparkling scarf stretched between her spread hands. "Something you care about that the thieves didn't get after all."

Zoe was absurdly pleased to find the shawl still whole, still jangling with its cheap charms. "Well, I think they tried very hard today, but they didn't succeed in any of their goals," she said. "They won't keep me from attending the dinner. They won't force me to be embarrassed by my attire. And they haven't destroyed anything that matters to me."

Annova brought her the shawl and Zoe wrapped it around her head, just to feel its familiar weight, just to hear the cheerful clinking of the beads. For a moment she closed her eyes, thinking how much simpler life had been when this item was the only thing of value she owned.

Then she stood up, tossed the shawl to the bed, and said briskly, "We'd better start getting me dressed. Obviously, this is one night I can't afford to be late."

There were too many people present at the dinner for Zoe to ascertain if any of them looked disappointed when she showed up, on time, and dressed in the height of fashion. By the time she was able to sort through the crowd to locate Alys—whom she considered the likeliest suspect—everyone had been ushered into the great dining hall and seated. The queen had had ample time to see Zoe and recover from any frustration she might have felt.

The banquet was a dazzling affair, and Zoe had to admit to a certain traitorous relief that she hadn't had to attend it in the plain, loose-fitting tunic and overrobe that Calvin had managed to obtain on such short notice. People would certainly have noticed. Everyone else wore gaudy silks, expensive imported fabrics, robes and tunics so heavily embroidered that they might be wearing wall tapestries thick enough to hold back a draft. She thought there must be enough money in the room—just in jewels and cloth-of-gold—to buy a fleet of Dochenza cars and a housing structure for them made out of imported marble.

No one she knew was seated at the table with her, and she was too far away from the central dais to get a good look at the guests of honor. So she spent the entire meal trying to keep a gracious expression on her face, responding properly when anyone spoke to her, and hoping she didn't spill anything on the one good piece of clothing still in her possession.

Through the welter of people in their expensive outfits, she did get a few glimpses of the royal table. One showed her Josetta, earnestly carrying on a conversation with a thick-bodied man dressed in a flamboyant and unfamiliar style—one of the ambassadors, Zoe surmised. She hoped the princess was practicing her Soechin and impressing the ambassador with her fluency. Another glimpse showed her Alys, moodily silent, staring back at her through the throng of diners. Zoe lifted her water glass in a silent toast, and the queen turned away without a flicker of response on her face.

Another time, she caught sight of Darien Serlast standing beside Alys's chair as if he had come over to greet her before the evening was done. He was bent down, listening, as she stretched up to whisper something in his ear. One of her hands clutched his arm where it rested on the back of her chair. While Zoe watched, he made no move to straighten up or pull away.

He did not particularly look like a man who hated the queen

as much as he'd claimed. Yet another lie from the Serlast man. Zoe turned her attention back to her food, though her appetite was entirely gone.

She was surprised, once the meal was over, to be approached by one of the royal servants. "Please, you will come with me," he said, so she rose and followed him, mystified but maintaining her look of composure. They crossed the echoing *kierten* to enter the men's wing, where he ultimately delivered her to a small chamber that reminded her of her green sitting room back in Christara's house. It was decorated more sumptuously, in shades of silver and icy blue, but it was obviously meant to be a comfortable place for intimate gatherings.

Mirti Serlast was already there, as was Nelson Ardelay. Zoe was relieved to see her uncle, and immediately crossed the room to stand in the shelter of his shadow. "What's this about?" she asked him in a low voice.

Grinning hugely, he gave her a quick hug. "A chance for the five primes to meet in private with the ambassadors," he said. "It's a chance for us to ask them about their lands, and form opinions of their honesty, and later be able to advise the king on his relations with them."

"I have always had mixed opinions about the people of Soeche-Tas, and my brother unequivocally disliked them," Mirti said in her gruff voice. "I welcome the notion that Vernon will hear opinions other than mine when it comes to dealing with them."

Zoe felt a slight alarm. "I am not used to forming opinions about *anyone* and then urging them onto someone else. Particularly when it's this important."

Nelson grinned at her. "It's always important."

The door opened and two more men stepped in. They were both strangers to Zoe, but it wasn't hard to guess their identities. The big man with the weather-beaten face, unremarkable brown hair, and clear disdain for fashion must be Taro Frothen. He looked like a creature made entirely of soil and clay—a little dull, a little slow, but powerful. Patient. The thought came to Zoe that he could wait a decade to destroy his enemies, but when he had the chance, he would crush them under his relentless weight.

Then he smiled at her, and she saw the other side of the *torz* personality—not charm, no, but a certain earthy appeal. "You must be Zoe Lalindar," he said, lumbering over and offering an enormous hand. She liked the methodical, assured way the blood pumped through his body. She liked its potent mix of useful chemicals and dormant beauty. "I had heard you were back in the city. I'm Taro."

"I haven't seen you here before, I think," she said.

He shrugged those massive shoulders. He was at least six inches taller than she was and maybe three times her body weight. "I don't have much interest in court matters," he said. "I don't care who is in favor and who is disgraced. In another few seasons, another few cycles, all of them will be nothing but dust anyway. Forgotten, and all their petty strivings forgotten, too."

She laughed. "I must confess, that is a philosophy that appeals to me," she said. "It lightens my heart to think I might do no deep and lasting harm during my brief time in this world."

"You could still do some harm," he said. "But in the end, all the works of men tumble down and fall away."

"I believe that," she said. "But I also believe it is important to bring good into the world while we are here. If we can."

"It is always possible," he said, "if you have the will. If you do not give up the attempt, no matter what the obstacles."

She tilted her head to one side. "I like that reasoning," she said, "though it is not precisely the *coru* way."

"Which is to abandon one plan if it proves untenable, and try another, and then perhaps another, until every course is exhausted."

She laughed. "Exactly! We are not much alike, but we understand each other, I think."

He smiled again. She thought he was the kind of man who always had a dog at his heels, a grandchild on his knee, a serving girl bringing him an extra portion. The kind of man who liked to surround himself with other people and who won their affection without even seeming to try. "Earth and water have a natural affinity," he said. "It takes both *torz* and *coru* to grow the crops, to dress the world in greenery and color."

"To wear down a mountain," she suggested.

Now his laugh boomed out, sounding like boulders falling.

"Exactly! Working together, *torz* and *coru* can accomplish anything."

Mirti's astringent voice spoke behind them. "And working together, *sweela* and *elay* and *hunti* can burn the world to ashes," she said. "Taro, it is so rare to hear you talking nonsense."

They turned to include her in their conversation and found her accompanied by the second stranger. He was tall, thin, and restless, with a crown of white-blond hair and mist-colored eyes blinking rapidly behind thick glasses. His hands nervously picked at his sleeves; he shifted from foot to foot as if he could not, *could not*, stand still.

"I never talk nonsense," Taro replied, wholly unperturbed. "So perhaps you should heed my words."

Mirti shook her head slightly and proceeded to ignore him. "Zoe, I don't believe you've met Kayle Dochenza."

He nodded jerkily but didn't offer a hand. Too bad; she would have liked to compare the makeup of his blood to Corene's, if she ever got a chance to touch the princess. "Hello," he said in a reedy voice. "Aren't you pretty? Or maybe it's just your youth that makes you seem that way."

Nelson was still standing nearby, and now he snorted with laughter. "A compliment or an insult? With a Dochenza, you're never quite sure."

Kayle looked surprised. "I didn't intend either. Just observing. You look like your father, I think. I suppose he's dead."

"He is," Zoe said. It seemed impossible that Kayle would be thrown off by any abrupt change of subject, so she said, "I like your smoker cars very much."

His lean face took on a blaze of enthusiasm. "Yes—they're magnificent, aren't they?" His hands carved invisible shapes from the air. "Speed and function and *elegance*, all in one."

"And expense," Mirti said dryly. "Don't forget that."

He looked surprised again. "Cost is irrelevant in any endeavor."

"You might get an argument on that point," Nelson said cheerfully. "Cost might not hold you back, but it's always relevant. What you pay so often determines how much you like what you buy."

Mirti ignored the general laughter that followed. "Quickly," she said. "We only have a moment or two."

Zoe glanced at her, bewildered, but the others were nodding. Nelson laced his fingers with Zoe's right hand; Taro engulfed her left hand with his. The others were quickly clasping hands as well. As soon as Kayle and Mirti completed the circle, Zoe took a swift, hard breath.

Beneath her feet, the world seemed to do a complete, giddy revolution; the air in her lungs expanded to the point of pain. Her body flushed with heat and her pulse hammered. She could have traced the route of her blood over every inch of bone, under every loop and fold of skin.

Then everything settled. She was struck with a sense of certainty, of rightness, of completion, more powerful than anything she had ever experienced. Her thoughts cleared; her feet seemed rooted in the heart of the world itself.

"Everything in balance," Mirti murmured. "Wood and bone."

"Fire and mind," Nelson said.

"Air and soul," Kayle said, his voice barely a whisper.

"Earth and body," Taro rumbled.

"Water and blood," Zoe finished up.

For a moment, their fingers locked even tighter; Zoe felt her hand crushed by Taro's. For a moment, she could not have said where her body ended, where any of theirs began. She was all of them; they were all a part of her, every element poured into her single, individual frame. Yet she saw herself endlessly replicated, in their faces, in their bodies, in the bodies of everyone in the palace, in the city, in the world, all of them made up of the same materials, just mixed in different proportions. She understood, suddenly, what made all of them human, what made all of them the same. There was no difference.

Then Taro and Nelson released her and she almost pitched over. Laughing, her uncle caught her around the waist and hauled her upright again. "Takes you by surprise, doesn't it, the first time?" he said. "Kayle actually fainted."

"I didn't," Kayle said in his breathy voice. "I merely collapsed on the floor to recover my senses."

Zoe clung to Nelson's arm. "I feel the way I do when I first climb out of the water," she said. "It's as if I'm too heavy to stand. As if I've forgotten what it feels like to just walk around like an ordinary person."

"Of course, you're hardly an ordinary person," Mirti said. "You're a prime."

"Does it feel that way if any five people do that?" Zoe asked. "I mean, five people with different elemental blessings."

Mirti shrugged. "I don't know. I've never tried it with anyone else." She looked as if she might say more, but then she paused, seeming to listen. There were voices down the hall, people on their way to join the five primes. "Try not to act as if you're drunk," she said, and positioned herself to be the first one the king's guests would see when they stepped through the doors.

Zoe thought the strange bonding experience with the other primes might impair her ability to concentrate for the rest of the evening, but, in fact, just the opposite was true. All of her senses felt particularly acute; details presented themselves to her with astonishing clarity. Completely in harmony with her own countrymen, she was able to form quick opinions of these visitors from Soeche-Tas.

Fairly soon, she was certain she didn't like them.

All four guests had a self-satisfied, well-fed air that marked them as individuals of wealth and privilege. Their clothes were layered, colorful, and intricately designed, with a great deal of trim along the sleeves and hemlines. The men each had two sets of earrings dangling from their lobes; the women each sported five or six pairs. All of them wore a profusion of rings and bracelets, exotic perfumes, and lavishly applied makeup.

They had a tendency to stand too close and touch too often. "I simply *love* the colors in your robe," one of the wives exclaimed to Zoe, reaching out to stroke the sleeve. She took a pinch of fabric between her fingers and rubbed it together with sensual satisfaction. "Not just color, but texture. It looks as if it would be cool against the skin, even in a heated room."

Her accent drew out the words and burdened them with complicated *R*'s and *ooo*'s, but her voice was melodic and rich. Zoe had to concentrate to understand her. "Thank you," she said. "It was a gift from a cousin."

The ambassador's wife reached up un-self-consciously to brush her fingers along Zoe's cheek. Zoe tried to check her strong reaction to that, as her body rushed to make an analysis. What she received back was a tangled impression of heat and cruelty and alien chemicals.

"And this face? So piquant and winsome? Was that a gift as well?" the woman cooed.

"I suppose so. Bestowed upon me by my father and my mother at my birth."

The woman laughed, flattening her hand on the side of Zoe's head. Her fingers were astonishingly warm. "Ah, in my country, wealth will buy a beautiful face and perfect skin. These are not surgeries you possess on this side of the mountain?"

"I do not believe so."

The Soeche-Tas woman patted Zoe's cheek again and finally dropped her hand. "Then perhaps that is something we might trade for, your country and mine."

Zoe was infinitely relieved that the woman was no longer touching her; now if she would only step another pace away. "And what could we offer in return?"

"My husband and the viceroy believe your transportation technologies would please them exceptionally well!"

"And do you agree?"

"I am not one who loves horses overmuch. If I could travel the land and no longer be dependent on such animals—oh, yes, I believe that would be worth a great deal."

"Then Kayle Dochenza is the person you want to talk to. The thin man with the white hair. He's the inventor of the machine."

"But, *zhisu*, you are the one who interests me," the lady replied with a laugh. "In this room of old ones, you are so young! I find age so appallingly dull."

Zoe forced a light laugh. From the corner of her eye she had seen Vernon and Elidon enter the room, and she assumed the rest of the wives could not be far behind. "Queen Romelle is younger than I am. You might like her."

"Oh, yes! The pretty dark-haired one. I sat beside her at dinner and enjoyed her company very much. But she has retired to her room—some unfortunate trouble with her stomach, I think it was? She ate very little during the meal."

So whatever illness Romelle had complained of at breakfast

had followed her through the day. Zoe briefly felt sorry for her, and briefly jealous. She would be glad of an excuse to leave this uncomfortable conversation right now.

Rescue came from an unexpected source as Alys rustled up to them in a silken robe of red and gold. "Qeesia, this obsession with youth!" the queen exclaimed in a teasing tone. "It is most unseemly."

Qeesia turned willingly to invite the queen into their conversation. "It is true. I am—what might your word be?— something of a parasite, greedily attaching myself to things that seem pure and uncorrupted. And that is much more likely to be youth than age."

Alys tossed her thick red hair. It was loose around her shoulders, but woven with bits of gold and chips of gemstones, so that it seemed to sparkle with a more than ordinary luster. "I am not so much older than Romelle or Zoe," she said.

"And your face is even more perfect," Qeesia agreed. "Again, I think, innocent of any surgeries?"

Zoe was starting to wonder exactly how old Qeesia was. She looked to be somewhere between Seterre and Elidon in age—forty-five, perhaps—yet if she had undergone one of these surgeries she kept talking about, she might be a decade or two older. Or, who knew? If someone could endure multiple operations, Qeesia might be seventy or eighty. Her hands were smooth and free of blemishes, but Zoe supposed the Soechin operation might rejuvenate the flesh of the entire body.

Alys was preening a little. "Indeed, yes. This is my face as it has always been."

Now Qeesia laid her palm against Alys's cheek with the same sort of questing hunger. "Yes—feel that softness— almost divine and impossible to replicate. I imagine your skin is flawless all over."

If Alys was repulsed by the attention, she didn't show it. In fact, she wore a triumphant expression, as if pleased that she had been able to steal Qeesia's interest from the Lalindar prime. At that point, Zoe thought it was safe to slip away.

The rest of the evening was not much different, except in degree. None of the other three guests were quite so blatant about their preoccupation with youth and their desire for physical contact, but both ambassadors and the other woman managed to brush against Zoe, or take her hand, or stand so close that she could almost catch the rhythm of their hearts. The encroachment didn't seem to bother anyone else as much as it bothered Zoe. *Sweela* Nelson unfailingly enjoyed contact, *torz* Taro was always open to the press of flesh, and *elay* Kayle was so ethereal he didn't seem to notice. Even the two *hunti* women in the room—Mirti and Seterre—seemed unaffected. Zoe thought that was because Seterre was determined to win favor with the visitors, and Mirti didn't mind saying in her brusque way, "Here. No reason to stand so near." Only Elidon seemed a bit put off by the closeness that the Soechins seemed to require—and Elidon, as the oldest wife present, was the one who drew the least attention.

The ambassadors from Soeche-Tas did not crowd too closely to the king. So he stood among them all, offering his hesitant, hopeful smile, shoulder to shoulder with Elidon for most of the evening.

Zoe was seized by a sudden whimsical notion. If she, *coru* prime, could read the blood in someone's veins, could the *sweela* prime read the thoughts in that person's head? Could Nelson look at Vernon and know what he was thinking?

And if he could, what thoughts would he find at the forefront of the king's mind this very moment?

TWENTY-SIX

Vernon never asked Zoe for a formal opinion about the Soeche-Tas guests, so that was one problem she stopped worrying about immediately. The other one—the vandalized wardrobe—was an ongoing source of annoyance, since Zoe was expected to make at least one appearance at some social function for the rest of the nineday. Once again, Keeli came to her rescue, arriving at the palace early the next day with a trunkload of clothing that belonged to her or Sarone.

"I only brought things that we have never worn to the palace—or worn at all—but even so, a few of them are out of date," Keeli said. "I'm sorry about that."

"Sorry! You've saved my reputation."

"You don't care about your reputation," Annova said, pulling out first one tunic, then another. "Oh, these are so lovely. Why don't I have the dressing of *you* instead of Zoe? You at least care what you look like."

"You don't want to work for her. She's demanding and ill-tempered," Zoe said, holding one of the overrobes up to her shoulders. It was so dark that at first it looked black, but just a touch of light revealed it as a haunted blue. "But I have to admit, she has excellent taste in clothing."

Keeli had settled in the middle of the bed, her face sunny as always. Anyone less demanding and ill-tempered it was hard to imagine. "So what were the Soechin visitors like?"

Zoe wrinkled her nose. "Unnerving. One of them—a woman named Qeesia—reminded me of a bat. Some creature that would fasten itself to your throat and suck you dry."

Keeli's blue eyes widened comically. "That sounds very disturbing! Were they all like that?"

"Yes, but she was the worst. It made me wonder. If the king were really to marry one of the viceroy's daughters, would she be that way, too? Seems like she would bring no end of havoc to the court."

"Well, I don't care if she's a jackal feeding on corpses," Keeli said. "I get to come to the palace for the women's luncheon tomorrow! So I like her just fine."

The luncheon, to Zoe's mind, was hot, crowded, and over-long. The shopping expedition that followed was marginally more enjoyable, but only because she was able to make some serious inroads into her wardrobe deficit. She also purchased two extravagantly expensive outfits for Keeli to thank her for the timely loan of her own clothes. They were both happy, for different reasons, when the afternoon coasted to an end.

Zoe yawned through the whole trip back up the mountain, wondering if she would have time to nap before the night's activities began. The king had planned a grand outdoor event—one of those breathtaking displays of light that would paint the palace in gorgeous colors. She remembered the last one she had witnessed over Quinnahunti changeday when she was living on the river flats with Annova and Calvin. It was almost impossible to catalog all the ways her life had changed since that day.

"Have you decided what I should wear tonight?" Zoe called to Annova as she entered her suite.

The other woman came hurrying through the door to the room she shared with Calvin. "I haven't had time to think about it," she said. "Calvin's had a stomachache all afternoon. I was giving him something to help him sleep."

"There must be an illness going around," Zoe said. "Romelle's been miserable the past few days, too. I hope you don't catch it."

"Or *you*! Even worse! Come along, we've got work to do before you're fit to be seen tonight."

"We'll be outside in the dark. How beautiful do I have to be?"

"As beautiful as Elidon. And how do you think *she* will be dressed?"

Zoe sighed and submitted to Annova's ministrations. In truth, it was difficult to know exactly what to wear. Winter was not as punishing here in Chialto as it could be in the northwest provinces, but it was still Quinnelay, and the nights could be extremely cold. Meanwhile, the king, his wives, his visitors, and many of the other invited guests would be viewing to-night's spectacle from boats rowed out into the middle of the lake that snuggled up against the palace grounds, and the air just off the water was sure to be icy. Zoe insisted on dressing for comfort as much as style, and Annova reluctantly acceded.

"Are you going to come outside and watch?" Zoe asked as Annova finished crimping curls into her hair.

"I might. It depends on how Calvin is feeling."

"Well, that's not the only reason I hope he's much better soon!"

They ate a light meal together as darkness was falling. Annova took a bowl of soup to Calvin and came back to report that he thought he was improving.

"For dessert we have these lemon bars that Elidon sent— and these chocolate drops from Alys—and I don't know what these are from Romelle," Annova said. Nearly five ninedays after the rescue on the river, the queens were still supplying Zoe with tangible expressions of their gratitude. "Fruit tarts? I think they've gone bad."

Zoe stood up, brushing crumbs off her robe. "Maybe I'll have a sweet when I get back. I hope you get to see the enter-tainment!"

A few minutes later, she was in the *kierten*, milling around with fifty or sixty others, waiting to hear how they would be organized for the event. The royal family and the visitors from Soeche-Tas had gathered into a small, isolated group. Qeesia was standing too close to Josetta, patting the girl's fair hair with a look of intense satisfaction. Seterre stood nearby, smiling fondly. Zoe shivered and looked away.

There was a commotion near the grand front entrance as the royal herald stepped forward and announced that boats had been drawn up to the water's edge and anyone who wanted to witness the exhibition from the water should stroll down to the bank. "Only the royal family and their invited guests will be allowed on the king's vessel," the herald added, raising his voice above the noise of the crowd in motion.

Zoe didn't care if she watched from water or land, but she docilely followed everyone else outside. The dark of night was pushed back by a forest of brightly burning torches, though the flames did little to warm the crisp air. Servants helped men and women onto the ranks of rocking watercraft, some large and elaborate, some barely bigger than rafts. A number of guests showed no interest in the boats, but arranged themselves in chairs that had been set up along the edge of the water. Zoe even saw a few blankets laid out for anyone who wanted to recline on the ground to watch the palace painted with color—or who wanted to wrap up against the frosty air.

"A *coru* woman not rushing to take her place on the river?" said a voice behind her. She turned to see Darien's teasing smile. "Surely you would find a welcome among the royal family. What holds you in place on land?"

"A disinclination to spend more time than I must with people I don't particularly like," she replied.

"New acquaintances or old ones?"

She laughed. "In this case, the new ones. Why are *you* not at the king's side, as you always are?"

His expression was rueful. "I admit, the Soechins do not appeal to me, either. I claimed I was worried about overcrowding on the boat, but that was a lie."

"Because lies come so easily to you," she said, but she couldn't put any venom into it.

He laughed. "But it is really quite spectacular to see such an exhibition from the water. I have instructed the servants to reserve one of the smaller boats for me. Would you care to join me and row out into the middle of the lake?"

She gestured down at her fine clothes. "I am not dressed for rowing. I am dressed for sitting at my ease while people around me labor."

He laughed even harder. "I misspoke. Would you care to sit in a boat with me while *I* row us out into the water?"

"Yes," she said, "I believe I would."

She took his hand and they picked their way down the uneven ground of the bank. Some of the smaller boats had already traveled some distance from shore, but the king's stately vessel was just now casting off. Fragments of conversation drifted over the Marisi, eerily disconnected from the speakers.

"I can't believe *you* wanted to come out onto the water," someone said in a nasty tone. Zoe thought it might be Alys.

Josetta answered, her voice casual. "Oh, I'm not afraid of the river. At least not here, where it's so calm."

Zoe was grinning when a servant helped her into one of the smaller watercraft where Darien had already taken the oars. Unlike Nelson's boat, this one didn't have a selection of benches where different rowers could take their seats; this one just featured a long narrow hump that bisected the boat from stern to prow. Darien sat with his spine pressed up against a back support, one leg on either side of the divider.

"Elegant," Zoe said as she climbed in, trying to minimize the shifting of her weight so the boat didn't rock too badly.

He grinned. "At least the bottom's dry."

"So far," she said darkly. "I'm glad I didn't wear my expensive shoes."

As soon as she was settled, a servant pushed them into the water. She watched the palace recede as Darien rowed them smoothly away from shore. She loved the sound the river made as the oars dipped in and pulled back, water slapping against the side of the boat, dripping from the edges of the wood. All around them were similar noises, echoing across the surface of the river, embroidered with muffled laughter, occasional shouts, the creak and rattle of the oars straining against their guides. The king's boat and two of the other big ones were bright with torchlight, but everything else on the water moved in darkness. The star-chilled air felt unexpectedly delicious against Zoe's skin.

Darien shipped the oars and the boat came to an incomplete standstill. She could feel the current eddying around them, nudging them gently toward the southern border of the lake.

"Is this good?" he asked. "Are we far enough away?"

"This is perfect," she murmured, "even before the exhibition starts."

He laughed softly. "I thought you would like it out here. Are you cold?"

"Yes, but I don't mind."

"Here. Scoot back by me."

She glanced at him over her shoulder, ready to mock. But he was pulling on her arm, urging her to slide back along that center bench. "We'll tilt into the water," she said.

"We won't. Come on. Lean against me. You'll be more comfortable."

She couldn't resist. Gliding carefully, so she didn't snag her overrobe on any rough edges, she moved back until she could settle against Darien's chest. The boat danced under them, the stern sinking a little, but Darien extended his legs along either side of hers and they steadied. He wrapped both of his arms around her waist and snugged her closer.

"Isn't this better?" he whispered in her ear.

She felt a giggle rising. "You've done this before."

"Not for a long time."

"How can I believe that," she said, "from a man who lies so easily?"

"Shh," he said. "The show's starting."

Indeed, on some signal that Zoe missed, the torches were abruptly extinguished, which was when she realized that all of the palace windows that faced the water were also dark. Gasps from the crowd rose from across the water.

Then suddenly the whole front surface of the palace was lit with a showering sizzle of gold, bars of color sparking and spiraling down. The watchers had barely expressed their awe at this sight when it was swept away by great swaths of purple and blue and orange that bloomed and faded along the stone canvas of the palace.

"How can something like this be *possible*?" Zoe asked in a whisper.

"Some Dochenza invention," Darien replied, his mouth at her ear. "Controlled gases and some kind of pigment. I don't pretend to understand it."

"Are they here? Running the display?"

His head was so close to hers she could feel him nod. "If you look closely enough, you can see shadows running up and down the base of the palace."

"Kayle?"

"Not him. Two of his sons and one of his nephews, I believe."

That caught Zoe's attention as much as the twisting green ribbon—maybe twenty feet wide—that coiled and curled along the turrets before dissipating into the velvet dark. "Is one of them Wald? I'd like to meet him."

Darien's arm tightened warningly around her waist. "Don't look for ways to cause trouble."

"I'm not," she said, breathless. "I'm just curious about him."

"Watch the show," he whispered against her cheek. In the cool night, his breath was warm against her skin. He loosened his hold, but just a little. She made no protest.

The coiling ribbon was followed by sheets of color, one laid over the other so that scarlet melted into saffron and dripped ochre along all of the palace bricks. An emerald wave washed the whole surface clean, and then suddenly was pierced with random dots of color like wildflowers in a summer meadow. Some of the dots puffed up into great floating bubbles of fuchsia and melon; the rest fizzed in place and disappeared.

Zoe leaned back a little and turned her head toward Darien's. "Down on the river flats," she murmured, "all the squatters are sitting outside their tents, watching the show. Did you know that?"

"Not tonight," he said.

"Why not?" she asked, and then she remembered. "Oh. Important guests in the city. The squatters have been relocated. Well, when people are allowed to live on the river, and the king throws a party like this, they can see the whole display. It's like watching magic."

"This is better," he whispered back, and he kissed her.

She closed her eyes and felt color painted across her skin

while his mouth pressed against hers. Everything was in motion—the boat drifting gently with the current, the sky swirling around them, the blood speeding through her veins. She felt his pulse, as rapid and disordered as her own. He kissed her harder, tightening his arms around her. For a moment she wrapped her hands around his wrists, clinging, and then she pulled away, struggling for air.

"And was *that* a lie?" he asked in a quiet voice. What she could see of his face shifted from purple to violet to a ruddy red as the colors flamed against the palace and reflected off his skin.

"I don't know yet," she gasped.

"You do know," he said.

"Maybe I do," she said. Not speaking another word, she faced forward again, setting her backbone against his ribs. She could still feel his heartbeat, faster than usual, but so strong. So reliable. Ruffled just a little by emotion, maybe, but steady enough to withstand any punishment, any reversal, and too stubborn to fail.

All men failed eventually, of course; every pulse faltered to a halt. But Zoe leaned into Darien Serlast's heartbeat and felt as if she had found the source of the engine that powered the world.

It was easy to slip away into the crowd that slowly disembarked from the fleet of boats with the aid of the waiting servants. All the torches had been relit and the path back to the palace was clearly delineated. Darien had made no move to stop Zoe as she climbed out of the boat; neither of them had attempted much conversation during the rest of the exhibition, which was over in another ten minutes. She wanted to get inside. In that short span of time she had grown cold enough to start shivering—though that might have been from excitement, from fear, from uncertainty. She wanted to return to her room and burrow under her covers and remember the colors and think about Darien Serlast.

The minute she stepped into her rooms, she knew she would have little chance to carry out that excellent plan.

The suite smelled harsh, unpleasant, wrong. All the lights, doused for the festival, were still off, except for one dimly spilling out through the door to the servants' room. The foul odor emanated from the same direction.

Tense with misgiving, Zoe strode to the source of light. "Annova? Calvin? Is something wrong?"

She found Calvin on the bed, deep asleep, and Annova lying on the cool tiles in front of the circulating sink. The stink of vomit was stronger here, and streaks of it clotted the floor and the front of Annova's tunic.

"Annova," Zoe said sharply, dropping to her knees. "Are you all right? Do you need me to send for help?"

Annova shook her head weakly. Even her dark skin looked pale, leached of color by pain or purging. "I'm better now. I think it's all—out of my stomach finally."

"How long have you been throwing up?" Zoe asked. She laid her hands on Annova's cheeks and forehead and was relieved to find no trace of fever. From what she could tell just by touch, the blood was clean of infection.

"About an hour."

"You must have caught whatever it was that hit Calvin this morning—is *he* all right? Should I fetch the king's apothecary?"

With Zoe's help, Annova struggled to a sitting position. "I think both of us will recover on our own. Can you bring me some water? I think I can keep it down."

Zoe filled a glass from the spigot, then wet a towel, and she began wiping Annova's face while the other woman took careful sips. "You need to get out of these clothes. Can you stand enough to strip down and wash yourself off? I'll clean everything up."

Annova didn't make any protests about Lalindar primes looking after lowly servants. But she didn't answer the question, either. "Zoe," she said, her voice faint but threaded with urgency, "I think it was poison."

Zoe's hands froze in place. "Poison? Someone was trying to *kill* you?"

"*You.*"

After a moment of absolute silence, Annova continued. "Though not trying to kill you, I think. Just make you too sick to attend important events."

Zoe's hands had cramped around the wet towel. She felt a

murderous rage turn her blood to acid. "You think you ate something someone intended for me. You and Calvin both."

Annova nodded. "The chocolate drops. He only had one. I had four. And about fifteen minutes after I had the last one—"

"Alys," Zoe said, her voice glacial.

Annova gave an exhausted cough, then sucked down a little more water. "It probably didn't occur to her that your *servants* might eat something that had been given to you. Her own wouldn't."

"And she knows I like chocolate."

"She must have thought that if you ate one before the shopping expedition—or before the exhibition tonight—"

"Or before the luncheon tomorrow, or the dinner tomorrow, or any of the other activities that have been lined up *endlessly* for the rest of the nineday—"

"That you would get sick. You wouldn't be able to make an appearance."

"Which would insult the king's guests and displease the king and embarrass *me*."

Impossibly, Annova was able to conjure a smile. "Good thing for you that you have such greedy servants."

Zoe sent the damp cloth in one last pass across Annova's face. "Good thing for me I have such dependable friends."

It took another hour for Zoe to wash Annova and scrub down the tiled room. The sharp, clean smell of disinfectant chased away the acrid stench of vomit and made all of them feel better. Then Zoe spent a few minutes hovering over Annova and Calvin, making sure they had water at their bedsides, making certain no fever had made an unexpected appearance. But both of them breathed easily, their skin cool against their pillows, their dreams seemingly untroubled. Zoe decided that if they were well by morning, she would allow her concern to seep away.

Finally she slipped into her own room, stripped away her own clothes, and bathed herself in water as hot as she could stand. It should have been cold water—to bank her rage—but instead she wanted steam. She wanted heat. She wanted to burn away the rot that she was sure clung to anything that had passed through Alys's hands.

TWENTY-SEVEN

In the morning, Zoe arrived late to the daily breakfast in Elidon's suite. The first wife gave her a reproving glance, but forbore to make any pointed observations. Mirti was the only guest present besides Zoe and the queens, and everyone showed marks of a late night. Seterre and Alys were yawning, Elidon and Mirti both looked tired, and Romelle leaned her chin on her hand and appeared to be dozing at the table.

"I suppose everyone has already talked about how wonderful the display was last night," Zoe said, helping herself to a generous slice of bread and spreading it with honey. "I've never seen anything quite like it."

"Yes, Kayle says sometimes he thinks he could make a fortune from festival exhibitions if he'd give them as much attention as he gives his cars," Mirti said, her dry voice amused. "I can imagine many a rich family willing to pay for such a display at a wedding, for instance."

"Weren't the Soechins funny last night?" Alys said with a trilling laugh. "I think Qeesia was actually afraid that something would catch on fire and the whole palace would burn down." She glanced at Zoe and instantly looked stricken. "Oh—I forgot—you weren't in the boat with the rest of us. Sorry."

It was such a halfhearted dig that no one bothered to respond. Zoe took a big bite of her bread and served herself a healthy portion of an egg-and-cheese dish. "No, I went out in one of the smaller boats," she said. "At first I thought I would regret it, because the motion of the water upset my stomach, but then I was fine."

Her eyes still closed, Romelle spoke up. "I hope you don't get sick with whatever's been bothering me."

"We *all* hope we don't catch that," Seterre said.

"I don't think I will," Zoe said brightly. "I feel fine this morning." She consumed the eggs with relish. "But I wondered if all of you would do me a favor."

Mirti was watching her with narrowed eyes; this early-morning buoyancy was not in Zoe's usual style. Elidon appeared to be on the edge of annoyance. "What kind of favor would that be?" the first wife asked, her voice far from encouraging.

Zoe had brought a small basket with her, and now she opened it to pull out the chocolate drops, still wrapped in their pretty confectioner's bag. "Alys sent these to my room yesterday, which was so kind of her, because she knows that I love chocolate. But I had one and I just thought it tasted—a little off. Like it had been overcooked or undercooked or something. I hate to throw the whole bag away, because I really do love these chocolates, but I won't keep them if there's something wrong."

She picked up an empty bowl and poured about a dozen candies into it. They made a small, cheery clinking against the porcelain. Smiling, Zoe held it out in a general invitation. "Anybody?"

Nobody moved. Everyone was staring at Zoe, even Romelle, who had opened her eyes without lifting her chin from her hands.

"Both of my servants were quite sick last night," Zoe went on in a chatty voice, keeping her arm extended. "Vomiting all over the place—! Take my word for it, the smell was overpowering. Of course, I'm *sure* they wouldn't have eaten my candy without my permission, so it must have been something else that made them sick."

Now the silence in the room was thick, heavy, exerting an

actual pressure on everyone around the table. Mirti's mouth had pressed into a grim line, and she was still staring at Zoe, but everyone else had shifted their attention to the redheaded queen.

"Alys?" Zoe said, offering the bowl and shaking it just enough to make the contents rattle. "Would you like to try one? Tell me what you think?"

Alys tossed her hair over one shoulder, clearly deciding to brazen it out. "No, thank you," she said. "Breakfast isn't the time for chocolate."

Zoe put the dish down, widening her eyes as if a thought had just occurred to her. "I don't suppose—Romelle, did Alys give *you* chocolates, too? Is that why you're sick? Could there have been a whole *batch* of them that were bad?"

Romelle had finally lifted her head and pulled herself upright, striving for a look of dignity. "Not chocolates," she said. "Alys gave me some glazed *fruit* the other day, but—but—she ate some, too, and she seems to be fine."

"This is ridiculous!" Alys exclaimed, allowing anger and indignation to roughen her voice and flush her cheeks. "What are you implying, Zoe Lalindar? What terrible things are you saying about me?"

Zoe dropped her cheery manner; her voice became quiet, intense. "I'm saying that I think that you don't like me. You want to discredit me, make me look foolish, keep me from the responsibilities I am expected to carry out while I am a guest under your husband's roof."

"I don't know why you think—"

"I'm *saying*," Zoe went on, raising her voice to drown Alys's out, "that someone came to my rooms three days ago and destroyed every piece of clothing I own, hoping to keep me from attending the banquet to honor our Soechin visitors."

"Well, you can't suppose—"

"And that was petty and pointless, but then yesterday someone brought doctored candy to my room, hoping to make me sick." She gestured at Romelle. "And someone could very easily have poisoned Romelle using the same method."

"Zoe," said Elidon in a warning voice. "These are serious accusations, and you don't have any proof. Calm down. Think things over."

Instead, Zoe stood up. She could feel rage running through her veins like a spring flood down a canyon, too wild to pen up. "I have a little proof," she said. "I know that Alys brought the candy to my room. I know that my servants grew sick on it. I know it was intended for me. Therefore, I think I can be forgiven for assuming that Alys wishes me ill."

"I will talk to her," Elidon said, earning a burning glare from Alys.

"Oh, *I'll* talk to her," Zoe said. "I'll ask her questions. Why did you just try to make me sick? Why didn't you try to murder me? It's clear you won't balk at killing if you want to get someone out of your way. Look at Princess Josetta. *Someone* paid off her escort so that the girl would go over the falls. Am I wrong in thinking that was you?"

Crystal shattered to the floor as Alys leapt to her feet. "You miserable bitch!" she cried. "How dare you say such a thing about me? I didn't try to hurt Josetta—I wouldn't try to *kill* anyone! How could you—"

"Shut up," Zoe said fiercely. She heard chairs scrape back, dishes rattle, anxious voices lift all around them, but she had attention only for Alys. She raised her hand, palm upward, half-cupped as if to catch raindrops. "I don't care if you admit it," she said, her voice low. "I don't care if you destroy anyone else in the palace—or the city—or the kingdom. But don't you *ever.* Don't you *ever* try to harm me, or anyone close to me, again. And don't try to harm the princess—*any* of the princesses. Do your scheming, I don't care. But not against me. Or I will hurt you."

She clenched her fingers into a fist and Alys gasped in real pain, shuddering unsteadily on her feet. From the corners of her eyes, Zoe could see the other women staring in stupefaction, their gazes swinging between Zoe and the queen. But Zoe kept her eyes on Alys.

Whose face began to redden, as if with a blush, and then with a sunburn, and then with a bruise. "Zoe," Alys whispered, lurching forward a pace. Under her smooth cheeks pooled a slowly spreading stain of purple; dark half-moons gradually became visible beneath her eyes.

"Stop it!" Elidon shouted. "Zoe, stop what you're doing! Release her!"

She didn't want to obey. She wanted to call up a lesion on Alys's face, open the skin so that the blood drained out, running down her cheeks like tears. She wanted to draw all the blood to Alys's head, leaving her knees weak and her feet unreliable. She wanted to make the queen stagger and fall, from dizziness or from fear.

But she didn't. She took a deep breath and splayed her fingers. Instantly she felt the abrupt cessation of pressure, the snapping of the invisible conduit that had sucked Alys's blood up through her body as it yearned toward Zoe. Alys gasped for air and collapsed gracelessly into her chair.

"An excellent decision," a voice murmured in Zoe's ear. Suddenly she was aware of a presence at her side, a pressure on her own arm—Mirti Serlast, her fingers laced around Zoe's wrist. Mirti's gray eyes burned into hers. "What you can do to Alys, I can do to you, or something very like it. You can call blood, but I can shatter bone. And I will do it if you ever try such a trick again."

For a moment Zoe stared back at her, her mind somewhere between rebellion and rage. She could hear Elidon and Seterre fussing over Alys, shushing her, assuring her she would be just fine, her face showed only the slightest bruising. She was only just beginning to realize how much power she truly had in her hands. How much power Mirti had. Any prime.

Then she jerked free of Mirti's hold and shot back, "Then *she* can't do all the dreadful things *she* does."

"We will see to it that she doesn't," Mirti said.

It was clearly a dismissal from the room—possibly from the palace. Zoe gave one quick nod, paused to glance at the scene of chaos around the breakfast table, then stalked toward the door without another word. She slammed the door behind her.

Romelle caught up with her before Zoe had taken three steps. The fourth wife looked horrified, excited, worried, and sick, all at the same time. Zoe was surprised she'd been able to overcome nausea long enough to go chasing down the hall. "Thank you for speaking up in such a way," Romelle said. "I have often wondered if Alys would try to harm me or Natalie. Sometimes I've thought—but there was never any proof—and the things were always so subtle—"

"She's a greedy, wretched, selfish, ambitious—woman," Zoe said, ending lamely on the last word because she couldn't think of anything bad enough to call Alys. "I don't think you can ever be too careful where she's concerned. Watch her. And watch out for Natalie."

"I will," Romelle promised. "And you—watch out for yourself."

There was no doubt that was a goodbye. Obviously Romelle believed Zoe couldn't stay at the palace after today's display. Zoe nodded. "I certainly will."

She turned to go, but Romelle surprised her again by putting a hand on Zoe's shoulder to hold her in place. "I've never met anyone like you," Romelle said. "I'll miss seeing you every day."

Zoe only nodded again, dumbstruck by one more revelation coursing merrily through the queen's blood. Romelle smiled, dropped her hand, and slipped back into Elidon's suite, where the rising sound of feminine voices portended one tempestuous argument.

Zoe closed her eyes and leaned briefly against the wall. She didn't sense poison in Romelle's veins, oh no, but there was definitely an interloper aboard. There was an alien presence, a tiny entity feeding on the queen's blood and struggling to manufacture its own. Romelle was pregnant.

Feeling buffeted by so much knowledge and so much rage, Zoe made her way carefully down the halls, up the broad staircase, and into her suites. Calvin and Annova were sitting together companionably over their own breakfast, though from the array of bland foodstuffs laid out, they were eating gingerly after the previous night's discomforts.

"You're back early," Calvin said.

Annova was already on her feet. "What's wrong?"

"I hope you feel well enough to help me pack," Zoe said. "Good thing I haven't accumulated too many new clothes."

"You're leaving again?" Annova asked.

"*We're* leaving. All of us. This time for good."

T he manager of the expensive hotel was happy to provide a suite for Zoe Lalindar this time, to accommodate her servants as well as the prime. She toyed with asking him to deny access to anyone who might come looking for her, but she knew it was pointless. One of Darien's spies had probably followed her down into the city; if she truly wanted to hide, she would have to be far more clever than she had been so far.

Calvin liked the new quarters, but Annova was restless. "This isn't a place for *staying*," she said. "You need someplace you can feel more settled."

"A *coru* woman never feels settled," Zoe said.

Calvin shrugged. "Maybe it's time to go back to the river," he said.

"You can't abandon me now!" Zoe exclaimed.

"I mean, all of us," he said. "You, too. It's only a few ninedays until Quinncoru. A fine time to be living on the flats."

Annova spared him one scandalized look. "The Lalindar prime does not live down on the river!"

Zoe sighed and flopped into a chair. "Oh, this Lalindar prime remembers those days on the river as some of the happiest in her life," she said with a sigh. "But, no, I don't suppose I can try for such a refuge again." She sighed a second time. "Anyway, that's the first place Darien Serlast would come looking for me if I disappeared."

Annova bent her gaze to Zoe. "Is Darien Serlast likely to come looking for you soon, since you left the palace so abruptly?"

Zoe nodded. "I think he's afraid I will cause some kind of trouble if I'm not under his watchful eye."

Calvin cackled. "Seems like he's right about that."

"Then you ought to have something nice to wear when he arrives," Annova said. "Let's go to the Plaza of Women. We still have a lot of shopping to do."

Zoe found it more enjoyable to buy clothes when she didn't have to think about trying to impress four queens and a foreign delegation. The excursion made her so cheerful that she sent Annova back to the hotel with the packages while she made a detour by Sarone's house to see if there was any fresh gossip.

"Zoe!" Keeli squealed when she was ushered inside. "What have you done *now*?"

Before Zoe could answer, Sarone hurried into the room, arms outflung. "Zoe! *What* is happening up at the palace?"

"What do you know already?"

"Nothing! Josetta came looking for you, very upset, and we had to tell her we had no idea where you were."

"I'll send her a note," Zoe said.

"But Zoe, what *happened*?" Keeli demanded. "Josetta said you just left? Moved out of your rooms?"

"No other news has filtered down the mountain?" she asked. Impressive if Elidon had managed to keep the details of the altercation a secret—but then, she would have plenty of motivation to do so. Accusations of murder and threats of retaliation put everyone in a bad light.

And raised hard questions.

And made everyone afraid.

"Josetta said you had an argument with Alys," Sarone said. "But no one knew what it was about."

"What happened?" Keeli begged.

How much to tell? Zoe was not secretive by nature, but this was pretty incendiary material. She settled on the portion of the story she was certain was true. "I think Alys sent tainted candy to my room—just enough to make me sick," Zoe said. "I didn't eat any, but both my servants did, and they were throwing up all night. I was so angry! I brought the candy in and told everyone what she'd done, and then I accused her of tearing up my wardrobe as well."

"Did she admit it?" Keeli asked.

"No—and I don't know if anyone else believed me. But I was furious. I—well—I should probably be ashamed of this. I caused her blood to rise to her face and bruise her skin."

Keeli and Sarone both stared at her mutely. When the silence had gone on for a while, Zoe added in a faint voice, "I was hoping that was something Christara had done a time or two, but by the expressions on your faces, I suppose not."

"I think my mother *could* do it, but she never did," Sarone said quietly. "She was very aware of the fact that she commanded power, and she didn't want to abuse it."

"Mirti said something of the sort," Zoe replied.

"Mirti was there?"

Zoe nodded and didn't give specifics. "So, I think it's pos-

sible I've behaved unforgivably," she said. "Maybe I'll be exiled again—this time for my own crimes, not my father's."

Sarone looked even more apprehensive. "How badly did
you hurt the queen?"

"Not as badly as I wanted to." *Not as badly as I could have,*
she thought. "But her face will probably show bruises for a
couple of days. Elidon was very angry with me, and rightfully
so, I suppose. I'm sure she'll tell the king, and perhaps he'll
forbid me to return to the palace."

"Or Darien Serlast will," Sarone said quietly, "since he
sometimes makes decisions for the king."

Zoe thought about that kiss in the boat under the painted
sky. Could that have been only last night? It seemed like it had
happened a year ago, or not at all. As if Zoe had dreamed it,
or wished for it so hard that imagination had supplied her with
all the details of sound and sight and touch.

"He likes you, I think," Keeli said. "Doesn't he? Maybe
he'll tell Vernon your behavior was justified."

"Maybe," said Zoe. Or maybe he would cast her out altogether.
What was a kiss, after all? "I can't guess what to expect next."

"Well, one thing that *won't* happen, even if you're banished," Sarone said briskly. "We won't lose track of you
again. Promise me, Zoe. Even if you disappear, you will not
disappear from *us*."

Zoe put her hand out, palm raised, and Sarone flattened her
own hand against it. For a moment, she felt it again, the reassurance of blood to blood, the markers of family, of belonging.
"Promise," Zoe said. "I am used to leaving things behind. But
you will not be one of them."

She didn't want to go back to the hotel—either because she
didn't want to face Darien Serlast or she didn't want to learn
he had not come looking for her. Zoe couldn't decide. So instead, upon leaving Sarone's house, she simply wandered, trac-
ing a meandering path through the wealthy neighborhoods
where she had lived as a child. As Calvin had noted, it was
nearly Quinncoru; soon the world would remake itself. The
thin, naked shrubberies would dress themselves in greenery
and blossoms. Nervous, impatient birds would peck at the

dirt, hoping to surprise unwary beetles lumbering between stalks of early grass. Even today, despite the chilly air, the sunshine was extravagant, the breeze gentle. It was no hardship to walk another block, another mile.

She found herself, not planning it, in front of the house her parents had owned, the place where Darien's mother and sisters now lived. A few ninedays ago, Zoe might have been able to convince the king that the property should be hers again, but she doubted Vernon would believe such courtesies were owed to her now. She could probably afford to buy it outright, however. If she wanted it.

She stood in the street for about ten minutes, staring up at the facade. The house was four stories high with three or four rooms on every floor. She had spent many days running up and down those stairs when she was a child, mostly because the adults were too fatigued by the exercise to chase her for long. She had begged to be given the small room on the top floor as her very own, because she loved the view and the sense of freedom, but her parents had thought her too young to sleep so far away from them at night. "When you're older," her mother had promised. "When you're fourteen."

Of course, Zoe had celebrated her fourteenth birthday in the village with her father, and her mother had been dead nearly three years.

She doubted she would have much interest in that high, isolated room these days. And the memories inside the house were more likely to be painful than comforting. She turned away, blundered on down the road, surprised to find her way blurred by tears.

Not looking for one, she came upon a temple, set back from the road and surrounded by a thicket of bare shrubbery just waiting for spring to muscle into full bloom. She followed the curving stone path to the low door and felt a certain peace settle over her as soon as she stepped inside.

She did not have the patience to move from bench to bench, meditating herself back into a state of balance, but she did make one slow circuit around the small room, acknowledging all the elements. Then she crossed to the deep, handsome basket set on a central podium and stirred the coins before she pulled out a blessing.

She was getting awfully tired of seeing the glyph for change.

The second blessing was synthesis, a symbol she recognized although she had never seen anyone pull it before, ever. She turned the disk over and over between her fingers, trying to decide if she should keep it or throw it back to be found by the next supplicant looking for direction. In the end, she slipped it into her pocket and trusted the acolytes to refresh their blessings on a regular basis. She had no idea how the blessing applied, but that it was portentous—and that it pertained directly to her—she had no doubt.

No more wisdom was offered. The third coin was so smooth, so worn that it was almost blank. A ghost blessing. A signal that even the elemental forces could not advise her in the trials to come.

Zoe pursed her lips, then shook her head. *This* was a coin she would not bother to keep. She flipped it into the basket and left the temple, rather less peaceful than she'd been when she walked in.

TWENTY-EIGHT

Zoe couldn't tell if she was relieved or dismayed to find Darien Serlast waiting in her hotel room. Annova had made him comfortable, seating him at a pretty little table before the window, offering him fruited water and sweet crackers. The minute Zoe stepped into the room, Annova grabbed Calvin's arm and said, "We'll be back in an hour." Zoe let the door click shut behind them before she made the effort to stroll across the room and face her visitor.

"What happens now?" she asked, not bothering with subtlety. "Am I banished?"

He finished off his glass of water and folded his hands on the table. He gazed up at her, seemingly calm. "Alys would like that, but no," he said. "Under—intensive—questioning, Alys was persuaded to admit that she had, indeed, sent tainted candy to your rooms in the hopes of making you sick. But she was adamant that the chemical wouldn't do you any real harm. And she insisted, with such vehemence that I'm tempted to believe her, that she had no hand in Josetta's mishap on the river. But sending you doctored food is a serious offense, even if she did nothing worse."

"And so?"

"And so everyone agrees that—extreme and wrongheaded

as your reprisal was—you had some justification for your behavior today."

"Who constitutes *everyone*?"

"Why don't you sit down?" he said, waving at the chair across from him.

"I'd rather stand. Who's everyone?"

"Vernon. Elidon. Me."

"And who else knows what happened at Elidon's breakfast?"

"For now, as few people as possible. *Coru* luck must have blessed you today to make sure there were no servants in the room when you—expressed your opinions—and Elidon can keep Seterre and Romelle in check. Alys has little incentive to repeat the story, for it reveals her in a bad light as well, and Mirti understands the urgency of keeping such a matter private. For now, the king and I are the only other ones who know. But I can't predict how long the events will remain secret."

"How will Alys explain the marks on her face?"

"Some story is being worked out, I suppose. I was not interested enough in the details to linger."

"So I'm not banished."

"Not from the city, no. But it is thought it might be generally wiser—for the time being, at any rate—for you to take up quarters outside the palace."

She gestured at the room around them. "As you see, I already have."

"You might consider investing in something more personal. More permanent."

"Maybe it's time for me to go back to Christara's house."

"No," he said sharply.

She raised her eyebrows, waiting.

He came to his feet in a leisurely fashion, as if trying to move casually. But once he was standing, she could tell that his whole body was coiled with some strong emotion. Anger, she guessed. Anxiety. Maybe something else.

Maybe he, like Zoe, was expending a lot of energy to *not* think about that kiss last night. That kiss three or five or eight years ago.

"There are upcoming events where your presence will be expected," he said. "Taro and Kayle are both committed to staying for the next nineday, and they have even less interest in living in Chialto than you do. You ought to be present as long as they are."

"What is so important that all the primes are instructed to linger?"

He clearly debated how much to tell, but then decided she was unlikely to be moved by an incomplete answer. At least, that was how she interpreted the look on his face.

"The viceroy of Soeche-Tas arrives here early next nineday," Darien said. "To do him honor, all the primes are requested to be at the palace during his visit."

"The viceroy of Soeche-Tas was here a year ago, and the Lalindar prime was not at the palace showing him any particular respect," she reminded him.

"Your aunt Sarone and your uncle Broy attended many functions in your stead," he said. "The viceroy was thus saved from affront."

"I'm glad that my Lalindar relatives made themselves so agreeable."

"They seem to have that skill," he agreed. "Though you do not."

She laughed, a harsh, angry sound. "Come, you have been so restrained! Why don't you berate me as you would like to do? Tell me how foolish I have been, how vindictive—"

"How childish," he shot back. It was clear his iron control was slipping. "How ungoverned. How irresponsible."

"I was angry."

"*Everyone* experiences anger from time to time! I would go so far as to say I feel *rage* right at this moment. But I don't indulge in it! I don't smash things and destroy things and *threaten* people. You accused Alys of trying to kill Josetta! Very well, even if she had, how are you any better than she is if *you* try to kill *her*?"

"I did nothing more than bruise her face," Zoe replied hotly. "Though I *wanted* to do more. I *could* have done more."

"Oh, I believe that! Mirti said you wore the look of someone who suddenly found a weapon in her hand that she had no idea how to use. But she said she could see you figuring out how to turn it to good account."

Zoe laughed sharply, not amused in the slightest. "And then she whispered in my ear that *she* could break all my bones if she wanted to. I don't know why everyone is so outraged at *my* behavior if *all* the primes have some kind of destructive elemental power. I'm betting Kayle can suffocate a man merely by willing it—or Nelson can make a man go mad."

"You might win that bet," Darien retorted, "but they have shown no inclination to do so."

"Well, here's a question that's been vexing me," she said, taking a step closer. "If the primes are so powerful, why do we need a king? What can *he* do that they cannot?"

"He can withstand them," Darien said.

She just stared at him. "I don't understand."

"As you say, all the primes are capable of murder. But when they ratify the king's selection of heir—as all primes must do—they endow that heir with the ability to survive their assaults. They cannot kill him and thus it is in their best interests to support him." He shrugged. "There are obvious flaws in the arrangement—any one of them could hire an assassin, for instance—but the system has worked for Welce for hundreds of years." He gave her a dark look. "And works better if none of the primes abuse their powers, no matter what inducement they might be offered."

She wanted to sneer at him or stamp her foot or throw a tantrum, but he was already rebuking her for appalling behavior, and she didn't want to continue to prove his point. Maybe this was why Christara had wanted to have the raising of Zoe once she realized that *power* was more than a blessing charm hanging on Zoe's bracelet. Maybe Christara would have taught her how to control not just her ability, but the desire to use it. After all, there was no one Christara had hated more than Navarr Ardelay, and she'd done nothing more than ruin him.

But she had really wanted to kill him.

"I will focus on learning how to control my rage—and my power—no matter how great the provocation," she said in a cold voice.

"Yes, for there are always provocations," Darien said. "How he responds in the face of disaster is how you judge a man. Or a woman."

"Well, then certainly a *hunti* man has the advantage there," Zoe flung at him. "He will give in to no emotional excesses! Stubborn as wood and unyielding as bone!"

"It would not harm you to allow a little *hunti* resolve to give some shape to your restless *coru* days," he said steadily.

And are you the hunti *man to guide me?* she wanted to demand. *Are you a man of such principle and determination that you can take a woman of blood and water and turn her into a solid, a reliable, a dependable form? Will you wrap your body around hers to contain her, to give her a place of rest and safety? Or will you merely stand, stiff and disapproving, and watch her dissolve and melt away?*

Instead she responded, her voice cutting, "I have not found the *hunti* ways so much to my taste that I want to submit to their guidance." *You kissed me,* she was saying, *but that doesn't mean I liked it.*

He nodded, making it clear he perfectly understood her message. "Then I will not burden you with my unwelcome presence," he said. "I will just reiterate that the king wishes you to stay in the city. That your attendance will be expected from time to time at the palace. And that you have not been put under any interdiction." He gave her another nod, though this one was more of a bow, and strode toward the door.

"Wait," she said. "I remembered something I had to tell you."

His hand touching the knob, he paused to look back at her. He could not shift emotions as quickly as she could; he still looked both angry and hurt. "What is it?"

"Or rather, something to ask you."

He didn't bother to speak again, merely waited.

"Did you know Romelle is pregnant?"

His hand fell; astonishment wiped everything else from his face. "That's not possible," he said.

Zoe shrugged. "Possible or not, it's true."

He came a few steps back into the room. His frown had returned, but the rage had been replaced by bafflement and concern. "Did she tell you this? I hadn't thought you and Romelle were on such good terms that she would confide in you."

"She followed me after the argument this morning and took my hand. I could feel it inside her. The blood of someone else. A baby." She saw he was not convinced and said, with some heat, "It doesn't matter if you believe me or not. It's true."

"Does she realize she's pregnant?"

Zoe gave him a scathing look. "I don't know. We're not on such *good terms* that she confides in me."

"She's said nothing to anyone."

"Nothing that's been repeated to *you*," Zoe felt compelled to point out.

He brushed this aside. "If Elidon knew, she would tell Vernon, and he would tell me. But if Romelle doesn't yet realize the truth—"

"She's been sick for the past few days. I thought Alys was poisoning her, too," Zoe said. She couldn't help grinning, though of course it wasn't funny. "No wonder Alys was so incensed. She probably hasn't done anything to Romelle. Romelle's just been throwing up because of the baby."

Darien was still frowning, apparently trying to calculate calendar dates. So Zoe asked the obvious question. "Who's the father?"

Darien shook his head. "I have no idea."

"I suppose that's a lie," she said.

He offered her a strained, reluctant smile. "Oh, I wish it were." He shook his head. "I could believe it of Alys. I could believe it of Seterre. Each of them would take lovers without consulting the king. But Romelle? She's always been the most biddable of the four. If she's pregnant—then there are serious lapses in palace security. Which is as troubling to me as the fact of the pregnancy itself."

"I guess you can't just ask her for the truth," Zoe said, sparing a moment to enjoy imagining that conversation.

"Not until she's made a public announcement, I can't."

Zoe shrugged. "Then I don't suppose there's much you can do about it."

"Thank you for letting me know," he said. The astonishment seemed to have knocked the last of his anger out of him; now he looked tired, and a little sad. Not for the first time, Zoe thought he probably had responsibilities she knew nothing of, and none of them easy.

She said, "It doesn't seem to have lightened your burdens, however, so perhaps I shouldn't have told you."

"It never occurred to me that you had any interest at all in lightening my burdens," he replied.

She laughed out loud. "*You* were the one who came seeking

me out, Darien Serlast. You have now tracked me down—what, four times?—when I gave you plenty of reason to abandon me forever. My only conclusion must be that you actually *like* the turmoil I bring into your life."

This time his smile was a little warmer. "I told you. I am merely fulfilling a promise I made—to your father and to mine."

"Consider that promise kept," she invited. "Consider your duty discharged. If you ever have reason to come chasing after me again, let it be on your own account."

He studied her for a moment in silence and then nodded sharply. "All right, then. I will." He reached the door but turned back. "But you're not to run away again until after you have shown some respect to the viceroy."

"I suppose I can agree to that," she said. "You wouldn't have time to come looking for me, anyway, until after he was gone."

He allowed himself a slight laugh. "Exactly so," he said. "I think we understand each other."

"I doubt that," she said, "but we are at least in agreement."

"Which is more than I can usually hope for."

"One more thing," she said as he opened the door. "Will you tell Josetta where I am? She came looking for me at my aunt's."

Now the amusement was gone from his face and he looked, once again, wary and displeased. "Josetta? I thought I had made it clear—"

"I haven't been whispering secrets in her ear," Zoe said, irritated. "I've been making sure she knows how to swim. A useful skill, don't you think? If anyone ever tries to drown her again?"

"That's just an excuse. You're trying to build a relationship with her. Because she's your sister."

"Yes, I am," she said cordially. "And I will continue to do so. I'll be discreet. I won't reveal the lies you are so determined to pretend are true. But I'll make myself her friend. And you can't stop me, so it's no use growling at me like that."

"I'm not *growling*. It's just that—"

She waved him toward the door, coming close enough that she could shut it behind him once he finally left. "It's just that you don't like it. Well, I'm sorry. Actually, no, I'm *not* sorry. Go home, Darien. Worry about the things you can control. This isn't one of them."

This time he actually managed to open the door before he was stopped by one more thought. "If you leave the hotel," he said, "you will let me know where you move?"

"Surely your spies will tell you that before I've had a chance to send you word?"

"It gives me the illusion that you trust me if you tell me of your own free will."

She shrugged. "All right. Then I will notify you if I change my residence. Does that satisfy you?"

He was silent a moment, watching her, his face gone suddenly serious. His right hand was still on the door, but now he lifted his left hand and touched two fingers, very gently, to her lips. "No," he said, "but I suppose it will have to do." Smiling at her bewilderment, he bowed again and strode from the room.

Zoe was left first to stare at the closed door and then to collapse against it, dazedly reviewing the last exchanges of that conversation. It took her a moment to remember what she'd asked that had prompted him to reply in the negative.

Does that satisfy you?

She had spoken the truth. They would never understand each other.

But there were days she thought they might reach an understanding, even so.

Josetta was not happy with the news that Zoe did not plan to move back to the palace anytime soon.

"What does it matter?" Zoe asked. They were visiting in Zoe's hotel room before heading to Sarone's for an afternoon swim. "I never talk to you when we're at court anyway, and you can come see me anytime you like."

"You just *feel* farther away when you're down here. Why did you want to leave the palace? No one will say."

This was certainly one of those secrets Darien Serlast would not want her to reveal. Zoe temporized. "I had a disagreement with Alys. I thought both of us would be more comfortable if we didn't have to worry about running into each other in the hallway or the *kierten* every day."

Josetta made a scoffing noise. "*Everyone* disagrees with Alys. No one would be living at court if that was a reason to move out."

"Perhaps my quarrel with her was more bitter. But don't worry. I'll be there for the important events. I understand the viceroy of Soeche-Tas will be here in a few days."

"Yes, and I can't wait."

"You're looking forward to seeing him?"

"No, I can't wait for him to take Qeesia and all the rest of them back to Soeche-Tas! I can't stand them. They're so—odd. And they stand too close. And they touch me all the time. Me and Corene. It gives me the shivers. And it gives Corene nightmares."

"I thought Corene rather liked it when they paid attention to her."

"Her mother told her to encourage them, but I think she hates them even more than I do."

Zoe couldn't think of a delicate way to phrase the next question so she just asked it. "Do you like her? Corene?"

Josetta shrugged. "Sometimes I do. She can be so spoiled and sure of herself and *mean*. Then other times she's nice. Everybody else brought me flowers the day after the regatta, but Corene brought me a doll because she thought I might be having trouble sleeping. She's so smart, and she can speak so sharply, that sometimes you forget she's just a little girl."

"Whose mother isn't very nice."

Josetta nodded. "Trying to be what Alys wants Corene to be would make anybody mean, I think."

"Well, if you ever want to bring her along to go swimming, I'm sure Sarone wouldn't mind."

"No," Josetta said, without pausing to think about it. "That's something I want to keep just for me."

The day was so fine that, once they left Sarone's house, neither Zoe nor Josetta could bear the idea of going back inside. So instead of having the driver take the Cinque toward the palace, they instructed him to follow a slow, narrow, snak-

ing roadway that paralleled the Marisi on the eastern edge of
the city. When they neared the river flats, Zoe had him stop
the car so they could climb out. The guard Foley immediately
scrambled out after them, but he maintained a respectful distance as they picked their way to the overhang above the hard,
broad expanse of the squatters' campground.

It was entirely empty now, of course, with the transients
moved to some less visible spot while the Soechin visitors were
in Chialto. The river that rushed by an open, echoing arena
was much higher than the one Zoe remembered from when she
had taken refuge on the flats. She lifted her eyes to gauge
the volume of water pouring down the rock face behind the
palace. Harder to tell from this distance, but the falls seemed
plumper, too, gorged with excess and roaring joyfully down
the side of the mountain. It seemed the Marisi approved of
Zoe's continued presence in the city.

She and Josetta settled on the lip of the rocky bank, dangling their feet over the flats below. Foley stood a few yards
behind them, close enough to dive after Josetta if she fell—
close enough to hear their whole conversation, Zoe thought.
"All year long, but mostly during the warm seasons, people
live down here," Zoe began.

Josetta nodded. "I can see them from my bedroom window.
My mother says they're dirty vagrants, but sometimes I
think—it would be nice to live down here. Maybe. For a little
while."

"I don't think it would be the right life for a princess," Zoe
said with a smile. "But if—if something ever happened to you.
If you ever felt you had to get away from the palace, suddenly,
in a hurry, telling no one where you were going. You could
come to the river. And once I knew you were missing, I would
come here to find you."

Josetta turned to give Zoe a searching look. "Why would I
ever need to suddenly get away from the palace?"

"I don't know. Sometimes scary things happen. It's good to
have a plan."

"Would I be safe down here? With—with the vagrants?"

Zoe smiled and glanced over her shoulder at the guard, who
was listening intently. "Bring Foley with you. He'll take care
of you, I think."

Leaning back on her fists, Josetta swung her legs a couple of times and then stuck them straight out in front of her. Her feet were clad in lacy slippers as delicate as spiderwebs. "All right. But I'm not sure how far I'd get trying to come down here without a coach or an *elaymotive*. My shoes would wear through before I was halfway down the mountain."

"Don't you have anything sturdier than those?"

"I used to have boots, but I've outgrown them, and my mother says I don't need new ones again until next winter."

Zoe jumped up, catching Josetta's arm and hauling the princess to her feet. "Now, *this* is a problem I can take care of," she said. "Let's buy you some walking shoes."

The instant Zoe and Josetta stepped through the cobbler's door, the shopgirl called out for Ilene, who had made it her habit to wait on Zoe personally whenever she dropped by.

"And what can I help you with today, Zoe?" Ilene asked in her usual brisk style. "Or shall we be looking at shoes for your companion?"

"For my companion," Zoe said, wondering how quickly Ilene would recognize Josetta. Foley was waiting outside, so there wasn't much pomp to tip her off, but Ilene was a smart businesswoman. A princess in the shop meant money, and Ilene never overlooked money. "She might need a couple of pairs."

"Casual? Formal? Custom-made? Ready-to-wear?"

"Definitely something casual," Zoe said. "Something with a bit of a sole that could stand up to hard usage. Ready-made would be fine."

"Sit here and let me examine your feet," Ilene said to Josetta, and proceeded to take very thorough measurements. "I think we have some choices that would be quite suitable."

In fact, Josetta was delighted by two pairs of sturdy shoes and one pair of knee-high boots, the latter heavy enough to withstand a wade in the Marisi. "Can I have them all?" she whispered.

"If you want them, you can."

"Oh, I do."

"Excellent," Ilene said, carrying the collection of footwear over to the counter and tallying up prices before the customers could change their minds. "Would the princess like to take them with her now or send a footman to pick them up later?"

Zoe and Josetta laughed at that. "How did you know?" Josetta exclaimed.

Ilene gave her a prim little smile. "It is my business to know," she said.

"We'll take them with us," Zoe said. "I'm sending her straight back to the palace as soon as we leave here."

"I wish you were coming with me," Josetta said, her expression as close to a pout as she ever allowed it to be.

"Well, I'm not. You can make it through dinner just fine without me."

At that, Ilene looked up from her task of wrapping the shoes in fine brown paper. "Oh—if you don't have other dinner plans—perhaps it's too forward of me to suggest it, but Barlow will be eating with us tonight," she said. "If you were free, we'd be happy to have you join us. I wouldn't want to presume too much, of course."

"Of course you're not being too forward!" Zoe exclaimed. "I would *love* to have dinner with your family tonight. Nothing would make me happier."

TWENTY-NINE

The royal carriage dropped Zoe off at her hotel and continued on toward the palace. Zoe hurried inside, already wondering what to wear that evening. Ilene would be disappointed if Zoe didn't dress to her station, but court clothes would look ridiculous in the small apartment above the shoe shop. Something elegant but simple would be required.

"Annova, I went by Ilene's today, and she invited me to dinner," Zoe called as soon as she stepped into her suite and knocked on the connecting door to the servants' quarters. "Barlow will be there, too. Annova?"

But Calvin was the one who opened the door, his face alight with mischief. "Good, you're finally back!"

She stepped into their room, impressed as always by how quickly Annova managed to turn a bland, ordinary space into something personal and inviting. There were bright rugs on the floor, dried flowers on the nightstand, rich and relaxing scents hovering in the air.

Annova turned away from the window, where she was tacking up a gauzy red scarf to turn plain sunshine to fire. "He's been waiting all afternoon to talk to you."

"Did something happen? Something good or bad?"

"Something interesting," Calvin said. "Sit down."

"I don't have much time. I have to change clothes and be back in the shop district in an hour."

"You have time for this."

She glanced at Annova, who shrugged. "He won't tell *me*."

Both women settled on the bed, made cozy with extra blankets and a mound of quilted pillows. "So tell me," Zoe said.

Calvin was too excited to stop pacing. "Today I was wandering through the Plaza of Men, and I saw one of the palace carriages pull up. Not one of the *royal* carriages," he clarified. "Not one the king would ride in, but one of the vehicles that carries servants to market and back. I thought I might know whoever had come to the Plaza, so I waited while he got out, and I heard him tell the driver to come back for him in an hour."

He paused for dramatic effect, so Zoe asked, "And did you know him?"

"Recognized him," Calvin said, "though he probably wouldn't remember me. He was the king's valet." When this didn't elicit much of a response, he added, "The king's own man. Who takes care of all of his most personal needs."

"All right," Zoe said, still not enlightened. "So did you talk to him?"

"No, but I was curious about what he might be doing in the Plaza, so I hung back a little and followed him. But he didn't stay in the Plaza. The minute the carriage was out of sight, he hurried out to the Cinque and caught the first tram that came along. I was barely in time to jump on behind him. I made sure he didn't see me," he added, pleased with himself.

Zoe glanced at Annova, trying to hide her amusement. "Where did it take him?"

"He got off by the southern canals," Calvin said.

That did make Zoe raise her eyebrows. "What would the king's man be doing in a district like that?"

"That's exactly what I wondered! So I kept following him. He was a little nervous, you could tell, because he kept glancing over his shoulder like he was afraid a thief would pick his pockets."

Zoe kept a straight face as she said, "I hope he didn't notice you."

"No, he did not! I walked on the other side of the street and kept bending down to adjust my shoes whenever he looked back. And I ducked into an alley when he finally went into a shop." He said with heavy emphasis, "An apothecary's shop."

Now he really had Zoe's attention. "He was buying drugs for King Vernon? In a seedy shop down by the canals? Why?"

"He could have been buying something for himself," Annova suggested. "Something he didn't want anyone at the palace to know he smoked or swallowed."

"That was my first thought," Calvin admitted. "But still. I thought it was curious. So I dawdled along the street until he came out—trying to make sure no one robbed *me*!—and then I waited a few minutes and dashed into the apothecary's like I'd been running. It was a dreadfully dirty place," he added, shaking his head. "Smelly and dark. There was only one man working there and he looked *evil*. I wouldn't want to buy my drugs there."

"So what did you do?" Zoe asked. "Bribe him to tell you what the king's man had bought?"

"I pretended he'd sent me," Calvin said, clearly proud of himself for having come up with this subterfuge. "I said, 'My master says I'm to buy another half order of the prescription, if you've got more on hand. We'll have a need for it.'"

"That was smart," Zoe said.

"Yes, and it didn't make him suspicious, like he would have been if I'd started asking questions," Calvin said. "He just shook out something that looked like dried dirt and rolled it up in paper and said, 'Three gold pieces.'"

"Three *golds*?" Zoe demanded. "*I* don't even carry that much with me most of the time!"

"Well, I'd thought to shop at the Plaza of Men, so I had a pocket full of coins," Calvin said. "Even so, I was astounded. What could cost that much?"

"Well? What could?" Annova said.

Calvin threw his hands in the air. "I don't know! I could hardly ask him after I'd bought it pretending I knew what it was."

"Of course I'll repay you," Zoe said. "But let's see this expensive medicinal! Maybe one of us will recognize it."

Calvin perched on the bed beside them and carefully undid the twist of paper. Indeed, the finely ground dried leaves resembled nothing so much as dirt, except for their pungent, unpleasant smell. As of rotted fungus sprinkled with urine, Zoe thought, wrinkling her nose. Gingerly, she poked at the brown dust, but she was too leery to touch her tongue to her fingertip and take a taste.

"Can I borrow this?" she asked Calvin.

"It's yours," he said.

"I know someone who might be able to tell me what it is."

Dinner at Melvin and Ilene's cluttered, well-stocked apartment was a happy affair. Barlow greeted Zoe with an exclamation of surprise and a hug, demanding to hear what had happened to her once she had left his company. Ilene rarely sat still for more than five minutes, constantly jumping up to fetch another tray of food or to bring Barlow something she was certain he would enjoy, whether it was a book or an item of clothing or a glass of wine. Melvin, as usual, sat quietly and said little, but beamed contentedly at the people gathered around his table.

Zoe lightly told the more respectable parts of her recent past, then asked after Barlow's business ventures. "I assume you're still partnering with Jaker?" she asked. At Barlow's grin and nod, she said, "Tell him I asked after him. What are you two trading in these days?"

"Oh, as always, whatever looks unusual enough to command a good price," he said. "We took some seeds from the southern coasts all the way to the northern mountains and sold them to a few of the farmers who live near Lalindar property. Shipped in from lands a thousand miles from here—kind of thing that only grows in a wet, cool climate. Ought to do really well up by the river."

"How long are you in the city? Where are you going next?"

"We're waiting for one more shipment to arrive—ought to be four or five days from now, and then we're off again. Probably going straight west this time." He smiled. "Well, with detours now and then. You know how it goes."

She smiled back. "I remember."

The dinner was delicious, the dessert was sinful, and Zoe expressed the belief that she might not be able to waddle home on her own. "Barlow will drive you," Ilene said. "He's been using our smoker car while he's in the city."

Zoe was amused. "You have your own *elaymotive*? I'm impressed!"

"Bought it a quintile ago," Melvin said with satisfaction.

"Of course, it was ridiculously expensive," Ilene said. Her voice conveyed disapproval, but Zoe could read the truth in her eyes. She was delighted to have achieved the level of wealth that would enable her to own such a thing. "Such a waste of money."

Zoe started gathering her things. "I hate to leave, but it's gotten so late! Barlow, if you don't mind taking me home, I would love your escort."

Once they were in the car and Barlow was carefully navigating the narrow streets of the shop district, Zoe said, "I'm glad to have a few minutes with you alone. I had a question I didn't want to ask in front of your parents."

He cut her a sideways look, halfway between amusement and alarm. "Something personal?"

"Not really. I wondered if you could identify a—a drug that came my way under mysterious circumstances."

Now he looked alarmed and intrigued. "Probably not, but Jaker could. He's the one who deals in produce and spices and herbs. And drugs."

"Could I ask him? Now?"

"He'd be glad to see you."

In another twenty minutes, Barlow was showing her into a squat, unfashionable building in a crowded neighborhood on the western edge of the city. The district seemed safe enough, just unkempt. "Bachelor's quarters," Barlow told her with a grin. "Mostly single men. And men who live with other men. No one spends much effort on upkeep."

The door opened onto cramped rooms that were cluttered with boxes of merchandise and stacks of paper—receipts, maps, banker's notes—but the living surfaces were clean and orderly. Jaker exclaimed with pleasure to see Zoe and he came over to take her in a big hug. She remembered with a rush of fondness how much she liked his tanned face, his relaxed friendliness.

"Things have certainly changed for you since we left you

up by the mountains," he said, crinkles springing up around his blue eyes as he smiled. "Every time I hear *Zoe Lalindar*, I think, 'Is that really our Zoe? She seemed so quiet when we knew her.'"

"Surely you can't have heard my name that often."

Jaker and Zoe settled on comfortable chairs around a scarred old wooden table while Barlow fetched drinks from a tiny kitchen. "There was some story about the king's regatta," Jaker said. "It sounded pretty exciting."

"Oh. Yes, I suppose *that* tale was repeated often."

Barlow joined them, handing drinks all around. "You'll like this," he said. "Cost a fortune if you were to buy it in some tavern."

It was both sweet and strong, with a light fizz and a powerful kick. Zoe wanted to guzzle the whole thing down but, watching how slowly Jaker sipped his, she thought it wise to follow suit. "You ought to sell this up at the palace," she said.

"We're already working on that," Jaker said with a laugh. "But I think there's a bigger market among the Five Families. They like to outdo each other when they entertain."

"So how's business been?" Zoe asked, and they spent another fifteen minutes talking trade in a little more depth than they had with Ilene and Melvin.

"All of that is very interesting," Zoe said, and she meant it sincerely. "But I had a question that Barlow said you might be able to answer." She pulled out the twist of paper and slowly unwound it, flattening it on the table. "Do you have any idea what this is? And what it's for?"

Both men leaned forward, Barlow merely curious but Jaker appraising. Like Zoe had, Jaker prodded the loose, dried leaves, taking a pinch between his fingers and rubbing it to dust. He sniffed at the residue and then cautiously tasted the end of his finger. When he straightened up to look over at her, his face was very serious.

"Are you dying?" he asked.

Zoe stared at him. "Am I—no. No, I'm fine—this isn't for me. But you're saying—" She couldn't absorb the implications. "Whoever would take this drug is sick? *Really* sick?"

Jaker nodded. He hadn't lifted his gaze from her face; he seemed to be trying to reassure himself that she wasn't lying.

"This is a pretty high-quality batch," he said. "Not cut too many times with sugar or garbage herbs. Very potent. Risky, though. If you *are* taking it, Zoe, I can find you something a little safer."

"I'm not. Jaker, I swear I'm not. If I seem stunned, it's because—the person who is using the drug—it's a little shocking."

Jaker nodded and didn't press for more details. "Where'd you get it?"

"A shop down by the canal shanties."

"I hope *you* weren't the one buying it, then," Barlow put in. "That's a bad place to wander."

She shook her head. "No, a friend of mine saw—someone—entering the shop. He got curious and followed, and then bought a sample for himself. But we didn't know what it was."

"It's called renaissance," Jaker said. "New life."

"And someone would only take it if he was—if he was *dying*?"

Jaker nodded again. "That's its primary usage. It slows down the progress of a couple of the worst diseases. Adds maybe a year to your life. Maybe two. And takes away a lot of the pain, so they say."

"Sounds like a pretty good drug, then! I'll keep it in mind if I'm ever stricken with something fatal."

"But it's got consequences," Jaker warned. "Sometimes it eliminates your symptoms so completely that you forget you're sick. You show fresh energy—you think you can do what you want. You push yourself too hard and—" He cocked his head to one side, eyes shut, tongue protruding, mimicking a dead man. Straightening up, he said, "You can die just like that."

"What other side effects?"

Jaker tapped the side of his head. "You start to lose some mental ability. You forget things. Some people turn childlike. They say if you take it too long, you can actually become senile or demented. I saw an addict once, raving like a lunatic. Not a pretty sight."

Everything he said made Zoe turn colder and more afraid, though fear had clamped hard on her heart with his very first reaction to the drug. King Vernon was dying. There was no other explanation. Dying, and Darien Serlast knew it. And

Darien was using the riskiest imaginable method to keep him alive another season, another year. And lying to everyone else in the palace while he did it.

Who else knew about the precarious state of the king's health?

Zoe was also puzzling over something Jaker had just said. "If people take it too long, they get senile," she repeated slowly. "Take it too *long*."

He nodded. "Years. I've seen it."

"But if the only people who take it are dying—does it really keep them alive for years?"

"Oh, it has another use," Jaker said. "Not one *you* would be interested in."

Now Barlow was grinning. "Renaissance," he said. "Gives a man new life."

At Zoe's look of bewilderment, Jaker added, "Improved virility. Enhances his ability to perform. There's a certain kind of professional man who needs renaissance just to do his job."

Barlow burst out laughing at that, but Zoe was just in a deeper state of shock.

She knew now who had fathered Romelle's baby.

THIRTY

Zoe's tendency was to share everything with Annova and Calvin, but even she realized that this information was too dangerous to repeat. Begging them to forgive her, she asked if they would leave her alone to meet with Darien Serlast, whenever he deigned to respond to her urgent summons. She had gotten home from Barlow's place at midnight; the message went out at dawn. In reply she had gotten only *As soon as I can*. But he would come. She knew he would.

"I'm so sorry," she said to Annova for the hundredth time. "But you'll have to leave as soon as he gets here."

"Stop apologizing," Annova said. "Do you think I tell *you* everything? Everyone has secrets."

"You'll find it out soon enough, I suppose," Zoe said. "But it shouldn't be from me."

True sunset was just streaking through the false sunset of Annova's gauze curtains when Darien presented himself at Zoe's door. They had laid out a light repast, not sure when he would arrive or if he would be looking for a meal. Zoe had been nibbling all afternoon, but it wasn't as if she was hungry. Her stomach was still a knot of worry and consternation. How could the king be dying?

Annova ushered Darien inside, then took Calvin's hand and

hurried out, closing the door behind her. Darien waited in the middle of the room, watching Zoe as she stood near the window. She had a sudden need for sunshine, for as long as it lasted before the onrushing night.

"Every instinct tells me I'm not going to like what you have to say," Darien observed in a quiet voice. "Has there been an attempt on your life? Have you discovered another half sister? Have you decided to leave the city despite all my entreaties?"

"I have learned one of your secrets—the worst one, I hope," she said.

His expression shifted instantly from an open look of concern to a closed mask of neutrality. "It's true I have secrets," he said. "I'm not certain which one you would consider the worst."

"Which fills me with deep disquiet," she said, "that you could think you have more than one that is as bad as this."

He came across the room, his face troubled. As was the case so often, he was dressed all in black; his wool overrobe swirled almost to his ankles as he walked. He was a dark, steady presence, a wedge of mountain, a massive oak that could not be brought down by any storm. She would have trusted him, too, if she had been dying, if she had needed some bulwark against that greatest of all terrors.

She almost whispered her question. "How much longer do you expect Vernon to live?"

He closed his eyes and swayed backward, for just a moment trembling against a high wind. Then his lids snapped open and he braced himself, planting his feet more firmly on the floor as if determined not to lose his balance.

He didn't deny it, which she considered a great gift. Instead, he said merely, "How much do you know?"

"He is taking a restorative drug known as renaissance. It will extend his life by a year or two, though it will slowly sap his mental acuity. I am only guessing, but I think he has been taking it for a year at least. Which means he can't have much more than another year to live."

He nodded and said, "And how did you discover this?"

"My friend Calvin followed the king's valet into a south city apothecary's shop and ordered the same drug, just for curiosity's sake. Someone else I know—a trader—told me what it was for."

Now Darien's eyes closed for a longer stretch of time; he appeared to wait out a spasm of pain. "Then all of them know—all your friends—"

"No," she said sharply. "I did not share with Calvin the details of the drug, nor did I tell the trader the identity of the patient. I know you think I am careless and indiscreet, but even I know that some things do not bear repeating."

He was regarding her again, his gray eyes a little warmer. "I have that to thank you for, then."

"You haven't answered my question."

He hesitated, then sighed and moved toward the table with its assortment of tempting foods. "Can we at least sit?" he said. "I am tired unto death myself."

They settled at the table and Zoe found herself uncharacteristically moved to take care of him, pouring his water, filling a plate with delicacies, asking if he needed anything else. He looked exhausted, and no wonder. No doubt he spent most of his energy every day maintaining the fiction that the king was healthy. She rarely felt sorry for Darien Serlast, but at this moment it was clear he deserved some kindness.

He ate three dainty sandwiches, finishing each one in two bites, and drained his entire glass of water. Zoe poured him another one, stirring in a teaspoon of crushed fruit. "The king fell ill early last year," Darien said with no more prompting. "In early Quinnelay. Everyone was sick with one cough or another, so at first no one thought much of it. But he did not get better and he did not get better. Elidon was worried, but, of course, we had to proceed with caution. When you send for a physician to see the king, the whole nation is uneasy. Particularly when his daughters are so young—and none has yet been named heir."

"One of those problems he could have solved quite easily," Zoe pointed out. "Just pick his successor."

"Two things made the selection a far from simple process," Darien said. "One, Natalie had not yet been born, and Vernon wanted to see if Romelle might bear a son."

All of Zoe's sympathy for Vernon evaporated in an instant. "Of all the narrow-minded, ill-considered, disastrous reasons to put your entire kingdom in jeopardy—"

Darien managed to produce a faint smile. "I am in complete

agreement with you," he said. "I am prepared to believe women make much better leaders than men do. Mirti and Elidon, for instance, would be splendid rulers, either one of them."

"So once Romelle only managed to produce another girl, what kept him from choosing his heir? You said there were two reasons."

"Any choice would have had to be ratified by all five primes," Darien said, "and one of the primes was missing."

Zoe stared at him for so long that he had time to eat another sandwich. "Are you telling me—after all this time—after all the reasons you gave me, all the lies you told me about why you came to fetch me from the village—this was the *real* reason? This was why I suddenly had to be in Chialto, at the palace, under your watchful eye? So I could fulfill my part as prime?"

He bowed his head in acknowledgment, though he still watched her from under his lowered brows. "It was an urgent necessity that you be present to ratify the choice of the king's successor," he said in a quiet voice. "The stability of the kingdom depended on it. And yet, all of the other reasons I gave you were true. The king *was* negotiating with his wives, and your name *was* put forward as a choice for his fifth bride. I *did* promise your father, and my own, that I would come for you when Navarr was dying. These were not lies. But they did not matter to me as much as the knowledge that the fifth prime had to be on hand or we could never choose the next ruler of Welce."

She made a strangled sound of exasperation and shook her head, trying to dissipate her incredulity and her ire. But how could she be surprised or even annoyed? It had always been clear he had secrets, some of them monstrous. She was not sure she could entirely blame him for concealing this particular ungainly and terrifying truth.

"Very well, then, you came searching for me, but at the same time you did what you could to keep Vernon alive," she said, bringing the conversation back to its original topic. "When did he start taking the drug?"

"By the middle of Quinncoru last year. As I said, we went to some trouble to bring in a physician in stealth, and we pretended that Elidon was the sick one. She spent a great deal of time languishing in her quarters and depriving herself of food, so that she would look pale and thin. Vernon came to her rooms to be present when the physician examined her." Darien shrugged. "He was fairly quick to make the diagnosis and to lay out our wretched options. He was honest about the repercussions we might face with the renaissance, but the alternative was unthinkable. The king to be dead within a quintile. We all agreed we would risk the drug."

"Who was in on the agreement?"

"The king, Elidon, and me."

"And the doctor."

"An *elay* man. Elidon's nephew and utterly reliable." He must have seen the skepticism on her face because he almost smiled again. "Obviously, or this news would have gotten out long before now."

She was forced to agree that was true. "So none of the other wives know?"

He shook his head.

"And none of the other primes? Not even Mirti?"

"I would not be surprised to learn Mirti has guessed. But she has said nothing—at least, to any of us. Kayle and Nelson and Taro—no."

"The king's valet—the one who buys the illicit drugs—*he* must know something."

Darien nodded. "Again, I'm sure he has his suspicions, but he has not voiced them. He is utterly loyal. He has been with Vernon since they were both boys."

"Still. You must know this is a secret that cannot be kept forever."

"I am astonished it has not been discovered before now."

"How much longer do you think he has before—he has to live?"

"Two quintiles, maybe four. For a while, his deterioration was so greatly slowed that I began to think he had been misdiagnosed. That he was actually recovering. He seemed quite strong last summer—in fact, the only symptoms I even saw in him were the ones caused by the drug."

Zoe remembered the king's oddly vulnerable manner that day in Ilene's shop, his inability to choose a buckle for his shoe. "A childishness in his behavior," she murmured. "A loss of focus."

"Exactly. But other than that, he seemed quite healthy. Hearty, even."

"When did you realize that this burst of vigor was not, unfortunately, a sign of recovery?"

"When we decided to take him off the drug for a couple of ninedays. Actually, it was only a few days. That quickly we saw him lose ground. His pain returned. His nausea. He couldn't sleep for the headaches. We put him back on the renaissance—and increased the dosage at that." He shook his head. "There was no more lying to ourselves. He is a very sick man."

"So you have until, perhaps, the end of the year before he dies."

"Yes. And less time before he becomes so weakened it will be impossible to conceal his condition."

"So now it has become urgent that his heir be identified."

Darien nodded. "It is our constant conversation to discuss the strengths and weaknesses of the three girls. Josetta is the oldest and thus the one who will soonest be an adult, which means the regency period would be that much shorter. But if, as I would hope, the next queen sits on the throne for thirty or forty years, perhaps a regency that is only three years longer should not be a foremost consideration. Is Corene the better candidate? She certainly has more strength of will than Josetta. She is quick-witted and passionate, while Josetta is cautious and sometimes timid. I am far from certain who would be a better queen."

"You don't even consider Natalie?"

He shrugged. "She is barely a year old, and I, at least, cannot judge her personality well enough to gauge how fit she would be to rule. But an even bigger barrier, I think, is the idea of a twenty-year regency. Certainly *I* am not eager to spend so much of my life in such a role."

"And are you so convinced that *you* would be picked for the position?"

His face showed the ghost of a smile. "Who else?"

"I can think of a couple of women who would consider themselves qualified to stand beside their daughters and lead."

"I would trust Elidon's guidance, but Seterre or Alys as regent? Seterre would divide loyalties and pit factions against each other, leaving the court fractured and at odds. Alys would beggar the kingdom and then send us into war to refill our coffers. She would randomly elevate favorites and banish those who disagreed with her. Who knows? She might dispatch assassins in stealth to rid herself of the councilors she particularly distrusted."

His tone was so bitter that Zoe had a hard time hiding her astonishment. "You despise her more than I realized."

"And even more than that," he said.

"What happens if the king dies without naming his successor?"

Darien slumped back in his chair, weariness once again evident on his face. "Oh, then I suppose the brangling and the scheming and the plotting begin in earnest. The queens will each lobby for their favorites, but the primes will have to do the real job of choosing the next monarch. I hope you can bring yourself to be impartial."

Zoe smiled. "Who do you think the other four would favor?"

"Kayle would choose Corene, for Wald's sake," Darien said instantly. "Nelson is new enough to power this time around that he would probably follow your lead. Mirti always has her own agenda, so she is hard to predict. But she's unlikely to change her mind once she makes it up. As for Taro, he likes little Natalie because he is fond of Romelle."

"You realize there is yet another option, one that is sure to be obvious to everyone very soon."

He caught his breath. She thought he might actually have forgotten. "I am not used to including a fourth child in my calculations," he admitted.

"I think you must," Zoe said. "I think we have solved the mystery of who sired the child Romelle is carrying now. The renaissance drug has given Vernon new virility, and that baby is his. The king's subjects—and the primes of the Five Families—might simply decide to hand over the crown to the only one of the four children who is truly the offspring of the king."

Darien watched her for a long time with narrowed eyes. "You know nothing for certain yet—or so I assume. Until the baby is born, you will not be able to decode its blood."

"That's true," she said. "But if, as you say, Romelle has had no other lovers—"

"That I know about," he interrupted. "I am willing to believe her abilities of subterfuge overmatch my skills of surveillance."

"Let us assume she has been chaste," Zoe said. "This child is the king's. Shouldn't his legitimate son or daughter be the first choice for heir?"

"We have gone to a great deal of trouble to make the king's subjects believe that all of his supposed daughters are, in fact, legitimate," Darien countered. "To suddenly retract that would render the whole kingdom uneasy, don't you think? Would make them wonder what other lies have been perpetrated at court?"

"I think these simple country folk you worry about already believe there is a great deal of lying going on at the palace," Zoe said. "And I think most of them don't care. They want order in the realm. They want safe borders and opportunities for profitable trade. It doesn't matter to them who governs as long as he or she governs well."

"In which case, you have lost your own argument," he replied. "Why must the next ruler be blood of the king's blood?" He leaned forward, his pose almost accusatory. "And, since *you* are the only one who can—or *claims* she can—determine a child's parentage simply by touch, you might have a hard time making anyone else believe you. Or, if they believe you, care. Josetta and Corene and Natalie have all been presented as heirs of the king's body. This fourth child is unimportant, almost inconvenient. He or she will not be a factor in the upcoming struggle for power."

Zoe regarded him for a moment in silence. She wished her uncle Nelson was here, or Taro Frothen—either one of them, she thought, would answer her truthfully; she was less sure of Mirti Serlast and Kayle Dochenza.

"Do you seriously think that such a gift was given only to the *coru* line?" she asked softly. "Don't you think your aunt Mirti can squeeze a man's hand in hers until she feels the alignment of the bones? Don't you think Taro Frothen can rest his fingers against a girl's wrist and read the heritage in her skin? I don't know how Kayle Dochenza analyzes the souls of those he meets—perhaps he has to kiss them on their mouths; perhaps he only has to feel their breath against his cheek. And

I am even less certain what skill Nelson uses to read a man's mind, but I have no doubt he can do it. I am not the only prime who can decipher your secrets, Darien Serlast. The others either have not been in a position to make discoveries—or they have decided to keep their knowledge to themselves."

Now she was the one to lean forward. "If you must rely on the Five Families to anoint and protect the heir, you had better let them know that a fourth candidate is on the way—and that *this* child is truly born to the king. Because if they discover that fact after they have bound their power on behalf of one of the other princesses, I promise you, the whole court will be in an uproar. You will see alliances shattered and vows revoked. And your own days of power as confidante to the throne will be irretrievably behind you."

"I do none of this to increase my own consequence," he snapped. "Is that what you think? I don't keep secrets and try to influence events merely to feel like an important man. I would have happily shoveled my responsibilities onto someone else's shoulders anytime these past two years! But Vernon chose me to trust and I had no choice but to be trustworthy. Perhaps that is not something a *coru* woman can understand. *I could not bend.* If you think that makes me ambitious, then fine. Think the worst of me. It does not change that I have done the best I can."

She tightened her lips and straightened in her chair. "Perhaps you have. At any rate, there is no point in wishing the past reconfigured. It is the future we must contend with. And if I were you, I would make sure Romelle's child has a place in that future—even if just to be considered and rejected. Or you will pay for that secrecy in ways I do not believe you can foresee."

He sat very stiff and straight for a moment, and then nodded jerkily. "I perceive the wisdom in what you say. But there are formidable obstacles to honesty in this case."

Zoe felt a smile brush her lips and disappear. "The fact that Romelle herself may not know she is pregnant? Surely that obstacle will disappear very soon."

He spoke with chilling deliberation. "The fact that, the minute someone believes Romelle is pregnant with the king's true heir, both Romelle and her baby are in danger of their lives."

Zoe stared at him, feeling as if she had been punched in the stomach.

"Surely you haven't forgotten that someone tried to kill Josetta," he said, speaking still in those cold, precise tones. "I have wondered if Natalie's constant discontent has been the result of subtle poison being administered to her diet. I have had some changes made to the kitchen staff, with the result that Natalie has been a much more cheerful child in recent days. Someone is maneuvering to put Corene on the throne. I cannot believe such a ruthless person would hear Romelle's news and quietly cede the crown. I think someone would hear that news and intensify attempts to dispose of all rivals."

"In which case, once any of the girls is named heir, her life is in danger."

"Perhaps. But once the decision has been made, I can be excused for marshaling more resources to protect the child named as successor."

"I would think you would be better served marshaling those same *resources* to discovering who is harming the princesses *now*," she said sharply.

Abruptly, he pushed back from the table and sprang to his feet. "Do you think I am *not*?" he demanded. "Even now, I have men in Chialto and Soeche-Tas, hunting for the two sailors who crewed Josetta's boat in the regatta. One of them shipped out on a merchant vessel that is due back in port within a nineday—one of them crossed the mountains with a peddler's caravan. It might take me another year, but I will find them and I will discover who paid them. I have other inquiries afoot—" He paused and shook his head, as if annoyed that he would stoop to justify himself to her. To anyone. "It doesn't matter," he said. "I have done what I can. I *will* do what I can. Believe me or not, as you will. I am done here."

He gave Zoe an abbreviated bow as she slowly stood up. "I thank you for sharing with me the knowledge that you stumbled upon," he said. "I would ask you to refrain from repeating it for as long as your conscience allows. And I would reiterate my hope that you join Vernon and the rest of the Five Families to celebrate the viceroy's visit when he comes." He bowed again. "That is all."

He strode for the door. "Wait," she said.

More than halfway across the room, he turned. His expression was bleak. "Waiting seems to have done me no good at all up to this point," he said.

Her smile was painful; she was surprised he was even able to attempt a joke. "I apologize," she said.

His expression didn't change. "Surely I misunderstood."

She smiled a little more naturally as she took a few steps in his direction. "I did not mean to imply that I thought your attempts were—inept. Or insufficient. Or ill-advised. I doubt I would have managed as well as you have in circumstances this complex and fraught with danger. I was merely expressing my own worry and fear. Clumsily, I suppose."

He had not moved from where he had frozen at her command. *Hunti* man, unbending. Not making it easier for her in any way. Forcing her to come all the way to his side. While they had sat before the window, the lingering gold of dusk had illuminated their conversation, but this deep in the room there was nothing but shadow. She could no longer see his face clearly.

"If I were the king, I would trust you, too," she said, once she was close enough to practically whisper the words. "What I fear is that no one, not even you, can keep everyone safe."

"I fear the same thing," he said, his voice very low. "I am—worried—that even now there are events unfolding that I know nothing about and cannot control."

"What kind of events?"

He made an indeterminate motion with his hands. "Something to do with the viceroy. The king seems more excited about this visit than I would have anticipated."

Zoe grinned in the near-dark. "Maybe he is feeling healthy enough to reconsider that fifth wife," she said. "Maybe the viceroy will be bringing one of his daughters with him."

"That *would* be momentous," Darien agreed. "Though I would argue vociferously against a marriage with the people of Soeche-Tas. My father visited the place some years ago—on an expedition that also included your father, as a matter of fact—and he told me stories about their customs that shocked me to the core."

"Those are stories I might want to hear someday."

"When you're in the mood for a gruesome tale, perhaps,"

Darien said. He shook his head. "I can't think another marriage is on Vernon's mind, and yet something clearly is. For the past year he has consulted me on every decision, no matter how small. For the past two or three ninedays, that has not been the case. It worries me." He sighed heavily. "Everything worries me."

"I am sorry to have added to your burdens," Zoe said, and she meant it.

"Sometimes you are the thing that worries me most," he said, and reached out and pulled her into his embrace.

It was what she had hoped for, so she did not resist. She merely lifted her face to meet his kiss, hungry and searching on her mouth. His arms around her were so strong that for a moment she could allow herself to be utterly weak; she could drift against him, knowing he would not permit her to melt away. She wanted to fit herself to his body, her soft surfaces against his solid bulk, sheltered at last, in a still, calm cove of ease and safety.

His arms tightened; for a moment, *sweela* heat washed over them, a reminder that both wood and water were susceptible to fire. She clung to him, willing to be swept away, but only if he came along with her. But he groaned against her lips and grudgingly loosened his hold.

"I find myself trusting you," he whispered. "But everybody knows that only a fool puts his faith in a *coru* woman."

She laughed against his mouth. "A fool or a desperate man," she whispered back. "Which are you?"

"Both," he said.

"You fascinate me," she murmured, "but everyone knows that a *hunti* man makes for a stern and joyless lover."

"I would like the chance to prove to you that the conventional wisdom is wrong."

"Now?" she asked, teasing.

"If only that were possible. But with your friends returning at any moment and the king plotting who knows what catastrophe—"

"Perhaps once the viceroy is gone," she suggested, still speaking against his mouth. In between sentences he was snatching quick kisses, brief and breathless. "Perhaps the world will slow down and time will stretch out. It sometimes happens."

"Although time is more likely to speed up and then fall to pieces, but we will hope for some balance in our lives sometime in the coming season," he said. He kissed her again. "I must go."

"One thing I'd like to ask you," she said.

He had released her from his embrace but his hands were on her shoulders, as if he couldn't quite let her go, and her wrists were hooked around his forearms, as if she wanted to hold him in place. "Again, I'm filled with foreboding," he said.

"Tell me your last secret."

There was a brief silence. "You'll hate me for it."

"That's ominous."

"It's what I fear."

"I didn't hate you for this one," she reminded him.

He kissed her with an air of finality, and dropped his hands. "Oh, but this time the risks are so high," he said. "After the viceroy is gone. When the world stabilizes. We'll talk some more then."

She felt some of her giddiness fade—at the thought that he wouldn't confide in her, at the realization that he was actually leaving, she wasn't really sure. "The world never stabilizes," she said. "It only changes."

He bent in to kiss her on the cheek, a curiously comforting gesture. "But some things endure," he said. "Word of a *hunti* man."

Josetta was back the next day, trailed by two guards in addition to the watchful Foley. "Darien insisted," she said when Zoe asked about her expanded escort as they traveled to Sarone's. "He says there is too much chaos because of the plans for the viceroy's visit, and things can go wrong. Corene has three guards following her everywhere, too, *and* Natalie. Although Natalie goes nowhere without Romelle, and Romelle scarcely leaves the palace, so I don't know how much danger she could possibly be in."

"Is Romelle still feeling unwell?"

"Yes, but only in the mornings. *I* think she just doesn't want to go to Elidon's breakfasts anymore."

"Now, that's something I should have thought of when I

lived at the palace! Although it's tedious to pretend to be sick. Every day, at that. I think it's much better for me just not to live in the palace at all."

Josetta wrinkled her nose. "I don't think I would want to live in a hotel all the time, either."

"It has its disadvantages," Zoe admitted. "Keeli has found a house for me here in the city but I haven't had time to look it over. Would you like to go see it today?"

Josetta agreeing to that suggestion with enthusiasm, they cut short their swim by about twenty minutes to tour the house Keeli had picked out. It was not nearly as large as Sarone's place, but Zoe had asked for something small enough to be manageable, and she considered it charming. Public rooms and necessary spaces were thoughtfully laid out on the bottom story, while upstairs a cluster of bedrooms offered places for the owner and any guests to sleep in comfort. All the walls were covered in paints or papers of soothing blues and greens; there was a fountain in every room. Even the *kierten* featured a wall of running water endlessly splashing down a slab of malachite into a grillwork drain. It was clear a *coru* family had lived here in the past.

"I love it," Josetta said, "but no room for a pool!"

"Close enough to walk to Keeli's," Zoe said. "And not far from my uncle Nelson, either. It does seem perfect."

"Then I think you should buy it."

"Then I think I probably will."

On firstday, Nelson invited her to dinner, a small affair where only family members were in attendance. It gave her a good opportunity to observe Kurtis's son and daughter, rambunctious ten-year-old twins with hair so red it lit the darkness. She liked the way they tumbled through the room, rarely in their seats for more than five minutes at a stretch, but she had to admit the mood was much more peaceful after the meal, when their mother took them up to bed. The rest of them moved to a sitting room filled with extravagantly plush furniture and more candles than she had ever seen in one place at one time. The flames were reflected from dozens of small mirrors, doubling the light.

"You'll be at the palace tomorrow afternoon for the reception?" Kurtis asked.

"I've been issued an invitation that read more like a command," she answered with a laugh. "I would not dare miss it."

"Did you see the viceroy's convoy arriving this morning?" Rhan demanded. "There had to be fifteen carriages, one right after the other! Traffic on the Cinque was snarled for hours."

"I saw that! I pushed to the front of the crowd, because I wanted to get a good look at the viceroy's face. I spotted him once before during a parade and I thought he looked like someone who was not very nice."

"I don't believe he is," Nelson spoke up. "Your father met him years ago when he and Damon Serlast and a whole delegation went to Soeche-Tas. I think the word Navarr used to describe the viceroy was 'debauched.'"

"So you *know* he has to be a lecher or a drunk if a *sweela* man despises his excesses," Rhan said with a grin.

"What did he do that was so awful?" Zoe asked. Darien hadn't told her, but she didn't think her uncle would be so squeamish.

Nelson squinted, as if that would help him remember details. "I think it was the whole Soechin society that repulsed him. He said the viceroy sent concubines to his room every night and was astonished when your father turned down their services."

"My father did?" Zoe said dryly. "I find that surprising."

"They were girls. Ten and eleven years old," Nelson said in a quiet voice. "Each night, they sent him someone younger, thinking the problem was that he considered his potential bedmates too old." He shrugged. "The whole country is obsessed with youth, but I admit this was a particularly disturbing story."

Zoe took a deep breath. "No wonder he was so opposed to the alliance with Soeche-Tas."

"Yes, though I think he tried to argue against it for political reasons, not cultural ones. I'm not sure how widely he told the story of the concubines sent to his room. He knew his own reputation might turn it into a ribald tale, instead of a tragic one. Damon Serlast only told the tale once that I overheard it, but it was clear he never cared much for the viceroy, either."

"No, and now I hate him as well!" Kurtis exclaimed. Zoe wondered if he was thinking of his own red-haired daughter and how poorly she would fare in the viceroy's land.

"How long will he be here, do you know?" she asked.

"Five days, so I hear," Nelson replied. "And all his attending advisors go home with him, which will finally put the city back to normal."

"I'm looking forward to his departure," Zoe said.

"As are we all," Nelson said. "I'm eager to spend my days at court talking about something besides Soeche-Tas." He laughed. "Now that I am welcome *back* at court, at least let me have conversation that matters!"

Zoe did not see Darien Serlast during those intervening days, but he did send a small package to her hotel room on the morning of the viceroy's reception. Annova and Calvin watched with great interest as she unwrapped it to reveal a small wooden box, gorgeously inlaid with strips of cherry, mahogany, oak, and teak. Inside was a pin fashioned of some wood so dark it was almost black, and polished to an onyx shine. It featured a kneeling woman bent over a flowing river; she apparently had just lifted her hands from the water, for droplets fell from her fingers in tiny sapphire chips.

"Well, that's about as pretty a piece as I've ever seen," Annova said in an approving voice. "A most thoughtful gift for a *hunti* man to give to a *coru* woman."

Zoe had gone to the nearest mirror to try the pin against the shoulder of her plain green tunic. Naturally, she would change into a much more elegant ensemble for the reception. "Do you think I should wear it tonight?" she asked.

Annova snorted. "Of course you should wear it tonight! That's why the man sent it today!"

"Unless you want to tell him to stop wasting his money buying gifts for you," Calvin said. He was grinning hugely; for some reason, he liked Darien Serlast. "Then leave it at home."

"But if I do wear it, am I sending some other kind of message?" Zoe asked. She had planned to wear something pink and floaty, but this piece would look wrong with such an outfit. She had a new overrobe, a heavily textured weave of copper, cobalt, verdigris, and sky. The pin would look stunning against that backdrop.

"Well, forgive me if I'm wrong," Annova said, "but I assume that's the message you *want* to send to Darien Serlast."

Zoe turned to make a face at Annova, then laughed and returned her attention to the mirror. "How long do you think it would take to make such a thing?" she asked. "When would he have had to commission it to have it ready by today?"

"I don't know," Annova said. "When was the first time he touched your hand? As long ago as that, I imagine. But he waited to give it to you until after he'd kissed you."

Zoe whirled around, ready to pretend indignation, but it was impossible to keep from blushing, which did not make a denial credible. "You see too much," she said.

Calvin was smirking. "Some things are easy to see."

THIRTY-ONE

The reception was scheduled to begin in midafternoon; Zoe was dressed an hour early and spent the rest of the time sitting quietly so she didn't muss her hair or clothes or makeup. She was waiting in the hotel *kierten* when Nelson's smoker car pulled up, and she climbed in beside him and his sons.

"I suppose if I'm going to live in the city, I'll need to buy my own vehicle. And hire someone to drive it. It seems like a lot of trouble," she remarked as they began the ascent to the palace. The way was clogged with dozens of other *elaymotives* as well as horse-drawn vehicles, making progress slow.

"It *is* a lot of trouble," Nelson said.

Kurtis demurred. "It's fun! I take the car to the country estates and drive it myself. Come visit this summer and I'll teach you."

She remembered that rambling journey with Jaker and Barlow, so long ago it seemed like a different life. "I've driven a smoker car," she said. "It *was* a lot of fun. But I don't think I'd enjoy trying it in the city with all the traffic."

Rhan was eyeing her with narrowed attention. "I sometimes think I don't know half of the stories you could tell about your life," he said.

She laughed. "None of them as interesting as you might hope."

"I would like to hear them and judge for myself."

They finally made it to the mountain plateau that held the palace and its attendant lake. For a day in deep winter, the weather was unexpectedly fine, and the king had taken advantage of this fact to set up tables and refreshment booths in the courtyard. Already, dozens of guests were milling about, holding drinks and visiting with friends. The slanting afternoon sunlight glinted off the moving surface of the water and gilded the planed surfaces of the palace. Braziers ringed the courtyard to provide extra warmth; torches and tall stands of candelabra were strategically placed to offer illumination later in the evening. Zoe wondered if they could expect another light-and-color extravaganza as part of the night's festivities.

She vividly remembered that last exhibition—parts of it, at least. She put her hand up to the pin on her left shoulder and briefly stroked the smooth wood.

"Let's find something to drink and someone to talk to," Rhan said, and they all climbed out of the car.

Zoe didn't make much effort to stay with the Ardelays, but instead allowed the eddies of the crowd to separate them. She drifted through the throng, restless, unwilling to talk for long with one group or individual. Soon enough, she found herself in the great echoing *kierten* of the palace, even more crowded with revelers than the courtyard and more heavily stocked with refreshments. A low stage had been erected near the entrance to the men's wing, decorated with banners depicting the colors of Soeche-Tas as well as the king's multicolored rosette motif. Vernon was planning some announcement, then. Probably news about a commercial alliance or even a military pact. Zoe didn't really think the king would take another wife, from Soeche-Tas or elsewhere. He had too much other business to attend to during his few remaining quintiles.

She sampled the foods offered at the various stations in the *kierten*, finding them all tasty though some were so unfamiliar they must be Soechin delicacies. None of the liquid refreshments was as good as the sweet fizzing drink she had had in Barlow and Jaker's apartment. She didn't want to get tipsy on alcohol, so she was grateful when she found servants handing out glasses of fruited water. Accepting a large goblet, she continued to roam the hall.

She knew why she couldn't settle. She knew she was hoping to encounter Darien Serlast. Even though she realized that was unlikely. He was no doubt with Vernon in the royal quarters, going over final schedules for the evening and, perhaps, if he hadn't yet learned it, trying to discover what grand idea the king planned to announce tonight. Darien would have no time to give Zoe more than a nod, a brief smile, assuming she could even catch his eye amid all of the color and noise. But still she searched for him; she found herself longing for a glimpse of his face.

Sounds from the courtyard—laughter and applause—made her drift back outside to see what entertainments were on hand. Jugglers were tossing bright balls in the air and magicians were causing small items to vanish and reappear. Music threaded through the crowd, though at first she couldn't place its source. Eventually she realized that an energetic quartet had been set up on the third floor of the men's wing, in an open window embrasure; the individual notes seemed to spatter down like rain from overhead.

Darien Serlast was nowhere in sight.

Zoe braved the chilly air outside the heated courtyard and wandered down to the edge of the river. She stood for a moment contemplating the assortment of boats tied up at the bank. None of them looked as if they had been cleaned up and organized for an excursion tonight, so perhaps there would not be an after-dark lights festival after all. There would certainly be no reason to step into one of these little dinghies and glide into the middle of the lake, wrapped in Darien Serlast's arms . . .

She shook her head and turned back for the palace.

When she entered the *kierten* again, the royal family had finally made an appearance. They were mingling with the rest of the revelers, moving through the crowd in one loosely formed knot. The king was surrounded by his four wives and three daughters, while various attendants hovered nearby to do their bidding. Darien followed the king so closely he almost appeared to be mimicking Vernon's movements. If, upon entering the scene, he had spent a few moments searching the throng for Zoe, he did not do so now. All his attention appeared to be on his liege.

A second constellation of prominence moved in tandem with the first, the Soechin delegation following the gravitational pull of the royal family. Zoe saw that the ambassadors and their wives had been augmented by three people—the viceroy, whom she remembered from his previous visit; a very beautiful, very bored woman who looked young enough to be his daughter; and a thin, hawk-faced man with an unpleasant expression. Zoe guessed he was a personal guard of some sort, and further guessed that more Soechin soldiers were stationed nearby, within call if their viceroy needed them.

The thought made her glance up and search the *kierten* for figures she was sure she would find. Yes—unobtrusively backed against the walls and lurking in the shadowed archways were twenty or more of the king's own militia. Zoe looked until she located Foley, his expression neutral as always, all his attention on Josetta.

She returned her gaze to the viceroy, her instinctive dislike even stronger now that she had anecdotal evidence of his depravity. As before, he was opulently dressed in many layers of purple and red and cloth of gold; even from a distance she could see diamonds glittering at his ears and weighing down his hands. Small braids gave texture to his flowing white hair; his lips and cheeks were so rosy she would not be surprised to learn he wore cosmetics. Qeesia and the other ambassador's wife hung on either arm, fawning over him. His smile was somewhere between triumphant and exhilarated, as if he had just ingested a potent exuberant drug or won a hotly contested game. She shuddered and looked away.

A flutter on the corner of her vision caught her attention, and she turned to see Josetta waving from the inviolable circle of her family. Zoe smiled and waved back, nodding enthusiastically when Josetta gestured at her own ensemble. It was a delicate confection of blue lace, blue tulle, blue embroidery, and blue ribbons. Corene's outfit was similar, except constructed from shades of ivory accented at carefully casual points with tiny carnelian roses. Even her red hair had been laced with off-white ribbons dotted with budding flowers. She looked as if she had just stepped out of a milk bath that had been strewn with blossoms that now clung randomly to her skin.

Beautiful, Zoe mouthed at Josetta. Corene intercepted the exchange, so Zoe added silently, "You, too." Corene smiled and tossed her red hair.

Darien Serlast never bothered to look Zoe's way.

Zoe was tempted to go back outside, except the motion of the crowd was against her. News seemed to have traveled quickly through the courtyard that the king and his exalted visitors had joined the celebration, because all the other guests were pouring inside, eager to catch a glimpse of royalty. She couldn't even retreat toward the women's wing because the press of the crowd was too great. Instead, she was caught in the middle of a sea of people, helplessly shifting in whatever direction they tended and hoping she didn't suddenly suffer a suffocating sense of panic.

Unexpectedly, she found her cousin Rhan beside her. His presence was reassuring; she clutched his arm as if he represented an anchor. "I hope you don't mind," she said somewhat breathlessly. "I find myself—overwhelmed—by the crowd."

"I need someone to hold on to myself," he replied, putting an arm around her shoulders, which seemed to isolate her from the mob, if only a little. "I don't think I've ever seen this many people shoved into this space before."

"Why didn't some of them stay outside?" she said in a petulant voice.

"Someone said there was going to be an announcement. Everyone wants to hear."

Indeed, now it became clear that the king's cluster of family and the viceroy's knot of advisors were both moving toward the dais in as straight a line as possible, given the constraints of the crowd. It seemed to take forever for them to arrive at their destination and then ascend the makeshift stairs in a carefully calibrated order of precedence. First the king, then the viceroy, then Elidon, then the beautiful Soechin girl.

She must be his daughter after all, Zoe thought. A slight uneasiness threaded through her stomach, making her wish some of the wine undrunk. Possibly Vernon *was* going to announce his fifth betrothal. The renaissance had left his body feeling stronger and his mind more susceptible to fantasy. She watched as the remaining three queens climbed the stairs, one right after the other, Romelle carrying a squirming Natalie in her arms. One ambassador and his wife flanked Josetta as she mounted the steps. Corene was escorted up the steps by Qeesia and her husband, who remained very close to the princess once they stood on the stage, rather unnervingly near the front edge. Darien slipped up last, after everyone else was in place.

"Look at how they paw at poor Corene," Rhan murmured in her ear. "She's putting a brave face on it, but I can't imagine she much likes having them touch her like that."

Indeed, Corene's expression seemed fixed in an unnatural smile and her skin was oddly flushed. Zoe didn't know her well enough to judge if she was excited and trying to hide the emotion, or terrified and trying even harder.

"I keep wondering about that Soechin girl," Zoe whispered back. "Do you think she's one of the viceroy's daughters? Do you suppose they're going to announce that she's marrying the king?"

"It crossed my mind," Rhan admitted. "But I've heard no gossip to that effect."

Have you heard gossip to the effect that the king is dying? she wanted to ask. "I suppose we'll find out very soon," she replied.

Indeed, Vernon was stepping forward, raising his arms to call for quiet. Instantly, the murmur of the crowd died down. Zoe felt the whole assembly press forward, carrying her another five inches closer to the stage.

"My subjects—my friends," Vernon called out, his voice barely strong enough to carry through the whole *kierten*. He was smiling; he looked pleased with himself, Zoe thought. Her sense of foreboding intensified. "As you know, we have long been interested in creating deeper bonds between our kingdom and our friends to the north in Soeche-Tas."

"Speak louder!" someone shouted from the back of the hall.

The king took a big breath, obviously hoping to comply. "And what better way to unite our two nations than through a marriage?"

Zoe glanced up at Rhan, who gave her an expressive look and shook his head. "Madness," he leaned down to say in her ear.

Zoe turned her attention to Darien Serlast, who stood stony-faced beside Elidon, but *his* expression she could read. He was worried and displeased and braced for worse to come. She kept her eyes on Darien as Vernon continued talking.

"That is why today I am pleased to announce that you have all been invited here to witness a wedding that will be held this very evening!"

"Tonight?" Rhan whispered. "That's eager!"

The king turned slightly to the left, then slightly to the right, as if with his open arms he would embrace everyone on the stage with him. "A wedding between Harmon Koel of Soeche-Tas and my daughter Corene!"

"*What?*"

Zoe thought she screamed the word, but perhaps she only breathed it. At any rate, her single shocked syllable was wholly devoured by the noisy reaction of the crowd. Some people were applauding; a few were cheering; even more turned to their closest neighbors to express surprise, uncertainty, speculation.

"I don't think I like that," Rhan was saying in an under-voice. "She's what? Eleven? Twelve? Considering what my father was telling us the other night—"

Zoe scarcely heard him. She scarcely heard anyone. She was staring at Darien Serlast, who had staggered as if from a fatal blow. He instantly pushed his way past the queens to the king's side and began arguing furiously. Vernon tried to turn his head, waving away Darien's protests, but Darien leaned closer, talked more loudly, gesticulated more wildly. He looked as if he was having to restrain himself from pushing the king off of the dais.

As for herself, Zoe was shaking so badly that for a moment she thought the floor was rocking beneath her feet. Her lips were moving, but even she could not have said what words she was trying to form. Her eyes were still on the stage, where Qeesia had laced her hands with Corene's and lifted their arms up in a gesture of victory. Corene was still offering that strange smile, waving at the crowd, bowing once toward her affianced husband. Zoe couldn't tell if the princess was feeling smug or terrified.

Rhan nudged her. "Zoe? Are you all right? Zoe?"

She shook her head. "No," she said, her lips finally finding the word they had been searching for. *"No."*

Rhan grabbed both of her shoulders and forced her to look at him. "Zoe? Zoe! Is something wrong? Can I do anything for you?"

For a moment she stared up at him, seeing his smiling face creased into concern for her. Oh, but Zoe wasn't the one he needed to worry about. That the sick, mad king would sacrifice his daughter in such a way. That a child should be bartered to a lecherous old man for the sake of a political advantage. She could feel horror building up in her veins, or perhaps it was rage, or perhaps it was power. "No," she said.

"No, what? Are you all right?"

"No," she said, breaking free of his hold and starting to push blindly through the crowd. "No—no—*no!*"

Maybe she clawed at them, drawing blood; maybe the tone of her voice was so odd that she frightened them, but people moved back from her, gave her room. Scarcely even conscious of her motions, she spread her hands as wide as the fingers would go, palms down, as if she was bracing herself against the floor. She felt the thrumming of the pipes in the levels below the *kierten*, carrying water to the palace from the nearby river. She felt the splashing of every fountain set up in the public spaces, the private rooms. She felt the rushing force of the Marisi roaring through those spectacular falls and briefly calming itself to a lake before dropping down the rest of the mountain on its way past the city to the sea.

She collected every drop of that water and began drawing it in her direction.

If anyone spoke to her, she didn't hear it. If anyone touched her, she didn't feel it. All she could hear, all she could feel, was water. Crystalline, bountiful, and beyond restraint.

The great bronze fountain on the back wall of the *kierten* began spewing jets of spray into the gathered crowd. A few people swore and moved hastily back; others murmured surprise and dismay. Those murmurs grew louder as the water in the basin began overflowing, pouring steadily onto the marble floor.

"What's wrong? Can someone turn that off?"

"I'm soaked! Did you see my shoes?"

"Look out! The water's coming!"

Servants hastened toward the fountain, seeking shutoff valves, showing each other frightened faces when none of their efforts had any effect. A cook came dashing up from the back corridor, crying, "Help us! Somebody! A pipe has broken and there's water all over the kitchen!"

The crowd's voice grew louder now, more alarmed. There was a wet and slippery surge toward the doors and the safety of the courtyard—and a series of screams from the first few people to stumble out the exit.

"The lake is rising! The river—unbelievable! *The river is flooding over the falls!*"

Now the revelers were starting to panic; now there were wails of fear and a few angry shoves as people fought to get clear of danger. Someone shrieked and pointed, and dozens of people wheeled around to stare at the corridor to the queens' wing, where water was gushing into the *kierten* from some unknown source. It was not too hard to imagine water pouring down those varicolored marble stairs like the largest and most beautiful fountain in the world.

Deep beneath the foundations of the palace, an ominous rumbling started.

"What's that?" someone shouted.

"Get out! *Get out!*"

"But the lake is rising! We'll all be carried away!"

"We're all going to drown!"

A sudden sheet of water erupted from the men's wing, drenching Soechins and subjects alike before subsiding into an unbroken oncoming stream. The king and his guests had been milling about on the dais, as stunned and distracted as the mob below, and this only made them worse. The ambassadors and their wives were shouting; the queens were weeping and clinging to each other. Vernon stood stupidly at the edge of the stage, staring at the mayhem around him. Only Darien Serlast seemed to be moving with any purpose, herding Josetta and Corene and Romelle toward the middle of the stage and what might be a modicum of safety. His eyes darted around the great room, searching for causes or searching for escape routes, and his gaze snagged on Zoe.

"Stop this now!" he roared at her, his arms around Josetta and Corene. *"Stop the flood!"*

In reply, she lifted her arms, fingers still spread, and water began rising up from the foundation of the palace itself, pulled from the aquifer deep inside the base of the mountain.

The viceroy and his daughter held hands and leapt from the stage with a magnificent splash, then plowed through the rising waters for the door. Vernon turned his bemused face toward his most trusted advisor and said, "What are we to do, Darien? There is water through the whole palace!"

"Zoe!" Darien shouted. *"Stop the flood!"*

Oh, but she was not ready to still the waters yet.

Most of the *kierten* had emptied out by now, though fifteen or twenty hardy souls still stomped through the swirling water, churning up great gouts as they attempted to open drains or close off access points. Three men struggled back inside, waving their arms frantically.

"Majesty! Majesty! The Marisi is almost to the palace door! You must evacuate now—everybody—out of the palace!"

For the first time, the king looked frightened. "Darien! What should I do?"

Now Darien's expression was pleading; his voice was hoarse. "Zoe! Zoe, I beg you—"

In a pool up to her knees, she waded forward, her woven robe so sodden it weighed her down. But she could not discard it, not decorated as it was with the *hunti* pin Darien Serlast was probably very sorry he had given her. "I'll take the older girls," she called up to him, as if she was offering him reasonable aid for which he would be immensely grateful. "You watch out for the king and his wives and Natalie."

"Zoe—"

She held her hands out. "Josetta! Corene! Come to me and I'll take you to safety."

"No!" Seterre cried as Josetta, without a moment's hesitation, ran across the stage and vaulted down into the rising water. "Stay with me—"

Zoe hugged Josetta and beckoned again to Corene. "Come with me! I'll take care of you."

Clearly afraid, Corene glanced worriedly at her mother, at

her father, at Darien. "Go with her!" Darien shouted, and that decided her. The girl scurried to the edge of the dais.

"Catch me," she said, and jumped into Zoe's arms.

For a single heart-stopping moment, Zoe staggered under her weight, under the impact of her body and her blood and its encrypted secrets, and then she set the girl on her feet. Taking hold of Josetta with one hand and Corene with the other, she said, "Ready?"

Then the three of them raced through the frothing water, plunged down the inundated steps, half swam across the courtyard in water up to their hips. Then, still clinging to both girls, Zoe flung all of them headlong into the rising river.

THIRTY-TWO

The river lashed around them, but Zoe and her two companions floated in water that was mysteriously smooth, mysteriously calm, though it whisked them along with alarming speed. Josetta was not afraid, Zoe could tell; she used her recently acquired skills to keep her head above the surface, but otherwise let the river carry her where it would. Corene was more frightened, clinging to Zoe, gasping out little cries every time a thrust of the current sent them briefly bobbing below the surface. Zoe held her tightly with one arm and murmured reassurances, all the while keeping part of her attention on Josetta and part of her attention on the landscape so swiftly passing by.

It took only minutes for the Marisi to rush them through the short initial fall and then the few miles south to the broad stone apron of the river flats. "Josetta! To the shore!" Zoe called as she saw the channel open up, and they both started stroking toward land. It was instantly clear this wouldn't be a haven for long. The hollow bowl of the flats was rapidly filling up as the Marisi collected water from all over the city and sent it galloping through the palace before letting it flow downriver. The whole place would soon be underwater—and then the flood would start spreading west until it covered the city itself—

"Up! Up!" Zoe cried once Josetta dragged herself out of the water, coughing a little. Zoe and Corene were right behind her, and they all scrambled for the comparative safety of the overhang. Corene was still clinging, and now she was openly weeping, but she didn't hesitate when Zoe pushed her toward higher ground. Josetta clambered up first, then leaned down to haul her sister to the top, and moments later Zoe was beside them on the rocky ledge, only a few feet from the rising river.

Now that they had paused from their intense exertions, the cold air of Quinnelay hit them with miserable force, made worse by their waterlogged clothing and little hope of immediate shelter. Corene started crying even harder. Josetta hugged her sister tightly and turned big eyes toward Zoe.

"What do we do now?" she whispered.

Zoe wrapped her arms around the two girls, drawing them into a brief protective circle. "I need to stay here a few minutes," she said, explaining as well as she could. "I called the river, and I need to contain it. I know you're wet and cold and wretched, and I'm sorry, but as soon as I can, I'll take you someplace warm and safe. Corene, listen to me. I know you're afraid, but I—"

Corene lifted her face from where it was pressed to Josetta's shoulder. Tears were still streaming down her face, or maybe it was water dripping from her bedraggled hair. Her ivory gown clung to her in sloppy wet folds; the scattered rosebuds were augmented with bits of river debris. "Thank you!" she sobbed. "Oh, Zoe, *thank you!* I was so terrified of that man—I told my mother I didn't want to marry him, but she said I had to. She said it would be good for me, and good for the kingdom, but I *hate* him. I hate all of them and I didn't know what to do—"

Zoe hugged her again, relieved that at least her wild rescue had pleased the person she had tried to save, no matter who else would be devastated by the event. "Good. I'll get you to safety, I promise you, but first I—"

"Zoe," Josetta interrupted. "There's somebody coming down the river."

Zoe whirled around and, sure enough, there was a body tumbling through the currents, not being treated nearly as gently as Zoe and the princesses had been. She spread her fingers

and imagined caressing the tempestuous surface of the un-
bound river, smoothing its choppy waters, slowing its tumultuous descent. The man shouted at her, waving his arm as if
hoping she would throw him a rope, but she could do better
than that. She directed the Marisi to deliver him to the shore,
and he came splashing and sputtering out. He climbed up beside them, then fell to all fours, wheezing and panting.

She didn't recognize him, but he wore what had started
out as finery, so he was no doubt a wealthy man. "Do you
need help?" she asked him a little fearfully, but he mouthed
the word *no*.

"I just need—to catch my breath," he gasped. He shook
his head and sat back on his heels. His eyes were glazed with
exhaustion and disbelief. "Never—I have lived in Chialto my
entire life—and *never* have I witnessed something like that.
I can't even understand what happened."

Josetta, her arms wrapped around Corene for warmth, just
looked at Zoe, who shook her head slightly. This didn't seem
to be the time and place to claim to be the Lalindar prime, who
could make rivers and fountains overflow at her command.
"You'd best go find shelter and dry clothing," Zoe said.

He didn't seem to be thinking clearly enough to respond
with the logical, *And so should you*. He merely nodded, sat
there another moment gathering his strength, and then pushed
himself to his feet. He loped toward the curiously empty back
streets that tangled around shacks and small businesses this
close to the flats.

Deserted, Zoe realized. People had evacuated as soon as the
river started rising. A few hardy and curious souls peered out of
second-story windows or clustered several yards upriver, watching the water race past, but most everyone else had run away.

"Zoe!" Josetta called again.

She turned back to the river, where two more bodies were
spinning in the water. Again, she guided them to the bank;
again, they showed no disposition to linger. Servants this time,
she thought, and even more speechless about their adventure
than the first man.

The fourth person she pulled out of the water was Foley.

He scarcely required her aid, swimming strongly to shore
and swinging himself up to the overhang with swift, economical

motions. Zoe felt her whole body loosen with relief. He would take care of the princesses, leaving her free to control the river.

"Foley!" Josetta cried when she saw him. She didn't go so far as to fling her arms around his wet uniform, but she might as well have; she looked that glad to see him. "I knew you would come for me—I knew it."

He nodded at Zoe, which she took as a mark of approval for the havoc she had wrought in pursuit of one desperate goal. "Saw you go into the river and thought you would end up here," he said. "We need to get you warm and dry. All three of you."

Zoe pointed toward the nearest buildings, which appeared to be a couple of storehouses and one dilapidated repair shop. "I think everything's been abandoned. You might be able to break in and take clothes or blankets. Maybe build a fire."

"How long do we have to stay here?" Corene asked. "You said you'd take us someplace."

Zoe nodded. "I will. But not just yet. I have to—I have to make sure the river doesn't do any more damage."

"A foot higher and it'll breach the banks all up and down its length," Foley said. "Flood the whole town."

"I know," she said. "But I can stop it."

"We'll wait here with you," Josetta said.

Zoe glanced at Foley, wondering if he would argue, but he was merely nodding. Not his place to question a princess, Zoe supposed; his job was to make sure she lived through whatever she decided to do. "I'll see what I can find," he said and headed off toward the deserted buildings.

Zoe turned back toward the river, bubbling higher in its channel, only inches now from the top of the overhang. Upstream, she knew, there were a few places where the river might already have gone spilling out of its course, sending wet destruction through the streets. Well, she had called the river; now she needed to control it. She needed to stuff it back into its underground cisterns and passageways, send it sinking back into the soil.

Zoe knelt on the edge of the overhang and poured her heart into the Marisi.

She rocked it like a crying baby; she stroked it like a hissing cat. *There, there,* she crooned wordlessly, patting its indignant cheeks, smoothing its disordered hair. *All better now. Lie quiet now. Be still. Be peaceful.*

At first the water resisted, petulant as a willful child, but she continued to murmur, continued to soothe, continued to coax. And slowly, slowly, the water began to sigh and simmer in its banks. Its high boil shrank down; its gushing pulse grew tame. The agitated gallons summoned from underwater reservoirs went chattering down the southern miles toward the sea. The ordinary flow of everyday water resettled in its banks, churning up an occasional feisty spray, but otherwise resuming its ordinary volume. *All better now. Calm, peaceful.*

"Zoe."

Her own name snapped her from a deep reverie. She drew a swift breath—and then another one, surprised to learn that full dark had fallen while she had been communing with the river. A little disoriented, she pivoted away from the Marisi, trying to regather her thoughts. She found Josetta, Corene, and Foley sitting around a busy little fire, all of them wrapped in blankets that looked none too clean. Corene lay with her head on Josetta's lap; it appeared that she might actually be sleeping. Zoe realized that she was absolutely freezing. Her hands and feet were completely numb, though someone had draped a blanket over her shoulders while she hadn't been paying attention. How long had she been standing here, cajoling the river back inside its banks?

"Zoe," Josetta said again. "Is it time to go yet? Foley's hired a man with a cart if you have someplace to take us."

"I do," she said. *I think I do.* "You're right. It's time to go."

Foley rose and began stamping out the fire, while Josetta woke Corene up and shepherded her toward a bulky shadow squatted on the nearest street. Zoe could just make out the shape of a horse and driver. She turned to follow the others, but paused to take one quick look up at the mountain, where tiny lights always outlined the palace against the night.

There was nothing to be seen. The palace—or at least every candle, every lamp, every flame in the building—had been washed away.

Jaker opened the door on Zoe's first knock, and then stared mutely at her entourage. She had never before seen his blue eyes so blank.

"Good, I was afraid you might have left town already," she said. "Can we come in?"

He nodded and stepped aside, still staring. Barlow's voice sounded from the other room. "Is someone here? Jaker?"

Zoe motioned the others inside, and then shut the door under Jaker's hand. "You might have heard there was an incident at the palace this afternoon," she began.

Barlow wandered into the common room, dressed only in a towel. "Is—Zoe! And—oh! Who are all these—I'm sorry, let me get dressed." He disappeared again.

Corene had instantly collapsed onto the well-worn sofa, but Josetta was looking around with interest at the boxes and books and oddments. Foley stood stiffly by the door, his face showing the first signs of disapproval Zoe had noticed all night. *He doesn't mind if I bring the palace down to save a princess from a disastrous marriage, but he doesn't like the girls to be brought too close to common men,* she thought. It was hard to restrain a somewhat hysterical giggle.

"Zoe," Jaker said, his voice quiet. "Am I mistaken, or are these two of the king's daughters?"

"Josetta and Corene," she said, pointing. Just then Barlow hurried back into the room, so she repeated the girls' names, and then identified everyone else. "Foley, their guard. Jaker, Barlow. Two traders who are friends of mine."

"It's very nice to meet you," Josetta said politely.

Jaker cut Zoe a look from his blue eyes. His face was beginning to thaw from disbelief to amusement. "This is even more astounding than learning you are the Lalindar prime."

"Does anyone want anything to eat or drink?" Barlow asked, heading toward the kitchen.

"I'm starving," Zoe said.

"There's not much in the house because we're leaving in the morning, but you can have anything we have," Barlow said. "Then everyone sit down! And tell us just what's going on."

Even Foley consented to taking a seat—though not until Josetta told him to. They all shared a meal of stale bread, withered fruit, and some of the dried rations the men had prepared as provisions for their journey. Regretfully, Zoe turned down Barlow's offer of that delightfully sparkling wine; she was feeling fuzzy enough already. But Jaker took a small glass and drank it down in two swallows.

"We learned today that the king planned to marry Corene to the viceroy of Soeche-Tas," Zoe said, making the story as concise as she could. "He's a man so loathsome even my father despised him, and I couldn't countenance the notion of a girl her age going to his bed. I called up the river. The palace started flooding. I grabbed the princesses and jumped into the Marisi, and a few other people got swept away. Now the river's back in its banks, though I imagine there has been some damage. I am *not* returning the girls to the palace until I'm certain there is no more talk of such catastrophic weddings, so I thought you could take them with you. No one will know where to look for them if they're with you."

Jaker started laughing. "Oh, Zoe," he said. "It was a grand day when the elements swept you into our lives!"

"We'll be happy to take them," Barlow said. "If you don't think we'll get hanged for treason if the girls are found with us."

"Treason or worse!" Jaker exclaimed. "Two grown men making off with two young girls!"

Foley spoke up for the first time. "I am concerned about that as well," he said in a mulish voice. "You say these men are friends of yours, but can you be certain you have not delivered them into a fate even worse than the one that awaited Princess Corene in Soeche-Tas?"

Barlow looked mildly offended, but Jaker nodded. "Exactly."

Josetta stirred. She was sitting very straight on the sofa, Corene asleep against her shoulder. "We will write letters and have them delivered to the palace, explaining that we are safe and in Zoe's care," she said. "No one will worry."

"People will still worry," Jaker began, but Foley interrupted.

"But you won't be in Zoe's care, and you can't know if you'll be safe with these—these men," he finished up.

"Zoe? You're not coming with us?" Josetta asked.

"That's assuming we take you with us to begin with," Jaker said under his breath.

Zoe shook her head. "I have to stay here at least a few days. I have to see what damage my hasty action has caused—and mend it, if I can. I have to—well, I have to learn what will happen next. To me, to you, to your father, to everyone."

"You can stay here while we're gone," Barlow offered.

"I hoped you'd say that. I must assume people will be searching for me, but no one will know to look for me here. How long will you be away from Chialto?"

Jaker shrugged. "You know how we travel. Maybe four ninedays, maybe more."

Josetta looked intrigued. "Where are you going? Where are *we* going?"

"South, then west, then north, unless we pick up a load of goods that takes us south again," Barlow said with a laugh. "But we're aiming for Lalindar country by early Quinncoru."

"Good," Zoe said. "I'll be sure to be at my grandmother's house by changeday, and you can bring them to me there. Maybe the world will be sane by then."

"I've never been out of the city," Josetta said.

"You'll enjoy the trip, then," Barlow told her.

"But two grown men and two young girls—it's not right," Foley said urgently.

Zoe laid her hand on his arm, conveying as much reassurance as she could. "They are not interested in girls," she said gently. "And you will be along to keep them safe from whatever other hazards arise."

Foley's face had sharpened at her first words, and relaxed at her last ones. "I *will* accompany them," he said. "No matter what anyone says."

"Oh, we want you along, believe me," Jaker said. He shook his head, sighed, and then laughed. "I suppose we will really do this. I'd better have some more of that wine, then, while we figure out the details."

The next four days were among the strangest of Zoe's existence, and she had thought parts of her life were pretty strange up to this point.

Jaker, Barlow, Josetta, Corene, and Foley left very early the next morning. Barlow had shown her where they kept an impressive cache of spare coins—"Take what you need"—and Jaker had told her she could wear anything she found in the closets, though he couldn't promise her a fashionable or even attractive wardrobe. She had repeatedly kissed the girls good-bye, but she was relieved when they were finally gone, off on a journey so unplanned and meandering that no one would be able to find them unless by sheer, astonishing luck.

Now to deal with the consequences of what she'd done.

She found a pair of trousers and a tunic that fit her well enough to wear in public, wrapped her head in a scarf so she could conceal her face in its shadows, and stepped out of the apartment to see what she had wrought.

The Cinque was chaos; it turned out to be faster to walk than to try to ride an omnibus. Despite the cold, the Plaza of Women was filled with crowds, though no one appeared to be buying. Instead, visitors stood in small clusters, gossiping, exclaiming, and repeating their stories of the night before. Zoe moved through the splintered crowd, catching snatches of conversation.

"—water down the street, but it never got as far as our house, for which I am everlastingly grateful—"

"—the wagon lost in the flood, and the horses were terri-fied. But only one of them was injured, a gash on his right foreleg, and we think he'll be fine—"

"—mud as deep as my ankles in every room—"

"—a complete loss, but I can salvage the linens—"

She overheard no story of children drowning, old men be-ing swept away, water rising so high it brought down a house. She might have caught it in time; she might have destroyed nothing except the palace.

Though the palace was not actually *gone*. By daylight, she could see it limned against the mountainside, looking curi-ously hollow. For the longest time, she could not identify ex-actly what seemed different about it from this distance, since it still stood as tall as ever, flags at its turrets, ivy on its walls, the bend of the river making a placid pool beside it. Then she realized—every door and window of the lower level was gone, leaving behind the skeletal remains of the foundational pillars and crossbeams. If she stared hard enough, she thought she could make out swarms of human shapes at work on every aperture, cleaning away mud and making repairs.

She imagined even more of that work was under way inside the *kierten*, where the damage was no doubt the worst.

She didn't linger long at the Plaza of Women and went nowhere near the Plaza of Men. It was too close to the palace, to the wealthy districts where the Five Families lived. She was too likely to encounter someone she knew, and she could not bear to face any of them. Well, she was also likely to be arrested for wanton destruction of municipal property, so she didn't want to encounter a palace servant or a royal guard or anyone who might recognize her face and call the nearest authorities to take her into custody.

She kept on walking toward the river.

About a mile inland, the effects of the flooding began to show, as streets and alleys were caked with mud left behind by the receding waters. The closer she got to the Marisi, the higher the waterline on the buildings that had been affected when the river escaped over the lowest point of its banks. Most of the damage appeared to be centered in a neighborhood about halfway between the flats and the palace, midway between the Marisi and the Cinque. Here the waterline was about four feet above the ground. A few tumbledown buildings—which didn't appear to have been too steady even before the waters came rushing in—had buckled against the river's insistent pushing. A public well had been contaminated, and a small city park had turned into a quagmire of matted grass and fallen trees.

Residents were organizing themselves into teams to haul branches out of streets and to clear away the broken lumber of the ruined houses. Zoe paused at the tainted well and rested her hand on the low stone wall, rimed with ice on this chilly morning. She spent a few moments sifting the dirt and rubble out of the reservoir and calling on clean water to come bubbling up from below.

Then she turned toward the nearest crew finishing demolition of a small house and threw herself into the task of cleaning up after the flood.

Zoe was walking back through the Plaza of Women that night, sore and exhausted, when she heard the first whispers about Vernon.

It wasn't quite dark yet, but there was a sense that the workday was over. Those who had been engaged in hard labor had simply quit; those who had tried to keep shop and carry out normal commerce all day had given up pretending. As they had this morning, people gathered in knots all along the Plaza, sharing shards of gossip.

"Did you hear? The king has collapsed."

"Vernon is sick. They say he can't even move from his bed."

"At first someone said he was injured in the flood, but now I hear he's had a serious illness for some time now."

"My mother's cousin's son works at the palace, and he says the king has a terrible disease—so bad it can't be cured—"

"The king is dying!"

"The doctors have been giving Vernon a strange drug, but they say it's dangerous—anyway, it's stopped working—"

"Who will be queen if Vernon dies?"

Zoe kept walking, catching the bits of tangled conversation like buzzing insects, then releasing them and moving on.

The king was sick; the king was on his deathbed. That had been true for a year now, but apparently he had been so distressed by her theatrics yesterday that his body had lost whatever strength it had been able to conserve. She had not intended to reveal his secrets; she had only thought to thwart his mad plan. But she found she was not entirely sorry to have his lie exposed. He was dying, after all. His subjects deserved to know. Welce deserved a chance to prepare for what would come next.

Who will be queen if Vernon dies?

The next day, and the next, were much the same. In the mornings, Zoe wound through the Plaza of Women to catch the day's gossip, and then headed toward the river to help the cleanup and restoration effort in whatever way she could. There turned out to be more than one contaminated well, though each of them was functional again once Zoe sauntered by. There were a dozen houses to tear down, and two dozen to shore up with boards and beams and makeshift measures. There were dead shrubs to clear out of the parks, sidewalks to sweep, benches to scrub. There was a whole city to put to rights.

The evening of that third day, Zoe threaded her way through the Plaza of Women again, spending a few of Barlow's coins to buy a wrapped meat pie to take home with her.

"Any news about the king?" she asked the vendor, a middle-aged woman with *torz* blessings embroidered on her overtunic.

"No change in *his* condition, but now all the talk is about Romelle!" the vendor exclaimed.

"Romelle? The queen? What about her?"

"She's pregnant! And nobody knew!"

"That's good news, isn't it?"

The woman threw her hands into the air. "Who knows? Three princesses and a baby that's not even born yet, and we still don't know who the king wants as his heir. How hard can it be to make that decision? Pick one! Settle this! I can't imagine what they do all day up at the palace. I really can't."

Zoe shook her head. "I can't, either."

She could, though, and as she sat on the tattered couch and ate her dinner, she tried to picture the chaos that must be roiling through the palace walls. Vernon moaning on his bed in the men's wing . . . Seterre and Alys pacing through the women's wing, frantic to know the whereabouts of their daughters . . . Elidon and Darien trying to impose an iron calm . . . Romelle alternating between throwing up in her own quarters and tending Vernon in his. Meanwhile, workmen sawing and hammering in the *kierten* and the primes arguing over who should be ratified as heir.

She took a bite of the meat pie—spicy and flavorful and very filling—and thought it over. She still couldn't be sorry she'd done it.

On the fourth morning, as Zoe tossed through cheap fabric at a booth in the Plaza of Women, someone slid in place beside her and tapped her wrist. Zoe gasped and jerked back, then laughed out loud when she realized who had approached her.

"Annova! It is so good to see you! I have been wondering how I can get in touch with you."

"I knew you would come to the Plaza eventually," Annova said. "I thought I saw you yesterday, but I couldn't catch up in time. Are you all right? Where have you been staying?"

Zoe supposed she ought to entertain the idea that Annova had turned spy for Darien Serlast—or the royal army—but she didn't even hesitate before answering. "In the lodgings Ilene's son, Barlow, shares with his partner."

"Are the princesses with you there?"

Zoe shook her head. "Gone. With Barlow. I didn't know how else to keep them safe."

Annova glanced over briefly, raising her eyebrows at that definition of *safe*, but made no comment aloud. They both continued to pick through the fabric remnants as if the scraps of cloth held their full attention. "Calvin and I are over in the pavilion on the west edge of town where the river folk were relocated when the viceroy arrived," she said. "The flats are still covered with mud, but they'll be cleared off again in a nineday or two, and we'll move back there."

Zoe shook her head. "I've been afraid to try to get to my money, in case the royal guards are watching," she said. "But if I ever do have access again, I'll give you so much you can buy your own place. You won't have to sleep on the river anymore."

Wearing a sweet smile, Annova held up a bolt of sunset scarlet as if to offer it for Zoe's inspection. "I like sleeping on the river," she said. "I've missed it."

"Has anyone come looking for me?" Zoe asked.

"Yes. Men from the palace, sent by Darien Serlast. They were polite, however. They didn't arrest or threaten us. They seemed to believe us when we said we had no idea where you were. But every day we've seen one or the other of them lurking outside the pavilion. Watching us. Waiting for you to show up."

Zoe had to resist the urge to look over her shoulder. "Do you think some of them may have followed you here?"

"I walked around the Plaza for a long time before I approached you," Annova said. "If they followed me, I think they have lost track of me by now."

"I've heard whispers," Zoe said. "Gossip spreading through the Plaza. Vernon is dying and Romelle is pregnant."

Annova nodded. "Change is coming to everything. The gift of a *coru* woman."

Zoe gave a faint laugh. "I'm not sure anyone at the palace considers my recent actions to be a *gift*."

Annova had moved to the other side of the vendor's table to examine a translucent sheet of fabric spangled with bits of silver. She lifted her head to give Zoe one quick, level look. "I'm sure the princess felt her freedom was a gift beyond measure."

Zoe glanced around to make sure no one was close enough to hear them discussing royalty, then she replied in a low voice. "Yes, I believe so, too. And that makes this whole maelstrom I have created much easier to accept."

"What will you do now?" Annova said. "You cannot live in Barlow's place forever."

"I know." Zoe shrugged. "Once the king's men finally catch up with me, I'm sure I will be punished in some fashion. Banished, perhaps. Denied my place as prime, assuming they're able to take my power away from me. I wanted to stay in the city a few days to do what I could to atone, but I think it's time for me to go. Tomorrow or the day after, I will return to my grandmother's house on the river and wait there to see what fate will befall me next."

Annova nodded. Such a fatalistic plan of action appealed to a *coru* soul. "Meet me here tomorrow," she said. "I have your mother's shawl and the few things I was sure you'd want. I left everything else in the hotel room."

Zoe felt a rush of gratitude and relief. She would have safety of a sort; she would have shelter, as long as her mother's shawl was around her shoulders. "Gladly," she said. "You have been the dearest of friends. I hope someday to do half as much for you as you have done for me."

Annova smiled. "What makes you think you have not?"

THIRTY-THREE

Z oe arrived at Christara's house at midnight on a bitterly cold Quinnelay night. She had cut a gold coin from her mother's shawl and recklessly offered the whole piece to the driver she had hired on Calvin's recommendation—a cousin or son or nephew of a friend of the river, and wholly to be trusted. He had a small *elaymotive* and a son of his own, and they took turns driving as day turned to night and back to day. They made the long journey in a remarkable four days.

Hoden had greeted her at the door, as unruffled as if she had just returned from an afternoon's shopping in the village. Her bedroom had been readied for her—a fire in the hearth, fresh sheets on the bed, subtle incense released into the air—as if he had known she was coming. Perhaps he had. Perhaps the wooden timbers of the house had told the *torz* man that the prime was on her way. She had stumbled into bed and didn't wake up until the following afternoon.

She slept for most of the next four days. Whenever she woke—to eat, to bathe, to exchange a few words with Hoden—all she could see out of any window was rain. Though she had not consciously wished for wet weather, she was sure her presence had called the storms.

If anyone came to the door asking for her during those four

days, Hoden did not admit them or even mention their names to Zoe.

Even after the rain tapered off, leaving the skies sullen with clouds, Zoe felt little inclination to leave the house. She spent most of her time in the green sitting room, staring through the symmetrical scallops of the fountain to the churning river below. It had been dangerously high the night she arrived, wild and fractious in its banks, but it had subsided considerably as Zoe regained her peace of mind. She knew that if she made her way down the mountainside and knelt at the river's edge, her hand wrist-deep in the water, she could soothe the Marisi from a torrent to a stream to a trickle to a dry bed.

It was an odd thing to know.

Only one of many odd things her mind held now.

The morning of Quinncoru changeday, Zoe woke at dawn. She asked the servants to draw a scented bath and set out her favorite perfumed lotions. She allowed a maid to style her dark hair, teasing it into curl and texture, and she arrayed herself in a simply cut tunic of woven gold. It was so long, it fell to her toes, completely obscuring the matching trousers beneath it.

Over her shoulders she draped her mother's festive shawl. She had spent part of the last nineday sewing more gold coins into its much-mended hem. It was clear to her that she was poised to run—at the least, to be disinherited; at the gravest, to be arrested for treason and sabotage. Armed with her mother's remembrance and a small amount of treasure, she might have another option. If she had the chance, she could simply walk out the door and disappear.

Another bend in the river. Another change in the life of a *coru* woman.

But her heart, it seemed, was not entirely certain that flight was in her future. She had pinned the bright wrap in place with the *hunti* brooch Darien Serlast had given her before that final day at the palace. Around one wrist she wore a wide, flat bracelet of matching dark wood; on the other, her blessing bracelet dangling with power, love, and beauty.

She had proved she was powerful. Today she had gone to

some trouble to make herself beautiful. It remained to be seen if she could be loved.

She stood in the *kierten*, in front of the window overlooking the river, and spent an hour watching the empty road. There was sunshine for the first time in days, and it fell greedily on the landscape as if famished for the taste of green. It poured in through the *kierten's* vast windows and pooled on the burnished floor like sheets of caramelized honey.

A little before noon, she caught the first glimpse of a small smoker car wending its way upward. This wasn't one of the spacious palace vehicles that could carry six passengers plus a driver and a guard; this was compact and maneuverable and probably seated no more than two. At the moment, it held a single occupant, who traveled so slowly he might be dreading his arrival at his destination.

Zoe watched as Darien Serlast navigated between the fountains, cut the motor, and stepped out of the car. He stood for a long time gazing at the front of the house, though she was fairly certain the glare on the windows made it impossible for him to see inside, then he stepped out of her field of vision as he came close enough to ring the door chimes three times. She heard his voice lifted in a brief exchange with Hoden, heard their footfalls as Hoden ushered him inside, heard the clamoring unregulated excitement of his heartbeat as he caught sight of her again.

Hoden bowed and disappeared. Darien stood where he was, watching Zoe. As they had once before—a day that seemed like years ago, though it had not even been two quintiles—they studied each other from across the width of the room.

She had not planned to be the first to speak, but a thought skittered through her mind and she found herself voicing it. "If you had known, the first time you saw me in this room, what would have transpired between us by the next time you found me here, I wonder if you ever would have set foot inside my grandmother's house."

"I was asking myself much the same question as I drove up the mountain," he said. His voice was composed, neutral, giving nothing away. But she could still hear the clatter of his pulse, too fast for an indifferent man.

"What answer did you find?"

He shrugged. "What permanent answers does one ever find with a *coru* woman?"

She wanted to face him coolly, tranquilly; she did not want to betray restlessness or unease. But she could not stand still. She turned away from him and began a slow and measured pacing around the room. Darien stood where he was, pivoting slowly to track her progress.

Coru woman, who could not be contained. *Hunti* man, who could not be moved.

"Let us have plain speaking between us, at least this once," she said, a slight tremor in her voice despite her efforts to sound serene. "If you have come to tell me the dying king wants me stripped of my position, I will turn over whatever trappings I can divorce from my body and leave the mountain today. But don't come here and merely look at me and force me to ask what you want from me *this* time."

His face relaxed into a smile of true amusement. "But all I want from you *this* time is a chance to see your face, which I have missed. I have no other official agenda, and no commissions from my king."

That was impossible to believe. She came to a ragged halt, flinging words at him as if they were rocks. "Not even questions? Not even accusations? Not even exclamations of horror? *Zoe, you flooded the palace and ruined half of the city and destroyed any chance of alliance with Soeche-Tas!* Surely you have some recriminations to heap upon my head—if not the king's, then your own."

"Officially, there is a great deal of royal consternation at your actions, and I am afraid the Lalindar estate will have to bear some of the cost of paying for the damage which your heedless flood caused," he said seriously. "Unofficially—" He paused, shaking his head. "Unofficially, if it had been within my power to do so, I would have brought the whole palace down in huge chunks of stone that crushed the heads of all of them. The king, the viceroy, their scheming friends. I would not have bothered with anything so insubstantial as water."

She stared at him, struck speechless.

He took a tiny step toward her. "You knew—surely you knew, you *guessed*, that I had had no knowledge of plans for such a marriage. My father had told me stories about the viceroy of Soeche-Tas that turned my blood to ice. I never would have allowed or ever *approved* any arrangement that gave that man a child-bride. Before I say another word, tell me you knew that. You believed that."

"I believed it," she said.

He nodded. "So, I cannot condemn your actions—but there is no denying that there has been a great deal of suffering by a good number of people who *also* had no hand in arranging the marriage. Those are the ones you must reassure and reimburse."

"I will make restitution, and gladly," she said. "But even so, I am sure there are plenty who will find my deliberate destruction hard to forgive. Surely there are questions about whether or not I am fit to be prime—"

"Questions," he admitted. "But not asked by anyone who matters." When she gave him an inquiring look, he added, "By that I mean the other primes. Mirti and your uncle Nelson repeated the stories brought back from Soeche-Tas by my father and yours, and Taro and Kayle have flatly refused to condemn you. There is no way Vernon could strip you of your title without their cooperation. And he is too weak to try, at any rate. Your position is intact. Your standing among the people of Chialto is seriously weakened," he said, attempting another slight smile, "but if you show remorse and largesse, you are likely to retrieve their goodwill."

"I'll build them a fountain right in the spot where the water was most destructive," she said. "That will be my memorial of regret. And I will hand out money, too, as long as it is still mine to give."

"The coins will be even more welcome."

She didn't want to move away from him, but she couldn't hold her feet in place. She resumed her pacing. "But there are still so many questions," she said. "If not you—if not Mirti and the other primes—who was helping the king plot this obscene marriage? Because I do not think, in his confused state, Vernon was likely to have come up with such an idea on his own."

"No," Darien said. "As far as I can tell, his only advisor for this particular course was Elidon."

She whipped around to stare at him again. "*Elidon?* But why? She despises Alys, of course, but she is not petty enough to take out that hatred on a child."

"She is being very close-lipped about it, but her reasoning seemed to go like this: Alys wanted Corene to be named heir, so Alys had made several attempts on Josetta's life. Elidon decided Josetta would not be safe unless Corene was removed from the picture—but Elidon is not coldhearted enough to murder Corene. So she sought to marry her off instead. In its way, a clever solution to an intolerable situation, if barbaric in this particular instance. She swears she believed the marriage would not be consummated until Corene was of a suitable age. I am inclined to believe her, though I still do not condone her actions."

"But I thought you were not convinced that Alys had been the one trying to harm Josetta. Have you changed your mind?"

Briefly, he looked tired beyond endurance; his frame sagged a little, as if those *hunti* bones had failed him. "No, in fact, I am pretty sure I have located the villain, but Elidon was convinced Alys was the guilty party. A belief she seems to have come to," he added, "when *you* made your furious accusation at the queens' breakfast."

Zoe brushed that aside. "I only said what many people thought. But you have found the person who is truly responsible? One you are sure of?"

He nodded. He still looked weary. "Though the discovery gave me no pleasure," he said quietly. "I finally tracked down one of the sailors who abandoned Josetta's boat, and told him he would spend the rest of his life in a cell if he did not identify his employer. He was quick to give a name, which led to another name, and eventually led to Wald Dochenza. Kayle's nephew." He gave Zoe a swift look. "The man who always seemed most likely to be Corene's father. He wanted to see a daughter of his on the throne. Which he thought seemed more likely if Josetta was dead."

"Ahhhhhh . . ." Zoe said with a long sigh of both comprehension and dismay. She realized she was pacing again, slipping from one square of glorious sunshine to another, and finding no peace in any of them. "It is an answer that makes sense but breaks the heart. Has he admitted it?"

"When confronted, Wald confessed the whole, and then began sobbing hysterically, in a way that led me to believe he is not quite sane," Darien replied. Now she understood some of the weariness in his stance. "The scene was even more unpleasant than you might think questioning a would-be murderer could be."

She slewed around to face Darien again. "Was his uncle involved?"

"I am convinced Kayle had no part in the scheme, though he has taken his nephew's treachery very hard. He asked that he be the one to administer justice and I agreed. My thought is that Wald—a child of air—will never again be granted his freedom. It is difficult to know which of them will find this punishment most bitter."

"It is all the more tragic because, of course, Wald Dochenza is not Corene's father."

Gazing unwaveringly at Zoe, Darien slowly straightened his posture, leveled his hunched shoulders, planted his feet—braced himself, she thought, for whatever wild storm she might conjure next. "You took hold of the princess when you snatched her from her Soeche-Tas suitor," he said in an uninflected voice. "I suppose that was the first time you decoded the secret of her blood."

Zoe said, "Corene is your daughter."

A long shuddering sigh shook Darien's body. He stayed silent, briefly closing his eyes. Zoe added, "She's your daughter, though you claim to despise her mother above all others. So I wonder how that liaison came about."

As if he could not have this conversation while he was standing still, Darien opened his eyes and began to pace the perimeter of the room. Now Zoe was the one to stand firm, watching him, turning slightly to keep him in view. "I was twenty-one," he said. "Still the eager romantic, willing to do anything to serve my king. I had seen your father work in stealth to help Vernon produce an heir. I thought it was my duty, I thought it was an honor, to be asked to give the third wife a child."

"You were in love with her," Zoe said.

Still pacing, he nodded. "I was in love with her, or I thought I was. She was all red hair and wicked beauty. She was—life and desire and excitement and endless fascination. She was—" He shook his head.

Zoe said, "A *sweela* woman makes a *hunti* man burn."

"Maybe," Darien said. "But she burned very fast through whatever fuel my soul had to offer. It wasn't long—less than a quintile—before I began to see her for the woman I now know her to be. Scheming, inconstant, ambitious, selfish, jealous—I could spend the next hour coming up with unflattering words to describe her."

"She still has feelings for you, though—deep ones."

He shrugged. "Maybe. She says so. I think she is just petty and possessive. She thinks that because once she thought she owned me, she should own me forever."

"She doesn't like the notion of any of her past lovers showing a preference for someone else," Zoe said. "When one of her friends merely *spoke* of Wald Dochenza with affection, Alys went to some trouble to get her ousted from the palace. I would not be surprised if—in the past ten years—other women you were interested in found themselves the targets of Alys's unfriendly attention."

He paused long enough to throw her a humorous look. "Hard to be certain," he said. "Since there have been very few other women in whom I have shown an interest."

Zoe did not bother mentioning her own wardrobe, slashed to ribbons by the malicious queen. "So what made you fall out of love with her?"

"What could it have been?" he said in a mocking voice. "The fact that she entertained other lovers and told me about them? The fact that she offered love or withheld love in order to control me? The fact that she was endlessly and inventively cruel? Pick your reason. There were many."

"If she had a lot of lovers, how could she be sure who Corene's father was?"

He shook his head. "She couldn't be, of course—and neither could I. She pretended to be certain that Corene was mine, but my guess is that she pretended to be certain with Wald Dochenza as well. And maybe others—who knows? But I have always known Corene *could* be my daughter. It has given me a tenderness for her, even though I have tried not to show it. I have showered her with many a small gift, pretending it was from the king, saying only that it came from her father. I figured that, at least on some level, what I said was true."

"She is a sharp and difficult girl, but she was very glad to be saved from the viceroy's wedding bed," Zoe said. "I don't think Alys has entirely ruined her. It might require some very public battles, but you could claim her as your own and do what you can to change her life."

Darien came to a halt only a few feet from Zoe and nodded gravely. "I would like that," he said.

"Of course, that would mean revealing a terrible truth about her. About *all* the king's daughters."

His face showed a ghost of a smile. "You are behind on the gossip, then," he said. "Shortly after Romelle revealed she was pregnant, the four primes still in the city announced that they were ready to ratify her unborn child as the next successor to the throne. That was when they also announced that none of his other three daughters were actually heirs of Vernon's body."

"That must have created pandemonium!"

"It would have, I think, if everyone wasn't already so numb from all the other shocks. And then a few people stepped forward to say they had known it all along—the blind sisters had told them so—or they had always suspected such a thing was true." Darien shrugged. "It has gone very quickly from being the greatest secret of my life to commonly accepted fact. Under no other circumstances do I think that would have been the case."

"When the primes revealed that the princesses were not sired by Vernon," she asked, "did they also reveal the various fathers?"

"Not yet," Darien said. "I suppose they will convene to discuss that at some point, perhaps debating how much damage the revelations might do to the reputations of the men."

"Well, my father's reputation could hardly suffer more," Zoe said cheerfully, "and I am eager to claim Josetta. So, I hope it is time to tell these truths very soon. Of course, we have to make sure Josetta and Corene hear the news first—they might be devastated to learn how their stations have changed."

Darien glanced around, as if expecting to find the princesses suddenly materializing from the corners of the *kierten*. "I have been authorized to let them know how the situation currently stands at court," he said. "And to bring them back with all speed. So, if you send for them now, I can begin to tell them their own stories."

"Unfortunately," Zoe said, "they're not here."

"Not here?" he repeated.

She shrugged. "I didn't know how the situation would unfold at the palace. I didn't know if madness or reason would prevail. I didn't know who would be the first person to show up at my door, demanding I return the girls. So they're not here."

He nodded. "It makes a sort of convoluted *coru* sense," he said, almost smiling. "So where are they? In the village where I first found you more than a year ago?"

"I considered that as a hiding place," she admitted. "But I decided it would be the second place you looked, after you came to this house."

"The third place," he said. "I first searched for you among the river folk."

"So I gave them over to the care of friends, who will bring them to me when their travel takes them this way."

He stood very still, watching her, clearly torn between disapproval and worry and a hard-won trust. "I told Seterre and Alys they were in your hands," he said at last. "It was the only thing that allayed their fears. I told them the princesses were safe."

"They are."

He bowed his head. "Then I believe you. Please bring them to Chialto as soon as you can once they are back in your care."

"I will," she said. She paused and then went on in a tentative voice, "Unless you wish to wait here for their arrival."

He smiled briefly. "I do wish it—very much. But I am greatly in demand at the palace, as you might imagine, for it is still in utter turmoil and I have, for the most part, a steady hand. I am not even sure how well the many factions will survive my absence for as long as it will take me to complete my journey here and back."

"Then I will feed you and send you on your way again," Zoe said, trying to conceal her sudden sharp disappointment.

Darien blinked in surprise and then smiled with so warm an expression that for a moment he looked like a *sweela* man. "I hoped to be allowed to stay a little longer than that," he said. "I hoped to be invited to remain overnight, at least, so that we have the opportunity to talk of things that truly matter."

Zoe made a sweeping gesture. "What could matter more

than the subjects we have already discussed? The fate of the realm and the safety of the two girls we care about most—my sister and your daughter?"

"Talk of *additional* things that matter a great deal," he amended. "Things important only to you and me."

"There can only be one or two subjects with such a narrow focus," she said.

Now he was on the move again while she stood still, but this time he was narrowing the distance between them. He came very close; he was near enough to lift a hand and lay his palm against her cheek. She felt the unyielding bones wrapped in the calloused flesh of his hand; she felt her own wayward blood leap in response to his touch.

"One subject, in fact," he said. "The affection that lies between us—the fascination that holds us both in thrall."

"There is nothing but heartache for a *coru* woman and a *hunti* man," she said, deliberately contrary. "He cannot control her and she cannot change him."

"He never fails her and she always moves him," Darien corrected. "She can trust his strength, and he can be lifted by her joy."

"I have been forced to move on from too many things," Zoe said. "I would be happy to flow from shallow rapids into deep, still waters."

"I have had to stand so firm," he said. "I have had to be unbreakable for so long, immobile in darkness and silence. I look forward to bending just a little—to moving into sunlight—to remembering what it is like to unclench my hands and give in to emotion."

She laughed at him. "This is a most peculiar proposal—if that's what it is."

He laughed back, moving closer, wrapping his arms loosely around her waist. She felt sheltered but not trapped, protected but not oppressed. "The first time I met you," he said, "during that long trek to Chialto, I fell in love with you. I told you I was bringing you to my king so that you would marry him, but I wanted you as my own bride."

"That time? That trip?" she said derisively. "I scarcely spoke! *I* scarcely knew who I was! *You* could not have learned me well enough to fall in love with me then!"

"I knew you wouldn't believe me," he said. Keeping one hand at her waist, he used the other to rummage in a pocket of his long tunic. When he pulled out a scroll, he presented it to her, shifting his body away just enough so that she could hold it in her hands. "Note the seal," he said.

An irregular circle of wax had been imprinted with the glyph for certainty, the official motto of the *hunti* family that ran the booth of promises in the Plaza of Men. "Most impressive."

"Note the date."

It was a day from Quinncoru of the previous year. "This is just about when we arrived in Chialto," she admitted.

"If you open it, you will see," Darien said. "I made my way to the Plaza of Men shortly after you disappeared. I went to the promise booth and recorded my vow that I would find you, and I would marry you. A copy of this oath is permanently written in their books."

She looked doubtfully from the scroll to his face. "Open it," he urged.

Carefully, to avoid splitting the wax, she slipped her finger under the seal and unrolled the parchment. The words were printed in a professional scribe's clean lettering: *I, Darien Serlast, do vow and attest that I will marry Zoe Ardelay or I will marry no one. In this I shall not alter.* It was signed with a messy scrawl in which only the *D*, the *S*, and a boldly crossed *t* could be discerned, though the word *Hunti* was very legible beneath the name.

Darien had crowded closer to read it along with her; he still had one arm around her waist. "You see—this was before you had taken your grandmother's name," he said, tapping the scroll. "It was before everything had happened. But I still knew."

She could not resist leaning into him just a little, just to feel his reassuring strength against her shoulder. "But that is my point exactly," she said. "Who I am now and who I seemed to be then are two very different people."

"Not so different that I cannot recognize you," he said. "No matter how much you change, you will always be familiar to me."

She let the scroll flutter to the floor and drew him closer with her own urgent embrace. "And I will change," she said, peering up at him anxiously. "But not so much that I will ever forget how secure I feel when you are beside me, tethering me to the world. In all the madness of this past year, you are the only thing I have relied on, the only thing I believed in, the only thing I trusted to keep me safe." She stretched up to press her mouth against his. "The only one I loved."

His arms tightened around her, and he kissed her. For a moment, she was air and fire, breathless and passionate; she was earth, tingling along every inch of flesh. She was water, she was wood; she was herself and her lover both. She understood the weighted balance of the world, the completed elemental circle. She was whole.

"I love you," she whispered against his mouth. "No matter what changes, that will always be true. Spoken from the heart of a *coru* woman."

"I love you," he answered. "And that will not change though the rest of the world is made over. Word of a *hunti* man."

Quatrain

From National Bestselling Author
Sharon Shinn

Sharon Shinn's "outstanding" (*Publishers Weekly*) Twelve Houses novels have fascinated readers and critics alike with their irresistible blend of fantasy, romance, and adventure. Now, in *Quatrain*, she weaves compelling stories set in four of the worlds that readers love, in "Flight," "Blood," "Gold," and "Flame."

Now available from Ace Books!

penguin.com

M495T0711

THE ULTIMATE IN FANTASY FICTION!

From magical tales of distant worlds to stories of those with abilities beyond the ordinary, Ace and Roc have everything you need to stretch your imagination to its limits.

Marion Zimmer Bradley/Diana L. Paxson

Guy Gavriel Kay

Dennis L. McKiernan

Patricia A. McKillip

Robin McKinley

Sharon Shinn

Steven R. Boyett

Barb and J. C. Hendee

penguin.com/scififantasy

M12G0610